THE SYSTEM SERIES

THE PRIZE

BOOK ONE

HEATHER LIN

Dear Reader,

In these pages, you'll find romance, intrigue, space travel, and gun-slinging. *The System* is like science fiction and romance had a baby, but instead of a cute genre name like "Romantasy," the best I can come up with is "Science Fucktion," so we'll just not give it a cute genre name.

The best part of this story, however, is finally getting to share it with you.

You see, I'm a recovering perfectionist. Since 2008, I have rewritten this book five times. I wrote it, and, based on various feedback, I changed it. I made it more descriptive, less descriptive, more literary, less literary, more original, less sexy, and sexier. I submitted the novel to agents, had it published briefly as an eBook by a now-defunct publisher, and finally self-published it out of frustration.

I pulled it, of course, because it still wasn't *perfect.*

But through college, marriage, two kids, a dozen new stories, and a couple of career changes, one thing stayed the same—*this* story, Brody and Capri's story, niggling at the back of my mind.

In early 2025, I had a sudden burst of clarity: **I am an idiot.** (Unfortunately, wisdom only comes with age.) How many people get to write their favorite book? Why was I letting it sit on my hard drive when this was the one story I'd always wanted to share?

No more waiting for permission, for the "right" time, for *perfection.* Life is short. Everyone says it, but it's true. I'm putting this story out there now simply because someone else might enjoy it—someone like you.

So, **thank you** for noticing this book, for picking it up, for giving it a try even if you decide it's not your cup of tea. It isn't for everyone (see trigger warnings below), but that's okay.

I wouldn't change a thing.

Happy Reading,

Heather Lin

TW: sexual assault, grooming, graphic violence, alcohol depen-dence, suicidal ideation

CHAPTER 1

"Where the hell is he?" Haddaway barked.

Brody remained quiet as his superior officer yelled through the linker in his ear. He didn't believe in speaking unless it was necessary, and he knew Haddaway didn't really expect an answer. Roy and Desdemona, the two guards he and Sullivan were supposed to be relieving, were understandably anxious to leave their posts and get some sleep. Their expressions grew darker with each minute that Sullivan remained absent.

"I'll come down until he shows the hell up. Then I'm scheduling a meeting with King Ekon. He needs to know this kid isn't working out."

Brody turned to the guards. "Haddaway's coming up."

"I hate the new guy," Desdemona said.

"I think everyone does," Roy agreed.

Brody only grunted. He didn't really care unless something directly affected him or his family. It had made his former job as a professional killer simpler. But after a week of being forced to be Sullivan's partner, he was certainly starting to feel affected.

The stairwell door opened, and a young blond man with a boyish face burst through. At the same moment, the elevator doors opened, and Haddaway met him in the hallway. He was a head taller than the new recruit, grizzled and commanding authority.

"09:00 means *09-fucking-00,*" he yelled, jabbing a finger into the younger man's chest. "There are plenty of guards on this kingdom who would kill to be in your position right now, so how about you act like you give a shit about this goddamn job before I *let* them?"

Even from where they stood, the trio of guards could see the younger man's face flush scarlet. They exchanged glances and poorly suppressed smirks. It was true. For some reason, this asshole had gone from the training academy straight to guarding the Maiden

Dorm. It should have taken months, maybe even years, for him to work his way up.

The King of Mars, who Brody assumed was responsible for his placement, was about to get an earful from Haddaway about why they had a fucking promotion ladder and not an elevator.

Sullivan muttered what Brody figured was an apology and then hurried to join him on the opposite side of the door. Roy and Desdemona had turned and walked the other way before they were forced to acknowledge him.

"Sorry, Shots," he muttered as he passed.

Brody only glared at him. He caught a whiff of something floral and feminine. Was that why he'd been late? Was he fucking around with one of the other palace employees? It wasn't his business until the fucker made it his business. But at least if he was getting it out of his system elsewhere, he might be able to make it through a shift without staring at the girls.

That was another thing about him that pissed Brody off. Everyone knew the Maidens were for King Ekon—and *only* King Ekon.

He leaned back against the cool metal wall beside the door to the Maiden Dorm and settled into the first boring hours of his shift. The girls would be in lessons right now, which meant he'd spend at least an hour staring at the same cream-colored wallpaper that lined the walls of the palace. The ceilings looked as if they were made of plaster, the floors tiled and heated to keep the often bare-footed girls from catching a chill. The whole palace was designed to be rich, warm, and inviting, but space was cold, and it only took one touch of the unforgiving wall to break the illusion that they were anywhere but on a massive, decommissioned spaceship.

That's what the Kingdoms were, after all: 500-year-old migration vessels that had been shut down and put into orbit after the people of Old Earth had moved from the failing planet to this solar system. The four Kingdoms were named after planets from the old system, while the three inhabitable planets were called Earth 1, Earth 2, and Earth 3.

Whoever had been in charge at the time did not get bonus points for creativity.

It hadn't really gone according to plan, however, and the U.N. only managed to keep control of one planet, now called New Earth.

The other planets, the rebel planets, were renamed Tycho and Ptolemy, the latter of which happened to be Brody's home planet.

It wasn't a nice place. That was why he wanted to move his family here. That was why he was standing here, bored out of his skull, working with this asshole.

Brody scratched his strong, clean-shaven jaw and glanced over at Sullivan, who held his rifle in position against his crisp uniform. Upon further inspection, Brody saw that his head was tilted back, and his eyes were closed.

He snorted. It was a good thing they were just glorified escorts. If the girls ever actually needed protection, he'd be on his own. He took his rifle in one hand and stretched his long arm to poke Sullivan in the temple with the tip of the cold barrel. The younger man started awake and pointed his gun hastily, and poorly, in Brody's direction. His eyes narrowed, and his cheeks flushed.

"Fuck you, Shots," he muttered.

Brody laughed, a rough sound that didn't soften his demeanor. The nickname had followed him from his home planet. He was the best in the business back in Sector 25 and probably could have earned enough money to move his family to Mars in half the time just by contract killing. But having this job on Mars put him in a better position to be chosen to live there once he'd saved enough to apply.

His little girl was three, and she and her mother were waiting for him back on the rebel planet. He hated being away from them, hated thinking about the breaking glass, gunshots, and catcalls that were lulling them to sleep right now—the same sounds that had been his lullabies growing up. But this job was their ticket out, their ticket to a better life.

If they could stick it out for just a couple of years, they would be able to reap all the benefits that came with living on New Earth and the Kingdoms.

The door to the dormitory hissed open, and the men stood at attention. Lady Agatha, a stunning woman in her early thirties, peered around the frame. She had smooth, dark skin and striking amber eyes. Despite her beauty, The King of Mars had retired her and given her this new role as den mother. It was his way. He acquired new playthings and redistributed old ones.

The Maiden Dorm's newest resident, Capri, was with her. King Ekon had escorted her to the new quarters himself, which was enough to tell anyone she was the Rising Favorite. Ekon's current Favorite, Marianne, would soon lose her seat beside him at the high table.

Capri was well-formed, with dark curls and hazel eyes, but Brody couldn't see any of them the way Ekon did. Maybe it was because he had Jillian, and he was happy—or maybe he just couldn't understand the appeal of counting down the days until he could fuck a young girl.

Sullivan didn't suffer from that problem. Even now, his eyes raked over her.

"Our Capri needs to use the facilities, and I'm afraid I'm in the middle of mediating an argument," Lady Agatha said in her enduringly calm, but commanding, way.

Brody tried not to let his annoyance show. *Glorified fucking escorts.*

"I'll go," Sullivan volunteered.

"No," Brody growled. "I'll take her."

Sullivan glared at him but didn't argue in front of Agatha. The pretty boy might have been promoted faster than should have been possible, but Brody still held seniority. He made the calls. And he didn't trust the other man.

He walked Capri down the hall to the bathroom and peeked inside to make sure it was clear. It was protocol, not because he expected there to be any real danger. King Ekon took far too many precautions.

The girl looked up at him with a wide, trusting gaze, and he nodded for her to go ahead. Conversing was forbidden. She went inside, and he leaned against the outside wall to wait, ignoring Sullivan who was within sight just down the hall.

Capri had only been in the Maiden Dorm for two months, but at fifteen was the oldest of the five residents. The girls could only leave the children's dormitories when they began their monthly cycle, and until they became Ladies, they were required to wear their hair loose and don only knee-length white dresses.

Sacrificial fucking virgins. That's what they reminded Brody of. Ekon kept them from the time they arrived, the most exquisite female specimens in the solar system, until they turned seventeen when they were meant to become a Lady and lie with him. In five years' time, when the King turned forty-five, he'd begin trying to produce an heir with one of them. Maybe more than one of them.

Brody knew it was despicable. The King groomed the girls from a young age, brainwashing them to be his devoted lovers until he grew tired of them, but Brody was also a realist. He knew exactly what the alternative could be for the girls, especially if they came from Ptolemy or Tycho.

On Mars, the girls had rich food, soft clothing, and hot baths. They were constantly reminded they were special—they'd been *chosen*. Whether they were there because their parents had begged Ekon to give them a better life or their origins were a little murkier, they could do a lot worse.

When Capri was finished, he walked her back to the dorm and knocked. Agatha let her in with a nod of thanks and closed the door.

"I could've taken her," Sullivan said. Once Agatha was out of sight, he slumped against the wall, sulking.

"The girls are off limits."

"No harm in looking."

"She's fifteen."

"Looks grown to me."

Brody rounded on him. He was a head taller, and Sullivan flinched. "Then you've never been with a grown fucking woman."

They spent the rest of the shift in silence. Sullivan was angry, but Brody didn't give a rat's ass. If Ekon knew he'd even *thought* of fucking with one of his beauties he'd never see daylight again. Brody wouldn't miss him.

"Gotta take a piss," he grunted to Sullivan, who didn't acknowledge him.

He went to the far end of the hall and rounded a corner to the employee bathroom. He was only gone about five minutes, but when he returned Sullivan was nowhere to be found. Panic lanced through him.

He knocked on the door to the dormitory, and Agatha answered. She was putting in an earring, and he could see the flurry of girls getting ready for dinner behind her.

"Yes?" she said.

"Where's Sullivan?"

"The other guard? A note came from the King. He's taking one of the girls to the upper dining hall."

A muscle ticked in Brody's jaw. He already knew the answer, but he asked anyway. "Which girl?"

Agatha's brow furrowed. "Capri. Is something wrong?"

"No."

She gave him a look that said she didn't believe him.

"Wait here," he said. "Lock the door. I won't be long."

She nodded and shut the door. He waited for the click that told him it was secure and then headed for the elevator. If he was a horny little prick, where would he take an impressionable teenage girl?

He rode the elevator down to the first floor, and the doors opened to reveal a spacious entry hall. He'd been in a few rundown hotels over the years, either to stay or to shoot someone, and the palace's layout reminded him of the big, block buildings. A front desk with guards and clerks blocked the public from accessing the King's sanctuaries. A network of stairs, elevators, and winding hallways took those who were allowed to enter where they wanted to go.

Brody went through the busy kitchens at a normal pace to avoid drawing attention, heading straight for the back stairwell. There were plenty of shadowy corners for someone to hide on the twisting, turning steps and landings, and Sullivan would be familiar with it.

For all Brody knew, Sullivan had done his job, and the girl was in the upper dining hall right now, seated with Ekon at the high table. For all he knew, he was wrong about Sullivan. But he hadn't survived thirty-two years in the roughest sector of Ptolemy by having shitty instincts.

Brody heard voices as he approached the fifth-floor landing, confirming his suspicions. A girl giggled. He took the last steps silently, holding his rifle in one hand like a club and his revolver in the other. He watched them from the shadows, quiet for a man of his size. In his usual line of work, he had to be.

Sullivan was too close to Capri. She was blushing.

"I can't believe I got us lost," he said sheepishly, feigning embarrassment.

Brody's anger spiked at the lie.

"Don't worry." Capri's voice was shy. "I'll tell the King it was my fault."

"I don't want you getting in trouble."

"I won't."

"Thanks. You can't tell him we've been talking, either, okay?"

He sounded too fucking convincing. Sullivan reached out to brush her arm with his hand, and the blush rose higher in her cheeks.

"He's so selfish, keeping you from talking to other men."

Capri looked down. She'd been conditioned to see Ekon as a god, and Sullivan was fucking with her head, making her feel conflicted. Brody had underestimated him. He wouldn't just look at the girl; he wouldn't even take her into a corner and have his way with her. He would make her think she loved him. He would make her come to him.

He really was a piece of shit.

"Sullivan!" Brody barked.

Fear, then anger, flickered across the man's face. But he landed on an expression of feigned innocence. "Hey, Shots, I just—"

"You're just gonna shut the hell up and get to your post."

"He got lost," Capri intervened. Her voice wavered, but she was determined.

Brody gave her a sideways glance, and her mouth snapped shut, eyes returning to the floor. He was sure the look had been hard, angry, but *he* wasn't going to break the rules by talking to her.

"Now," he ordered, gesturing with the butt of the rifle.

"You'll report me," Sullivan said, dropping the act and growing sullen.

"You're goddamn right I will."

Capri flinched, but Brody's vision was red. Cursing was the kindest thing he could do.

"Fine." Sullivan knew he was done. He spat on Brody's shoes, turned on his heel, and stomped down the stairs.

They watched him go. When Brody turned back to Capri, her wide hazel eyes were filled with confusion. She looked at Brody, seeking reassurance, but that wasn't his place. Now she'd know better than to trust anyone, even the ones who were supposed to protect her, and especially the ones who pretended to be nice.

He gestured for her to follow him, and after a moment's hesitation, she obeyed, letting him lead her up the final flight of stairs to where she belonged.

CHAPTER 2

Heads turned when Capri stepped through the side door. She was late and coming from the servants' stairs. She kept her head down. Her soft slippers and graceful feet made no audible sound. She felt mortified, as if they must know what had happened. As if they must know she betrayed the King by letting another man speak to her and try to worm his way into her affections.

She was supposed to love Ekon and no one else.

Capri stepped up to the long table where the King sat with his advisor, two couples unknown to Capri, and Marianne. There was one empty chair, on the King's right-hand side, signifying beyond the shadow of a doubt her status as his Rising Favorite.

Guilt assaulted her, and she stumbled a bit as she bowed. When she found the courage to meet her King's gaze, he lifted one dark eyebrow, but his brown eyes only held amusement. He nodded to her, indicating that she should take her place. She breathed a sigh of relief, taking a brief moment to admire the lines of his chiseled, clean-shaven jaw, the thick, wavy black hair that was always perfectly styled. His warm smile. How could she ever have found that guard Sullivan attractive, even for a moment?

Capri settled primly into her chair and thanked the server who placed a glass of cucumber-and-lavender-infused water in front of her.

"Is everything alright, Capri?" Ekon asked in his rich, smooth voice.

"Yes, King. The guard was lost."

"Shots?"

"No. The other one."

"Ah."

For reasons unknown to Capri, he glanced at Marianne, who turned her eyes toward her plate. She slipped a dainty bite of steamed carrot through her perfect, painted lips and pretended not to notice her King's scrutiny.

Marianne's expression was less welcoming than their King's. The current Favorite was nineteen, with long, blond hair, lily-white skin, and deep brown eyes—and she knew what Capri's presence meant. In two years, she would be replaced.

"Shots took over, did he?" Ekon asked.

Capri's cheeks turned pink as she remembered the way Sullivan had looked at the other guard, spat on his shoes. She'd thought for a moment Shots was intimidating, but she'd been wrong. She still felt shaken.

"Yes, King."

"Very good."

The meal passed with polite, sometimes flirtatious, conversation. Music played softly in the background. An aerialist performed during dessert, and Capri was even allowed a small glass of wine with her chocolate mousse. It was enough to make her drowsy and the evening seem dream-like. At the end of the performance, King Ekon took her small hand in his large, brown one and kissed the back of it gently.

"Until next time, sweet Capri."

She blushed and offered her King a shy smile. He disappeared through a private exit with Marianne on his arm. His own personal guards followed him, but he left one behind to escort Capri back to the dormitory.

She took a last look at the clear, domed ceiling. It was the only place in the palace where one could see the endless space surrounding Mars. She watched a ship fly overhead on its way to the docks, and she stood, awestruck.

The evening—most of it, anyway—had been magical. In two years, this would be her life. She would always be by the King's side at the high table; she would be dressed in bold, daring gowns like the ones Marianne wore, and *she* would be leaving with him at the end of the evening.

The guard cleared his throat, and, reluctantly, she let him lead her from the room.

***

To Capri's relief, Sullivan was nowhere to be found when she returned to the Maiden Dorm, only Shots. Capri glanced at him. His face was set in a deep scowl, and she imagined the events of the evening had worn on him. She felt responsible, but she couldn't apologize. Rules were rules. All she could do was learn from her mistake and forget about the fair-haired guard. That would be easy enough. He was nothing next to a King. She could still feel the tingle of Ekon lips on the back of her hand and tried to keep the sensation with her.

The other girls had returned from the lower dining hall hours ago, and they met Capri at the door.

"What was it like?"

"You sat *next* to him?"

"Oh, I can't wait until it's my turn!"

Before she could answer, Lady Agatha cleared her throat, and they quieted. "Girls, let Capri breathe. It's time to get ready for bed."

They all filed to the bathroom to brush their teeth and use the facilities before returning to dress in white nightgowns. The right side of the dormitory contained a row of vanities, one for each girl, and they all brushed or wrapped their hair to prepare for bed. A large, open doorway at the back of the room led to the lounge, where they relaxed and studied during the day.

The beds were lined to the left with Capri's farthest from the door and closest to the walk-in closet they shared. Thick rugs softened the hard floor, and there was always a fresh, woodsy scent and the sounds of birds in the air. Capri had learned during a history lesson that just after the Migration, there was a pandemic of despair. People from Old Earth couldn't stand being on a big metal box in the sky. Adding ambience had helped stop the suicides.

In an atmosphere wrought with competition, finding a true friend was difficult. Capri was lucky to have Gina in the bed next to hers. They both snuggled under down comforters and rested their heads on soft pillows, facing one another. Gina was the only person Capri had ever seen with red hair and green eyes. She'd moved up to the Maiden Dorm two years before Capri, though she was only thirteen years old now.

Capri fully expected to be ousted as the Favorite as soon as the younger girl turned seventeen. Gina's father had made the journey from Tycho to Mars when she was an infant, hoping King Ekon would accept her into his fold. Many parents came to the palace with the same hope, but it wasn't often that their child was unique enough to captivate Ekon. In Gina's case, he hadn't hesitated to reimburse her father and give her a home.

"Are you reading tonight?" Gina whispered.

"No, I'm too excited," Capri replied in the same low tone.

"I've only been asked to dine with him once, and I was at one of the lower tables. I'm so jealous."

"He'll ask you again. I know it."

Gina smiled wide. "I'm going to start curling my hair. I bet that would attract his attention."

Capri laughed. "You don't have to do anything to attract his attention. Anyone can see that hair from a mile away."

Gina sighed. "I just can't wait, you know?"

"I know."

They smiled and turned away in unison. Lady Agatha had an adjoining room, but she kept the door open. If they stayed up talking too long, she'd reprimand them. Sleep was an important part of staying healthy—and beautiful.

Capri stared at the ceiling for a long time before falling asleep.

CHAPTER 3

The next day, the Maidens had lessons. The mornings were for History, Math, Literature, and Exercise. The afternoons were for Dancing, Fashion, and Etiquette. Each morning, they woke in soft, white beds beneath soft, white blankets, filed to the bathroom in soft, white robes, showered, and filed back to the dormitory.

They put on white dresses, tended to their hair, and were escorted by Lady Agatha and one of the guards to breakfast in the Lower Dining Hall. There, they indulged in a hot breakfast with fresh fruit and infused water.

This all occurred before 9:00am, for which Capri was grateful. All five girls were safely back in their room before the guards changed shifts, which meant she didn't have to face the big guard, Shots, again. She assumed Sullivan had been let go. She hoped so. Whether that was because she believed he *should* have been fired or because she was simply too mortified to face him, she wasn't sure.

With stomachs full and legs stretched, the group retired to the lounge. The room was small with a plush, high-backed chair for Lady Agatha and poufs arranged in a semicircle for the students. Capri and Gina chose seats next to one another, as always. The girls sat primly, with their calves to the side and ankles crossed.

The children's dorms, meant for those undeveloped girls aged six and older, had been more lax when it came to things like posture. Capri had been the oldest in the dorm by three years, and her studies had plateaued long before she became a Maiden. If it wasn't for Gina's help over the last two months, much of which involved gentle reminders to straighten her shoulders, she'd still be embarrassingly behind the other Maidens.

The other girls in the dorm—Carissa, 12; Dayani, 13; and Tessa, 14—weren't unfriendly, but they were very aware by the time they reached the Maiden Dorm that this was a competition. They would all be Ladies, but those who gained Ekon's particular favor received more attention, the best apartments, the most expensive gifts. They weren't about to help anyone gain an advantage.

And Capri already had an advantage.

She wasn't sure how it had happened, really. She'd been thirteen at the time; Gina had just moved up to the Maiden Dorm. She was wandering the gardens, bored, while Lady Helena taught a newcomer about floral scents, when she found a songbird that had fallen from its nest. She'd stood on a tree root to put it back, and when she'd turned, Ekon had been there, guards on either side, watching her. He'd wiped a smudge of dirt from her cheek, told her it had been a kind thing to do, and then begun asking her periodically to sit in the upper dining hall.

It was a clear sign she'd won his favor, long before most had the opportunity.

"Yesterday, we discussed the roles each Kingdom played in settling the System," Lady Agatha's voice broke into her thoughts, which had fast been becoming a daydream of sitting at Ekon's side in grand outfits like Marianne's. "Dayani, do you remember what I taught you about Venus?"

"Venus provided medical services during the Migration," the dark-haired, dark-eyed girl answered promptly. "Venus's sponsor migrated medical teams before sending the ship back for civilians."

Agatha nodded and turned to the others. Carissa correctly answered that Jupiter had been responsible for agricultural success, and Gina recited Mercury's contribution of construction crews.

"Tess," Agatha said, addressing the second-oldest. "What role did Mars play during the Migration?"

Tessa tossed her long braids behind her back. They were interspersed with gold threads and matched the color of her eyes. Capri deflated slightly. That was the easiest question by far, and they were out of Kingdoms, which meant she'd have to answer something else, something harder.

"Mars was the first migration vessel to arrive," she said with a note of pride. "We transported military personnel, and once the three planets had basic infrastructure, we worked with the other Kings and Queens to retrieve U.N. citizens."

"Very good," Agatha said. "Although it's important to remember that at this time there were no kings and queens. The sponsors and their ancestors were granted that honor only after the Migration vessels were decommissioned and placed into orbit."

She turned her sharp brown eyes to Capri, whose mind had begun to wander again.

"Today, we'll be learning more about the planets. Capri, did you notice that Tessa mentioned three planets were settled?"

"Yes, Lady Agatha," she said obediently.

"But there is only one New Earth today. Can you tell me why?"

This was not a review question. Capri had to sift through her brain to yesterday's reading, which seemed very long ago. As the oldest in the dorm and a Rising Favorite, Lady Agatha expected more of her. She understood it, but she didn't like it. She glanced at Gina who gave her an encouraging smile.

"The U.N. prepared three planets for settlement," she said slowly. "But—"

"Don't wrinkle your brow," Lady Agatha interrupted gently.

Capri relaxed her expression before continuing. "But the U.N. struggled to maintain them. New Earth, where the U.N. District is housed, received priority. The people of Tycho and Ptolemy—as they're known now—grew impatient and rebelled. The U.N. had to leave them to their own devices."

It hadn't been a strong finish, but Agatha nodded her acceptance. "That's the general idea, yes. Someone had to be first, didn't they? But the early settlers of Tycho and Ptolemy couldn't handle that fact graciously. Territories on the rebel planets are known as sectors, and there's no point in trying to keep track of how many there are and where they are because they change all the time."

"Why?" Gina asked, raising her hand but voicing the question before Agatha had called her name.

"Border wars, mostly," Agatha responded softly, a faraway look in her dark eyes. Then, she came out of her reverie. "In the last two centuries, New Earth has begun building a relationship with the rebel planets, allowing some import and export activities, U.N. bank operations, and scholarship programs. Still, it comes down to circumstance."

Agatha began pacing in the limited space at the front of the small room. "The rebel planets are inhabited by poor criminals who raise poor criminals. New Earth is civilized and safe—for the most part. However, the Kingdoms are the most desirable places to live.

"Not only does King Ekon allow a select few families to immigrate to Mars, he is the only ruler who scours orphanages, listens to the pleas of parents, and gives a chosen few the comfort, security, and affection we sometimes take for granted. We are all among the lucky few."

She paused, letting her words sink in. Agatha's passion for Mars and King Ekon was obvious, and she held the girls in rapt attention.

"Now," she said, turning to lift a stack of readers from a shelf. "Read over chapter twelve of your history book. One day, we'll see the name Ekon written in these texts."

Capri straightened her back and lifted the reader to her eyes—hunching over was forbidden—but Agatha's spell was broken, and part of the lesson didn't sit right with Capri. She was from New Earth, but she hadn't been rescued. She'd been forcibly taken from her home and offered to King Ekon at the age of five in exchange for payment. Her memories were vague, but they were there. Perhaps her King had believed the men who brought her to him were her parents.

It was easiest to believe that—that Ekon had meant well. And there could be no doubt that he provided her with safety, security, and comfort no one on New Earth could rival, even her own family. Her mind seemed to fizzle out at the thought of them, before she could summon a clear image, and her reader came back into focus.

She hadn't read one word.

CHAPTER 4

Something was wrong. Capri lay still, blinking against the fog of sleep and trying to figure out what had woken her. There was light. That wasn't right. The dormitory door was open, but why?

She sat up and looked around. Everyone was sleeping soundly, or seemed to be. She crept out of bed to look in Agatha's room. She didn't stir. Capri turned to close the main door herself, deciding there had been some kind of malfunction, when she came face to face with Sullivan. He clamped a hand over her mouth before she could scream.

With one lean arm, he pinned her arms to her sides. She struggled and managed to break free, tried to claw his fingers away from her face. He cursed under his breath but held tight. The room was dark now, and he wrapped her up again. She couldn't breathe. No one was waking up. No one saw what was happening. Why weren't they waking up?

Oh, God.

She felt wet breath in her ear. "Don't make a sound. Don't fight me, or I'll kill them."

Relief mingled with terror. They were still alive. She swallowed. Then she forced her body to still, and she nodded. He released her mouth but moved so that both arms were wrapped around her from behind. She'd never get away.

"What did you do to them?" she asked in a whisper.

"Chloroform. They'll be fine—" He nipped her ear, and she shuddered. "—as long as you don't put up a fuss."

His teeth caught the skin of her neck. Her stomach lurched. Before entering the Maiden Dorm, every girl was given a lecture on the science of sex. Every girl was told exactly what would be expected of them when they turned seventeen. It sounded wonderful, beautiful—the joining of two bodies, minds, and souls.

She knew that some twisted version of that was about to happen now, and she knew it would be nothing like what it should have been.

He dragged her into the closet, and she experienced a flash of memory. She was five years old, being dragged from her home and locked in a small room on a spaceship destined for Mars. She thought of her parents clearly for the first time in years, yearned for them. But she relied on Ekon for protection now. Only, he wasn't coming. Her parents weren't coming. *No one* was coming.

Sullivan closed the door. Capri swallowed again. Her heart was beating too fast; her mouth was dry. At least it was dark. At least she wouldn't have to look at him. But the light flashed on. He wore that smile she'd once, somehow, thought was sweet and began unbuttoning the pants of his uniform.

"It would be a shame if I didn't get to enjoy all this beauty while I ruin it."

CHAPTER 5

Brody rolled out of a bottom bed in the men's employee bunk room. He was one of a few workers whose home wasn't on Mars—yet—and tonight he slept on the second floor of the palace with just three others, some kitchen help and another guard.

After his shift the next morning, he'd hitch a ride back home with his brother-in-law, have two days with his family, and then return to Mars. He kept a picture of Jillian and Maxine in a ring that acted as a data storage device, and anytime he wanted to see them he could bring it up on a reader. But nothing compared to the feeling of his family in his arms.

He rubbed his hands over his face and went to the bathroom across the hall to answer nature's call. It was occupied. He growled under his breath. The clock read 2:00am, U.N. time, and he just wanted to get the hell back to sleep. He went back to his bunk, grabbed his shoes and gun, and headed for the third-floor bathroom.

Years of life on Ptolemy had taught him to keep a weapon with him at all times. Even in a safe place like the Mars palace, he couldn't break the habit. Maybe he'd try to recondition himself when they were finally gone from Ptolemy, but that wouldn't be as soon as he'd like.

He was in his uniform pants and a plain white shirt. The palace was quiet, but he noticed there were now guards monitoring the stairwell. He nodded to them as he passed. On his way out of the restroom, he glanced down the hall, toward the Maiden Dorm, and stopped dead. The hall was empty. There were supposed to be two guards outside the doors at all times. He reached for his radio, to call his superior, but it was in the bunk room three floors below.

Brody was fully awake now. He unclipped his holster and went to investigate, putting his ear to the door. An eerie silence answered him. He considered knocking, then keyed in his pass code, allowing himself the element of surprise. The door slid open, and he caught a whiff of something chemical. Chloroform. Growing up on Ptolemy had taught him all the tricks of every heinous trade.

His heart beat harder in his chest, pumping adrenaline through his veins. He knew there was a threat, but where, and from whom? He moved quickly and silently through the dormitory, looking first in Agatha's room and then at each twin bed along the opposite wall. No one stirred. They were all knocked out—all but one.

The last bed was empty.

A light shone beneath a nearby door, and the sounds coming from within made Brody's stomach turn. He didn't hesitate. One second could mean the difference between life and death. He burst into the closet, already knowing what he'd find, red-hot fury bubbling in his chest.

God, he hated being right.

He grabbed Sullivan by the throat and hauled him off Capri, throwing him to the floor and slamming a fist into his jaw. There was a crunching sound. A panicked cry. He punched Sullivan again and again until a scream broke through the haze. Agatha.

"Call for backup," he told her, breathing hard from exertion. "And a medic."

She hurried to the call box by the door while Brody landed one last blow to the side of Sullivan's head, knocking him unconscious. His pants were still around his ankles, and Brody left him that way. He stood, then, and blocked the closet door with his bulk while Agatha spoke frantically into the phone. Some of the other girls were beginning to wake. A redhead vomited over the side of her bed.

Capri was still in the closet, curled on her side with one hand covering her face and the other holding the hem of her nightgown over her knees. Brody took a robe down from a hook near the door and cleared his throat. The girl looked at him through slender fingers. Her eyes were red-rimmed, but it was obvious she'd run out of tears long before he arrived.

She sat up slowly to take the garment, wrapping it around herself and staring at the floor. Mars was supposed to be *safe.* The thought of something like this happening here, where he would bring his wife and child, sent him into a rage.

Lady Agatha appeared behind him. "More guards are on their way, and—Capri?"

She pushed by him to get to the girl, and Capri threw herself into the older woman's arms, bursting into fresh sobs.

"What happened?" she asked Brody, looking as helpless as he felt.

"Exactly what it looks like."

Agatha shook her head, and tears poured from her own eyes. Brody turned his attention back to Sullivan. He couldn't do much for the girls, but he could make damn sure the pile of shit paid for what he did. Brody had reported him, and he was supposed to be on the first ship off the kingdom. How the hell had he ended up back here? Brody scowled and gave him one last kick in the ribs before a team of guards ran into the room, led by Haddaway.

Brody's superior officer was going prematurely gray at the temples, and worry lines creased his forehead.

"What the hell happened?" he asked.

"He knocked everybody out and then raped one of the girls."

Haddaway's eyebrows shot up. "He *raped* her? Which one?"

"The Rising Favorite."

"Capri."

Brody nodded.

"Shit."

Haddaway ordered two of his men to stay with Agatha and the girls and two to search for the missing guards. He turned back to Brody.

"The King's going to want to talk to you in the morning."

Brody shook his head. "I'll make a statement now. I have a ship to catch tomorrow."

"You better wake up early, then."

Brody ground his teeth together but didn't bother to argue. What the King wanted, the King got. He watched Haddaway and a burly guard drag Sullivan out of the room toward the elevators, knowing they were headed for the rarely used prison on the lowest level. Then, he left the dormitory to try and get a few more hours of sleep.

***

Brody woke early, dressed in civilian clothes, and met Haddaway at the private elevator on the first floor. Haddaway eyed the casual clothes and his packed bag.

"It's my day off," Brody growled. "I'm going to tell Ekon what happened and then I'm going straight to the docks."

Haddaway shrugged. "Your clothes are probably the last thing on his mind."

They rode the elevator up to Ekon's suite. The doors opened into a parlor with a large desk in one corner. It was the first time Brody had been invited to the suite, and it was every bit as opulent as he expected. The scent of a fireplace and old books reached his nostrils. Being raised on a real planet with real smells, the artificial ones always left him feeling slightly nauseous.

The King's advisor, Alexander, greeted them. Despite the early hour, he was dressed sharply in a pressed suit, his white hair combed neatly to one side.

"Hello, Shots. Haddaway. Thank you for coming."

Brody nodded, and Alexander turned to a set of four guards. They blocked the closed, ornately carved doors to the King's bedroom. Real wood. It was a precious commodity on the Kingdoms.

They could hear muffled voices through the thick panels, the sound of a man and woman arguing. Their voices continued to rise.

"...your idea!" yelled a man

"...just trying to help!" shrieked a woman.

Brody and Haddaway glanced at each other. Ekon and Marianne. A flush rose in Alexander's cheeks, and he gestured hurriedly at the guards. One of them knocked, announcing their arrival. For a moment, all went quiet, and then the doors opened. Ekon stood before them, looking grave. He was still dressed for bed, in pristine silk pajamas and a matching green robe trimmed with gold thread.

Brody caught sight of Marianne sitting on the edge of a bed behind him. Her piercing brown eyes found his and narrowed, telling him clearly to mind his own business. The doors closed, and he looked back to the King.

"Shots, thank you for coming." Ekon moved to the large wooden desk in the corner of the parlor and motioned for them to follow. Brody and Haddaway sat in chairs opposite him.

Ekon's gaze was dark and serious, filled with concern. Maybe he really did love the girls, in his own fucked-up way. "I need to know what happened."

Brody clenched his jaw, loath to relive the events of the previous evening. "I was on the floor to use the bathroom. The guards weren't at their post."

"Yes, they were found injured in the Maiden bathroom." He glanced at Haddaway. "Any word on their condition?"

Haddaway nodded. "Yes, King. They'll live."

Ekon nodded and turned his attention back to Brody. "Go on."

"I smelled chloroform. Most of the girls and Lady Agatha were unconscious in their beds."

"Most of the girls?"

"All except the one Sullivan took."

The King of Mars looked as if he might be sick. He'd know the details by now. He was just hoping they weren't true. "Which girl was it?" he asked quietly.

"Capri."

Ekon slammed a hand on his desk, but when he spoke his voice was a whisper. "No."

He looked to Alexander as if the older man would tell him this wasn't happening. But he only offered a look of sympathy.

"No," Ekon said again. "What will we do with her now?"

Brody frowned. He wasn't upset about what happened to the girls. He was upset because it meant Capri wasn't a virgin, wasn't his for the first taking anymore. How could he count this against her? Brody's eyes narrowed, and he felt Haddaway nudge his foot, telling him to keep his mouth shut, and he did. He had his own goals to consider, and even if the King of Mars was a sick bastard, he needed this job.

"King," Alexander interjected. "She may still be of use to us."

"Oh?" The King raised a perfectly shaped eyebrow, but the advisor seemed hesitant to discuss his idea in front of present company. The King nodded. "Wait for me in the sitting room, Alexander. And tell

Marianne to return to her apartment. Haddaway, will you escort her back to her room?"

Haddaway stood and nodded. "Of course, King."

A moment later, Marianne appeared, head held high and her pretty mouth set in a thin line. The air between them sizzled with tension. Briefly, Brody smelled the same floral scent he'd noticed when Sullivan appeared late to his shift. Before he could analyze the meaning of it further, she nodded coldly to her King and allowed Haddaway to take her into the elevator. That left Ekon and Brody alone, save for the four silent guards around them.

Ekon's gaze lingered on the closed elevator doors for a few moments more, then he turned back to Brody. "Shots," he began, "can I get you something to drink? Tea?"

He gestured to the steaming pot and cups on the heavy desk. Brody spied a bottle of whiskey on a shelf behind him. Ekon followed his gaze and gave a knowing smile.

"Of course."

He poured the whiskey for Brody and tea for himself, and they sat in silence while Ekon stirred sugar into the brew. Brody watched him, waiting, knowing the other man wanted something from him.

"You do the occasional side job, is that right?" the King asked.

Brody eyed Ekon warily. "Yes."

"Moonlighting isn't against the rules. In fact, your...*particular* skill set is one of the reasons you were hired."

Brody said nothing but took a long sip of his drink, waiting to see where the conversation was headed.

"How much, on average, do you charge per kill?" Ekon asked.

"Depends," Brody answered. "If they're important and hard to track down...maybe twenty thousand. If they're sitting ducks, ten."

"Do you dabble in torture at all?"

Brody shifted uncomfortably. "Not really my style."

"Shame." Ekon took a sip of tea, then looked straight at him. "As you know, a death sentence in the Kingdom of Mars is rare. But Sullivan will die for this. I'll give you fifteen thousand to do the job."

Brody relaxed and downed the rest of his drink. *Was that all?* He'd killed better men for less.

"Done."

CHAPTER 6

Capri had a private room in the palace infirmary. The smell was anti-septic, but the staff had tried to mask it with the scent of lavender. Everything about the room, from the pale blue walls to the babbling tabletop fountain, was designed to relax a patient.

But Capri felt nothing at all—unless she moved. Then, she felt the ache, the reminder of what had taken place just a few hours before.

She knew about rape. One of her favorite books was a collection of *Grimm's Fairy Tales*. That anthology was an introduction to all the horrible things that could befall a person—and many fantastical things that couldn't. All of it had seemed so far away, so very separate from her clean, comfortable, sheltered life. She could count on one hand the number of times she'd been cut or bruised during her time at the palace.

But the stories were true. Monsters did exist.

Lady Agatha slept in a comfortable chair beside the bed. Another Lady had been called to stay in the Maiden Dorm. The girls had been examined in the room, given tea or warm milk, and told to rest. Agatha had remained by Capri's side during the invasive physical examination and the guards' questions. She'd been given the same pill the Ladies were given every time they were visited by Ekon, to keep unwanted babies at bay. Then, Agatha had read aloud to her, in an unspoken effort to distract Capri from her pain, until her exquisite chin touched her chest, and she dozed.

But sleep wouldn't come for Capri, and she'd refused a seda-tive. The last time she'd taken one, she'd fallen asleep on New Earth and woken up on Mars. Memories of that night had come back to haunt her, too. The terror and helplessness she'd somehow blocked out in the wake of King Ekon's kindness and the opulence of palace life. There was too much to think about, too much that made her feel ill, and she was glad when a knock sounded on the door and pulled her from her thoughts.

Lady Agatha started awake, smoothing her hair and straightening her posture before calling for the person to enter. Even wrenched from sleep, in her robe, Lady Agatha managed to be lovely. She was a work of art, the kind of natural beauty Ekon coveted most. It was what he'd found in Capri. How must she look now?

As if her thoughts had summoned him, she realized the person on the other side of the door wasn't a medic but a King's guard—and the King himself. Then came his advisor, Alexander, and a woman in her mid-twenties, who Capri recognized as Lady Briony, a former Favorite. A second guard followed. Capri tried to straighten her curls, to look presentable, but deep down she knew it was no use.

Lady Agatha stood and curtsied, but Ekon shook his head and stepped around the bed to take her hand in his. "No, Lady. You sit. You've had a trying night."

"Thank you, King," Agatha said and sank gratefully back into the chair.

Then Ekon turned to Capri. She looked down but felt it when he sat on the edge of the bed. She could see the blue fabric of his shirt, the khaki color of his slacks. He reached out to brush a limp curl away from her face, and she raised her head obediently, so that he could tuck it behind her small, perfectly formed ear. He watched her intently, compassion in his gaze, and her heart filled.

He wouldn't look at her that way if he didn't still care for her—would he? He took her hand between his warm, smooth palms, and her breath caught at the intimate gesture.

"Capri, my darling, how are you feeling?"

"Better, King."

He smiled, but it was a sad smile, tinged with regret. Capri could feel her stomach drop. Her heart pounded in her ears, and she felt dizzy. Instinctively, she knew whatever was coming next wouldn't be good.

"You will be…my most missed opportunity," he said softly.

She swallowed hard, holding perfectly still, as if by doing so she could stop time. He seemed lost in thought, just watching her hand, trailing a fingertip around her knuckles. She felt sick with grief, even before he said the next words.

"You know that, through no fault of your own, you and I can never be."

She squeezed her eyes shut against a fresh rush of agony. She'd been stupid to let herself feel hope. The rules were clear. Ekon would not accept a girl if she was not intact. Capri, now, was undeniably broken.

"However," Ekon continued gently, and she opened her eyes. Hope rose again, almost of its own accord. "There is another way you may please your King."

He raised his eyes to hers.

"Anything," she whispered, perhaps too eagerly.

"You are still a rare jewel, Capri, and a valuable part of my collection. Nothing could ever change that. There are others, throughout the System, who come to this place, who tour the lower levels of the palace, *just* in the hope of glimpsing one of you. Did you know that?"

Capri blushed and shook her head. She'd begun to relax. She was still beautiful. She was still wanted.

"Imagine what one of them would pay to bed you."

Icy terror rippled through her, constricting her throat. She couldn't be sure of what he'd say next, but she knew it would be something she didn't want to hear. It would be something she didn't want to do.

Capri looked at Agatha. The other woman kept her eyes firmly on her hands, clasped so tightly in her lap her knuckles paled. Otherwise, she betrayed no emotion.

"Once you turn seventeen, you'll be offered up to auction every two weeks. A man—or woman—may have you for one night."

He squeezed her hand, drawing her gaze back to his. She felt dizzy and knew she must look as scared as she felt.

"Lady Briony will walk you through what's expected. The doctors will perform a minimally invasive procedure to ensure no offspring comes from your unions. After recovery, you'll go straight to your own apartment. You know of the apartments?"

She nodded.

"They're private, luxurious spaces, and they're reserved only for Ladies."

Capri swallowed again and managed to speak. "But I won't be a Lady."

Ekon reached out and lifted her chin so she had to keep looking into his soft, brown eyes. "You will still be a Lady, Capri. You'll still have the title. You just won't be *my* Lady."

Capri dropped her chin again as soon as he released her. He released her hand, too, and she felt the loss keenly. The moment she'd been waiting for since she was brought to Mars ten years before would never come. She and the King would never consummate their love—because he would never love her. Not in that way. She was too broken.

She would have to endure the attentions of strangers instead. And what choice did she have? If she wanted to keep her warm bed and the King's respect, she would do this. Like so many years before, the decision had been made for her. Like so many years before, she would take the path of least resistance and comply.

Tears burned her eyes.

"Yes, King," she muttered.

He gave her one last, sad smile, kissed her chastely on the forehead, and stood to leave. "We will see each other again, Capri. Just never again at the high table and never as we had hoped."

He sounded so sad, as if he'd lost something that night, too. She squeezed her eyes shut, feeling the first stab of guilt, that maybe she could have done something to prevent this. If she hadn't talked to Sullivan in the stairwell. If she'd followed all the rules.

She heard Ekon address Lady Agatha. "You'll be needed in the dormitory. Briony will take good care of Capri."

Capri looked up. She didn't want her to go, but the Lady bowed to her King, gave her a sorrowful look, and obediently took Briony's place in the procession.

Capri and her newly appointed Attending Lady were left alone. Briony hesitated before taking Agatha's place in the bedside chair. She tried to sound bright and cheery, as if her tone of voice could fool Capri's heart.

"Let's focus on your rest and recovery, shall we? Then we'll worry about everything else. Shall we play a game? Chess, perhaps?"

Capri looked at her briefly. She had a kind face. Under different circumstances, they might have gotten along fine. But she rolled away from the blond and let the emotions she'd been holding back crash into her.

She cried for a long time. Briony didn't touch or speak to her. Mercifully, she let Capri pretend she was alone.

And as far as the former Rising Favorite was concerned, she was.

CHAPTER 7

The new guard for the Maiden Dorm was a sturdy blond woman from Tycho named Tamara. She'd been moved up from the front entrance. That was how it should have gone in the first place. The fact she was female likely helped in her promotion, too, but Brody suspected she admired the Ladies as much as most of the men.

She didn't talk much. He didn't talk much. They got along fine.

Over the last month, the shock had eased for Agatha and the girls, and now all seemed back to normal. Brody took a reader from his back pocket. It was a clear, paper-thin sheet that he could connect to the data ring he wore. Most people wore them. Not the girls, though. They had to take their readers directly to hubs in the library to access information and load books onto their readers. A ring for them would probably mean too much freedom.

Readers also told time, which was what Brody was interested in at the moment.

"How much longer?" Tamara asked with mild interest.

"Five minutes," Brody answered without looking up.

"Wanna grab a drink?"

"I've got a ride to catch. Maybe next time."

Tamara shrugged. When the two relief guards appeared, Brody headed for the employee bunk room. He gathered his rifle, revolver, clothes, and personal hygiene products from a locker and shoved them into a reinforced duffle bag. He took off his uniform jacket but didn't bother changing yet. He'd shower on the ship.

He nodded to the guards at the front desk. There was always a crowd of people near the grand, automatic doors. Some were citizens invited to see the King, some were there to file complaints, and many were tourists. He pushed through to the outside and took a deep breath.

Although there was no such thing, really, as fresh air on the glorified spaceship, the air in the domed, artificially lit community seemed easier to pull into his lungs. Everyone traveled by bicycle, public shuttle, or foot. Beneath the street and sidewalk were hundreds of apartments, just like the one he hoped to move his family into one day. Above ground were the houses of the grossly rich or favored citizens, as well as public buildings like a school, shopping center, restaurants, menagerie, and more.

It was common for the streets to stay packed during the day. Everyone went underground at night. Right now was the in between, twilight. People were taking after-dinner walks and leaving the restaurants. But Brody's destination was adjacent to the palace, and he made it to the dock entrance with time to spare.

He showed his papers—via the reader—to the security guard on duty at the footpath entrance, though it was purely formality. They knew each other by sight. Traveling back and forth between Ptolemy and Mars had been part of the deal. It was hard at times, but he was doing it for his family's future. Soon enough, they'd be close by. It would be a ten-minute walk to the tunnels instead of half a day's travel by his brother-in-law's spaceship.

Thanks to his bonus from Ekon for putting a bullet between Sullivan's eyes, he only had eight months to go until he could afford to buy one of the apartments outright—a requirement, since he wasn't a born citizen. If he could squeeze in a side job or two while he was home, it would take even less time.

But Jillian didn't like him being away on his only days off, and he didn't particularly like going. Either way, they'd be off Ptolemy before Maxine was old enough to remember her barren roots.

"You're in Bay 5 today," the guard told him.

"Thanks."

Brody found the large craft. All short-distance space vessels looked relatively the same, an echo of the space shuttles of old but upgraded to allow for more storage, more people, more fuel conservation, and, therefore, longer flights. They were like big, aerodynamic boats in the sky. Long-distance space vessels, like the ones that had brought the people of Old Earth to the System, had only been available to the U.N. and were decommissioned as soon as the Migration was complete.

Colin's spaceship was called *Task Eternal*, some reference to a poem that had meant something to him when he was young. Brody and Colin had run in different circles then. It was purely by chance he'd met his sister, Jillian, at a party. He'd been fresh off a kill and thought it was the adrenaline, the excitement, that had them in bed together—but he couldn't stop thinking about her. Somehow, she'd felt the same way.

That was five years ago, when he was twenty-six and she was twenty-five. Colin had been long gone, two years out of college on New Earth and already the master of his own vessel. Brody and his brother-in-law got along well enough. They both loved Jillian. But Brody knew Colin shuttled him to and from Mars only because it happened to fit in with his delivery schedule.

Brody pressed the intercom outside of the ship.

"Go ahead." The clipped voice belonged to Jax, Colin's second-in-command.

"It's Shots."

There was a clanking noise, and a small hatch in the hull of the ship slid back to let an elevator descend. It could fit two people, max, but it was an easier and less invasive method of boarding than opening the big ramp at the back of the ship. He stepped inside and pressed the button that took the metal cage into the loading bay.

The ship, true to its captain's form, didn't have a lot of frills. Everything was bare bones and metallic. Functionality over aesthetics. It was the opposite of Ekon's palace, which showed exactly what could be done to spruce up a flying metal box—or to mask the truth of a thing.

The loading bay was lined with storage shelves stacked with tools and whatever miscellaneous someday-useful items had been accumulated over the years. Colin had spent the first two years manning the vessel himself—a difficult feat—before taking on the twins, Jax and Leroy. Jax was an admirable pilot. Leroy was a competent, if annoying, mechanic.

A couple of motorcycles, the preferred method of transportation on the rebel planets, and an old, beat-up electric sedan took up half the bay. The other half was reserved for whatever cargo they carried.

It was empty now, since they'd just made a delivery to Ekon.

Brody headed for the corridor behind the car. On the right were three doors, each leading to an identical room with an identical set of bunk beds, shower, and toilet. At the end of the row, nearest to the cockpit, was the captain's room. Brody didn't know what it looked like inside, but he assumed it had one big bed and was a might bit nicer than the others.

He tossed the duffel bag in the first room he came to. No one occupied it, and there was some junk piled in a corner. Then he went in search of Colin, passing the closed, massive room used for over-flow cargo, the kitchen and mess area. He found Leroy in the last room, the lounge, looking at a reader and fiddling with some delicate piece of lap-sized machinery.

"Shots!" Leroy's caramel-skinned face broke into a wide grin. "Welcome back, man."

He had thick, tightly curled hair that he and his brother both kept long and pulled away from their faces. They both dressed the same, too, in the warm, heavy-duty coveralls that were typical of space crewmen. Still, Brody never struggled to tell them apart. Leroy was full of excess energy and chatter. Jax was quiet and serious. It took one look at their faces to know who was who.

"Leroy," he greeted with a short nod, continuing on to the cock-pit before the younger man could trap him in some excited, long-winded explanation of what he was doing.

The door to the cockpit was almost always open, and he found Colin in the pilot's seat with Jax to his right. They were turned toward one another, leaning a little closer than necessary, like magnets ach-ing to touch. He wasn't sure they realized it had become obvious there was something going on between them, but Brody would be the last one to mention it. They sat huddled over readers, discussing routes, pick-ups, and drop-offs like normal. Brody caught the tail end of it, and his interest was piqued.

"...and then Sector 45 on Tycho is getting the insulin, but only up charge 50% since it's medical."

There was a .5% chance that whatever they were discussing was a legal run. He was in no position to judge, but he knew his wife was under the impression that her brother ran a clean operation. Brody had suspected otherwise for a while, but it was the first confirmation he'd received. Colin either trusted him with the information or had simply decided to do away with pretense.

Brody leaned against the doorframe, waiting while Jax finished writing notes on his reader with a stylus. He always wore two data rings, personal and professional. Colin looked up and nodded to his brother-in-law. He had the same red-brown hair as Jillian, but his eyes were brown where hers were blue. He favored their father and she their mother, so he was told. They'd both been killed in a border war long before he and Jillian met.

The sectors were constantly changing and guarded only by militia. There was usually some semblance of government—often corrupt—and when the population or the boss's greed exceeded the provisions of the sector, it was common for war to break out. Jillian's sector had lost ten square miles in that battle.

Brody was in a neighboring sector, Sector 25. It was easily one of the meanest on the planet with one of the fiercest militia. They were rarely challenged and rarely made a bid to expand the territory. There was enough crime and lack of properly-trained medical professionals to keep the population under control, and the governor was constantly being ousted—in one manner or another—for being too corrupt or not corrupt enough. They were careful to never make alliances with other sectors, so they couldn't be called on as a whole to fight someone else's battle.

They were known for being the loner sector, the one that bred the System's worst criminals—and its best fighters.

"Brody," Colin greeted. "Good to have you on board again."

He was always pleasant enough but careful to keep an air of authority about him. His commands would be obeyed, and his decisions were final. Brody couldn't blame the man. He'd worked hard to get where he was, and he wouldn't let anyone or anything come between him and his accomplishments—even Jax, he suspected.

In that way, the two were very similar.

"Need help with anything?"

"No. Takeoff is in half an hour."

Brody nodded and headed back to his room to shower. It would take about twelve hours to get to Ptolemy. He'd spend most of the time sleeping and be home in time for breakfast. He'd have two days with his girls, and then he'd catch a ride back on *Task Eternal* in time for his shift on Sunday.

It didn't always work out that Colin would be back in time to pick him up, and on those occasions he had to pay a hefty sum for passage back to Mars. If it wasn't for Colin, working on Mars wouldn't make any sense.

He owed the man for sure, and he hated owing people. But falling in love and starting a family had forced his pride aside. He'd do whatever it took to give them the life they deserved.

CHAPTER 8

Brody walked home from the docks. It was early morning. Ptolemy was the farthest habitable planet from the sun, and it was always cold, prone to spontaneous flurries and a persistent icy mist.

He wore an insulated coat, a black knit hat pulled down over his ears, and a thick glove on the hand holding his duffle bag. His heavy boots crunched on the thin layer of snow beneath his feet. His right hand stayed in his pocket, finger on the trigger of a loaded revolver.

He passed a few drunks blacked out on the stairs of crumbling buildings. Some of them would freeze to death. On the streets closest to the docks, hookers called out to him and flashed their goods, nipples at full attention in the blistering cold.

He barely noticed them.

Drifters were as much a part of his home sector as the pitted roads and piles of junk. The U.N. had placed the infrastructure for a settlement, just as they had on New Earth. The intention had been for Tycho and Ptolemy to remain under U.N. control, but when the citizens began protesting and asking to live on New Earth, where there was plenty of room and a more temperate climate, they were denied.

They got angry. They rebelled. And the U.N. wrote them off and left them to fend for themselves.

Brody's apartment was a few miles away, on the outer edge of all the noise and debauchery. When his wife took Maxine out, it was never at night. Jillian would walk the streets the same way he did, alert, listening for the sounds of alarms or gunfire. One hand would hold Maxine's, and the other would be in her pocket, wrapped around her snub-nosed revolver. It was second nature for her, too.

They both wanted Maxine to remember something different, to run down the sidewalk with other kids, to see a garden that wasn't just half-dead weeds. It was the life she'd get on Mars.

He turned a corner on the broken sidewalk. A man stepped out of the shadows, but Brody bared his teeth at him, and he retreated. He was a notorious panhandler and pickpocket, and they'd already had one run-in. Brody reckoned he didn't want to risk making more than his nose crooked by crossing him again.

His building was ugly and covered in graffiti, but it was sturdy and the rent was fair. He'd gotten an apartment on the fourth floor—far enough from the ground they wouldn't be targeted for a break-in, but low enough that they had a good chance of getting out if the old wiring caught fire and they had to evacuate.

There was an elevator that no one used. It was either broken or likely to break. The stairwell smelled like piss and garbage, but when he reached his painted door and keyed in the code to unlock it, he was met with warmth and the smell of bacon.

He'd barely closed the door when his auburn-haired daughter crashed into his knees. He reached down to steady the two-year-old and scooped her into his arms.

"Daddy!" she shrieked, wrapping her arms around his neck in a surprisingly strong hug. "I pee in the potty, Daddy!"

"Well, ain't you a big girl?" he said, carrying her over a sea of blocks to reach Jill.

She was leaning against the door frame of their tiny kitchen with a smile on her face, waiting patiently for her turn to greet him. He tried putting Maxine down, but she hung on his neck, laughing, so he wrapped them both in his arms.

"You made it in time for breakfast," Jill said, tucking her short hair behind her ears. She wore faded jeans and a sweater. He flicked a speck of peeled paint from her shoulder. "Guess we gotta put some fresh paint on that, too."

She turned to flip the bacon, and Brody frowned. She hadn't said it with any hint of resentment. This was a great place, by Ptolemy standards. But by Mars' standards, it was practically a hovel.

"Daddy, play blocks?" Maxine requested, finally sliding down to the floor and stacking a few blocks on top of one another. He plopped a couple more on, and she knocked them over with both chubby hands.

"Boom!" she shrieked with glee.

He raised an eyebrow at the mischievous brown eyes. They were dark and deep and exactly like his own. The girl was the perfect product of their love—her hair, his eyes. Sometimes Brody thought his heart might burst. Before Jillian, he hadn't even been sure he had one.

"Breakfast's ready," Jill said.

"We'll play later," Brody promised.

"And Daddy read book?" she said hopefully.

Brody glanced at Jill. Reading wasn't exactly his strong suit, but if that was what his daughter wanted, she'd get it. "Sure thing, Maxi."

"Yay, Daddy!" she hugged him tightly around the knees before squeezing into her chair at the kitchen table.

Jillian caught Brody by his shirt and pulled him around the doorway, out of Maxine's line of vision. She clasped her fingers behind his neck.

"Finally, a hug all to myself," she murmured.

He grinned and wrapped his arms around her waist, pulling her close and kissing her deeply, searching her warm, familiar mouth with his tongue. God, he missed her when he was gone. He groaned, desire and frustration, but she broke the kiss before their daughter decided to investigate.

"Later," Jill promised, moving toward the kitchen.

He smacked her butt, and she laughed, plopping bacon, French toast, and sliced apples on a plate for herself. Maxine's was already cut up and cooling, and Brody helped himself to what was left.

"What do you think about going to the park today?" Jillian asked around a mouthful of food.

"Yes!" Maxine squealed.

"I'm asking your father."

Brody shrugged. The "park" was an empty lot where a building had once stood. A few half-dead trees managed to hold their own in the empty space, and Jill would bring chalk and let Maxi draw on the patches of concrete between the greenery.

It hurt, knowing the kinds of safe places kids had to play on Mars. But he'd get them there soon. Brody glanced at his daughter's eager face. Every time he came home, it was like he was being introduced to a whole new person. She learned so much in the days he was away; he had a hard time denying her when he was home. Jill already knew his answer.

"Sure." He smiled.

CHAPTER 9

Brody waited until Maxine was asleep for the night, then he kissed Jillian goodbye and ventured out into the dark streets of Sector 25. She'd begged him not to go, not to spend his two-day leave killing—but she'd also confessed they had another babe on the way. It had sent him into a panic. This couldn't wait. He had to get them out.

So, they'd made love, and he'd left. He wore a thin, bulletproof vest beneath his coat and thermal shirt. He loaded two pistols, ammo, a revolver, a grenade, sights, and silencers into a backpack and strapped a rifle across his chest. On Mars, he had a license for the revolver and the rifle. On Ptolemy, that type of regulation didn't exist. He had a stockpile of weapons, kept safely locked away from Maxine.

Brody went down to the basement of the building where he kept his motorcycle in a storage unit. The bike was decent, considering what was available on the rebel planet. A reliable ride and high-quality guns had been necessary when his only form of employment was shooting and speeding away. He was good at it, and the money was decent.

And that's why he was here now, despite his wife's pleas. Even an easy kill could bring them a month closer to buying an apartment on Mars. He knew he wasn't invincible; there were risks, but he hadn't died yet. She just needed to trust him.

Brody hauled the bike up to the first floor and rolled it outside. Then he secured his goggles and took off into the night. His destination was about five miles away, in the worst part of the sector, the one in which he'd been born. He slowed as familiar buildings came into view. The potholed streets were bright from neon signs and open doors, but the corners were dark. A couple of guards might be seen patrolling, courtesy of the governor, but they didn't try to stop crime so much as clean up after it.

No one could stop crime in Sector 25. Residents just found the type that suited them and protected their own as best they could. It was survival of the fittest. Kill or be killed.

Brody parked next to some other bikes outside of *Leo's Bar* and pulled a fuse to deter theft. The bar was busy, smoky, and smelled like sweat and spilled beer. He'd spent much of his boyhood in this bar with his father, learning about guns, drink, women, and—most importantly—how to secure a job.

Leo was the man to talk to, and Brody squeezed his way between the tables and past the serving girls, nodding at a few familiar faces, until he made it to the bar in back. He sat on an empty stool between two men.

"Shots!" Leo greeted from behind the bar. "Lookin' for a whiskey? Or has that fancy Kingdom in the sky, er, *refined* your tastes?"

Brody glared at the squat man but didn't dignify the jeer with a response. Leo put his hands up in mock surrender and poured him a double shot of cheap whiskey. Much as he hated to admit it, Mars *had* affected his taste. He'd never recognized the drink as cheap before.

Still, he slugged it back and tapped the bar for another. As Leo poured his second round, he leaned in close, demanding the other man's attention.

"I'm lookin' for work. Anything come through?"

Leo stole a glance at Sledge, the short, wiry merc next to him. He sported a shaved head and didn't seem very intimidating at all—until a person saw his face. Besides the long scars on either side of his mouth, his eyes were near-black; even when he smiled it looked like a sneer. At the moment, he was deep in conversation with the woman on the other side of him, Spinder, who was a skilled assassin in her own right.

"All I got's left is a rough-up job for somebody in the next sector."

Brody clenched his jaw. If he'd gotten there earlier, he might have gotten something better, but he'd wanted to see Maxine off to sleep. She deserved that much. He'd be gone by the next evening.

"What's it pay?"

"Fifteen hundred."

"That's it?" Brody growled, frustration making his fists clench.

"Don't shoot the messenger, Shots," Leo warned. "You want it or not?"

Brody considered briefly, but he already knew it wasn't worth it. That was the kind of work for odd-job men, who had nothing to lose and would do anything for a quick buck. Brody needed more to make it worth the risk.

"No," he said finally.

"Come back tomorrow. You never know when somethin'll come in."

"I'm leavin' tomorrow night."

"Sorry, Shots. Maybe one of the others'll go in with you."

Brody only grunted as he sipped his second glass of whiskey. A scuffle broke out to his right. Sledge was getting into it with Spinder, and he jostled Brody's elbow, making him spill his drink. He grabbed the other man by the back of the neck and slammed his head down on the bar. It was an automatic reaction, especially in his agitated state. Sledge slumped to the floor. Conversation paused only for a moment.

Spinder had a knife drawn, and her gray eyes narrowed. She was annoyed. Brody had stolen her thunder.

"I guess you can have his half of the job," Leo said, glancing down at the body over the bar and refilling Brody's glass.

"It's mine now." Spinder turned the tip of the knife towards the sixty-something bar owner, even though she knew better than to actually try and hurt him. His security was top-notch. She wouldn't get two feet out the door.

"You know damn well that's a two-person job if there ever was one." Leo smirked.

Spinder glowered at the small man but lowered her weapon. She eyed Brody, sizing him up. They only knew one another by reputation. Hers was good. His was better.

"What's it pay?" Brody asked, addressing Leo.

"Thirty thousand. Sector 72."

Fifteen thousand each, minus the cost of a plane and Leo's cut. *That* was more like it. He'd have the money to get on a waiting list for an apartment in six months. That put them on Mars before Jill's due date.

He grinned and turned to Spinder. "You got a bike?"

"Yeah."

"Then let's get goin'. You can tell me the details on the plane."

Spinder was still annoyed that this change in plan had been decided for her, and she hesitated.

Brody leaned close to her round face, framed by short, black hair. "Do you want the money or not?"

She shoved him away from her, being sure to dig her nails into his forehead. Brody was unfazed; the relief was too sweet. Spinder turned, pulled a warm cap over her head, and stalked out, expecting him to follow.

Brody glanced back at Leo. "Take the drinks and damage out of my pay."

"Will do." Leo tipped an invisible hat, and Brody went to catch up with his partner—and one hell of a payday.

CHAPTER 10

Brody was sweaty, exhausted, and covered in blood that wasn't his. He was also twelve thousand five hundred dollars richer. He parked his motorcycle in the storage unit beneath his building and locked the door. He had a few cuts and bruises from rolling around in underbrush, which Jillian wouldn't ignore. She'd use it as proof that he was putting himself at risk and should quit, even if it meant having a goddamn kid on the living room floor again. He just couldn't let that happen.

Killing was only dangerous if a person was bad at it, and he'd been born and bred for it.

Going to Leo's with Spinder to present proof of kill and collect his money had taken longer than expected. He'd be cutting it close for the rendezvous with *Task Eternal*, but Colin's bike was chained around the corner. The captain would be visiting with Jillian and trying to decipher Maxine's toddler babble, giving Brody enough time to shower and change before he had to say goodbye to his girls.

It always hurt, but he wouldn't have to do it for much longer now. Soon, they'd be saying goodbye together—to their old life, to the whole goddamn planet.

As he approached the fourth-floor landing, he felt relaxed. In just one night, he'd brought them two months closer to their goal. Jillian couldn't argue with that.

But when he stepped off the stairs and started toward the end of the hall, the smug smile fell from his lips. His apartment door was ajar, and Colin was leaning against the wall, waiting for him. His arms were tight across his chest, and he was staring at the floor. His coveralls were stained with blood, and as he got closer, Brody saw that his hands were, too. Finally, with effort, he lifted his head and looked his brother-in-law in the eye. Brody's heart stopped.

Colin was composed now, but he hadn't been. His auburn hair was wild, and his eyes were red-rimmed. Brody clenched his fists, bracing himself for whatever blow was coming.

"What?" Brody growled through gritted teeth when the other man still didn't speak.

Colin's gaze flitted to a wall behind Brody. In a moment of uncharacteristic weakness, he couldn't look Brody in the eye. "They're dead," he said flatly.

Then he looked at him again. The bad news had been delivered. Brody stared. He wanted to punch him in the face. What the hell was he playing at? His words didn't make any sense. But even as his brain denied them, his heart knew that they were true and broke. For a long moment, Brody couldn't move. He could only stare at the grim line of Colin's mouth in disbelief.

Then he was nothing but movement.

He burst into the living room, dropped his bag, and found Jill on the floor. She'd been dragged from the couch, probably by Colin, who would have tried to revive his sister. But it was clear from the blue of her lips, the pallor of her skin, the blood where her heart would be—she was dead.

"No," Brody muttered.

He turned toward his daughter's room.

"No," he said again.

He moved to the open door. *They.* Colin had said it. Colin had warned him, but he still had to see for himself. If he didn't, he would never believe it. She lay sprawled out as she always did when she slept—his baby girl and all of her brains and blood.

"No."

The scent of blood, metal, and death were unmistakable. He'd been the cause of it often enough. But it was never supposed to reach here. Not here. Not them. *No.*

He realized he was screaming the word, clutching his daughter's legs, but they were already cold. She was no longer his daughter, just an empty vessel where half of his heart used to be.

She was dead. Jill was dead. And with them went all his hopes and dreams and everything he loved. *Sledge.* It had to have been

Sledge. And that meant that this was because of him, because he'd crossed the bastard. This was *his* fault.

Jill worried about him. She worried he would be hurt or killed. She worried *he* would be taken from *them.* Neither of them had considered that she and Maxine might be in danger. But this was *his* sector, *his* world, *his* goddamn profession.

He should have known.

He should have known that cold-cocking one of the meanest sons of bitches in Sector 25 and then taking a job out from under him would have repercussions. But he hadn't set out to do that. The opportunity was there, and he'd needed the money. Anyone else would have done the same thing—the same goddamn thing for *themselves.* Brody was doing it for his family, and wasn't that noble?

Now he had no family. He'd gotten them killed.

No more smirks, soft kisses, and sweet caresses from his Jill. No more laughing and stumbling through bedtime stories with his Maxi. He'd never even get to meet the second babe.

Red clouded Brody's vision. The pain was unbearable. It consumed him, begging for release. He screamed and put his fist through the closet door, but it wasn't enough. He wanted to burn the whole fucking building to the ground, but it would never be enough.

When his vision cleared, his knuckles were bleeding, his throat was raw, and his chest heaved with exertion. He'd torn his daughter's room to pieces, but she remained untouched, a red-haloed angel.

Something else caught his eye. Jillian's snub-nosed revolver, the gun that had murdered his daughter, was on the floor beneath a cracked dresser drawer. He picked it up, considered joining them in the nothingness. But he slipped it into his pocket instead. He might take that route, but first Sledge had to die. Sledge, who had murdered them with his hands. Then Brody, who had murdered them with his own fucking stupidity.

When he turned, he found Colin standing in the doorway. He might have seen Brody unravel, but he was too deep in his own pain to care.

"Who would do this?" he asked.

"I know," Brody rumbled.

"Then what are we waiting for?"

Brody stepped past Colin and grabbed his backpack, still heavy with his favorite guns and all the ammo he could fit. He wouldn't deny Jill's brother his part, so long as he could keep up. He took one last look at his dead wife, at the apartment that had been their oasis in Ptolemy's desert of crime and corruption for four years. Then he turned and walked away.

Brody hauled his bike up to the road. Colin was waiting for him. Neither said a word. Brody took off, hell-bent on finding Sledge and showing him far less mercy than he'd shown his family.

CHAPTER 11

Capri's apartment smelled of roses and vanilla.

Her closet was the same size as the one in the Maiden Dorm, but it was filled with lavish dresses, jewels, and lingerie rather than modest clothes in hues of white. Instead of several beds, there was just the one, piled with pillows and set in an upholstered frame that matched the near-white blue of the walls. It was large and inviting. The crystal chandelier hanging above made it clear that it was the main attraction.

In the back of the room was a private bathroom with a tub big enough for two. There was an alcove with two wingback chairs and a table between, perfect for intimate conversation. She had a small, carved vanity—a gift from the King—and a mini bar.

Most Ladies, when they moved to their apartment, decorated with scarlet, silk, and furs. They were given free rein when it came to preparing the space in which they would entertain the King, and they fretted over it as if they were choosing their wedding gowns.

Capri would be entertaining all kinds, and every part of the room was designed with her future role in mind. It could be anything she— or the person who won her—wanted it to be. Briony had tried to involve her in the design process, but Capri wanted nothing to do with it. The only choice she'd made was the artwork. A reproduction of Bernini's *The Ecstasy of St. Teresa* sat like an exquisite gargoyle in one corner of the room.

Capri glanced up from her reading assignment, a book by Leopold von Sacher-Masoch, to look at the nun. Her expression was the epitome of pleasure and pain, and it made her feel less alone.

A knock sounded on the door by the vanity.

"Come in," she called.

Briony's room was adjacent to her own. She didn't have to knock. She did it out of courtesy, but Capri felt it was all pretense. An Attending Lady was something like a lady's maid, but, despite subservient appearances, Briony outranked her. She answered to Ekon. She used the power she had kindly and wisely, but she still held it.

The blond stepped inside. She wore a hunter green dress and held a paper note in her hand. Capri was lounging on the bed, naked beneath a soft robe. She hadn't bothered dressing after her bath.

"Hello, Capri," Briony said brightly. "How do you like the book so far?"

"It's interesting," she said vaguely, marking her place with a stylus and turning off the reader. She gave her tutor her attention, but there was still a distance between them. She imagined there always would be.

"It's good to know the philosophy behind various schools of sexual...flavor."

Capri looked away and pretended to pick a piece of lint off her robe. The idea of ever dominating someone in the bedroom made her feel ill. The idea of doing *anything* in the bedroom made her feel ill. She didn't want to talk about it. Her maidenhead had been stolen and with it the life she was supposed to have.

Briony was a woman who had gotten everything Capri never would, and a part of her would always resent her for that.

Capri was in a Lady's apartment, with a Lady's wardrobe, but she would never be a Lady. A *Lady* of Mars was a lover of the King—past or present. She would have the title, out of courtesy, but she would never be that. She was an other. A prostitute, if she thought about it too hard.

No part of her wanted that, but she still wanted to please her King. She was willing and unwilling. Her entire future, once so simple and bright, was now dark and dichotomous.

"You should dress for dinner," Briony suggested, still trying to infect Capri with her chipper attitude.

She swept into her closet and looked through her clothes. Capri looked away. She didn't like the closet.

White was prohibited for the ladies. Their dresses were colorful and daring. They still had to go past the knee, but attractive necklines and cutouts were encouraged.

"Here," Briony caught her attention, and Capri looked back to her Attending Lady.

She held a black chiffon number with floral detail. It was beautiful. Capri felt a small stirring of excitement. It took her back to when pretty things and the love of her King were guaranteed.

"Don't you think it's a bit much for dinner?" she asked.

"Not at all." Briony held out the note to her with a look of triumph.

The paper was wax-sealed, and Capri knew who had sent it immediately. Once again, she felt a rush. Her heart fluttered—then fell as she read the words.

She was invited to the upper dining hall, but not to sit at Ekon's table. Only to eat in his presence. It would be her first time seeing him since his visit to the infirmary, and he was asking her to take her place for all to see, not at his side on the dais—but at his feet on the main floor. She would sit beside those that the King was only fond of, next to those he had loved and those he never would.

Marianne would be there, and she would eat up Capri's fall in station like the beautiful monster she was.

"I'll be with you," Briony said softly, breaking through her turmoil. "I'm on your side."

Capri raised her hazel eyes to Briony's green ones. For a brief moment, the air cleared between them. She believed the woman was genuine. She tried to smile, but this was her burden to bear and no one else's. Briony couldn't carry the weight. She couldn't understand. This was Capri's future now, and she'd just have to find a way to make it through. She'd have to make it through seeing Ekon tonight, the next two years of her unorthodox education, and being whored out by the man she'd once adored—instead of loved.

She dropped her robe and slipped into the dress. Briony zipped her in and then styled her hair and applied her makeup. By the time she was done, Capri looked stunning. It was the only power she had left.

Everything was different now, but she was still one of Ekon's beauties. Tonight, she would remind him, his Favorite, and everyone else present that she had been one of the chosen ones, too.

She would hold her head high. She would make him his money. And she would make him mourn the loss of her.

CHAPTER 12

Capri began looking forward to dining beneath the King's dais—not because she longed for his touch, his approval, or his love—but because she knew that seeing her and being unable to have her was torture for him. Indeed, over the course of the next year and a half, he asked her to join him weekly, and each night, his hungry eyes found her. His pain and anguish were almost tangible. He regretted the chains with which he'd bound himself, and it brought Capri a certain amount of satisfaction.

Briony, who had a particular insight into his likes and dislikes, organized new, daring outfits for Capri to wear in his presence. She'd been chosen to be Capri's Attending Lady because she was unassuming, but she had a certain sensuality and brazenness about her that had captivated Ekon.

She'd confided that during her time as the favorite they had pushed even Ekon's sexual boundaries.

The King believed Briony could teach Capri to do the same, only for others. He wanted to be sure that she would be worth what the bidders paid, not only in beauty and bragging rights, but also in knowledge. She had to be whatever appealed most to a Victor—the man or woman who won her for the night—whether that was an innocent virgin or an experienced seductress. Ekon's plan was working; she was coming into her own—only *he* was being seduced, as well.

It was a small revenge, but it was enough, and she was careful not to take it too far. It wouldn't do to anger the King or Marianne.

An air of innocence and sadness that she did not need to fabricate clung to her like a low fog, breaking the King's heart even more. It was an asset, Briony told her. At some point, the blond's allegiance had changed. Capri did call her a friend. And now that she had a friend and a focus, she could sometimes go an entire day without thinking of Sullivan, a week without dreaming of that night.

She lay in her robe the night before her seventeenth birthday, reading a book of her own choosing for once. It was the biography of a soldier-turned-artist who had been there, at the start of the Migration from Old Earth to New Earth five hundred years before. This woman had been inspired to paint scenes from New Earth, before it was inhabited, as it was being built up for use by those lucky enough to gain passage.

Capri had only vague memories of New Earth. What had once been her home was a strange place now. She knew she would never leave Mars unless it was through a book, in the comfort and safety of her room. But, sometimes, her mind wandered, and she wondered what it might have been like if she hadn't been brought here.

Would she trade all this to have control over her own destiny? Some days, she thought the answer was yes. Most days, she knew she wouldn't survive a day away from her luxurious slavery.

A knock sounded, and Briony let herself in through the adjoining door. She was also in her robe, having just finished a bath, and joined Capri on the bed. Capri didn't look up. She'd been avoiding this conversation all day, and now the day was done. She could avoid it no longer.

"Did you get a chance to look at the files I sent you?" Briony asked gently.

"No."

Her time of unhurried opulence was at an end. In just three days she would meet her first Victor. She didn't want to think about it.

"Capri," Briony said. "You knew this day would come."

She pretended to be absorbed in her reading.

"Well," the blond continued in her usual, unruffled way, "lucky for you I brought my own reader. And a note from the King."

That caught Capri's attention. It wasn't Thursday. This wasn't a request that she come to dinner. It was something else, and she wanted to know what.

Briony held up the paper but kept it out of Capri's reach. "First, the contracts. You must know what to expect."

Capri sighed and sat up, putting her reader away to give Briony her full attention.

"Thank you. Why don't we move to the alcove? I ordered tea."

Capri chose the chair to the left and waited for her mentor to set the tray on the table between them. She hugged her knees to her chest, keeping her body covered by the robe simply because it was one of the last times she'd have a say in the matter.

Briony joined her a few moments later, and Capri accepted the warm China cup. It smelled of chai—her favorite—and despite her dark mood she began to relax.

Briony was understanding and kind and everything she'd seemed in the beginning. And meanness without reason wasn't in Capri's nature, either. Her fire fizzled out, and she was left feeling tired, detached, and anxious to get that note—even if it meant facing the reality of her fate.

"There are things we need to discuss before next week," Briony said, pulling up a written document on the screen of her reader. "We've talked about them before, but the day of their relevance is coming. We should go over the document again."

Capri nodded obediently.

"One night with a Lady of Mars will be auctioned off on a bi-weekly basis. The auction winner, man or woman, will be known as 'Victor'. They may state in the initial form if they prefer to be called by a different name."

Briony raised her eyes to be sure Capri was paying attention. "If they do give a different name, it's because they'd like you to use it. Make sure to say it. Especially during the act."

Capri nodded again, and Briony looked back to the document.

"You will maintain some autonomy over your wardrobe, but the Victor will express his or her preferences. These may include style, color, etc." Briony looked up again. "Take this into consideration. Remember that if you give a little in the beginning, you may be able to avoid further demands. Let the Victor feel that they are being heard, and they may not ask you for more. Some, of course, simply like to be in control. There isn't much you can do then."

Her eyes returned to the reader, but she paused. Capri glanced up, her interest piqued. Briony's perfect composure was slipping. She didn't want to be having this conversation any more than she did, despite the fact she'd never seemed to have an issue with any of it—or her role in it—before.

"Victors are not permitted to leave a mark," she said in a steady voice. Then her eyes met Capri's, and they looked pained. "This does not mean that they can't hurt you."

Capri looked away. She knew that. But the thought of exactly what that could entail sent a shiver down her spine. It was something she'd avoided thinking of until now; now, when she could no longer avoid it. All she knew firsthand of sex was Sullivan. All she knew was pain. The thought of it happening again made her want to vomit.

"If you feel someone is breaking a rule, press one of the five panic buttons in your room, or, of course, scream. There will be guards stationed just outside."

Capri nodded. Briony grasped her hand, urging Capri to look at her. She did so reluctantly. She didn't want to be here, discussing this. She'd rather be walking through the gardens or library. Dining, dancing, bathing, studying, singing—*anything* else. Briony, her constant companion, who had helped her pick up the pieces after Sullivan, knew exactly where her mind was.

"You are never powerless, Capri," she said. "You have to remember that. Use your knowledge, your beauty, and your body to your advantage. Oftentimes, you can control the situation without your partner ever knowing."

Capri looked away again. It was easy for her to say. She, like most of the women in the palace, had only ever been with Ekon. Capri would never know what it was like to be with someone she wanted. Any romance with Ekon was only an imitation of the real thing—even she knew that by now—but she had wanted him once, and if her circumstances were different, she would want him blindly still.

Now, she was broken, bitter, and expected to please a new lover every two weeks, never knowing who or what to expect. Briony could offer advice, but for Capri it would be different. She would always be different.

Briony squeezed her hand so hard it hurt, forcing Capri's eyes to meet hers again.

"You are *never* powerless," she said again.

Capri nodded, just so she'd let go. The blond cleared her throat and resumed the review with her usual composure.

"Just as the winning bidder will be called the Victor, you will be called 'Prize'. However, your given name is not to be used under any circumstances."

Briony put the reader down. "I'll be here to help you prepare. If you look at the last document, you'll see Ekon is requiring that your first Victor be 'a gentle lover suited to taking a virgin'. Although your virginity is not technically intact, the Victor is aware you've never had a man reach completion inside of you, and you've never reached completion with a man yourself."

"How generous," Capri quipped. "Can I see the note now?"

Briony handed it to her. The seal was already broken.

"It was addressed to me," Briony explained. There was a playful smile on her lips. "But it concerns you."

Capri looked over the contents, and her heart beat faster with every word. A party. She would have a birthday party. She hadn't thought she would be afforded the privilege. Ekon had even requested the first dance.

"This is for tomorrow?" Capri asked, rereading the words.

"Yes." Briony smiled. "And he's had a dress made as a present for you."

Capri smiled back. She could tell the other woman had been counting on this to brighten her spirits—and it had.

But she would never be fully free from the dread. Even if the evening was magical, it was still the only evening standing between her and the night she'd meet her first Victor.

CHAPTER 13

The dress Ekon had chosen was royal blue with a plunging neckline and asymmetrical skirt, placing Capri's exquisite legs on display as she walked through cascading waves of organza. She wore her hair down, woven with loose braids and beads of solid gold and silver. Her high-heeled sandals were gold and silver, too, and besides a pair of nude underwear, that was all she wore. Briony knew when to let her student's beauty speak for itself, and her coming of age party was one of those occasions.

A royal guard escorted them to the upper dining hall, which needed no added décor to become a place of elegant celebration. The glass dome gave a view of the night sky; simple gold centerpieces adorned the clear polycarbonate tables, which had been moved to allow for dancing. The music playing in the background was soft and lilting, something with violins. Guests were just sitting down to dinner, drinks, and conversation.

Ekon beamed when she made her entrance. "The woman of the hour!"

The guard entered just after with Briony. Capri was careful not to make eye contact. Getting too friendly with the men who were supposed to protect her was not a mistake she would make again.

Capri smiled demurely as the guests applauded her arrival. She approached the dais and bowed to the King. He looked at her ensemble with approval, and she noticed he'd dressed to match. She still was not permitted to sit beside him, which would have been tradition for a Maiden coming of age. Instead, he stepped down to stand with her.

Her status was uncharted territory for everyone present, including Ekon, but he was a talented diplomat. Every movement was intentional, making it clear there was nothing strange about this party for his broken beauty. It was tradition for a new Lady to share her first taste of champagne with the King, and he handed her a glass after taking two from a serving tray. They touched them together with a delicate *clink* and sipped.

Capri bowed again and sat at her table in front of the dais. Next to being on the platform, it was the highest place of honor. Ekon called for dinner to be served.

Of course, Capri was already well-versed in the art of alcohol. If a Victor wanted to share a drink with the Prize, it wouldn't do for her to gag on a sip of whiskey or overindulge on sweet wine. Briony held tastings regularly so that she was familiar with all kinds. Ekon knew this, but he kept up appearances.

There were plenty of people she didn't know at the party, invited because the King wished to have them there. Then there were others, like Agatha, who caught her eye and gave a graceful wave.

Her friend, Gina, had replaced her at Ekon's side on the dais. She'd be fifteen now. Marianne was studying her soup, lips turned down in what was becoming a trademark frown. It was an unexpected birthday gift, getting to witness Gina's rise and the beginning of Marianne's fall.

After dinner, Capri greeted her guests and thanked them for attending. She chatted with Agatha but glossed over the details of what Ekon had planned for her. The other woman still bore guilt for what had happened that night, and Capri wanted her to believe that she was content. Sometimes she nearly was.

Ekon rose, and the activity stopped.

"Now I would ask my newest Lady for the first dance," he said, smiling down at her.

"Of course, King," Capri answered.

He stepped down once more, and the dance floor cleared. He pressed a button on a remote in the pocket of his jacket, and music played. The song was upbeat. His fingers grazed her bare back, and he pulled her close when the steps called for it. The tempo of the music and the choreography didn't allow for intimacy or conversation. After the first verse, other couples joined in, and soon the floor was a sea of beautiful bodies dancing in pairs.

Ekon's Ladies weren't allowed to dance with other men, but they danced with each other. Some male friends or associates of the King were present, but anyone who stepped foot in the palace knew better than to break the cardinal rule if they wanted to remain in his good graces.

As the song ended, Ekon came to a halt, holding both of Capri's slender hands in his, a smile on his handsome face. He had exerted himself and was breathing heavily. Capri was breathless herself and had laughter on her lips. In that brief moment, she loved him again, and her heart clenched painfully. His dark, wavy hair had fallen across his eyes. He was guileless, almost boyish. The excitement of the night made everything shimmer.

"Capri," he said, the whispered word a commendation—and a lament.

Her smile faltered. He reached up, brown eyes focused on her mouth, and he ran the pad of his thumb across her bottom lip. Her face burned; her breath caught. She wasn't sure how to react to the King's anguish, and her own hurt was becoming anger. He continued to act as if this arrangement was beyond his control. As if he hadn't decided her fate.

The next song started, and he seemed to come to his senses.

"Happy birthday." He said, smiling once more before going to the dais and bowing to Marianne.

Capri tried to put the unsettling interlude out of her mind and danced with Briony, Agatha, and some of the other ladies in turn. She realized that Gina hadn't left the dais at all. She sat, looking poised and politely interested, remembering her schooling, in a white chiffon dress.

On a whim, Capri approached the platform and called up to her. "Gina! Will you dance with me?"

The redhead's eyes widened. She glanced around, looking to Ekon for approval, but he was otherwise engaged with a Lady whose impossibly dark skin made her look otherworldly. *Aphrodite of Knidos* in ebony, Capri thought.

Gina stood and descended, but her reluctance was obvious. Hurt slipped through Capri's euphoria again. She'd thought Gina would be pleased to spend time with her. Masking emotion had been an important part of her studies, and she retained her grace despite the pang of injured pride. They began moving to the beat. The girl's muscles were tense beneath her freckled skin. She couldn't look Capri in the eye. They continued at a friendly distance; to anyone else all seemed well.

"You don't have to dance with me," Capri told Gina softly. "I won't be upset."

The redhead looked up then, and Capri was surprised to find fear in her green depths. She stopped moving to focus on her.

"What is wrong?"

Gina swallowed. "Aren't you angry?" she asked, almost in a whisper.

Capri's brow furrowed. She glanced up at the table as if it held the answers. Ekon had returned to drink a glass of ale and was now watching them dance together with poorly concealed pleasure. Then she caught sight of Marianne's glower and understood. Gina thought she must hate her for stealing Ekon away, as Marianne had once hated her.

"Oh," she murmured. "That ship took off a long time ago. I'm happy for you."

"Really?"

"Really."

Gina relaxed, and they danced the next song as well. The younger girl gushed about how well Ekon treated her, how excited she was to serve him, and Capri listened enthusiastically. Her own rose-colored glasses were gone, but she wouldn't ruin this for her friend. Gina's dreams were coming true.

The song ended, and they parted ways. Briony whisked her away to the ladies' room to touch up her hair and fix her dress, keeping her a vision of perfection through the cutting of the cake.

Soon, it was time for the last dance. It would be something upbeat to keep the feeling of elation alive as the courtiers returned to their rooms. Capri had Briony's hand in hers, ready to pull her onto the dance floor.

But to her surprise, a melancholic love song began over the speakers, and Briony let Capri's fingers slip from hers as she looked at something over her shoulder. The hair on the back of Capri's neck stood on end. Ekon stood behind her, demanding the last dance as well as the first. The last dance always went to the Lady he'd be sleeping with. It wouldn't be her. It *couldn't* be her.

Still, the sweet strains of the music curled through her body like mulled wine, and she knew that this dance would not be casual.

She turned to her King. There was no predetermined choreography for this one, and most of the people on the floor were true couples, their bodies swaying and meeting to the slow beat. Capri barely noticed them. The King held her gaze and her body, moving in a way that spoke of his vast experience with the female sex.

Anger, resentment, reverence, and arousal all vied for Capri's attention, and the overload only served to heighten her senses, set her nerves on fire. Inside, she was torn between fight and flight. Outwardly, of course, she was the perfect partner, matching him move for move, graceful and sensual, giving into his silent demands without question.

He was, after all, her King.

Ekon held one hand in his and kept the other on her lower back. His eyes were dark with passion, and his mouth formed the charming grin Capri had once dreamed of. She forced herself to relax, to slip into the guise of the confident seductress that would soon mean her survival.

"Do you know how much the winning bid was?"

Ekon's husky voice caught her off guard. She hadn't thought he was looking for conversation.

"Do I get a share?" Capri asked lightly. "It doesn't really concern me otherwise."

The King laughed. "Maybe you will, if I receive a positive report from your Victor."

"I'll do my best, King."

Ekon looked past her for a moment, toward the dais, and a frown flickered across his full lips. Capri caught sight of Marianne's scowl and suppressed her own smile. Ekon brought his eyes back to hers, probably thinking she'd missed the exchange.

"She must be very good in bed," Capri said.

She was being impertinent, but Ekon only seemed amused. They both knew she didn't have much to lose by speaking out of turn.

"Are you wondering why she's the Favorite?"

Capri gave a delicate shrug. "There are others as beautiful, if not more. I doubt she's a great conversationalist. And, somehow, she's had the longest run so far."

Ekon smiled, but this time there was sadness in it. He reached out to tuck a curl behind her ear, her cheeks burned at the touch. She'd hoped the conversation would ease the strange tension between them, but it only seemed to intensify it.

"Be fair to me. You would have replaced her at my side tonight."

For a moment, she forgot herself, and felt sorry for him. Then her anger returned with a vengeance. Her entire future had become twisted into some sick imitation of what it was supposed to be, and the only reason for it was his own hubris. She'd gone from Rising Favorite to whore all at the whim of the man holding her so tightly.

She couldn't be sure of her feelings, but she knew it was something akin to hatred, and she was not supposed to hate her King. She certainly couldn't show dislike for the man in charge of her life. But she understood the restlessness she felt now, the dark knot that had settled in her chest when Ekon explained how she would be serving him and Mars.

She felt trapped.

"If you must know, she does please me in bed." Ekon's voice returned her to the present. "She's also a fine opponent in chess."

"Chess?" Capri was surprised. "Really?"

"Yes. Somehow she always manages to capture my queen."

Capri laughed, continuing the charade. She glanced back at Marianne and met her stony gaze evenly. So, Marianne's head wasn't empty, after all.

She found that very unsettling.

CHAPTER 14

The end of the night was a swift and silent arrow. Capri and Briony took the elevator to the fourth floor with a slew of other Ladies and a group of silent guards. The laughing, talking, and good wishes—some even genuine—continued until she and Briony entered her room.

Briony helped her out of the dress with clumsy hands as they chatted about the evening. The blond had drunk her fair share of champagne and was flushed. Laughter bubbled from her in the form of giggles that were quite unlike her. It made Capri laugh in turn, staving off the sadness that would envelop her once her friend was gone.

Capri only had two glasses of champagne during the party. She'd grown to prefer red wine, dry and bittersweet.

Soon, Briony retired to her own room, and Capri was left alone, her head perfectly clear, her last, shining moment already dimmed. Most new Ladies would be freshening up after their party, choosing lingerie to impress the King, and waiting with anticipation to hear from their newly appointed Attending Lady that he was on his way to bed them.

Capri didn't want that, but she wanted *something*. Something more.

She sighed, finished undressing, and donned a satin robe. She kept the beads in her hair because she liked them—a bit of luxury to comfort her. Briony recommended she sleep naked. Most Ladies did. They could be called upon at any time, and Briony insisted that it allowed a woman to feel more in tune with her body.

Capri, however, couldn't bear to feel so unprotected when she was at her most vulnerable, and her Attending Lady didn't push the issue.

She was tired but not enough to sleep. She wandered the room, sipping a glass of cold water, savoring the last night that her body would be hers. Her thoughts drifted to what would come next, what it would be like. Best-case scenarios and worst-case scenarios played in her mind until she finally decided she would go to bed, after all.

But then Briony burst into her room, dressed in her own robe, wide-eyed and mostly sober.

"Good, you're still awake," she said before Capri could speak. "He's coming."

"Who's coming?"

"Ekon."

The blood left Capri's face so fast she had to sit down. "What? Why?"

"Why do you think? He wants to bed you."

This couldn't be happening. She'd built her entire life around Ekon and then been forced to dismantle it. She'd gone through so much pain and grief because he'd rejected her. Now that she'd come to terms with it, now that she didn't even *want* him, he would still have her.

It wasn't fair.

"But…he can't."

Briony turned from the vanity where she was scrambling to find a particular bottle of perfume. Her gaze was sharp. "He's the King, Capri. He can do whatever he wants. Now let's get your dress back on."

"My dress?"

"Yes," Briony snapped. Then she took a deep breath and collected her patience. "He wanted you in that dress tonight so he could take it off you. I can't believe I didn't see the signs before. I'm sorry for that."

She spritzed Capri with the subtle perfume, and together they pulled the dress out of the laundry. Briony shook out the wrinkles, and Capri slipped into it once more. She was shaking; her heart was beating too fast. She was terrified and completely unprepared.

"You left your hair. That's good. Bare feet will be fine." She was talking to herself, checking off some mental list.

When she seemed satisfied, she took her protégé firmly by the shoulders and looked her dead in the eye. Her tone was urgent. "I'm not sure what to expect from him, Capri. I've never seen him like this. You're forbidden fruit, and that's something he's simply never had. Just remember what I've taught you."

Capri nodded automatically, before the words fully sank in. If Briony, of all people, was out of her element, what the hell could Capri do? Her Attending Lady stood next to her, and they'd barely turned to face the door when a sharp rap sounded. Capri flinched. Briony squeezed her hand tightly and then moved to open it.

"King," she greeted. "I apologize for my attire. We weren't expecting a visit."

"It's alright, Briony," he replied, barely looking at her.

He stepped inside, letting the door slide shut behind him with his guards on the other side.

"Is there anything I can get you?" Briony asked.

"No, thank you. You can leave us."

"Yes, King."

Briony nodded her head in acquiescence and shot Capri one final glance, her gaze filled with warning. Capri would need to handle this carefully.

And then she and Ekon were alone.

Capri swallowed, struggling to keep fear from showing. His eyes, dark with desire, ran down the length of her body, taking stock of all that was his. She didn't need experience to know that his self-control was hanging by a thread. She forced her voice to remain even.

"What can I do for you, King?"

"Oh, Capri," he breathed, keeping his distance but still seeming too close. "I've tried to resist you, but I just can't."

Capri's mouth was dry, but she thought if she turned in search of a glass of water he might pounce.

"I'm honored, King," she said softly. "But as you've said, I…" She fumbled here, and his eyes shot to hers. The show of weakness, of innocence, seemed to ignite him, and he moved in. She finished her thought quickly. "I do not meet the requirements."

"Yes," he murmured, almost to himself as he reached a hand up to massage the nape of her neck and toy with the clasp holding her top together. His eyes raked over her clothed breasts. With effort, he managed to focus on her and their electric conversation once more. "I think I've discovered a solution."

Capri didn't trust herself to speak. Her mind was going haywire, but she couldn't let him know. Every ounce of energy was put to keeping her body from trembling. If he knew her fear, it would be all-too easy for him to dominate her, to hold the upper hand, and even in her current state she knew she couldn't let that happen.

He pressed her against him then, and she could *feel* him. He whispered in her ear, "There are parts of you that are still untouched."

His hand gripped her ass, illustrating his point, and bile rose in Capri's throat. She knew exactly what he intended, and it was the last thing she wanted to do. Briony had told her it could be nice under the right circumstances. These were *not* the right circumstances.

Ekon himself had demanded a gentle lover to ease her into her new duties, and now he would take even that from her.

She nearly shut down then, just as she had when she'd accepted that there was no escaping Sullivan—or the men who had brought her to Mars in the first place.

Briony's words drifted back to her. *You are never powerless.*

She was wrong. She'd never been raped. Capri could not have escaped Sullivan—but he had been a monster. The King, she suspected, was just a man. A man overcome with desire for her.

Maybe that did give her power.

She took a deep breath, tamped down her fear, and very carefully took the upper hand.

"My King," she said softly, untucking his shirt from his pants so she could begin to unbutton it, her movements tantalizingly slow. He gasped as her deft fingertips grazed his skin. She took genuine pleasure in the sound, in the knowledge that she was bringing her King, the source of her woes, to his knees. "That isn't what you really want."

She pushed his jacket off his shoulders, and he rid himself of the shirt. His skin was smooth, light brown and chiseled. If he were someone else, he might have been perfect.

"I can't go back on my word," he said, voice husky, resolve cracking under her touch.

"King," she murmured, standing on her tiptoes to nibble his ear, "you know that no man has ever spilled his seed inside of me. I can promise that I am as tight as any Maiden. I want you." She paused to undo his belt, sliding it through the loops and letting it fall to the floor. "And you want me."

She looked him in the eye. It wouldn't do to blush now. His lips were a whisper away, but she needed him to close the gap, to sign the corporeal contract. She realized suddenly that he was trembling. She felt like a goddess.

"I've promised you to another," he whispered, his lips brushing hers.

"I won't tell if you don't."

He groaned then and kissed her fervently. Capri felt a rush of triumph. Her fate might never be her own, but she could twist it in her favor. Maybe she had some power, after all.

And maybe that would be enough to make her new life as the Prize bearable.

CHAPTER 15

"Shots," the captain's clipped voice sounded over the intercom in Brody's room, waking him from an alcohol-induced slumber.

His initial feeling was irritation, and it lingered. Passing out drunk was the best sleep he got. Waking meant remembering, and even a year and a half after the death of his family, the memories were agonizing when they found him. For a man who had been taught to rage against pain, this quiet, simmering anger had become his norm.

In his new life, that anger found plenty of outlet. His place in the crew of *Task Eternal* was never official, but it was indisputable. Colin made him earn his keep, and Brody was happy to look mean and shoot whoever needed to get shot. When the ship docked for supplies, he spent his earnings on drinking, guns, and sometimes women.

He wouldn't recognize any of them if he saw them again. They satisfied a need, warmed his bed, and let him pretend he wasn't such a miserable son of a bitch for an hour or two. When he thought back to the last time he'd felt anything more for someone, he only saw Jill.

He tried not to think back too often.

"Shots," the voice snapped again.

Brody fumbled for the button by his bed. "Yeah," he grunted.

"We're about to land on Tycho. Get right."

Brody grunted his acknowledgement. The dynamic of captain and crewmember seemed to suit them better than brothers-in-law. Brody didn't want to put too much thought into where he went or what he did next, and, with his increasingly risky ventures, Colin had plenty of use for one of the best gunmen in the System.

His self-destructive behavior was an unspoken agreement. *Don't let it interfere with the mission.* If he fucked up too badly, he was off the ship.

Brody stumbled to the tiny bathroom, barely big enough to contain a sink, toilet, and shower, and splashed water on his face. He ran a toothbrush over his teeth and didn't think to look in the mirror. He kept his brown hair cropped close to his head and waited too long to shave. Low maintenance. He pulled a clean shirt out of a drawer beneath his unmade bottom bunk. He put it on, selected the best guns for the job from his personal stash in a crate against the wall, and let the door to the main corridor slide open.

He looked far from impressive, but he functioned and did his job, and that was all anyone asked for. It was all he could give.

Today they were picking up a supply of Sector B25 moonshine from the rebel planet for Queen Mary of Venus. The liquor was popular, but few were willing to risk getting it. Especially on the lawless rebel planets, suppliers were often just as happy to kill the buyer and keep the money as they were to maintain a business relationship. Some of Colin's contacts had consistent reputations, but others were unpredictable.

This supplier was new, and they all figured it was better to err on the side of caution and go in with all the protection they could carry.

Everyone on the ship knew how to handle a gun, even Leroy, and they each had a part to play. Colin handled the business side of things. Jax would follow him to edge of the System if he asked, despite the fact Colin probably couldn't pay all he deserved for his skill level. And there wasn't anything on the ship Leroy couldn't fix except his running mouth.

Brody added a certain amount of credibility when they dealt with rebel planets. The twins were New Earthers, and as far as most of the "businessmen" they dealt with were concerned, Colin might as well have been.

They made a solid team. If their reputations preceded them, it would be unlikely anyone would fuck with them today.

But Brody really hoped they did.

He met Colin and Leroy in the loading bay. The ship had landed, but Jax was still in the cockpit, flipping switches and grabbing his own guns. Tycho was the closest habitable planet to the sun, and Brody braced himself for the heat. He was used to the cold of his home planet, of space, of Mars's thinly veiled steel. Dry though it was, the heat always made him feel uncomfortable, suffocated.

"Morning, Shots," Leroy said brightly.

Most ships, including theirs, opted to follow the time it was in the United Nations district on New Earth. It was the afternoon there.

"Shut up, Leroy," he growled.

"Enough," Colin said without looking up from loading his rifle.

Brody glared at the mechanic, who just laughed and pulled on a pair of tactical gloves before slipping a pistol into its holster. In the beginning, when Jill and Maxine were alive, Leroy had been a nuisance, a fly buzzing around his head. Now they were stuck in the same metal crate day in and day out, and Leroy had taken to pushing Brody's buttons for his own amusement. They both knew Brody could kill him faster than he could blink, but they also knew he wouldn't risk the repercussions.

It wasn't just his chipper attitude that got to Brody. It was what the chipper attitude meant—that he'd never felt pain, never known loss. It was a gift he'd hoped to give Maxine. It was a gift Leroy had that she never would, just because he'd had the good fortune to be born on the right fucking planet.

Every fucking day he took it for granted, and every fucking day Brody hated him for it.

Jax came from the corridor and nodded to Colin, who turned to Brody. His eyes flickered to the gunman's chest. Brody knew what he was looking for. It wouldn't be the first time they'd had this brief exchange, and it wouldn't be the last.

"Are you wearing gear?"

"No."

"You should."

"Is that an order?"

Colin's lips formed a thin line. "You know it's not."

Brody shouldered his rifle, placed a linker in his ear, and kept his face impassive. "Then let's go."

Colin and Brody took the elevator down. There were no official docks in the sector, so Jax had landed on a flat spot near their destination. He'd sent the coordinates to the group they were doing business with, and once Brody got past the initial blast of hot air, he spotted a truck about five hundred yards away, outfitted for desert driving and waiting for them.

Jax and Leroy hung back in case anything went awry.

The vehicle approached. A gray-haired woman was driving, and a man in the passenger's seat had his gun drawn but pointed down. A machine gun sat on the top of the truck, but it wasn't manned.

A dozen scenarios played out in Brody's mind, and he noted each one objectively. She could run them over. Shoot them where they stood. They might survive and return fire. There were only three or four of them. Two in the front and one, maybe two, in the back. The suppliers would assume there were more people in the ship. They wouldn't know how many. The odds weren't good for a fight.

But it could always go either way.

As the truck stopped, the hairs on the back of Brody's neck pricked. He was alert, anticipating, hoping. He gripped his rifle tightly, and all feeling slipped away as he achieved the perfect focus that kept his aim true and impartial.

The woman got out to meet Colin with a wary smile. Colin lowered his gun and shook her hand. Brody stayed ready, as did the woman's guard. She showed them the alcohol, let Colin sniff and taste the clear liquid. Maybe it was poisoned?

But to Brody's disappointment, the transaction was a smooth one. Colin showed her the jewels Queen Mary had promised. They made the trade. Jax and Leroy lowered the ramp to load the alcohol. The job was done, and it had been easy.

Brody scowled.

When they were in the air, he joined the rest of the crew for dinner. They made their own easy-heat meals or sandwiches, but they had to sit and eat one meal together. It was the captain's version of a meeting, a daily open forum, where they discussed upcoming jobs, plans, ideas that weren't urgent. Sometimes there wasn't much to talk about and conversation drifted to more casual topics.

Occasionally, Brody would forget himself and start feeling normal. But then he'd remember and grow restless, moody, waiting for the next move, the next distraction, the next chance to draw blood or have it drawn.

Today there had been no release for his pain, his anger. There had been no killing. There were no women. After dinner, he snagged the open bottle of moonshine from the loading bay and took it back to his room.

If he couldn't release his demons, he'd have to drown them.

CHAPTER 16

The fourth anniversary of his family's death found Brody on Mars. The ship still landed every few weeks to deliver fine Bourbon from Tycho and gems from the mountains of Ptolemy. Brody took it upon himself to lay low on these missions. All ships had to show papers stating the names of everyone on board. Ekon knew he was there. But he'd left the King's service abruptly, and he didn't want any lingering resentment to affect trade relations.

His services were rarely required in the civilized Kingdoms, anyway.

They landed in the docks by the palace. Brody helped secure the crates for delivery before Jax lowered the ramp. Two guards came aboard to confirm identification and escort Alexander, who inspected the goods and handled payment on the King's behalf.

Today, however, he lingered. Brody watched him from the doorway of the corridor, leaning against the cold metal, gun on his hip. Alexander would never cause that kind of trouble, of course, but Brody wouldn't let his guard down. Especially not today. He was on edge. It was harder to focus, harder to breathe, and he didn't want to think about why. Once the crates were unloaded and his unnecessary guard duty was done, he'd be hitting the bottle hard.

The only thing standing in his way was Alexander. Irritation burned in his veins.

The white-haired man beckoned the captain over to a corner of the loading bay for a private conversation. Colin nodded and said a few things that Brody couldn't hear. Then the advisor stepped down to oversee the crates as they were loaded into a small truck. Jax closed the ramp to the loading bay, and Brody was in the kitchen before the hiss of the air lock sounded.

He had a strong bottle of scotch he'd been saving for a shit day like today. Leroy was there, too, rooting around for food. He hadn't even bothered showing up for the exchange. Brody tamped down his annoyance with effort. Everything got under his skin today. He had to be careful, or Leroy would take the brunt of it. For once, he might not deserve it.

Brody opened the cupboard, found the bottle, and lifted it. Then, he pulled it down and stared at it, uncomprehending. It was empty. He caught movement out of the corner of his eye—Leroy, sneaking away. He froze when Brody's gaze landed on him.

"Sorry, Shots, I was going to replace it."

His shrug, so nonchalant, ignited Brody's anger in a flash. The bottle fell to the floor with a resounding *clank*, and his hand was around Leroy's throat before he was fully aware of what he was doing. He held back, grip loose but unshakeable as Leroy tried to pry his fingers away.

"It was in the kitchen! The kitchen is communal," he managed.

"The fuck it is."

"I was just going to have a glass! But that is some quality stuff. I killed the bottle before I even realized it."

"You're in the kitchen, Leroy," Brody growled, leaning in close to the mechanic. "Can I kill *you?*"

The younger man's breath came in gasps, from fear more than because his airway was constricted, but it didn't look good when the captain and Jax appeared in the doorway. Jax pulled his gun without missing a beat, but he'd wait for the captain's orders—even where his brother was concerned.

"Get the hell off him, Shots," Colin ordered in a low voice.

He knew better than anyone what this was really about. Brody met his gaze. His eyes had the same anger, the same haunted look as his own, but somehow he remained in control. That had never been Brody's strong suit, but he didn't want to lose his place on the ship. He released Leroy and stepped back.

The mechanic leaned against the table, hand to his throat. "Shit, I almost pissed myself."

Jax returned his gun to its holster but only gave his brother a glance.

"Get off my ship and don't come back until you're cooled down," Colin told Shots. Then he rounded on Leroy. "And what did you do?"

"What?" Leroy's brown eyes were wide, playing innocent, but under the hard gazes of both the captain and his brother, he faltered. "I may have taken something that didn't belong to me."

Colin glanced down at the empty bottle. "Then you'll replace it, and if you don't stop fucking with him I might just let him have his way next time."

Leroy's cheeks flushed. "Yes, sir," he mumbled.

"Now both of you, out. We've got a job to discuss at breakfast tomorrow. I don't want to see either of your faces until then."

Brody turned and stalked down the corridor. He took the elevator without bothering to remove the gun from his belt. Technically, he was still licensed to carry on Mars. He fidgeted with the data ring below his first knuckle as the metal cage descended.

He left the docks, still in search of a drink. There were no dive bars on Mars, nowhere his twice-worn shirt and unshaven face would really fit in. The closest thing was the bar by the far docks, which was frequented by other interplanetary travelers and off-duty security guards from the palace.

Still, just walking in made him feel unsettled, and he was already in a shit mood. Mars's worst place to grab a drink was better than the best in Sector 25. The scent in the air wasn't cheap alcohol, sweat, and vomit. It was something fresher, something better. Wood soap and citrus.

To the right was the wooden bar top. The barstools had seatbacks. To the left were intimate round tables, and in the back was a lounge. The faux leather couches were piled with more throw pillows than had probably existed in his entire apartment building on Ptolemy.

This was the life he'd failed to attain for Jill and Maxine. The names formed in his mind, unbidden.

He needed that drink. Now. He sat at the bar and glanced down at the reader. It had been preloaded with a menu and advertisements, but he already knew what he wanted. The bartender appeared with a ready smile before Brody could signal.

"That bottle of scotch." He pointed to a tall bottle with smooth lines on the top shelf.

"The fifty-year single malt?"

"Yeah," Brody grunted. The bartender hesitated, and Brody struggled to keep his anger under control. "I know what it costs."

It was midday. There were only a few patrons in the bar, but they turned at Brody's menacing tone. The bartender's face flushed.

"Sorry, yes, of course." He grabbed the bottle and poured a glass with swift skill, anxious to put the embarrassing incident behind him.

Brody downed the glass like a shot and poured another. On the third, he finally found some of the relief he'd been searching for. Warmth unwound his muscles, numbed the heat in his veins, and quieted his thoughts. He looked down at the reader again, starving, now that the knot in his stomach was abating.

What he found himself focused on instead was the full-page advertisement he had to view before he could get to the menu: *Now accepting bids for the King's Auction.*

He glanced through the details. One night with one of King Ekon's beauties. Starting bid $100,000. Brody had more than twice that in his account. He considered for a moment. Fine booze and a fine woman. It would be one hell of a way to get rid of the money that had been weighing on him for the last four years.

Once upon a time, that money had a purpose. Now it meant nothing.

Someone sat down next to him, too close, considering there was only one other person at the bar. He caught a glimpse of a palace uniform in his peripheral, instinctively alert even through his alcohol-induced haze. He didn't look directly at the person, but he sensed body movement. The person was leaning in to talk to him. Irritation rippled through him.

"Your new job must be treatin' you well."

The gravelly female voice was familiar, and it compelled him to turn. Tamara. They hadn't worked together long, but he'd liked her well enough—back when he'd let himself feel things for people.

"Tamara," he grunted in greeting.

He motioned to the bartender for another glass, and, out of habit, poured a generous amount. Tamara raised the glass in thanks and took a sip, closing her eyes in silent appreciation.

When they opened again, she pointed a finger at the ad on his reader. "You gonna bid?"

He made a noncommittal noise. He could tell she was joking.

"The last Victor paid $248,000. The first time she got $910,000. But I 'magine interest wanes a bit once you know she's been with six-ty-odd other men. And women." She winked.

"When did it start?"

"'Bout two years ago. Guess the King realized he had an untapped commodity on his hands and could spare a girl."

"Is it always the same one?"

Tamara took another long sip and nodded.

Brody glanced down at the ad again. There was no picture. No other information on the Prize. Just that tomorrow was the last day to make an offer. The following night the Victor would claim his—or her—Prize. Brody ran a hand over his jaw.

He didn't need any other information, and neither did anyone else. Ekon's beauties were known throughout the System, and there were plenty of people who would pay just to *see* one of them, let alone fuck one.

Brody was surprised the bidding might actually stay in his price range.

He'd never taken much moral issue with paying for sex. It was a mutually beneficial arrangement, no different than paying someone to cook a meal. He wasn't sure it was the same this time around. She wasn't selling herself, after all; she was being sold.

But he'd stopped caring about things like right and wrong four years ago. On impulse, he tapped the link that would allow him to bid. Tamara was busy downing the rest of her glass. He flipped open his ring and aligned the sensors. He bid $250,000. It was all the money he had, except for what he might need to survive.

Tamara glanced down just in time to see the confirmation.

"Shit," she breathed. "You were serious."

She raised her wide eyes to his. "You gotta get me a job on that ship."

CHAPTER 17

"Shots." A voice over the intercom wrenched Brody from sleep. Jax this time. *"The meeting's in ten. You've got a message from the palace."*

Brody didn't bother responding and bit back a groan as he sat up. He'd done a good job drinking himself into a stupor the previous night, but somehow he'd found his way back to his bunk. He fumbled for the drawer beneath his bed and rummaged around for a bottle of aspirin. He popped an indiscriminate amount in his mouth and chewed before stumbling to the bathroom for a few gulps of water.

He splashed his face, brushed his teeth, and changed his clothes. Then he pressed the heel of his hand hard against his throbbing temple.

A letter from the palace. The auction. Had he won or lost? Which did he want?

He stretched his neck from side to side, swung his shoulders back, and headed for the mess area. The others were already seated, eating cereal, twice-baked bread, dry meat, and easy-heat meals. A bowl of fresh apples kept from a job the previous week sat in the middle of the table. Brody scowled and downed a protein shake while he waited for his frozen eggs and biscuits to thaw in the quick oven.

Jax held up the official, wax-sealed note from King Ekon between his fingers without looking up from his reader. Leroy's interest was obvious, but he wouldn't be willing to engage the shooter in conversation any time soon.

Brody leaned against the counter while his breakfast spun in the heat and ripped open the letter.

Dear Victor,

Congratulations. You've won an evening with a Lady of Mars, a.k.a. The Prize. I can promise your money has been well spent. The

Prize has been trained in the art of seduction and its various forms. Her natural sensuality and flawless physique make a pleasurable evening inevitable.

A blood test and physical evaluation will be administered at your convenience, between the hours of eight o'clock and noon today. Pending favorable results, you will be asked to sign a contract and have the opportunity to fill out a form, which will be passed on to the Prize, stating your preferences and expectations.

Thank you for bidding in the King's Auction. I have no doubt you'll enjoy this night as I enjoy all of mine.

King Ekon of Mars

He shoved the note into his pocket, grabbed his meal, and sat with the others. Colin glanced up briefly from his own reader, curious but unwilling to delve into his gunman's personal business. Brody dug into his food, ravenous now that he was up and moving. Colin set down his reader and took a sip of coffee from a tumbler before speaking.

"King Ekon's advisor has work for us."

Brody's eyebrow twitched, his only outward sign of interest as he chewed. It was unusual for a job to come directly from Alexander.

"It's different from the jobs we usually take, but considering our good relationship with Mars, he thought we might make an exception. Anyone who wants in gets a cut. Anyone who doesn't won't be penalized."

Brody stopped chewing, his interest fully piqued.

"Alexander thinks the King is in danger. He wants extra security at a birthday party three nights from now. One of the new girls was brought to the King under...suspicious circumstances. Someone, maybe the father, has threatened to come and take her back by force. Ekon isn't taking these threats seriously, but Alexander has concerns. He talked the King into inviting us to dinner. Good food, beautiful women *that you cannot touch*"—he looked pointedly at Leroy as he said this—"and maybe some gunslinging. If you take moral issue, just want to stick to the usual gigs, whatever, that's fine."

He glanced at Jax, who poked his oatmeal with a spoon, lips pursed. He clearly disapproved, but he'd go where the captain went.

Leroy wouldn't want to be left out of the fun, and Brody...killing had never bothered him any. The captain gave them the day to think it over, but none of them needed it. They were in.

Brody pushed away from the table and tossed his tray and utensils down the garbage chute. It was all biodegradable, to be collected whenever they landed back on New Earth.

"I got somewhere to be," Brody announced. "I'll be back in time for the job."

Colin nodded, acknowledgement and dismissal. Brody went to his room to relieve himself and grab his gun. He looked in the mirror and clenched and unclenched his fists.

There was no coming back from this. The money he'd saved for his family's future spent on a high-class whore. It was the final chapter in his old life, the first chapter in a new one—one where there was no evidence left of his past and nothing to prevent him from giving himself wholeheartedly to the kind of darkness in which he was always meant to live.

CHAPTER 18

Victor #68 had passed his physical exam and blood test. His name was Brody, he liked the color red, and he drank whiskey. The rest of the form left much to be desired.

"It's not that I like it when they write a book of demands," Capri said to Briony, who was shifting hangers aside, searching for a tasteful piece of red lingerie for the coming night. "But they have to give me *something* to go on."

"Maybe he doesn't know what he wants," Briony murmured distractedly. Then, she smiled triumphantly and held up a pair of red satin panties and a matching lace cover. "I knew this was in here somewhere."

Capri raised an eyebrow, and Briony sighed and sat on the bed next to her. "It isn't a bad thing, Capri. If all he wants is to lay with a Lady of Mars, your job will be easy."

"Or it could end up like #32," she said ruefully.

That particular Victor hadn't written much because the things he wanted would not have been allowed. He'd demanded she call him Reaper, and he'd liked to bite—hard. She'd managed to reach the panic button but still bore a scar on her left ribcage.

She shook her head to keep the memory at bay, the fear away. It wouldn't do to think of the "unfortunate incidents," as Alexander liked to call them, when she had to perform tonight. Briony frowned, tender sympathy in her gaze.

Capri sighed and looked away but felt Briony's weight on the bed next to her.

"Wash up, Capri, and then I'll do your hair. Once you get through tonight, you'll have two weeks of lounging around reading, walking in the gardens, visiting the spa...And who knows? Tonight might even be fun."

Capri looked up and couldn't help smiling as Briony wiggled her eyebrows suggestively. She was right. These nights weren't always bad, and then she'd have two weeks of downtime. Ekon hadn't visited her since that first night. Once the forbidden fruit had been tasted, he'd seemed to lose his appetite.

"I'll run your bath," Briony said, patting her hand and standing. "And I'll find that perfume with guaiac wood. It pairs very well with whiskey."

***

Capri dimmed the lights in her room and checked herself one more time in the vanity mirror from across the room. Her curly brown hair was woven with braids and golden beads, and Briony had used a few swipes of makeup to highlight her already stunning hazel eyes and high cheekbones. Her panties were a deep red, the shade of a rose where the petals began to fold. A silk robe in the same shade blurred her dusky nipples. Her lips were plump, her eyes soft and sad. She was perfection.

Capri knew this, objectively. It was her job to look perfect, to *be* perfect, to make the Victor feel they'd gotten his or her money's worth. She moistened her lips with the tip of her tongue and glanced at the clock on her side table, which was partly obscured by a tray containing two glasses and a decanter of single malt scotch whiskey.

One minute to go.

Capri straightened her spine and went to the door. Alexander was never late. In thirty seconds, the guards would knock. She stood in front of the metal panel, took a deep breath, and closed her eyes. When the knock sounded, she opened them, relaxed her face, and pressed the button to admit tonight's Victor.

She recognized him immediately. *Shots.* The man who had guarded the Maiden Dorm, the man who had found her with...*No.* If her mind went there, she would never be able to perform.

It had been years since she'd last laid eyes on him, and she could tell he was no longer employed by Ekon. Although he wore clean clothes and was freshly showered, he was unshaven, and...harder. It was the only way she could think to describe him. His shoulders were rigid, his jaw tense, and his brown eyes—which hadn't yet risen to her face—were darker than she remembered.

When he'd finished perusing her body, he locked eyes with hers, and they widened slightly in surprise. She kept her own expression carefully blank. He might not want to be recognized.

"Can I offer you a drink?" she murmured, head tilted slightly to one side.

She was studying him, trying to determine what he wanted from her tonight. The way he swallowed, the fleeting look of doubt told her that Briony's assumption had been correct. He wasn't sure what he wanted.

"Yeah," he grunted.

She turned to her bedside table and poured two glasses half full but glanced at him with the decanter poised. He nodded, and she poured another generous amount into his. She handed it to him and took a long sip from her own. He watched her, probably expecting her to react to the strong drink, but she swallowed and licked a drop from her bottom lip. His eyes darted to watch, and then he lifted his own glass and downed the entire thing.

She raised her eyebrows slightly, unsure whether she should be worried or impressed. Tentatively, she reached out a fingertip and ran it across his bottom lip. His nostrils flared as she brought it back to her mouth to taste it.

"Would you like another?" she asked, surprising herself by how breathless she sounded.

There was something about him, his intensity. She couldn't quite predict what he would do, and that usually made her nervous—but she had a connection with this man, and that was something she'd never had with another. Something that—for once—allowed her feel something like trust.

Brody was quiet while he considered her. Then, he leaned down and touched his lips to hers. The movement was soft, experimental, and Capri felt a jolt run through her. He parted her lips with his tongue, the hair of his beard scraping deliciously against the soft skin of her chin and cheeks. She wound her arms around his neck, pressing herself against him, while his hands found her waist, deepening the kiss. She could feel him at her apex, though he remained fully clothed, and she found herself wishing intently that he was not. She was beginning to have very high hopes for tonight.

Then, just as suddenly, he released her. She gasped, almost falling over on wobbly legs.

"Yeah. Another," he grunted.

She swallowed and nodded, trying to regain her composure. She poured him another full glass, handed it to him, and turned to add another splash to her own.

"I guess this is why they warned me not to call you by your name—even if I recognized you," he said to her barely concealed back.

Capri took a very long sip of her drink before turning to face him again with a soft, practiced smile on her face.

"Rules are rules," she murmured.

"I was also told not to leave a mark," he said, eyes roaming her body as if looking for a reason the rule might have been instated.

"Do you like it rough?" she asked conversationally.

His eyes snapped back to hers and narrowed. "Do many of them?"

Capri glanced down, once again forcing unpleasant memories to the back of her mind. When she met his gaze again, her smile was serene. "Not many of you, no."

Brody grunted his acknowledgment and sat on the edge of the bed. Capri sat primly next to him, as if she wore a couture gown rather than almost nothing. She lifted the glass again. He had drained his and sat with his elbows on his knees, staring at nothing, his mouth a hard, thin line. She waited for him to do something, and finally he looked at her.

"So this is what Alexander meant when he said they could still use you? You get raped and then they whore you out?"

Capri had been called whore too many times to feel the sting anymore. But the blunt mention of her attack made her fake smile fall. She stared at the brown liquid as it swirled in her glass.

"I should have known it was Alexander's idea. Waste not, want not." She smiled wryly, still not looking at him, and took a sip. "It's not so bad, really."

She could hear Brody breathing next to her. His leg touched hers, and she still felt it, something electric, and wondered if he did, too.

"Do you enjoy it?" he asked quietly.

She looked at him then, allowing her pretty shoulders to slouch slightly, a sardonic smile on her lips. For the very first time, she felt like herself with a Victor, and the sensation was bittersweet. This man knew her origins exactly, had seen her at her worst, had rescued her once and now...now what? He would have his way with her, like every other Victor.

But at least she could be honest with him. "It's like being served a covered dish every two weeks," she said. "Most nights, I know what I'm going to get. But every so often, I just don't." She shrugged, and though he was once again staring at his empty glass, she knew he was listening. "It might be something delicious, or it might be poison. Either way, I have to eat it."

Brody looked at her for a long moment. "What am I?"

Capri studied him, then took the glass from his hand and set it down on the table next to hers. She swung her long, smooth leg over his lap, straddling him, making his breath hitch. She lifted her hand to his face so she could run the pad of her thumb across his lower lip. She gazed into his eyes, as though she might find answers in their dark depths.

"Something different," she murmured before kissing him.

He groaned deeply, then flipped her over so he was on top of her, their bodies aligned. He let his hand slide to her breast, and she moaned as his calloused fingers brushed her nipple, making it pucker. She squirmed beneath him, begging for more, and he placed his hot mouth on the other.

Capri reached between them to feel him through his pants, to stroke and encourage him, but when her nimble fingers began to undo his zipper, he let out a noise of frustration and wrenched away. He stood, gave her one last angry look, and left—just like that—with the bottle of whiskey.

That had never happened before. Capri felt hot and ready. Capri *wanted* him, and he was just...gone. She didn't know what to do. She felt the sting of tears in her eyes, and she wasn't sure what to do with that, either.

After a few moments' silence, a knock sounded on the adjoining door, and Briony poked her head in.

"Are you okay?" she asked gently. "That was quick."

Quick usually meant rough, painful. It wouldn't occur to her friend that the deed hadn't been done at all.

"Capri, what's wrong?"

Briony rushed over, breaking Capri from her daze. She realized then that she had tears streaming down her face.

"Nothing," she managed, swiping at the liquid on her cheeks.

"This doesn't look like nothing," Briony pressed, holding her gently by the shoulders and checking her over for signs of injury.

Capri pushed impatiently at her friend's hands. "He didn't do anything."

She stood and fumbled through her closet for a robe that actually covered her. She stripped off the other garments and left them on the floor.

Briony moved slowly to pick up after her.

"What happened?"

"He...changed his mind."

"He what?"

"He just...he left. I don't want to talk about it."

"Okay." Briony's voice was quiet as Capri got into bed, a bed that had not been unmade the way it usually was after a night with a Victor. After a few moments, Briony addressed Capri's back. "You seem...disappointed," she ventured.

Capri pretended to be asleep.

CHAPTER 19

Brody had to put last night out of his mind. When it came down to it, he just couldn't be another person who took advantage of Capri. He didn't want to care anymore about anyone—and the fact that he did meant he was still soft, still weak. He was angry at himself for not going through with it, but he couldn't live with himself if he had. At least his twenty minutes with the Prize had accomplished one goal: the money was gone. Now, he had a job to do.

He sat with the other three members of the *Task Eternal* crew in Ekon's upper dining hall. As far as anyone was concerned, including the King of Mars, they were guests. Alexander had arranged the invitation as a show of appreciation for their enduring business relationship.

Brody thought Alexander was right to worry. Even if nothing came of tonight, Ekon was getting reckless. He had acquired a new girl, Faye, five months before. She was fourteen and the oldest yet—*too* old. She wouldn't have only vague memories of her previous life, like the other girls, and that meant Ekon would have a harder time brainwashing her.

According to Alexander, she'd come willingly, but Ekon had received multiple death threats since her arrival. She was more trouble than she was worth, and Alexander had told him as much, but Brody wasn't surprised the King of Mars refused to listen to reason.

He wasn't known for thinking with his big brain.

From their vantage point at a table on the perimeter of the grand room, the crew had a perfect view of the hall's main and side entrances. Brody appeared casual, lounging in the clear polycarbonate chair, but his muscles were taut, senses on high alert. He'd exchanged his typical cargo pants and wrinkled T-shirt for slacks and a button-down to better fit in. It was a job, after all, and he'd do what was required—without complaint, unlike Leroy.

The twin kept pulling at the collar of a shirt he'd borrowed from Jax, who put them all to shame in pressed khakis and a blue button-down. Brody suspected he'd tried to dress the captain, too, but Colin had rolled up his sleeves and unbuttoned his collar, as uncomfortable among the aristocracy as Brody, thanks to their rebel planet roots.

They were the first to arrive, a feat organized by Alexander, who got them and their guns past security. That meant they were able to watch the couples from the Mars apartments trickle in, as well as courtiers who lived in the palace itself.

Leroy was seated to Brody's right, which had the worst vantage point, as the captain had rightly assumed he would be the least attentive. Jax sat across from the gunman, watching the main doors. Brody had a view of the stairs, and Colin had a partial view of both.

When the Ladies appeared, Leroy stopped fidgeting.

Ten of the gorgeous creatures poured in, each with their Attending Lady trailing a step behind. He turned to watch them take their seats at the center tables, trying to convince himself he wasn't searching for Capri among the fold. She wasn't there. He glanced at Leroy, and, partly to vent some of his own frustration, smacked him under the chin to close his mouth.

The twin shot him a resentful look but regained the little composure he had.

Once the Ladies were seated, the door by the dais opened, and Brody refocused. Two guards entered through a side door, followed by the King of Mars and a second pair of guards. The room went quiet. The guests stood as one and bowed to their King. Ekon waved briefly and took his seat in the center of the platform. Marianne, a deep scowl twisting her face, came next, settling two seats away on Ekon's left.

The far seat meant she was on her way to becoming a regular Lady now, destined for retirement or occasional use. While it would take some time for Gina to transition to the role of Favorite (she could always prove to be a disappointment), it was assumed she would soon take the blond's place. Tonight, she would sit directly to Ekon's left, while Faye—the presumptive Rising Favorite—would sit to his right.

"Wow," Leroy breathed, mouth hanging open again, and Brody glanced over to see what—or who—had caught his eye.

Gina, the girl of the hour, had entered with her Attending Lady. A dazzling green gown offset her thick, flaming red hair. Her freckled cheeks were flushed, and her adoring eyes were wide and set on Ekon. She looked like a blushing bride. Brody snorted at the farce. Colin shot him a look.

Ekon helped the girl up the steps of the dais and pulled out her chair. He offered her a glass of champagne, and Brody reached for his own. The crystal vessel was small, delicate, not meant to be handled by his calloused fingers.

"Thank you all for coming," Ekon said to his guests. "A toast—to the newest and, perhaps, rarest of my Ladies. Happy birthday, Gina."

He raised his glass, gave the infatuated girl a dazzling smile, and took a sip. The room followed his lead. Brody managed not to break the glass or spit out the bubbly liquid. Champagne had never been to his taste. The King sat down, and so did everyone else.

Then, it was the Rising Favorite's turn to enter.

She arrived through the main door, escorted by Tamara. The girl's skin was smooth and brown, and the white dress she wore skimmed the floor, making her look like some kind of Greek goddess. They could see her stunning blue eyes from where they sat, and her dark, voluminous hair, held away from her forehead by a gold headband, was like a nimbus around her head.

Even Jax and Colin raised their eyebrows slightly in appreciation. Leroy looked like he might fall out of his chair. Brody had to admit she was a rare gem. She seemed to know her own appeal better than the other girls and wasn't flustered by the King. He imagined it was the benefit of having had time to come into her own, on her own. Brody could see why Alexander was concerned. This was a completely different type of girl than the King was used to.

She approached the dais and bowed low. Ekon nodded his approval, and she climbed the stairs to take her seat. So far, there was nothing out of the ordinary, and Tamara returned to her post at the dormitory without ever realizing Brody was there.

Suddenly, the main doors opened, and Brody and Colin sat up straighter in their seats, hands on the guns they'd strapped beneath the table. Jax's eyes were narrowed shrewdly to assess the situation, while Leroy just stared curiously. Heads turned. Ekon's brow furrowed in disapproval.

It was only a late arrival, and the table relaxed—except for Brody.

Capri wore a full-length gown in some sheer, frilly fabric cinched at the waist, one delicate shoulder exposed. Her brown curls were loosely braided and interspersed with beads and ribbon. Brody thought she looked like spring.

She was far from the most exotic woman in the room, but with perfect poise and a secret smile, she commanded it. Everyone looked at her, whether with awe or envy, and even Ekon's expression of annoyance gave way to fondness.

For all her affected, seductive grace, something tragic still seeped through the facade. And because Brody knew her past, he saw it clearly and felt it more than he wanted to. He didn't need the distraction.

She seemed to sense his glare and glanced his way. Her lips parted in surprise, and he felt a sense of satisfaction at her break in composure. He held her gaze and threw back the rest of his champagne like a shot. The fair flesh of her throat moved slightly with a hard swallow, but she recovered and continued to greet her host and the guest of honor.

The conversation and festivities began again at the surrounding tables, but Brody's eyes remained on Capri. She bowed gracefully to Ekon, who nodded in return, and then she approached to say a few words to Gina. Brody was too far away to hear, but Gina's green eyes lit up when she saw Capri, and she reached out to squeeze her hand.

He remembered then that Gina had been in the Maiden Dorm the night he caught Sullivan on Capri. They'd been friends, only two years apart. He imagined seventeen had looked much different for Capri.

"Shots," Colin said quietly, drawing his attention away from her.

Brody looked at his captain, who jerked his head to the side. A man had entered through the stairs, wearing a servant's uniform. He was a little older than Brody. Nothing would have seemed out of the ordinary to the guards at the door, but Brody noticed the man's eyes were locked on Faye. Brody should have been the first to notice him, and he silently kicked himself before glancing back at the dais.

The Rising Favorite hadn't seen the man yet, but he centered himself between the tables, in her line of vision, and stepped forward. Gina caught sight of the movement and looked up. Brody, Colin, Jax, and—finally—Leroy reached for their weapons.

The man pulled a knife. Gina screamed and covered her mouth, drawing the attention of those near her. Faye saw what was happening. Her eyes locked on the man, and her mouth formed a silent question that confirmed Brody's suspicions: she knew him.

Dad?

Leroy stood slightly because, somehow, he'd wound up with the clearest shot—but a palace guard reached the intruder first, tackling him to the ground. Leroy and Jax slipped their guns back into place, assuming the danger was over. The guards had done their job, and the threat had passed.

Colin, who had been trained by the U.N., and Brody, who had been double-crossed enough times to know better, waited. They exchanged a glance. Something wasn't sitting right with either of them. Why had the man drawn a knife so far from his target? Why had he hesitated when his daughter recognized him?

The young guard who had apprehended him took the knife away—too easily—as two more guards came to assist.

Ekon was already standing, waving the hero of the hour forward. He couldn't have been more than eighteen, and Brody knew they didn't usually hire them that young. It was also unlikely someone fresh out of training would be assigned to the upper dining hall. Ekon brought him onto the platform and wrapped an arm around his shoulders.

The King sported a wide smile, and his easy attitude in the face of near assassination gave the rest of the court permission to relax.

"This young man has earned a seat at my table! He saved my life tonight!"

Brody looked at Faye, and despite the events of the last few minutes, despite her father being taken to the concrete cells below the palace at this very moment, she stared resolutely at her plate. She was hiding something, trying not to give something away.

Jax had sensed the mood, and his gun was drawn again.

"What's your name?" Ekon asked the guard.

"Tyler." He spoke clearly. There was no sign of nerves.

"Tyler! I'll have a special reward for you." He glanced out into the crowd, and Brody followed his gaze—to Capri.

Brody could tell that using her to reward heroic deeds had not been part of the arrangement. At first, her expression was one of shock, but it quickly turned scathing. Her cheeks were scarlet, and she opened her mouth as if to say something, but her Attending Lady placed a hand on her leg and whispered in her ear. She'd try to fix it.

Brody felt a familiar anger rise in his chest. For once, it wasn't on behalf of his dead wife and child—but he didn't want to feel it for *anyone*.

"Don't worry." The King waved his hand dismissively. "He'll wait the two weeks."

Capri remained tightlipped and went back to her champagne. Brody turned back to the dais with effort, forcing himself to ignore her, to stay focused. He was just in time to see Faye glance up at the guard. For the briefest moment, they made eye contact, and hers shone.

She wasn't flustered by a King, but she was flustered by this man. *Shit.*

"Actually, Ekon—" He didn't use *King* and that was significant. It rang some alarm bell in Ekon, and he stepped back. "I intend to take another beauty with me. Right n—"

He didn't get to finish the sentence. Brody had already pulled the trigger.

CHAPTER 20

Capri looked up just in time to watch the guard fall. It didn't seem real, but there he was, blood droplets from the bullet wound in his head becoming airborne as gravity took him down. It was quiet for a moment, and then the only sound was screaming. Ekon still stood on the dais, shocked and spattered with blood. Gina fainted. Faye, in a peculiar reaction, screamed and fell to the floor beside the guard, as if trying to help him. But he wouldn't survive.

Capri knew exactly who was responsible.

She stood and whirled around to find Brody. His gun was still pointed at the spot where the guard had been standing a moment before, his face impassive. Others were standing, too, unsure of what to do. Some headed for the door; others ducked for cover. Still others sat, frozen, at their tables.

Brody held up his hands, letting the gun dangle unthreateningly from his thumb as the palace guards descended on him and the other men at his table. Capri's heart thumped hard against the inside of her chest. She couldn't make sense of it. He'd shot a guard. What was wrong with him? She couldn't reconcile this cold-blooded killer with the man she knew—or *thought* she knew.

She caught a movement out of the corner of her eye and turned in time to see a servant running from behind the bar toward the dais, gun drawn, shooting as he went. There was more going on than she realized. He was running to Faye. This was about her. Through the clear polycarbonate of the high table, she had a clear view of the beauty on the ground, sobbing and covered in the young guard's blood. The servant's aim was careless, desperate. Two innocent party guests fell near the door.

Capri flinched and covered her ears as another gunshot sounded from the direction of Brody's table, and she watched the servant fall, too. Two men in uniform burst through the door to the stairs and began firing. The guards that had been ready to arrest Brody changed tactic, going after the more imminent threat.

Fear wrapped itself around Capri's heart, crushing it, making it hard to breathe. She couldn't move. A bullet whizzed past her ear, and Lady Agatha fell, blood spraying from the side of her head. Capri's stomach lurched, but all she could do was stare.

Briony grabbed her arm and yanked her to the floor.

Capri was shaking; her breath came in gasps. The tables were clear and most didn't have tablecloths. That meant they could see everything that was happening—and everyone could see them. They were easy targets.

"Breathe," Briony told her, tears streaming down her own face.

Capri realized then that the smaller woman was trying to drag Agatha under the table with them. She grabbed her around the waist and, together, they pulled her to fragile safety.

Somehow, Agatha was still alive. Maybe even conscious. But her eyes were wide and unfocused, and the sounds she made were incomprehensible. They tried to stop the flow of blood with cloth napkins. Capri's pretty peach gown was soaked with it. Sobbing, she clenched her fingers around the napkins until her knuckles were white, pressing down hard on her friend's wound.

Neither of them knew about caring for injuries. They were Ladies of Mars. Their specialties were in art, music, dance, literature, fashion, seduction. Most of them had never felt more pain than a twisted ankle, a bruised knee, or Ekon taking their virginity.

With pain, at least, Capri could empathize. She might not be able to save Agatha, but she could be with her, she could understand a fraction of what she was feeling.

It seemed like the gunfight went on forever, hours of screaming, shooting, and breaking glass all crammed into just a few minutes. The *pop-pop* noises that had been unbearably loud at first were now so constant they became background noise. Then, mercifully, reinforcements arrived. Whoever was to blame was outnumbered now, but there would be more fighting. She glanced up through her tears, trying to see if Brody was still standing and not sure if she wanted him to be. Wasn't this his fault? He'd taken the first shot.

He was still standing, still shooting. His aim was perfection, his focus absolute. She shivered. It was like he had been built for this.

"No. Oh, no." Briony's voice, thick with grief, forced her attention away from him.

Agatha was gone. With effort, Capri released the blood-soaked napkins, fingers aching with the effort it had taken to keep her friend's blood inside her body. A heavy thud sounded at the next table, startling them both. Briony squeezed Capri's hand reassuringly and crawled over to the man who had been caught in the crossfire, leaving Capri alone with her dead friend.

The guards struggled to restore order, to calm the Ladies, courtiers, and citizens who hadn't made it out of the dining hall. Slowly, they were weeding out the enemies, making arrests. Many of those in handcuffs were dressed as guards or servants. She began to fit the pieces together. The guard must have been an imposter. Faye's family had come for her.

They'd all known Ekon was treading dangerous waters by taking on a girl so old—but no one could have anticipated this. Mars had never experienced this kind of security breach before. What would happen now?

The pounding in her ears began to subside. She'd survived. She glanced up, eyes landing on the dais again. She spotted Gina on the ground, struggling to move, blood pouring from where a bullet had, hopefully, only skimmed her forehead. Then she realized there was another wound, lower, on her chest. Capri made to move towards her friend, but someone grabbed her around the waist and yanked her out from under the table.

She opened her mouth to scream, but a large hand covered her nose and mouth. She couldn't breathe. She struggled, trying to pry the meaty fingers away. Panic tore through her.

"Stop fighting," a familiar voice growled.

Brody. Confusion made her pause, and he released her mouth.

"My friend—" she gasped.

"Medics are on their way. Backup won't be far behind. We gotta go."

"Wha—?"

He covered her mouth once more, and she struggled to breathe through her nose. She shook her head hard, and he removed it. What did he want? Likely what every other man wanted. Maybe the battle had him riled up, and he'd decided to take what he was owed. That meant he would be done with her soon enough, then she could check on Gina and Briony and everyone else.

He guided her through the crowd, blocking most of her body with his bulk, heading for the stairs before the guards had the exits fully secured. He kicked open the door and half-dragged her down the stairwell. They heard footsteps, and he pulled her off to the side, into the shadows, covering her mouth again so she couldn't alert them. The memories were too vivid, the fear almost tangible. She could only see Sullivan in her mind's eye.

She wrenched away from him, again, only because he let her. Her heart was beating fast; she couldn't catch her breath.

"Don't do that," she gasped. "He did that."

She saw a flash of sympathy in his gaze before the brown eyes hardened once again. "Sorry," he said roughly.

"Where do you want to go?" she asked.

"The ship," he grunted.

"The ship?" she repeated.

"It's safest."

Without another word, he grabbed her arm above the elbow and led her down to the kitchens and into an attached warehouse. The guards that would have been stationed there were busy upstairs. Capri looked around as they hurried through the vast metal and concrete building. She whipped her head from side to side, trying and failing to get her bearings.

Brody, however, seemed to know exactly where he was going. He found a small truck used to transport goods between the warehouse and palace docks and jerked his head, gesturing for her to get inside. She did, not sure if his confidence and borrowed hat would be enough to get them to where he wanted to go, but they arrived at the ship without incident.

Capri got out of the truck and looked up at the vessel, awestruck. She'd never seen a ship like this up close—at least, not that she could remember well. The white hull wasn't exactly gleaming, but the ship was clean and well cared for. The words *Task Eternal* were written in swirled letters on the side.

"Is this yours?" she asked.

He laughed, a harsh sound that she felt had more to do with disuse than his mood. "I don't do the flying. I do the shooting."

Capri pressed her lips together. So, he was part of a crew. Bedding him was one thing, but he wouldn't expect her to…would he?

"You won't let them…Will you?" she asked softly.

His brow furrowed, and his nostrils flared. He looked offended. "'Course not."

She nodded, and he punched a code on a nearby panel to release an elevator. It took them into a loading bay packed with small vehicles, shelves with bins and machine parts, and what she assumed was crated cargo. He led her through a path in the clutter to a dimly lit corridor. The ship was silent, and she shivered as he stopped to unlock and open a door on the right.

A light turned on, revealing what she assumed was his room. Storage crates, totes, and a large lockbox took up one wall while a bare desk was tucked into one corner. There was a set of bunk beds, too, with only the bottom showing signs of use.

Brody kicked some dirty clothes into a corner and pointed at a door in the back. "Bathroom's there. Keep quiet. I'll be back."

He left and closed the door, leaving Capri alone and perplexed. What was he doing? She stood in the middle of the room for a few minutes, and when it was clear he wasn't returning anytime soon, let her guard down. The blood was drying on her dress, on her skin, and she couldn't seem to stop her hands from shaking. She didn't exactly want to have sex with Brody right now, but she also wasn't sure she wanted to be alone.

Her eyes shot to the door as the sound of clanking metal and male voices reached her ears. But they passed by, and Capri remained quiet, as Brody had instructed. She didn't know how loud running water was on a ship, so she didn't dare shower, but she couldn't stand being in the dress any longer. She unzipped it with some difficulty and stepped out of the stiffening fabric. The amount of blood on it made her feel dizzy.

She grabbed the twisted sheet from Brody's bed and wrapped it around her body before sitting down hard on the bottom bunk. The scent of his sweat, of him, was preferable to the metallic tang of blood that had filled her nostrils for the last hour. She closed her eyes, held the fabric to her nose, and breathed deeply. The tightness in her chest eased.

She wasn't sure how long she stayed that way, but after a while the door to the room slid open again, and she opened her eyes, blinking in the brightness of the room.

"Can I shower?" she asked Brody. "Before you take me…and before you take me back?"

He gave her an odd look before turning his back on her to remove his own bloodstained shirt. Capri swallowed, knowing what would come next, but he just replaced the formal shirt he'd been wearing with a white T-shirt.

"I don't want that from you," he muttered, not quite looking at her. "And I'm not taking you back."

She swallowed, panic coursing through her veins once again. She gripped the sheet tightly in her hands, and when she spoke her voice was a whisper. "What?"

The ship rumbled beneath them, answering her question before he could.

"Are you taking me off Mars?"

"Yeah," he grunted, unapologetic.

"You can't. You can't do that." She stood, keeping the sheet around her but feeling too small while sitting down. He had to understand. "You have to take me back."

"Why?" he asked easily. "You'd rather stay and get fucked sideways by whoever Ekon decides is worthy?"

Her cheeks flamed. No, she didn't want that. "I don't know what I want," she said aloud. "But you didn't bother to ask. And he…he won't let me go. You have to take me back!"

Panic made her voice high-pitched, and it cracked on the last word. The ship shuddered. It was taking off. Tears sprung into her eyes, and her chest heaved. If her life had been anything since becoming the Prize it had been predictable; the only anomalies were the Victors. But in the last two days her world had been turned upside down.

Brody closed the distance between them and reached out to cup her face in his hands. He looked into her eyes, his expression unreadable.

"You gotta breathe," he told her. "I know you're mad, but you gotta breathe."

"I'm not just mad," she managed, her voice wavering, body trembling. "I'm scared. He'll kill you."

"I'm not worried about that."

She pulled her face out of his hands. "How can you say that?"

"I know the risks."

"Do your crewmates?" She gestured frantically to the closed door. "You're putting them in danger, too."

A muscle in his jaw tensed. "They had nothing to do with it. I'll make sure they know that, if it comes to it."

"Then what about me?" Her voice wavered. "*I* care if you die. And I don't want you to die because of me."

He stepped closer, locking serious brown eyes on hers. "You listen good and well, Capri. If I end up in some kind of trouble, it'll be my own damn fault. Don't you ever feel guilty about it."

"I can't…" She shook her head. "I can't…"

Terror and confusion overwhelmed her. Spots danced across her vision. She couldn't get enough oxygen in her lungs to finish her sentence, to remember what she had been about to say. Brody took one of her hands in his and placed it on his chest so she could feel the rise and fall of it.

"Breathe," he told her again.

She struggled to match his rhythm, and, slowly, her breathing evened out. Her vision cleared. He dropped her hand abruptly and stepped back.

"Take that shower," he told her. "I have to talk to the captain."

He left, and Capri was alone again.

CHAPTER 21

What the fuck had he been thinking? She was right. Ekon would be looking for her. Colin would be pissed. Brody didn't regret his actions, but he also had not thought this through. He'd just seen the girl there, cowering under the table, and the man he'd once been saw the opportunity to save her—leaving the man he was now to deal with the fucking consequences.

He clenched his fists and hesitated before pounding on Leroy's door.

It slid open, and the younger man stood on the other side, a wireless ear bud in his right ear and a reader in one hand. Some kind of game flashed on the screen. His brown eyes turned suspicious when he realized who had disturbed him. Brody didn't blame him. He wasn't sure he'd ever sought out the mechanic.

"What's up?" he asked warily.

"I need to borrow some clothes."

He took out the earbud then and tossed it and the reader on his bed. He crossed his arms. There was a beat of silence, and then: "What the hell are you talking about?"

Brody scraped together his remaining patience. "There's a girl on board, and she needs a change of clothes. You're more her size."

Leroy hesitated, unsure whether to take his words as an insult, but his curiosity got the better of him, just as Brody had hoped. He glanced down the hall toward the gunman's room. "And the captain..."

"Doesn't know," he finished with a growl. The mechanic's eyes lit up. "Don't go thinkin' you got anything on me. I'm about to go tell him."

"Well, shit, let me get some popcorn."

For something like the 700th time in four years, Brody found himself wondering if punching Leroy in the face would be worth the repercussions. He clenched his teeth, biting back the surge of violence.

"Are you gonna help or not?"

"Sure."

"She's in my room."

Brody walked away, wanting to get the conversation with Colin over with.

"What, you want me to take them to her?" Leroy called after him.

"Yeah," he said over his shoulder, not giving the younger man a chance to argue.

He knew he'd go. That insatiable curiosity was why Leroy was so good at his job—and why he was so goddamn annoying. He set his jaw and braced himself as he approached the cockpit. Jax sat at the controls. Colin stood behind him, looking at the screens. His hands rested easily on the pilot's shoulders, and Brody felt his heart constrict. That simple, intimate gesture was enough to remind him of what he no longer had. If the couple wasn't so private, he didn't think he'd be able to stand working on the ship.

He cleared his throat, and Colin removed his hands, straightening to give Brody his full attention.

"I need to speak to you."

Colin raised his eyebrows slightly, waiting for him to continue.

"Alone," Brody clarified.

Jax was good at pretending to hear nothing when he very likely heard everything, and he continued pressing buttons as if this was nothing out of the ordinary. In fact, he could probably count on one hand the number of times Brody had asked for a private word. The gunman usually didn't care who heard what he had to say; he usually didn't care about anything. The captain led Brody to the empty lounge, but neither sat. He leaned against the wall, arms crossed, waiting for Brody to start. His expression revealed nothing.

Brody cut to the chase. "There's a girl on board."

Colin straightened, his brow furrowed. "What do you mean? A stowaway?"

"No."

"Well then why the hell is there a girl onboard?"

Brody hesitated, just long enough for realization to dawn and Colin's eyes to narrow. He thought he knew the answer, and he probably did—but he'd make Brody say it.

"I took her."

"You *took* her."

"Yes."

Colin paused, either to process the information or to ensure his tight emotional control remained intact.

"Where did you take her *from?*"

Brody thought the captain probably knew the answer to that, too. Colin seemed to give up briefly, and anger flashed in his brown eyes. "Shots, I swear to God, if you say the palace—"

Brody just looked at him, prepared for whatever wrath the captain threw his way.

"Just tell me it wasn't one of the Ladies."

Again, Brody said nothing, and the captain threw up his hands. "What the *hell,* Shots!"

"I knew her from before," Brody said. "I was one of her guards."

Colin stilled, eyes dark and penetrating. "And what else?"

Brody felt a spark of fury. He knew what the captain was thinking. He did bad things. He might even be a bad man, but he'd loved Colin's sister.

"It ain't like that," he growled. "She was a *child.* You know damn well I was true."

"Then what is it like? I'm losing patience."

"Somebody broke her before Ekon got the chance, so she didn't get treated like the other girls. Ekon auctioned her off, and then last night—"

"—he offered her up to that 'guard' as a reward," Colin finished, remembering the scene. "So, she came willingly?"

Brody didn't answer.

"Then she didn't mind her circumstances. *You* did."

Brody ground his teeth together. "She just doesn't think she has other options."

"Does she?"

"We can drop her somewhere. New Earth. I'll give her some money, and she can...get out."

Colin seemed to be struggling between pity and fury, but when the captain finally spoke, his voice betrayed neither. "We have to take her back."

Brody shook his head.

"We have to!" Colin came off the wall, his voice sharp. "It's not going to take a genius to figure out which ship left around the time the girl went missing. You put our trade relationship at risk. You put our fucking *lives* at risk."

Brody looked away. Just then, Jax poked his head around the doorway.

"Alexander from Mars just came through and wants to speak with you, Captain. Do you want it in here or the cockpit?"

"The cockpit," Colin snapped.

Jax raised an eyebrow at his tone and retreated. Colin turned back to Brody.

"We're going back to Mars in one week. You're going to explain what happened to Ekon, and I'll likely be lookin' for a new gunman." His voice betrayed no opinion on the matter of Brody's fate. "Until then, she's your responsibility. Make sure she knows how to use a gun and keep her out of the way."

It was Brody's turn to be caught off guard. "What the hell do you mean make sure she can use a gun?"

Colin got close to his face. "This isn't a passenger vessel, Shots. What's the number one rule?"

Brody didn't answer, but he knew it. No one rode the ship without knowing how to protect themselves and their crewmates—no matter how temporary their tenure might be. Their line of work was too dangerous for that.

"You wanted to show her a new life, Shots," Colin said. "So show her."

CHAPTER 22

Capri stood under the hot, comforting spray of the shower. The room was so tiny she wondered how a man of Brody's size managed to maneuver. She unbraided her hair, removed the beads, and scrubbed. She scrubbed until her skin was raw and the spray was freezing. Then she stayed beneath the water until her teeth chattered so hard, she couldn't form thoughts, couldn't focus on anything that had happened, was happening, or would happen.

When she finally stepped out of the confines of the bathroom, Capri grabbed Brody's bed sheet once more and used it to dry off before wrapping it around her. It did little against the cold, now that it was damp, but she couldn't bear to wear the bloodstained dress again. She kicked the ruined garment into the same corner that Brody had kicked his dirty clothes and refused to look at it again.

Just then, the door to the room opened, and she whirled around, coming face-to-face with an unfamiliar man. He was taller than her, though not as tall as Brody, and his curly hair was pulled back in a thick, dark ponytail. His cheeks flushed bright red beneath light brown skin, and the genuine shock in his brown eyes was the only reason Capri didn't feel more afraid.

"Sorry," he said hastily. "I thought Shots was fucking—messing—with me. Sorry."

Capri watched him, waiting while he looked around as if there was a button that could make this awkward exchange disappear. Then, he grinned, the gesture so wide and genuine that she felt the corner of her own mouth lifting slightly in return.

"I'm gonna try that again," he said, and shut the door.

Capri stared at the place where the man had been, then jumped, startled, when a knock sounded. She reached out and touched the panel to let the door slide open. The man was there, leaning casually against the frame.

"Hello, there. I'm Leroy," he greeted as if the previous interaction hadn't happened.

Capri laughed. She couldn't help it. He grinned in return, then stood straighter and held out a change of clothes.

"Shots asked me to bring you these."

"Thanks," she said, taking them, but the man remained where he was.

"Aren't you…you know…one of *them*?" he asked.

Capri furrowed her brow. "One of what?"

"From the palace."

"Oh. A Lady?" Capri offered.

He nodded. Her smile fell slightly, and she shrugged. "Sort of."

She noticed a small metal object in his hand and gestured to it, anxious to take the focus away from herself. "What's that?"

He glanced down, seeming to have forgotten it was there. "Oh." He rubbed the back of his neck. "It's part of the ship."

Capri raised her eyebrows. She didn't know much about ships and space travel, but she was pretty sure all the parts were supposed to be attached.

"It's nothing important," he assured her quickly. "The cockpit door is broken. They never close it, but they want it fixed."

He shook his head slightly, clearly thinking the task was a waste of time.

"You're a mechanic, then?"

"Yeah, I am." He beamed. "My brother, Jax, he's the pilot. The captain's the captain, and you already know Shots. That's everybody. Except for you."

Capri smiled. He was chatty, guileless. It put her at ease. She'd assumed everyone on board would be like Brody, hard and defensive.

"Well, I'll let you get to it," he said, glancing at the sheet barely covering her chest and blushing. "If you need anything, just let me know. I get bored. It's nice to have a new face."

He turned and headed back down the corridor. Capri closed the door behind him and locked it. It wasn't her room, but Brody would have the code to get in. He couldn't deny her some privacy.

She dropped the sheet, shivered, and dressed in the borrowed clothes. She couldn't remember the last time she'd worn pants. Maybe never. The fabric between her thighs felt strange. The T-shirt was white, like Brody's, and nearly see-through where her skin was still damp. Leroy had also loaned her a jacket, and she donned that as well.

She finger-combed her curly hair and braided it into a single plait. When she glanced in the mirror, she barely recognized herself. But there wasn't much point in worrying about appearances here. The knowledge felt strange, threw her off balance. So much of who she was—at least who she'd been for the last fourteen years—was tied to how she looked.

She felt completely out of her element, but what she felt most was exhaustion. She had no idea what time it was, when Brody planned to return, and what news he'd bring. She knew, however, that the lumpy, twin mattress on the top bunk looked more appealing now than her luxurious bed at the palace ever had.

She turned off the lights, climbed up, and slept.

***

Capri was no stranger to nightmares. She had them regularly, especially in the nights before meeting the next Victor. The uncertainty got to her, and Sullivan and some of the Victors that had come after liked to taunt her while she slept.

This time, however, her dreams were different. She wasn't in her room at the palace; she was in the upper dining hall. The floor was slick with blood. Lifeless faces surrounded her; bony hands reached for her, tearing at her skin, and she knew they meant to kill her. She tried to run but couldn't move. A gunshot sounded. She should have started awake then, but she didn't. She just stayed there, staring at the blood as it spread across her stomach, drenching the fabric of her frilly dress until it was dyed red.

Maybe she was dead. Maybe it was true that if a person died in a dream they died in real life. This could be the afterlife; this could be hell, standing still with nothing but terrified thoughts for company—forever.

Somehow, Capri managed to pull herself out of it. The sound of a cry bounced off the metal walls of the room, her own voice like a stranger calling back to her. She sat up and shivered in the darkness, wondering if she'd woken anyone. But she heard nothing, not even the sound of breathing in the bottom bunk. Brody hadn't returned. She was still alone.

A glance at the clock told her that it was two in the morning. She didn't know the layout of the ship or even if she was allowed to leave the room, but she was starving, and her mouth felt unbearably dry. She climbed down from the top bunk, intent on finding the kitchen, but as she reached for the control panel the door slid open. She jumped, startled. Brody held a steaming container in one hand and a bottle of water in the other.

"What are you doing?" he asked.

"Looking for that," Capri managed. "Is it for me?"

He nodded and stepped inside to set the food on the desk. She closed the door behind him and followed. He sat on the edge of the desk, one foot on the ground, leaving the chair free for Capri. She sat down, straight-backed, taking small bites despite her hunger. Brody had grabbed a beer for himself, and she felt him watching her as he took a sip.

She glanced sideways at him, trying to ignore the fact that she was level with his very muscular thigh, on which rested a very muscular forearm.

"What?" she said between bites.

"Nothin'," he said.

She gave him a shrewd look. She was sure it was something, probably that she was eating at the gunman's desk like she was sitting down to dinner with Ekon. But it was all she'd been taught. She couldn't turn it off just because she wasn't on Mars.

"What did your captain say?" she asked.

Brody settled himself more comfortably on the desktop, stretching out both long legs and downing the beer. Though his body language was casual, Capri could sense his tension, see the brief tightening of his jaw.

"We'll take you back. In one week. That's the next time we pass through."

"Oh. Good. Thank you." She wondered if her voice sounded convincing. She should be happy. The few friends she had were on Mars, as well as her belongings, and Ekon might show Brody leniency if he brought her back willingly. Returning to Mars was the right thing to do.

"The captain wants to meet you," Brody continued. "He wants you at breakfast tomorrow."

She nodded. "Am I…allowed to go on my own? Or should I wait for you?"

He stood and cleared away her dishes. "You're not a prisoner," he said. "Go where you like. Just stay outta the cockpit and the other bunks. Don't mess with the cargo."

"Okay," she agreed softly.

He looked at her face, and she wondered what he saw there. She was usually good at reading faces and masking her own, but she was out of her element, scared, and tired.

"Did you sleep?" he asked.

She nodded.

"Did you dream?" he asked.

She nodded again, tears welling before she could stop them.

"I was going to sleep in the lounge," he said.

The words were out of her mouth before she'd had a chance to think them through. "Could you stay here?"

He raised an eyebrow.

"In your own bed," she clarified hastily.

He laughed roughly. "Guard duty?"

One corner of her mouth lifted wryly, and she wiped away a tear that had escaped. "Like old times."

He nodded, putting her garbage back down on the desk and holding out a hand to help her stand. The feel of his calloused palm around her slender fingers was electric, and she glanced at him, wondering if he'd felt it, too. But his face was impassive, his jaw locked.

She climbed up to her bunk and lay down. He hesitated at the side of the bed, his face level with hers. She licked her dry lips, and his dark eyes darted to watch. Then he seemed to shake himself out of it and looked her in the eye.

"Nothing's gonna get you," he assured her in his deep voice, in which she was beginning to find more and more comfort.

She nodded, and her tired eyes drifted shut.

<h1 style="text-align:center">CHAPTER 23</h1>

Capri woke to find Brody standing in front of her bunk, watching her, in nearly the same position as when she'd fallen asleep. His close-cropped hair was still damp from a shower, and he was dressed for the day in heavy cargo pants and a T-shirt.

"Breakfast's in ten," he said, and she couldn't be sure if he'd been watching her or about to wake her.

She nodded and sat up. He held up a pair of heavy brown boots and socks that might have once been white. She'd been going barefoot on the cold metal floor since changing the previous day.

"Thanks," she murmured.

He nodded, set them down on the floor, and left the room. Capri blinked at the closed door. He'd said she *could* go to breakfast on her own; it didn't mean she *wanted* to. And why didn't she want to? The truth came unbidden. *She was afraid.* She'd never been allowed to go anywhere in the palace without an escort. She wasn't sure she remembered how to leave one room and enter another alone.

She resented the fear, and she resented the person who had made her afraid. Ekon had wanted to keep them safe, and in doing so had kept them prisoner. Now she felt like a pet bird, too scared to fly from an open cage.

Capri climbed down from the bed and went to the bathroom. She didn't have a change of clothes, so she smoothed the wrinkles as best she could, brushed her teeth with her fingers, rebraided her hair, and pulled on the socks and shoes Brody had left for her. She tested them, walking from the bunks to the crates along the wall and back again.

It felt like someone had tied weights to her feet. She would have a hard time walking gracefully in these. But she felt instantly warmer and was no longer afraid of stubbing a toe on the hard, industrial corners of the ship. She glanced at the clock, took a steadying breath, and left the confines of the room.

Last night, the corridor had been dim and quiet. Now, it was bright, and she could hear voices and clattering dishes from down the hall. The ship wasn't overly large. The door across from Brody's room was closed, as were the ones to her right. As she walked tentatively closer to the voices, she guessed the living quarters took up the right side of the ship while the left was reserved for storage and communal spaces. The cockpit was visible at the end of the hall.

She paused before entering an open door to her left, taking a moment to survey the room. There was a rectangular table in the center, surrounded by seven chairs. Cabinets and counters lined the walls, as well as a fridge, sink, quick oven, and trash chute. It wasn't so different from a normal house, and it took several seconds for Capri to remember how she knew this. It reminded her vaguely of the kitchen in the apartment she'd lived in with her family on New Earth. Her brother, mother, and father.

She swallowed hard, forcing back the memories, and crossed the threshold.

Brody was seated at the table, legs outstretched as he drank a protein shake. A man who could be Leroy leaned against the counter, eating cereal from a bowl and chatting with the other man who could be Leroy. Twins. That meant the man at the head of the table had to be the captain.

The gunman noticed her first and drew in his legs as if to stand, but the twin at the counter beat him to her. His face broke into a wide grin, and she knew for sure that it was Leroy.

"Capri!" he greeted, taking her easily by the arm, as if they'd been friends their whole lives.

He led her to the chair across from Jax and sat beside her, pretending not to notice Brody's legs were once again occupying the space. Brody glared at the younger man but removed his legs, standing to retrieve a mug of coffee and bowl of cereal for Capri. He set the dishes in front of her and turned his attention to the captain.

"Welcome aboard, Capri," Colin said with a tight smile, too polite to point out that the situation wasn't by his choice.

"Thank you," she murmured.

"We'll be circling back to Mars in about a week. We made contact with Alexander, so he knows you're safe, but he'll want to talk to you himself. I expect Shots'll have some consequences to face when we return."

He glared at the gunman, who gazed steadily back at his captain. Capri felt a flutter of fear at the reminder and averted her eyes to the bran flakes and milk in front of her. She lifted her spoon and took a bite. When she felt more composed, she raised her eyes to Colin again.

"We don't often run into trouble," he continued. "Even so, this isn't the cushy life you're used to. We'll do our best to keep you comfortable, but you've gotta make sure you stay out of the way unless we have an all-hands-on-deck situation."

Capri glanced at Brody again, who was glaring at the captain, his jaw taut. Then, she looked at Leroy, who shook his head quickly and waved a hand as if to say she had nothing to worry about.

Colin shifted slightly so he was addressing everyone at the table. "We'll be stopping on New Earth for fuel and supplies in Mexico Territory. They're a little more lenient about papers." He looked at Capri, who, of course, had none. "Even so, best to lay low until we're checked into the dock. We'll get fake documents while we're there, and Capri can get whatever she needs to get through the week. *Needs*," he repeated, looking meaningfully at her.

Capri felt slightly affronted. Did he think she meant to go on a shopping spree?

"Then we'll be doing a pickup in the U.S. Territory for a Tycho sector. A night landing. We'll get the goods, head for Tycho—"

"Tycho?" Capri said in surprise.

Everyone at the table looked at her, and she swallowed, once again poking at her breakfast with her spoon in an attempt to calm her nerves. "It's just...the rebel planets are dangerous. Aren't they?"

"They are," Colin said. "I understand you aren't familiar with much of the System outside of Mars, but the rebels have needs and money just like New Earth and the Kingdoms. So, yes, we choose to deal with them when most vessels don't."

"Shots and the captain are from Ptolemy," Leroy informed her with a grin. "They know how to get us through without getting us killed. So far, anyway."

Capri looked at Brody. She hadn't realized he was from a rebel planet. She could feel her cheeks burning. He raised an eyebrow but didn't look angry. She wasn't so sure about the captain.

She kept her mouth shut for the rest of the meeting.

***

After making the delivery to Sector 5 of Tycho, *Task Eternal* would collect fabric from 72—known as The Green Patch, since it was one of the few places on the hot planet where crops could grow—and bourbon from Sector 39. Then they'd head back to Mars, drop Capri, and with any luck still manage to do some business with Ekon.

They didn't mention again what might become of Brody, but it hung in the air.

"I mean, we did save his life. How mad can Ekon be?" Leroy asked.

"He's a King," Jax said bluntly. "He doesn't play by the same rules as the rest of us."

"Well, obviously. He has a fucking harem," Leroy said carelessly. "Doesn't the U.N. have some law against—"

"Let's stay on topic," Colin interrupted sharply.

Capri had finished her cereal and was now carefully sipping the strong coffee Brody had brought her, pretending not to be offended. Is that how the rest of the System saw Ekon's Ladies? A harem? She'd been relegated to the role of high-class prostitute, but she'd always been under the impression that most Ladies of Mars were revered, envied. Were they merely a spectacle?

She noticed the way Brody's hand clenched around his own mug, and she lifted her eyes briefly to see him staring daggers at the mechanic. There was something between the two of them, some deep-rooted conflict.

"We'll see what happens on Mars and go from there," Colin continued. "For now, let's get what we need on Mexico and then we'll talk more about the Tycho drop. Any questions?"

The crew gave various versions of "no" as they finished their meals. Colin downed the rest of his coffee and was the first to leave.

Jax departed next, and Leroy opened his mouth to say something to her, but then his brother's head popped back through the door.

"Did you ever replace the air filters?"

Leroy sighed and stood. "On it."

He shot Capri one last grin and left. Capri took another small sip of coffee. Maybe she could make the beverage last an entire day. She had no idea what to do with herself. It was just her and Brody now, and she raised her eyes to his.

"What do you do to keep yourself busy?" she asked.

He shrugged one massive shoulder. "Drink. But today I gotta take inventory before we land in Mexico."

"Inventory of what?"

"Weapons. Ammunition."

Her brow furrowed. "How many weapons do you have?"

"Enough."

Capri raised an eyebrow. She wasn't sure she wanted him to elaborate and took another sip.

"Speaking of which," Brody began. "Captain says I gotta teach you to shoot a gun. Can't do it on the ship, so plan on it right after we land."

Capri nearly spilled her mug. "What do you mean?"

"It's a rule. Everybody's gotta know how to shoot a gun, just in case."

"In case what?"

"In case there's trouble."

She stared at him. Was it really that dangerous outside of Mars? *Mars turned out to be dangerous, too,* she reminded herself. "Fine," she muttered.

Then, Colin's voice sounded over the intercom. *"Capri to the lounge."*

She started at the sound of her name and looked to Brody. He shrugged and jerked his head toward the door, indicating she should go. "Next room," he told her.

Capri stood and left, walking hesitantly next door. She found the captain in a comfortable room with two worn couches and video screens. He stood in front of the far screen now, arms crossed, back erect, but the look in his brown eyes was tired.

"I was able to reach Alexander."

He gestured to the blank screen, under which was a row of buttons and switches. She approached, looked at the unfamiliar controls, and then looked back at him.

"Do I push…this one?" she asked, pointing to a green button.

Colin's gaze narrowed, as if he wasn't sure whether the question was serious. He seemed to decide it was, and his demeanor softened slightly. "This one," he corrected, pointing to the next button.

She pressed it, and Alexander's face appeared on the screen, as well as a miniature image of herself and the captain in one corner.

"As promised, Alexander, she's alive and well," Colin said.

"And you won't bring her sooner?" Alexander demanded, barely glancing at her.

"Again, you have my sincere apologies, but we're on a tight trade schedule. A week is the best I can do. You're welcome to send a cruiser out for her."

Alexander released a frustrated breath. "Ekon is demanding a complete overhaul of palace security. He won't approve it."

"How's Gina?" Capri cut in.

Alexander looked at her, his gaze somehow bored and piercing all at once.

"Gina will recover."

Capri breathed a sigh of relief.

"There will be no avoiding a scar, however," Alexander added.

Capri felt a surge of anger at his words, surprising even herself. The tone had been similar to when they discovered Sullivan's assault, as if Gina, too, were now irreparably damaged.

"Is she still the Favorite?" Capri asked.

"That's not your concern, Lady Capri."

Capri pursed her lips.

"Make sure you keep her safe," Alexander continued. "Ekon is not in a forgiving mood after the fiasco at the palace."

"We did save his life," Colin reminded him.

"Yes, but you failed to protect his Rising Favorite and then kidnapped the Prize. He's not exactly pleased with my part in it, either."

"They're treating me well," Capri interjected, though Alexander had clearly not been speaking to her. "Brody only wanted to keep me safe. And he is a former guard, remember? Ekon trusted him once."

"How could I forget," Alexander replied dryly. "He failed to save you once already, didn't he? Then he left the King's service without any notice and had the gall to bid on the Prize years later. I'm still surprised he managed to secure you."

Capri felt Colin's eyes on her. She wasn't sure how much he knew about her interactions with Brody, and her cheeks flushed.

"My point is, he isn't some stranger who snatched me away. I want King Ekon to understand that. None of them deserves to be punished for this."

"That's not up to you. Or me."

"You're his advisor," she snapped. "Advise him."

Alexander looked affronted. Capri held her ground. She had to know that Brody wouldn't be killed upon their return, or she would… what? What could she do?

The idea struck her suddenly. Her most valuable bargaining tool was herself.

Alexander opened his mouth, but she cut him off, voicing the thought before she lost her nerve. "Or I won't come back."

Alexander's eyes widened. She felt Colin's lock on her, too.

Ekon's advisor was quiet for a moment, then he gave a gracious nod. "I'll see what I can do."

He ended the transmission, and Capri felt her knees shake. With effort, she turned to look at Colin, expecting anger, but he only looked curious, as if he didn't quite know what to make of her.

"You can go," he said, his voice betraying nothing.

She returned to the kitchen and found it empty. She sat and drank the rest of the coffee in her mug, though it had turned cold. Someone had cleaned up the rest of her dishes. Capri put her empty mug in the sink and studied a few buttons near the faucet, pressing one that said *auto wash*. Water and soap sprayed from the sides, cleaning the few dishes it contained. While the cycle ran, she looked through drawers and cabinets, partly to familiarize herself with the layout and partly out of sheer boredom.

She was inspecting a row of knives when Jax poked his head in.

"You wanna check out the cockpit?" he asked, and she realized it was Leroy.

"I'm not allowed in the cockpit," Capri said.

Leroy's bewildered expression told her he'd probably never paid attention to the words *not allowed* before in his life. "Would you rather stay here washing dishes?"

Capri hesitated for only a moment. "No."

CHAPTER 24

It was adaptation, no different than when a Victor entered her chambers and demanded she mold to fit his or her fantasy. No different than when she'd been told of her new role at the palace. Capri was sure her ability to adapt was the reason it only took one day of following Leroy around and watching him tinker to feel, not quite at ease, but not so out of place.

She handed him tools and listened to him talk about New Earth. They were both from U.S. Territory, but her home had been New York, a city, and he'd grown up on a farm in Washington. When he was seventeen, Leroy became a ship mechanic's apprentice at the local docks, while Jax had gone away to pilot school.

"I was only two years in," Leroy said. He was tuning up the motorcycles for when they landed in Mexico Territory while Capri held the bolts and other bits he'd removed. "The captain landed in the docks and needed a screen in the cockpit fixed. I was the only one still around. We got to talking, I found out he was putting together a crew, and he offered me a job. Jax had just finished school and had something lined up, but he ended up here. I think Mom and Dad might have told him to keep an eye on me."

He grinned good-naturedly, and Capri got the impression that it had always been that way between them, Leroy acting on impulse and Jax struggling to keep him in line. Capri's brother had been older. She couldn't even remember what he looked like, let alone if he'd ever felt protective over her.

"I didn't think he'd stick around, really," Leroy continued. "He could've flown for the U.N. if he wanted to. But then he and Colin started bunking together, and unless they fall out he's here for good. Colin got a scholarship to the U.N. Academy but as soon as he'd served his two years and saved up for *Task Eternal* he was out."

"Why didn't he want to stay with the U.N.?" Capri asked. "This seems a lot…harder."

"Oh, there's a lot of folks like him flying around. The rebel planets have a chip on their shoulder about the U.N. The U.N. set up Tycho and Ptolemy with the basic necessities, but New Earth got the most attention. When the rebels complained about the extreme climates and failing infrastructure, the U.N. basically left them to fend for themselves. He'd never settle down on New Earth with a cushy job. He'd see it as a betrayal."

Capri was quiet for a moment. It seemed the System's history wasn't as simple as Lady Agatha had taught them. Her heart constricted painfully as she thought of her friend.

"Do you think you'll move on?" she asked Leroy.

"Nah. No one else'll put up with me."

He gave her a self-deprecating smile, and Capri shook her head, suppressing a grin of her own. "And how did Brody end up here? Alexander said he left suddenly."

Leroy was concentrating now on removing a stubborn filter, but Capri didn't think the frown on his lips was due to frustration.

"Shots was married to the captain's sister. She died—and their kid. He showed up drunk a few days after it happened, and he's been here ever since. He's been a goddamn asshole, too, but you can't really blame him."

One of the screws Capri had been holding fell from her grasp, and she scrambled to find it. She felt like she'd had the wind knocked out of her. She'd had no idea. Leroy took the screws from her, put them where they belonged on the bike, and stood, wiping his greasy hands on his coveralls.

"I'd better get cleaned up. We'll be landing soon."

As if on cue, Jax's voice sounded over the intercom. *"Entering atmosphere on New Earth. Twenty minutes to landing."*

"Leroy." Capri reached out to touch his arm, and he turned back, brown eyes curious. "I just wanted to say thank you. I don't think I've ever spent this much time with a man without… expectations."

"Well, I wouldn't say no…" He grinned and waggled his eyebrows.

"Don't ruin it," she told him sternly, but a smile tugged at her lips.

"Fine, fine." He held up his hands in mock surrender, backing to the corridor. He shot her one last smile and disappeared through the doorway.

Capri stretched. She'd been sitting so long her muscles were stiff. There was a grease stain on her white shirt and dirt beneath her fingernails, which would never have been allowed at the palace. To her surprise, she didn't miss the cleanliness. This felt more honest somehow.

She moved toward the corridor to search for a snack. That was different, too. On Mars, she'd been allowed to eat when and if she wanted—so long as she kept her figure—but it was always brought to her. She'd never had the freedom to root through a fridge or cabinet and grab whatever looked good in the moment.

Just as she approached the doorway, Brody rounded the corner. She nearly bumped into him but stopped just in time. She was close enough to smell him, to feel the heat of his body. She wanted to sink into him, to comfort him now that she knew what he'd gone through, but she knew that would be unwelcome.

With effort, she took a step back, raising her eyes from his broad chest to his dark eyes. "You gotta go back to the room," he told her.

She raised an eyebrow. "Why?"

"They can search the ship if they want, to make sure there's nobody else on board except who we say. If I knock, find someplace to hide. Under the bed or in the bathroom. Won't be for long."

"Great," she muttered.

"They don't usually care much here," he said with a shrug. "Then we can do what we need to in the city."

Capri nodded her assent, but Brody didn't move to let her through. His eyes were focused on her face, on her right cheek. He brushed his thumb over the skin beneath her eye, and she sucked in a breath. He pulled his hand back and examined the pad of his thumb, which was now smudged with grease.

"Not sure one of Ekon's Ladies should be doing manual labor."

Capri laughed humorlessly. "I'm not really *his* Lady, am I?"

"Does that bother you?" he asked casually, leaning against the doorframe.

"Does what bother me?"

"Being the only one he never had."

Capri hugged herself and looked away. She'd kept Ekon's secret, had never spoken of his indiscretion aloud. But now, away from the palace, keeping his secret didn't seem so important. She shrugged.

"He had me," she admitted.

Brody came away from the wall, brow furrowed, the muscles in his jaw tight. "What do you mean?"

Capri echoed Briony's words on that night. "He's the King. He can do whatever he wants."

"So he's fucking you *and* whoring you out?"

"No," she murmured. "It was just the once."

He held her gaze for a long moment, and she looked away, afraid of what he might find behind her eyes.

"And you want to go back?" he said finally.

"I told you. I don't know what I want," she replied, meeting his gaze again. "I've never had the chance to figure it out."

Then, before she realized exactly what she was doing, her eyes landed on his lips. Because what she said hadn't been entirely true. She had found something she wanted. He just didn't want her back. Or he wouldn't let himself want her.

Thanks to Leroy's revelation, she knew nothing was as simple as it seemed with the gunman.

"Ten minutes to landing," came Jax's voice.

Capri swallowed hard and wrenched her gaze from Brody.

"I'd better go," she said.

He moved aside to let her pass, but at the last moment, he reached out and grasped her upper arm. She looked at him, and he looked down at her, his brown eyes stormy. She waited, breathless. But he only released her again and disappeared into the loading bay. Capri continued to his room, closing the door and sitting on the bottom bunk, drinking in the scent of him.

CHAPTER 25

As expected, the dock officials only performed a cursory search for undeclared passengers and contraband. Jax left immediately after they'd been cleared to get papers for Capri. Colin and Leroy were waiting for him to return and discussing what maintenance could and couldn't wait. Brody already knew what he needed to buy during their stay, and after a meaningful look from the captain knew exactly how he'd be spending the next few hours.

He found Capri in the kitchen, looking idly through cabinets while eating a sandwich. She glanced up when he entered. Those hazel eyes struck him the same way they had at the palace, when she'd been all grace and glamor. Even now, when she was dressed like Leroy, he had a hard time tearing his eyes from her. He'd almost given in to his impulses earlier, and the way her eyes raked over him almost every time she looked at him didn't help his resolve.

He jerked his head toward the door. "Come on."

Capri replaced a can of beans she'd been examining and closed the drawer. "Where are we going?"

"To shoot some shit."

"Oh. Right." She ate the last bite of her sandwich and brushed the crumbs from her hands before following him.

He was too aware of her presence behind him, of her eyes on his back as he led the way through the loading bay to the elevator. He hadn't felt so aware of another woman since Jill, and he struggled to focus on anything else, on the grate surrounding the elevator, the strong cables that made it function. They descended and stepped onto the dusty surface of Mexico Territory. Brody sent the elevator back up and started to walk away, but after a few steps, he realized Capri was no longer with him.

She was frozen, staring at the sky. Her chest heaved, and her eyes were wide, but she didn't look frightened. Overwhelmed, maybe. Brody stopped, waiting. The climate on Mars was perfectly controlled. Except for the menagerie in the middle of the Kingdom and the garden in the palace, there was no wildlife.

The girl had probably never experienced a breeze, never seen clouds or a blue sky, at least not that she'd remember. A bird of prey cried above them, and she started. She looked at Brody, red-cheeked. He thought she might cry, and despite his attempts at hardening his heart, he felt a sharp twist of pity.

"Ready?" he said.

She blinked and nodded. He walked with her to the very edge of the docks, an overflow lot. There were no ships and only one guard. Brody showed him the guns and gestured to the empty bottles he'd brought, trying to indicate he wanted a spot for target practice.

The younger man stood up from his chair and eyed him warily. Brody used a reader to indicate that he'd pay him to let them practice, which piqued his interest. Spanish was the main language in Mexico Territory, and he didn't speak much.

Capri stepped around him. "Necesitamos practicar," she said. "Haremos pagar."

The man nodded and held out his hand. Brody handed him the reader, and he used his data ring to accept the payment. He gave Brody a small wave and went back to his seat, pulling his hat down over his eyes.

Brody looked at Capri, who shrugged. "I had to learn the basics. A Victor could be from anywhere."

Brody tamped down his anger. Ekon had put so much effort into making it so Capri could be anything to anyone. Ater all she'd been through with Sullivan, Ekon had denied her even the privilege of being herself.

He set up the bottles on a railing and handed Capri a pistol. "Let's see what you've got to start with," he said.

Capri raised the weapon uncertainly. Brody straightened her arm and adjusted her grip and stance. Then he let her take aim at the first bottle. She missed, her arm jerking back with the force of the recoil.

"Shit," she breathed.

"Try again," he said.

Again, she missed the bottle. But then she took aim a third time, and this time the bottle exploded into glass shards. She shrieked happily before remembering where she was.

Brody stared at her. She shrugged demurely. "You used to escort us to archery lessons, remember?"

"Archery's different."

"It's all aiming, isn't it? I just wasn't expecting the kickback."

Brody continued staring at her. "Try it again."

She did, and again she hit the bottle.

"Well, shit," Brody breathed.

It took her five shots to knock down the last three bottles, which was better than Brody had expected for a Lady of Mars. He'd be surprised if Leroy did much better. He glanced at Capri's face. She'd seemed elated at first but was now staring at the gun in her hand with a faraway look.

He didn't want to care. He wanted to be able to turn his back on her and only tolerate her until they got back to Mars. But that ship had flown. He'd cared about her before his family died, and that had made it too easy for her to crack the hard surface of his heart now. It was the reason she was here at all. He'd wanted to do for her what he hadn't been able to for them.

"What is it?" he asked.

She looked up, eyes clearing as though she'd forgotten where she was. She gave him half a smile, and even that didn't reach her eyes.

"I was just thinking I would have rather had one of these than a panic button."

"Panic button?"

Her eyes landed again on the gun in her hand. "In case they got violent."

His eyes narrowed, anger flaring so fast it made his fists clench. He forced his fingers to relax, to open again so he could reach out and turn her face toward him. They were too close. He knew that. He could smell his shampoo in her hair, her dusty sweat, and a metallic scent that could be from helping Leroy or from the gun she still held.

"Did that happen much?" he asked.

She paused, not breaking eye contact. His hand was still beneath her chin. "No, not much," she said finally, softly, her mind was somewhere else. "Just enough to make me scared. Every time."

"Were you scared of me?" He hated that it mattered.

She shook her head, and he lowered his hand, but instead of dropping it to his side as he'd intended, it slid down her neck, rasping over the soft skin of her throat. She shivered despite the heat.

"Not when I realized who you were."

It was his turn to pause, to break eye contact, but his gaze landed on her lips. "I'm not the same man anymore," he said.

He finally managed to let her go, but she caught his hand in hers, pressing his palm against her cheek, forcing his gaze back to those wide hazel eyes. She turned her face slightly to nip the soft flesh at the inside of his thumb, sending a shock of desire through him.

"I'm not the same girl," she whispered.

There was no denying that. Brody groaned and moved his hand to the back of her neck, grasping the hair at the nape and pulling lightly, so her mouth tilted toward him. He hesitated, still conflicted, but she grasped the front of his shirt with her empty hand and pulled him down to her.

If he'd thought she tasted delicious before, it was nothing compared to now. There was no whiskey, no artificial scent, no affectation. He wasn't the Victor, and she wasn't the Prize. They were just a man and a woman, and that turned him on so damn much.

He took the gun from her fingers, deftly turned on the safety, and slipped it into the back of his pants without breaking the kiss, leaving her free to wind her arms around his neck. He kept one hand in her hair and moved the other lower, cupping her ass and pressing her hard against him. She moaned, and if they'd been on the ship instead of out in the open, he would never have been able to break away.

But he did, lingering for a moment, experimenting with the way her lips felt when he was gentle with them, and damned if that wasn't even better. She sighed as he stepped back, and he looked at the sky.

"We gotta get back," he said. "Captain'll want to discuss the plan for tomorrow."

She nodded. Her cheeks were flushed, and her hair was falling from its braid. His finger twitched as he considered smoothing it down for her, but something told him putting his hands on her again would only end with their mouths on each other. Besides, she might get the wrong idea. She might start to think that he could be something to her.

He couldn't be anything to anyone.

"Let's go," he grunted, and he turned away from her, leading the way back to the ship.

CHAPTER 26

When they got on the elevator together, Brody leaned against one side, as far from Capri as possible. She pretended not to notice.

They stepped out, and already the sound of voices and smell of food wafted from down the hall. Capri hadn't realized how hungry she was. Something about the fresh air, her first taste in fifteen years, had made her ravenous. Brody fell back to let her enter the dining room first, and Leroy immediately caught her eye and patted the chair next to him.

He, Jax, and the captain already had plates of steaming food in front of them, and someone—probably Leroy, since Brody had been left to fend for himself—had a plate ready for Capri. She dug in like everyone else while the gunman heated a plate. Once Colin finished eating, he cleared his throat and leaned back in his seat.

"Jax and I have a meeting tomorrow morning, and then Leroy and I'll go to haggle over a few parts that need replacing soon. Shots'll be restocking. Capri, you make a list of the things you'll need to get you through the next few days and give it to him."

Brody sat across from her now and was shoveling mashed potatoes into his mouth. He made eye contact only briefly before looking back at the captain.

"I want to be out of here by 15:00 so we can land in U.S. Territory by nightfall for the next pickup," Colin continued. "Any questions?"

"Nope," said Leroy immediately, while Jax shook his head and Brody grunted.

Capri raised her hand, and a look of amusement flashed over Colin's serious face, so fast she wasn't sure she'd seen it at all.

"Yes?"

"I'd like to go myself."

He was shaking his head before she'd even finished, as did Brody, whose mouth was still full.

"Why not? Brody said I'm not a prisoner."

"That's true, but we're also responsible for returning you to Ekon in one piece."

"Is Mexico very dangerous?"

"Parts of it. I'm not taking chances. None of us have time to take you sightseeing, and you're not exactly equipped to defend yourself."

"That's not true," she said, leaping on the opportunity to convince him. She turned to Brody. "Tell him."

Colin looked at Brody with a raised eyebrow. Brody swallowed his food and stared back at his captain, saying nothing. Irritation flashed in Colin's eyes.

"Well?" he said. "How'd she do?"

Brody glared at Capri, but she was unfazed. He'd wanted to free her, so he'd better damn well give her some freedom.

"She did alright," Brody grunted, going back to his food.

Colin studied her again, as if seeing something in her he hadn't before. Still, when he opened his mouth, she could tell the answer would still be no. Only, he didn't get a chance to speak.

"I'll take her," Leroy said. The captain closed his mouth and stared at him, as did the others. Leroy shrugged, completely unconcerned by their obvious displeasure. "I have some time before we need to meet at the scrapyard. I'll take her in and get her what she needs. Shots can grab her on his way back to the ship."

Colin looked at Capri again, who turned her grateful gaze away from Leroy, desperate to convince him. "This could be my only chance to see something outside of Mars for the rest of my life. I'm just asking for a couple of hours."

The captain's lips formed a thin line, but Capri knew she had him. "Fine," he said before turning back to his crew. "Brody, make sure she has a piece. And Leroy, if anything happens to her, I'll hand you both over to Ekon."

"If anything happens to her," Leroy said, "I'll pretend to be Jax."

His brother laughed. It was the first time Capri had ever seen him show any sign of mirth, even if it was at his brother's expense. "You could never," he said.

Leroy shrugged but didn't argue.

Capri kept her mouth shut for the rest of the meal and was the first to leave, refusing to give the captain the chance to change his mind. She went back to Brody's room and removed the dusty, grease-stained clothing. She showered and then put the pants and t-shirt back on. It was that or the dress, and it made her realize just how grateful she'd be for another change of clothes.

As she lay in the top bunk, staring at the cold metal ceiling with nothing else to do but not yet tired enough to sleep, her thoughts drifted to the kiss she'd shared with Brody. He wanted her. When he returned to the room tonight, would they continue what they'd started?

An hour later, he still hadn't made an appearance, and an hour after that she was feeling drowsy. The next thing Capri knew, it was morning, and someone was knocking loudly on the door.

Capri slid off the top bunk and tried to run her fingers through her hair, but it was becoming more tangled each day. She slipped an elastic band from around her wrist and pulled it back as she pressed the button on the control panel by the door.

"Hey, Leroy," she greeted with a yawn.

"Hey." He said with his signature grin. "Time to get going."

"Okay. Give me a second." She glanced behind her, already know-ing the bottom bunk hadn't been slept in all night. Still, there was a glint of metal on Brody's pillow. He'd left her a gun as the captain had ordered.

"He slept in the lounge," Leroy said. "You two have a fight?"

Capri snapped her gaze back to his. She could feel her cheeks flaming. "No," she said. "It's not like that."

"Oh. Okay." For the first time, the mechanic's grin irritated her.

"I'll be right back," she said.

Capri went to the bathroom and did what she could to tame her hair and clean her teeth. She sniffed her clothes, although there was no real way of helping the lingering scent of her sweat. She came back out, put on a fresh pair of socks with her boots, straightened her clothes, and strapped the gun into its thigh holster. Like the boots, its weight would take some getting used to.

"All set?" Leroy asked, tossing her an apple.

She caught it and took a bite as they walked to the loading bay together.

"So, if it's not like *that*," he said, putting air quotes around *that*, "what is it like?"

"Complicated," Capri replied shortly. "Why are you so interested?"

"Just curious," he said, handing her a helmet and pressing the code that lowered the ramp. "This is the longest I think I've ever seen Shots sober. At least for a few years."

Since his family died. The unspoken words hung in the air. Capri shrugged.

"I don't know what goes on in his head," she said, still stung that he hadn't returned the previous night. She suspected he regretted kissing her, and though she knew his feelings had to be complicated and she couldn't push him, rejection didn't feel good.

"It's not like him to get involved."

Capri gave a half smile and shrugged. "Lucky me." Then she finished the apple, tossed it in the garbage chute, and strapped the helmet beneath her chin, anxious for a change of subject. "How do I ride one of these things?"

"Just keep your helmet on and hold tight to me. If you let go, you'll probably fall off and die," he said cheerily as he put on his own helmet and straddled the bike.

"Oh. Great." Capri got on the seat behind him, adjusting her position slightly to feel more secure.

Leroy started the engine, Capri grasped him tightly around the waist, and they were off. For the first minute, she kept her eyes closed. Then, she peeked cautiously through her lashes. By the time they reached the marketplace outside of the docks, she was enjoying the ride. She imagined it was what it must feel like to fly and was tempted to let go, to spread her arms like wings, but she only relaxed her grip when he reached the center of town.

He pulled over and parked on a crowded street lined with shops and restaurants. "You'll be able to find anything you need here," Leroy said, removing his helmet. "The captain loaded up a data ring for you."

He handed the small device to her, and she slipped it on her finger. Then she took off her own helmet and watched as he pocketed a piece of the bike's engine.

"Makes it harder for someone to steal it," he explained.

"Oh." Again, she wondered just how common crime was outside of Mars. She took in her surroundings while dismounting.

Mexico Territory, like the other territories, paid homage to its Old Earth namesake, with both U.N. and Mexican flags moving in the breeze. When the people of the U.N. countries migrated five hundred years ago, there had been talk of creating a true melting pot, of taking those migrating and placing them at random on New Earth.

In the end, the importance of preserving culture had won out, and many of the people she was seeing now were direct descendants of the Mexicans of Old Earth.

"What's first on the list?" Leroy asked, breaking into her thoughts.

"A hairbrush," Capri said promptly.

The twin smiled and offered her his arm.

CHAPTER 27

An hour later, she had the necessities, including two changes of clothes, all tucked away in a lightweight backpack. She'd opted for practical cargo pants and t-shirt for her time on the ship but also bought one dress for when they arrived back on Mars.

She didn't think showing up in pants would go over well with Ekon, and his level of pleasure or displeasure would likely be in direct correlation with how harsh Brody's punishment was. Every time she thought about returning, her heart clenched. She was still waiting for confirmation that Ekon had agreed to her terms. She wouldn't be able to fully relax until then.

Now, she and Leroy were sharing an early lunch at one of the restaurants. She'd followed his lead when it came to etiquette in the stores and in sitting and ordering at the small café. There was so much she didn't know about the worlds outside of Mars, and that truth hurt. Ignorance hadn't been bliss, but it had certainly been simpler.

And if life outside of Mars meant huaraches like these all the time, she wasn't sure she wanted to return at all. Leroy laughed as she took a very unladylike bite of her food and tried to keep the generous filling from spilling out of the fried masa dough.

"It's good, right?" he said, raising a glass of tequila.

She clinked hers against his and they drank.

"Really good," she agreed.

Leroy wiped his mouth and glanced at the time on the wall. Capri followed his gaze. It was eleven o'clock.

"What time do you have to meet the captain?" she asked.

"11:30," he answered grimly. "Shots should've been here by now."

"We could go to him. Isn't he just a few blocks away?"

Leroy shook his head. "A few blocks makes a lot of difference here. He's on the bad side of town. *Real* bad. There's no way I'm taking you through there."

"Then why don't I just wait for him here? You go ahead."

Leroy glanced at the time again. "I'll get my ass kicked if I leave you here alone."

"I could go with you," she suggested.

"We're also going to a bad side of town."

Capri wrinkled her nose. "Why?"

Leroy shrugged. "Everything's cheaper there."

"And…legal?" She already knew the answer and only said it to tease him.

He moved his hand in a *so-so* motion.

"Won't the captain kick your ass if you're late?"

"Probably."

"Then go," she said. "I've still got half my food left."

Leroy hesitated. "Are you sure?"

She nodded, and she meant it. She still had an entire huarache in front of her, and they'd sat by the window so she could see the street.

"Take my linker," Leroy said. "It's already set to our frequency, so you should be able to hear if Shots comes through or reach out if he doesn't."

He removed a small, wired loop from one ear and handed it to her. She placed it in her own ear while he stood and pressed his data ring to the menu to pay for their food and drinks.

"I'll see you later," he said.

With one last grin, he was out the door. She watched him hop on the motorcycle, buckle his helmet, and speed off down a side street. Capri was alone. More than that, she was anonymous. No one knew who she was, where she came from, or where she was going. It was surreal, and, for the next hour, she enjoyed it.

She was dressed so plainly no one gave her a second look, and that gave her the freedom to watch them. They were just people, going about their daily lives, but Capri had never seen so many children or so much activity in one place.

However, by the time 12:00 rolled around, she'd finished her food and drink, and the server was beginning to give her furtive glances as more people entered the restaurant to eat. She'd overstayed her welcome.

Capri stood and exited the building but remained near their meeting point to try and contact someone from the crew. She had no clue how to use a linker, and she fiddled with the small object, trying to determine if it was on and how to speak into it. All the while, a voice in the back of her mind was trying to incite panic, saying Brody must regret their interlude at the docks so much he'd left her here to fend for herself.

She'd just replaced the earpiece, ready to attempt contact, when a motorcycle pulled to a clumsy stop in front of her.

She glanced up, and there was Brody, looking as if he'd run there rather than ridden. Unlike Leroy, he didn't wear a helmet, and sweat glistened on his brow. His breathing was labored. His dark eyes landed on her before sweeping the immediate area.

"Where the hell is Leroy?" he asked, voice rougher than usual.

Capri's initial relief at seeing the gunman turned to concern.

"I told him to leave," she said, approaching him. "What's wrong?"

He indicated the saddlebags on the motorcycle. "Grab the first aid kit."

"What? Why? What happened?" she asked, but she moved, unbuckling the pack nearest to her and digging through ammunition and—*Was that a grenade?*—before removing a white metal box with a red cross on the top.

Brody removed the pack from his back and lifted his jacket, revealing a red stain that was getting bigger the longer she watched it.

"Get some gauze and pack it," he told her. "I can't reach it."

"No," she muttered, shaking her head even though he wasn't looking at her. "I can't."

"You gotta," he told her.

He was so calm about it. No one around them had noticed anything was wrong. It looked like he might just need help adjusting a strap or something. With shaking hands, Capri managed to find gauze and tape, and she raised his t-shirt. Blood still oozed from the wound, forming a small rivulet down his lower back.

All she could see as she pressed the gauze into the wound was Lady Agatha, the napkins soaked with blood, her wild brown eyes, the way the light had left them. She squeezed her eyes shut as she pressed with all her strength, as though she could force the memory from her mind.

"Tape it down," Brody ordered through gritted teeth, and she forced her eyes open again. She found a large, square bandage and taped it firmly over the gauze. Then, she let go, holding her hands out in front of her as if she'd just dismantled a bomb, still half-afraid it would go off.

Brody tugged his shirt and jacket back down to hide the wound and swung his bag onto his back again. Then he looked at her. She still couldn't move, couldn't look him in the eye. Memories kept her paralyzed. He reached out, his large hands enveloping hers, his touch breaking the spell.

She swallowed and pulled her hands away to repack the kit and strap it into the saddlebags.

"So what happened?" she asked, still not looking at him. His moments of tenderness confused her, and she'd already learned they wouldn't last. She willed herself not to find too much comfort in him.

"Got jumped by some guy with a knife coming out of the gun & ammo shop," Brody said, and he handed her the only helmet.

"Are you okay to drive?" she asked. "Should we call someone?"

"I'm fine," he said. "Get on."

Capri hesitated only a moment before swinging her leg over the seat and wrapping her arms around him. The pack on his back kept her from pressing against his injury, but she was careful not to squeeze too tight.

The ride back felt longer than the ride there. It had been a fun adventure with Leroy, but Brody had brought reality crashing back down. Each time they hit a bump, she felt his muscles tense. But he got them safely back to the ship, and when they rode up the ramp and parked, he dismounted with only a sharp intake of breath to indicate anything was wrong.

He grabbed a larger first aid kit from one of the shelves, turned, and handed it to her.

She took it from him but didn't move. "What am I supposed to do with this?"

"You gotta stitch me up."

"What? No." She almost laughed at the ridiculousness of the idea. Staunching blood was one thing. Stitching human flesh…she couldn't. There was no way. "Wait until one of the others gets back."

"It's gonna be at least two hours. If there was any way I could do it, I would." His hard brown gaze softened slightly. "I'm sorry."

"I don't know how," she insisted, fighting a rising panic.

"You just do it."

"What if I hurt you?"

"Little pinpricks ain't nothin'." His reassurance was impatient, but it was reassurance nonetheless.

Still, Capri thought she might see a reappearance of her tequila and huaraches.

"Fine," she muttered.

She hugged the first aid kit to her chest and followed him to his room. He opened the door, tossed his rucksack and jacket to the floor, and peeled off his shirt. Then, he straddled the metal chair and waited. Capri dropped her own bag, swallowed hard, and approached him. She knelt tentatively behind him. She'd never been this close to his bare skin before, and it was obvious this wasn't the first injury he'd experienced. Far from it. His back was a testament to just how violent his kind of life could be.

And now he'd have another scar to add to his collection.

With shaking fingers, Capri sifted through the kit until she found a suture kit. She wiped her hands with alcohol and ripped open the tiny packages containing a curved needle and catgut. She struggled to fit the thread through the small hole, and finally Brody turned, took the items from her, and deftly joined them together.

"Do a lot of sewing?" she muttered, taking the needle from him, cheeks burning.

"I do enough," he grunted, turning back again.

She took a deep breath and removed the bandage. His skin rippled slightly in response, and she was glad to see, upon removing the gauze, that the bleeding had stopped. She raised the needle, bit her lip, and pressed the point into his skin. She was nervous and slow, using forceps to pull it through, and she stuck him clumsily more than once. He didn't complain, his only reaction a brief tensing of muscles, the sheen of sweat on his skin.

When she'd finished, she sat back to look at her work and was once again drawn to the array of scars on his back. Before realizing she was doing it, Capri reached up to trace a long, faded mark with the tip of her index finger.

She felt a tremor run through his body, and he turned quickly, grabbing her wrist. His brown eyes were wild, but she didn't feel afraid. She just held her breath, waiting to see if he'd push her away or pull her toward him. But he just held her in place.

"You gotta stop," he said.

Her cheeks flamed, and anger flared. Like this was her fault. Like this attraction was one sided. "You want me to stop?" she said. "You brought me here, against my will, because you wanted me to want more. Now I do, and you're telling me to stop. That's not fair."

Their eyes locked. She sounded petulant, and she knew it, but she was so damn *frustrated*. His grip on her wrist tightened, and she watched his jaw clench and unclench. She refused to back down, refused to be the first to break eye contact. Finally, he spoke.

"Fine," he growled.

"Fine?"

His eyes were dark, and she realized suddenly it wasn't anger in their brown depths; it was desire. He turned so he sat forward in the chair, still holding her firmly in place.

"I didn't mean right now," Capri said breathlessly. "You're hurt."

He tugged her forward, and she landed easily on his lap, straddling him, like she'd done this a million times before. The solace she felt in his nearness was unnerving.

"You want me to stop?" he said in a low, mocking voice. "That's not fair."

He moved his hands to her hips, holding her in place. Her breath had left her completely; she felt dizzy, drunk, impossibly aware of his hot skin through the fabric of her shirt, the hard muscles of his chest pressing against her breasts. The heady scent of his skin was overwhelming, and her lips were so close to his neck... She pressed a kiss to his throat and felt a ripple move through his body.

As if the gentle caress had flipped a switch, his grip tightened on her hips and he began guiding her back and forth on his lap. The movements were slow and deliberate, ensuring that she felt every inch of his erection. Capri moaned, amazed that something could feel so good through so many layers of clothing.

Somehow, a sliver of sanity infiltrated her haze of pleasure. "The door's still open," she whispered.

His only response was to dip his head and bury his mouth in the place where her neck met her shoulder, and Capri was lost. She moaned, moving her hands from where they gripped his arms to his shoulders, then his back, raking her fingertips across his exposed flesh.

He shuddered beneath her, letting her know she wasn't the only one enjoying this. Soon, he wasn't guiding her anymore, and she was moving herself shamelessly against him. He reached down to tug at the hem of her shirt until it was rucked up above the tops of her breasts, exposing her pert nipples to his hungry mouth. She moaned, vaguely aware that one of his hands was heading south. She leaned back to allow him better access—and to return the favor.

She stroked his hard length through the fabric, but when she went for the zipper, he grabbed her wrist and forced it behind her back, pushing her breast further into his mouth.

He didn't hold her there, but she got the message. She kept her hands above the waist, exploring his skin as he unfairly dipped a finger into the front of her unbuttoned pants.

Capri was vaguely aware of noises that had to be coming from her, noises she'd never made before in her life. She clutched Brody to her, his hard length pressing deliciously into her center while his fingertip teased her sensitive flesh. She squirmed and moaned, riding higher and higher, until she exploded within sensation. Brody's hand was firm on the small of her back, and she was sure it was the only thing keeping her from falling. Vaguely, she was aware that his lips had left her body.

Through the shimmering haze of her orgasm, she watched him watching her, and his brown eyes were the clearest she'd ever seen them, filled with hunger, wonder, and something else, something like regret.

It took a long time for Capri to come down, and she collapsed against him, gasping for breath. He removed his hand and licked his fingertip, eyes dark as he tasted her. But to her surprise, he relaxed back against the chair, as if his erection wasn't jutting up between them, and smirked.

"Feel better?" he asked.

The emotion she'd seen in his eyes had gone, and he was unreadable once more. Capri stared at him while her addled brain registered what his words meant. He'd done this to get her off his back, as if she was a horny nuisance and their attraction wasn't mutual—when it very obviously was.

And still he sat there, inches from her face, with that self-satisfied look on his face. Fury rose faster than she could have anticipated, and she felt the sting in her palm before she realized she'd slapped him.

He hadn't been expecting it, and his head snapped to the side. Before he could turn back, she removed herself from his lap and stalked to the bathroom to shower and change.

CHAPTER 28

Brody remained sitting, listening to the sound of running water, feeling strangely empty. It had been more than four years since he'd pleasured a woman for the sake of pleasuring her. He'd done it because Capri should know what it was like to have an encounter that wasn't transactional. He'd done it because a part of him hoped scratching her itch would be enough to keep their hands off each other. And he'd said what he'd said to make sure of it.

He hadn't anticipated how watching her, touching her, tasting her would make him feel. He didn't want to feel at all. But here he was, wanting her worse than ever. He would have liked to be in the shower scratching his own itch, but he settled for standing, adjusting himself, and trying to put the whole thing out of his mind. In an hour, they'd be heading for U.S. Territory to rob a fruit distributor. He needed to get his mind on the job.

As if on cue, he heard the loading ramp descend and the noisy return of three motorcycles. He shoved the chair back over to the desk, returned the suture kit to the first aid kit, and had just picked up his bloody shirt from the floor when footsteps sounded in the hall behind him.

Colin and Leroy were passing by, and they both paused at the sight of him, shirtless, holding bloodstained clothing.

"Is that from you or her?" Leroy asked, scanning the room with more panic in his gaze than Brody liked.

"Me," he grunted, narrowing his gaze while he tried to interpret the mechanic's sudden concern.

Leroy visibly relaxed, and Brody turned his back on them to throw his shirt in the corner of the room and rummage for a new one. When he turned back, they were still standing there, Colin's arms folded across his chest.

"Who stitched you up?" he asked.

"She did." He jerked his chin toward the closed bathroom door.

Colin looked mildly impressed, which Brody also didn't like. He pulled the shirt over his head and left the room, closing the door behind him and stalking to the loading bay, effectively ending the conversation.

He still had to unload the guns and ammunition he'd bought. The wound in his back was a nuisance, nothing more. He hadn't felt pain the same way since his family was killed. It was all a penance and none of it enough. It wouldn't be enough until someone or something finally managed to kill him.

Although this time, when he'd been fighting off the three men who had tried to rob him in the grubby alleyway, he hadn't felt the usual apathy. Capri was his responsibility, and he had to live long enough to see her back safely. When the knife had entered his back, he'd been worried for a moment that he might fail her.

Three hours later, when the ship landed in a field in midwestern U.S. Territory, he put on a bulletproof vest. He had a rifle strapped across his chest and two guns in holsters. Jax, Leroy, and Colin trickled in around 22:00.

Colin glanced at him. He'd be able to tell immediately that Brody had gear on under his T-shirt. He'd know better than anyone what it meant, that he wanted—more like *needed*—to survive.

But he also knew better than to mention it.

The captain addressed the crew while taking his own weapons from the makeshift armory in the loading bay. Leroy was pulling on gloves and checking his ammo while Jax leaned casually against the car they'd be taking, awaiting instructions.

"Leroy, you're driving us to the warehouse. There's an electric fence, so make sure you have what you need to get through it."

"Already packed." The mechanic grinned and patted the trunk of the car.

"We'll need you keeping watch while Shots and I get into the warehouse and load the goods into one of the trucks. Jax, I'll link you when we're fifteen minutes out. Be ready to fire up the ship."

The pilot nodded and pushed himself off the car while his twin swung into the driver's seat. Colin slid in next to him. As Brody opened the door behind the passenger's seat, he caught a flicker of movement in the corridor. Capri stood by the loading bay entrance, only half-visible, watching them go. They made eye contact, but her steady gaze gave nothing away.

He was the first to break it, sliding in the back to sit in the middle. He wasn't sure if she'd meant to be seen, if she'd come for him, if she was just bored after keeping herself shut in the room for hours. He only knew he had to stop thinking about her, about the why, about the way her body had felt in his hands.

Brody gripped the rifle more tightly, trying to replace the memory of her soft skin with hard metal, with reality. It was time to focus. It was time to get paid. After they delivered these goods to Tycho, they'd head back to Mars, and she'd be out of reach again.

That was a good thing, he reminded himself.

Jax lowered the ramp, and they drove away.

CHAPTER 29

Capri was starving. She hadn't wanted to sit across from Brody at dinner so soon after he'd brought her to the peak of pleasure just to shove her off it. She trusted that if she stayed in his room, he'd stay out of it; he'd respect the fact she was angry. Trustworthy and asshole didn't seem like they should go together, but somehow, with him, they did.

Her anger hadn't taken long to fizzle out. She wanted to hate him, but she couldn't. He was hurting, and no matter how strong the pull might be between them, he wasn't going to let himself have her. At least, not completely.

Capri found herself wondering where exactly he'd draw the line. Would he let her touch him? What would it be like to pleasure a man on her own terms? She felt herself growing flushed at the thought and left Brody's room before her imagination ran away completely.

Although Jax was floating around somewhere, the ship was as quiet as on her first night, only this time she knew where she stood, and she felt free to wander into the kitchen and search for food. She found a packet of easy heat beef stew and tossed it in a bowl in the quick oven. Just a few days before, she'd had no idea how to use one.

While she waited, she peeked in the lounge next door. The room looked much as it had when Leroy had given her the grand tour of the ship, but now one of the plush couches had a blanket and pillow shoved to one end. That must be where Brody spent the previous night, where she suspected he'd spend every night until they took her back to Mars.

Despite her best efforts, Capri felt slighted. She was a problem he'd ignore until it went away. She left the room abruptly and went to collect her dinner, sitting down, alone, to eat.

At first, she didn't mind the quiet. She could hear the hum of a generator somewhere in the belly of the ship. A door opened and closed down the hall, and Jax's footsteps receded toward the cockpit. The sound was strangely comforting, reminding her of when she was very small, falling asleep to the sounds of her parents' movements in their apartment.

And then she did mind the quiet. Maybe the constant activity on Mars had been the thing keeping her earlier memories at bay. She finally had a moment that was truly her own, where she could consider her life and what she wanted from it.

But she didn't want to think. What if she decided she was unhappy? What if she found she wanted a different life? She'd only feel angry she couldn't have it. She had to at least pretend this was her choice, or the lack of power over her own life would drive her insane.

Capri stood and placed her bowl and spoon in the chute and downed a bottle of water. She considered going back to the room but found herself wandering around the loading bay, glancing into open bins. On one shelf, beside the place she'd watched the crew retrieve guns and masks, there was a box of linkers. She pulled a device out and examined it, studying the small button on the side and the dial on the part that looped around the ear.

"What are you doing?" came Jax's voice from the loading bay entrance, startling her so she almost dropped the small object.

She recovered, straightening her spine and turning to face him, refusing to look guilty. She'd been snooping, but what the hell else was she supposed to do? "I thought I'd try to learn how to use one of these," she said.

Jax glanced at the linker in her hands.

"Didn't you use one of those in Mexico Territory?"

She shook her head.

"Leroy left you a linker and didn't show you how to use it?" He sounded more resigned than surprised.

Capri gave a half shrug, not wanting to throw his twin under the bus.

"I was coming to tell you we received a message from Mars. Alexander said Ekon agreed to your terms. No one gets hurt, as long as you return in the same condition you left."

Relief and disappointment washed over Capri in equal measure. But she didn't want to examine the disappointment too closely. Jax glanced behind him and touched the device that sat in his own ear.

"Come with me and I'll show you how to use a linker," he said. "I want to be close to the controls when they come through."

Capri followed him, trying not to seem too eager. She never thought she'd get to sit in the cockpit, but he gestured to the co-pilot's seat and, once she'd sat down, held out his hand. She placed the linker in his palm, and he pointed to the dial.

"The numbers on the linkers should always match to make sure everyone is on the same channel. Whenever we touch down somewhere, we monitor to make sure the channel isn't in use by someone else. Press the button on the inside—" He gestured to a nearly invisible button that she hadn't noticed before. "—to turn it on, and press and hold on the outside to talk."

He handed it back to her. "Thanks," she said, staring down at the object. It was a commonly used communication device. Again, she was struck by just how much she didn't know—how much Ekon kept her from knowing.

"You can try it," Jax said, gesturing to her ear. "They just got through the fence."

Capri followed his instructions to turn it on, then slipped it into her ear. She didn't hear anything right away, but soon it was obvious that Brody, Leroy, and Colin had separated and had begun using the linkers to communicate.

Colin's voice sounded first. *"Hotwire successful."*

Capri glanced at Jax. He was listening intently to his own linker. She was again amazed by how different he was from his brother. They had the same copper skin, dark curly hair, and honey brown eyes, but where Leroy was nothing but chatter, she knew better than to try small talk with Jax.

"The truck," he explained shortly.

She recognized a slight tension in his frame now and wondered if he was waiting for the signal to spring into action, or if he was worried about Colin.

A minute later, Leroy's voice came through. *"Um, guys. There's a dog."*

Then, Brody. *"Even you can handle a damn dog, Leroy."*

"Not that kind of—shit."

There was a silence then, during which Capri held her breath, and Jax seemed to be doing the same.

"Threat neutralized," Brody said finally.

"And what the hell about Leroy?" Jax muttered under his breath, echoing Capri's own thoughts.

"Jax, we'll be coming in hot," Colin said through the linker. *"No injuries."*

Jax released a breath and pressed his thumb against a sensor, flipping switches and pressing buttons to warm up the ship's engine. He hadn't told Capri to leave, so she stayed put, watching the procedure with interest. The pilot turned on screens that acted as windows, and within ten minutes, she could see the crew approaching. The old car that had sat in the loading bay led the way, and a big box truck followed.

Jax touched his linker. *"Lowering the ramp."*

Then, without a word to Capri, he got out of his seat and headed down the corridor. Capri hesitated for only a moment before following. Leroy was driving the car and pulled in first, leaping out with an excited look on his face.

"Jax! They had a Guard Dog!"

"That's bad, isn't it?" Jax answered mildly.

"Only if they recorded anything. I had to bring it with us to check."

The box truck pulled in behind, making it so there was barely room to move through the maze of vehicles and supplies.

"I can guarantee you he did not have to bring it with him," Jax muttered to Capri.

He remained beside her just long enough to watch Colin alight from the truck, unharmed, then headed back to the cockpit to finish initiating takeoff.

Capri felt the familiar rumble beneath her feet that occurred just before the ship became airborne. She glanced at Brody as he hopped down from the passenger seat of the truck, also unharmed. He locked eyes with her for only a moment before moving to replace the guns he'd taken from the loading bay. Capri slid her gaze to Leroy, who was hauling what looked like a pile of twisted metal from the back of the car.

"Mind helping me?" Leroy said, his eyes bright with a contagious sort of excitement.

"What is it?" she asked.

"A security robot."

Upon closer inspection, she realized the hunk of metal was actually in the form of a dog—or had been before someone shot it. Or maybe threw a grenade at it. She glanced at Brody's back.

She helped Leroy take it out of the back seat. It was easily the heaviest thing she'd ever had to lift. "Can you get my tool bag?" he asked breathlessly once they'd set it on the floor of the loading bay.

Capri found the sturdy bag where he'd left it after working on the motorcycles and carried it to him. After selecting a screwdriver, he began prying open a spot on the machine's head, tongue poking out the corner of his mouth, lost in concentration. She watched him work, vaguely aware that Brody was watching her watch him, but she kept her gaze fixed on the mechanic.

"It looks like a direct feed," he said after a few minutes, and Capri realized the captain was still there, too, waiting for Leroy's diagnosis.

The frown on Colin's lips told Capri this wasn't a good thing. Leroy took a reader from the toolbox and hooked it up to the Guard Dog, his fingers flashing through the touch screen and his eyes scanning numbers faster than Capri could make sense of them.

"Looks like he was triggered when we opened the warehouse door. He got me and Shots, but he couldn't see our faces. Nothing concrete."

"Still, I'll be happy to unload these goods," Colin said. "We'll land on Tycho tomorrow at 13:00. Then we'll pop over to the Green Patch and it's back to Mars."

CHAPTER 30

Capri had missed the brief look of regret on Leroy's face when Colin mentioned returning to Mars, but Brody hadn't. He also hadn't missed the more surprising look of regret on Capri's face.

All she had to do was say the word. He'd make sure she got wherever she wanted to go, even if it meant Colin having to hand Ekon his head on a platter. That knowledge, the fierceness of his feelings, scared him. He told himself it was because he'd known her before he lost everything, because he'd seen her as some kind of redemption.

It wasn't because he had feelings for her.

She was engrossed in the mechanic's explanation of the robot dog and his plans to rebuild it, which meant his plans to have it taking up space in the loading bay for the next year, and Brody took the opportunity to go to his room, shower, and change. Then he went back to keeping out of her way.

It almost worked.

At 3:00am, Brody was in the loading bay checking on the guns for the third time. He couldn't sleep, and it was something to do, some kind of action, something to make him feel useful. But as he tested the weight of a pistol and made sure it was loaded, his skin prickled with the sensation of being watched. He glanced toward the corridor and, again, found Capri peering around the corner.

The dim light of the hallway shone around her head, giving her an almost angelic look. It seemed she couldn't sleep, either. He straightened and watched her. She didn't turn away, didn't seem bothered by the fact that she'd been spotted. She walked toward him.

Brody closed and locked the gun cabinet, then turned back to face her. She must want to talk. What could he say? He might be what she wanted, but he'd never be what she needed.

Capri said nothing, however, and only stopped when her body was inches from his. She studied his face, searched his eyes. It was unnerving, but Brody couldn't tear his gaze away. He was remembering the way she'd felt in his arms, the touch of her skin, her sighs of pleasure, the way his traitorous body had reacted to hers.

The flush in her cheeks and her heavy-lidded gaze told him she was remembering, too. Even now, he could smell her unique scent through the floral shampoo she'd purchased in Mexico. Her gaze moved to his chest, and she brought her fingertips up to touch him through his t-shirt, experimenting, exploring, her caresses frustratingly light. She brushed his nipples, and he gritted his teeth against the pleasure, reaching up to close his fingers around her wrists.

His firm grasp didn't deter her. She leaned forward and raked her teeth lightly across his chest instead, sending a shiver through him.

"What the fuck are you doing?" He'd tried to make his words a warning, but they sounded more like a plea.

She didn't answer, moving her lips down his torso until she was on her knees, using her teeth to tug on his zipper. He released a frustrated groan and let her small hands slide through his so she could unbuckle his belt, unzip his pants, and release his straining erection.

She bit her full lower lip and studied his length, touched him with another feather-light caress. Then, she gripped him firmly and pumped her fist. Brody shuddered and watched her, mesmerized. She looked up, holding his gaze as she leaned forward to lick the tip. He grunted and closed his eyes, knowing he was fighting a losing battle even before her hot, wet mouth enveloped him.

She took his shaft inch by inch, working the base with her hand, until he was fully inside of her mouth. She swallowed, the muscles of her throat constricting around him, and sensation exploding in his veins.

He tangled his fingers in the curls at the nape of her neck, every muscle tense as he struggled to keep control. He didn't want to hurt her, didn't want to make her feel used, but it felt so goddamn good. His legs shook with the effort it took to keep from thrusting. She seemed to sense his desperation and doubled her efforts, closing her eyes and increasing the speed of her movements.

Brody gave up. He went hard and fast, hitting the back of her throat, but the noises she made around his girth were eager, encouraging. He couldn't hold back. With a groan, Brody exploded in her mouth, and she sucked and swallowed everything he gave her.

Finally, he was able to relax his grip on her neck, and she released him with a *pop*. Her hair was a mess, her lips red and swollen. He had a sudden flash of memory, of fooling around with Jill in their early days. It had been easy, fun, and the pain of loss hit him almost as hard as his orgasm. Capri stood, and he zipped up his pants, frowning.

What did she want from him?

But she only wiped her mouth on the back of her hand, turned, and left. Brody watched her go, breath still uneven, at war with himself.

***

The ship landed on Tycho, Sector 5 the following afternoon. Colin and Brody would go down on the elevator with a sample of the goods and receive the first half of payment in credited dollars. Once that exchange was made, Leroy would drive the truck down, and they'd get the second half in uncut diamonds.

They'd dealt with these individuals a few times before and expected the exchange to go smoothly. Still, Brody had put on protective gear, and he, Leroy, and Colin checked and rechecked their guns in the loading bay.

He grabbed a crate of apples and a container of some new hybrid berry and joined Colin in the elevator. He glanced back toward the entrance to the loading bay, immediately hating himself for hoping Capri was there. She wasn't.

Brody set his jaw and refocused as the elevator descended.

Tycho was hotter than Mexico Territory, but it was drier, too. The air was still, and fine dust rose around their boots when they stepped off the metal platform. Two men waited to greet them. It was customary—even numbers. Colin and the leader of the Tycho group both had guns strapped to their hips, but they kept them there as they shook hands. The second man kept his rifle pointed towards the ground.

Brody placed the goods in front of the buyer, then stepped back and held his rifle the same way.

The buyer looked through the crate. He was tall and lean, his skin tan and leathery from the constant sun. Visiting hot planets always made Brody miss Ptolemy. The man glanced at his colleague from beneath thick, dark eyebrows, and then his black eyes darted to Colin.

"This one looks worm-eaten," he said.

Brody clenched his jaw and glowered at the man. Was he really going to play this game?

"You know the price is good," Colin said calmly. "If you want to play games, we'll go to the next sector and offload it there. We might be looking at a bigger profit, too. What do you think, Shots?"

Brody grunted his agreement without taking his eyes off the men in front of him. The leader dragged his gaze over to the gunman, eyed the rifle, and looked back to Colin.

"It comes with the truck?"

"As requested."

The man nodded and glanced back at his own guard. He reached back to him for a reader and showed Colin proof of funds. With a hand-shake, they touched rings, and the first installment was transferred.

"The diamonds?" Colin asked.

The man retrieved a small sack from his guard and showed the contents. The guard adjusted his rifle slightly to make it easier to shoot them, should they try to snatch the bag before giving them the truck.

It was Colin's turn to nod. He pressed a button on his linker. "Leroy, it's on."

A moment later, the ramp to the loading bay opened, and the mechanic hopped in the truck. It took him a moment to get it started, and in those few moments, the ground around Brody and Colin began to move.

At first, Brody thought it must be the heat and the big, blazing sun making the earth look wavy. Maybe sandworms existed, after all. He didn't really know what to think until fifteen armed Tychos wearing masks and goggles leapt from the ground, guns trained on the outsiders.

Fuck.

Brody was taken off guard, and there were few things he liked less than that. His shock was brief, his rage was instant, and he aimed his gun at the leader. Colin had his gun out, too, but held up a hand to stop him from shooting.

"I thought we were building a rapport here," Colin said, only acknowledging the leader.

The other man smiled apologetically and cocked his gun. "Heard there was a reward for capturing some fruit thieves in U.S. Territory. We're looking to collect both. Nothing personal."

"You aiming that gun at my face makes it feel pretty personal."

Brody glanced behind them. Their backs were to the ship, and all the guns were in front of them. If they could make it to the loading bay, they'd have cover and half a chance at winning the shootout.

The roar of the truck's engine was the only distraction they'd get, and they both knew it. As soon as it sounded, Colin shot the man he'd been attempting to negotiate with in the stomach, and the two of them ran for it, shooting blindly behind them and dodging bullets. Leroy slammed his foot down on the gas, taking out three men as he drove and putting the truck between the ship and the Tychos, providing Brody and the captain with cover.

He scrambled out of the cab as bullets shattered the windows, landing with them, gun already drawn. The tires were punctured within seconds, and a stray bullet hit the engine, setting the electric battery alight.

"Jax!" Colin yelled into his linker. "We could use a little help!"

"Let's get to the ship and go!" Brody called over the gunfire as they fended off the small crowd of Tychos.

"If you want this ship to stay in the air we need the goods or the money!" Colin yelled back.

Brody's yell of frustration was lost in the noise.

CHAPTER 31

Capri sat in the lounge, reading a book that Jax had lent her. She'd held on to the linker for lack of other entertainment, and when the captain's voice came through, filled with urgency, she dropped the reader and stood immediately. Jax dashed past her to the loading bay without a second glance.

She felt the powerful urge to act but didn't know what to do, how to help. She went to the cockpit to look at the screens, to see what exactly was happening. Then, she froze, much as she had during the shootout at the palace. Outside was a similar scene, with Brody, Colin, and Leroy fighting for their lives against a group of men and women who were better armed.

They'd walked into a trap.

She expected to see Jax appear on the screen, as well, but she heard his footsteps echoing in the corridor again, getting closer. She whirled around just in time to catch the thin vest he threw at her.

"Put this on," he ordered, his brown eyes filled with nearly enough determination to hide his fear.

She did as she was told, then accepted the gun he thrust at her.

"Shots said you can use this."

"I mean…"

"Let's go."

They both ran for the loading ramp, moving toward the sound of gunfire when every instinct told her she should run away. But she swallowed her fear, feeding off Jax's energy. *No.*

This was her choice. Even if it ended up being the worst—and maybe last—of her life.

The air was so hot it burned her lungs, or maybe that was the dust, and the sun was so big and bright it would likely burn her fair skin. But she registered these observations only vaguely. Her focus was on the three men using the truck as cover, even as bullets tore through the metal siding and the flames in the hood grew higher.

"No!" Brody roared, lunging toward her. His brown eyes were wild, but the captain shoved him hard against the cab of the truck.

"Go to the back with Leroy and shoot whatever you can!" Colin yelled before getting in Brody's face and saying something he didn't like. Brody growled something in reply, then moved to the truck's headlights to spray bullets.

Jax ran to the duo, delivering what had to be the biggest gun on the ship and a bag that probably contained more weapons. Capri dove for cover behind the rear wheels, landing next to Leroy, who was peering around the back of the truck to take aim.

Capri turned off her pistol's safety and swung out to shoot, but she quickly realized that shooting a living, breathing person was very different from shooting a target or an empty bottle. She hesitated, and in that moment, a bullet whizzed past her ear. The sound of it was terrifyingly similar to the one that had killed Lady Agatha.

She scrambled back without taking the shot, breathing hard, fear making her frozen, useless. Leroy clasped her shoulder and forced her eyes to meet his. They were serious, fierce and understanding. In that moment, he looked more like Jax than himself.

"Get down and take the legs. It's easier," he said, pushing her toward the gap between the truck and the ground.

He was right. Capri aimed for faceless legs and pulled the trigger. She heard a cry of pain, and a man crumpled to the ground. She thought she might feel guilty then, once she saw him, but there was no time. He was still very capable of shooting her, and she ducked behind the tire just in time to miss another bullet to the head. She squeezed her eyes shut and took another breath.

Her heart was pounding. Violent images swirled in her head, the fantasy of nightmares mixed with memories of the bloodbath in the upper dining hall. She forced them back. If she wanted to live—if she wanted them *all* to live—she had to stay focused.

She opened her eyes and prepared to make the kill shot. Leroy glanced her way and gave her a questioning look. She shook her head slightly. They switched places so that he could do what she couldn't, and she fired at random from the back of the truck to keep the Tychos at bay.

He came over to her. "I can't do all your dirty work for you," he teased.

Even in this moment, he managed to make her smile. She shot another pair of legs, a woman this time, and her gun went flying. Capri shot her other leg to keep her from getting to it and then turned to fire at an ankle that had been getting perilously close to the truck— but it was already gone.

Confusion made Capri hesitate. She glanced toward the front of the truck. The others were unhurt and holding their own. Then fear struck her anew, and she leapt to her feet. She realized exactly where the missing pair of legs had gone. She glanced up to the roof of the truck and found a Tycho man with his eyes and gun trained on their biggest threat—Brody.

Suddenly, the decision to kill was easy. Capri raised her gun, aimed at the man's head, and pulled the trigger.

Nothing happened. She was out of ammo. All Capri could do was scream a warning.

It worked, in a way. It got Brody's attention, but it also got the shooter's attention. He turned the gun on her, the wrench in his plans, and fired. She turned away, but it wasn't enough. She saved her brain, but the bullet tore through her arm.

She fell hard on the dusty ground and gasped as the initial shock wore off and pain seared through her. She'd never felt anything like it. There was no ignoring it. There was no going to the place inside her mind where it wasn't happening. The agony was too demanding.

Capri had landed between the front and back tires, an easy target for anyone who bothered to glance under the truck as she'd been doing just moments before.

"Capri?" Leroy yelled.

His voice was laced with panic, but he couldn't get to her without leaving the back uncovered. She struggled to her hands and knees, effort preventing her from answering, but she thrust an arm out toward the mechanic in a weak attempt to let him know she was okay, at least that she wasn't dead.

The man who had shot her tumbled from the roof of the truck and landed a few feet away with a *thud.* She flinched. His brain hadn't been as lucky as hers.

Brody was beside her then, wrapping a strong arm around her waist, lifting and half-dragging her to the front. He pushed her back down to the ground and stood over her as he continued firing. He didn't look at her.

"This is getting outta hand!" Colin yelled, struggling for once to control his anger. "Get back to the ship!"

Jax ran for the loading ramp, using the truck and three other men as cover. Brody took a grenade from his belt and pulled the pin.

Capri glanced at the body of the man who had shot her. The dust had settled around him, and through her haze she spotted several small, shiny stones spilling from a bag on the ground beside him. *Diamonds.* She couldn't be sure it was the payment they'd been looking for, but it was something.

She forced herself upright and stumbled over to him. She heard Brody swear and hoped he'd put the pin back in the grenade. She grabbed the bag. A few shiny rocks fell out, and Brody grabbed her again before she could collect them. She hoped it was enough, enough to keep them in the sky.

Then he was pulling her back, out of harm's way, and he threw the grenade. They all ran for it, but the noise and heat of the explosion rattled Capri. Colin closed the ramp behind them and barked into his linker for Jax to take off.

CHAPTER 32

The little adrenaline Capri had managed to muster abandoned her, and her knees gave out with the first jolt of takeoff. Brody lifted her easily into his arms, and she gasped as the movement jarred her injury.

She still had the diamonds clutched tightly in her hand. Colin kept his eyes on hers.

"We owe you one," he said.

Capri's heart swelled with pride. He took the bag from her and found a cloth to stanch the blood.

"Get the kit and take it to the lounge," he ordered Leroy.

The captain and Brody took her and laid her on the couch closest to the door. She wondered vaguely how many times the cozy space had been used as an impromptu infirmary. This seemed to be standard procedure.

Colin replaced his hand with hers, telling her to press down as hard as she could. The pressure eased the pain, but there was blood everywhere. Her blood. She felt dazed. How much had Agatha lost before she died?

Leroy arrived a few seconds later with the medical kit. Everyone was hurrying to get her patched up, but no one was panicking. That was good, wasn't it? Maybe she wasn't dying. The captain stuck a syringe in her arm.

"What's that?" she asked.

"We haven't run medical supplies in a while," the captain said. "That's the best I can do for you."

"'Cause you gotta stitch me up," she murmured.

The captain motioned for Brody to take his place by Capri while he continued speaking to her. "We've gotta do a little more than that.

The bullet's still in there. Shots has the most experience. He'll handle it. You'll be okay."

Capri nodded, trying to feed off the captain's confidence, but she only felt fear. Brody pried her fingers away from her arm, and she gasped as the pain, and with it the blood, surged through her torn flesh. She glanced at his face; his eyes were dark and angry. A vein pulsed in his thick neck. She couldn't look away from it. Then she caught sight of something red in her peripheral. It was her hand, covered in blood, so much that it trickled down her arm.

Brody caught her wrist and moved it out of her line of sight.

"Don't look," he ordered in a low voice.

Capri obeyed, too dazed to resist. Brody pulled the cloth away to inspect the damage while Colin leaned against the doorframe. Leroy took a seat on the other couch.

Brody turned to his captain. "I gotta do some diggin'."

Colin moved forward. Brody found a scalpel and sloshed it around in disinfectant before wiping fresh blood from her arm and examining the angle of the wound.

"Digging?" she asked, shying away.

Brody set his jaw and looked into her eyes. "I gotta get it out. We don't have anesthesia," he told her bluntly.

Her first instinct was to resist, but she forced herself to stop cringing. It would be more dignified to accept the inevitable. Besides, Brody's eyes were still locked on hers, and she trusted him.

"Oh," she said, unable to keep the fear from her face, the tremble from her voice. The sound was so soft he was probably the only one who heard it.

Brody's eyes narrowed slightly, like he was fighting his own internal battle. A pair of strong hands, leaner than Brody's, grasped her arm. Colin was holding her in place. Brody looked down at his work, there was a moment of suspense, and then the knife cut into her wound. She jerked away.

"Hold still," Colin told her sharply, struggling to keep her arm steady. "You'll make it worse."

Every time Brody moved the blade, it felt like the bullet was tearing through her skin all over again. So much for remaining dignified. She twisted and pressed her face into the faux leather cushion of the sofa back.

"Found it," Brody muttered.

Capri bit down on the fabric to keep from screaming as he used forceps and the tip of the knife to half-cut, half-slide the object through the entry wound. Then it was over. She panted into the fabric, trying to regain a fraction of composure before turning back to her audience. Colin held the bloody cloth against her arm while Brody threaded a needle. He looked at her again as he knotted the end of the thread but didn't say a word.

"You got it from here?" Colin asked.

The gunman nodded without looking away from her, and the captain and mechanic made their exits, presumably to discuss their next course of action. Brody kept a firm hold on Capri's arm, but the prick and pull of the needle and thread felt like nothing after her previous surgery. *Little pinpricks ain't nothin'.* He'd been right.

Once he'd finished, he wrapped gauze tightly around her arm and continued sitting beside her, motionless, staring at her injury. To anyone else, it would look as if he was double-checking his work, but Capri could see the sheen of sweat on his brow, hear his labored breathing. Had he been injured, too? Had his old wound reopened?

"Brody?" she murmured, reaching out to touch his cheek with her fingertips.

His gaze snapped to hers, and she was surprised by the anger there. His body was controlled, but those dark brown orbs were wild. She retracted her hand.

"What the hell were you thinking?" he managed through his teeth.

"He was gonna kill you."

"I told you already, you don't worry about me," he told her in a low voice, still struggling to maintain control. "I'll get what's comin' to me eventually. You don't need to get yourself in the way of it."

She struggled to sit up, but dizziness assaulted her, and she couldn't quite get there. "Is that what you want?"

He stood abruptly, startling her, and slammed the palm of his massive hand into the back of the chair. It fell and slid across the floor. When he turned back, his pain and panic were obvious. He was reliving some nightmare, and Capri could guess what it was. He jabbed a finger in her direction.

"See, that's something we've always had in common. What we want never fucking matters."

Then he turned and left, taking the last of Capri's energy with him. She dropped back onto the sofa. The pounding pain had gone, leaving a tolerable ache in its place. The only sound was the white noise of the ship sailing through space, and it began to lull her.

She closed her eyes for a moment, fighting against the fog in her mind, but she lost the battle and slept.

CHAPTER 33

Brody was in turmoil. He had been ever since Capri showed up with Jax, that gun clutched uncertainly in her soft hands. And when she'd been shot…

He'd felt the same dread as when he'd found Colin waiting for him outside his apartment. He hadn't seen where the bullet landed at first, didn't have a chance to see how bad off she was until after he'd shot the bastard. He was prepared for the worst, the devastation he'd faced upon finding his wife's body on the floor, his baby girl dead in her bed.

The images came to him clearly, and he knew in an instant she would have been added to that list. His list of failures.

How? How had she managed to find all the soft parts of him and make him feel again? He ground his teeth together as he cleaned his gun in his room. His relief at discovering she'd only suffered a flesh wound was as devastating as if she'd died.

He fucking *cared*.

He just had to get her back to Mars. She'd be safe there. Sure, she'd be back getting fucked by whoever the hell Ekon or the auction decided, but she'd be safer than anyone was when they were with him. Today had proven that.

But the thought of her in someone else's arms put him into a rage, too, and he threw the unloaded gun across the room. He watched it bounce off the wall with a sense of satisfaction that could only come from violence.

He needed it, craved it, but here on the ship he had no outlet. They hadn't landed on the Green Patch yet. He couldn't go off-ship and find a bar. In a bar, he could start a fight over something, anything, and then he'd really get to lay into somebody.

But here, all he could do was punch the wall on the way out the door and find a beer to calm his nerves. He wanted whiskey, but even that would have to wait until they got to Sector 39 and he could restock.

"Brody," Colin greeted him distractedly from the kitchen table, reader in hand.

Leroy sat with him, looking miserable. Brody knew he was worried about Capri, and that didn't improve his mood. He nodded briefly to the captain and reached into the fridge. He ripped the top off a beer and downed it in a few gulps. He grabbed another.

"Should Capri see a doctor?" Leroy asked. "The Green Patch is the most civilized place we'll be between now and Mars."

Brody ignored him in favor of reaching for a third bottle.

"Shots," Colin said warningly.

Brody took a long sip. What the hell happened to Capri being *his* responsibility? Why was everyone so worried about her? He had his suspicions Colin had taken a liking to her, but that just couldn't be. How the hell would he finagle taking on a Lady of Mars as part of the crew? Brody wouldn't survive it, and, more importantly, neither would she.

Brody almost laughed. Taking on a useless girl. The captain wasn't that stupid.

But maybe this was a bigger opportunity for Colin—to exact revenge for the death of his sister. Colin had to blame him. There was no one else *to* blame, and someone always needed blaming. Brody was spiraling to the dark corners of his mind, but Colin's sharp tone snapped him back to the present.

"Shots."

He bit out a response. "Ain't nothin' a doctor can do I ain't already done."

Colin chose to ignore his tone and nodded his acceptance. He fell back into thought, sipping his coffee, considering their next move. Thanks, in part, to Capri, they had most of the money they'd been promised. They'd pick up the goods they were slated to deliver to Mars—likely at a discount—and hand them off along with Capri.

Only now, it was complicated. Jax had told them what Alexander said: Ekon agreed no action would be taken if Capri was returned in the same condition as she'd left. How would her injury count against them? And why was she being treated like some fucking rental cruiser he'd be checking for dents?

This wouldn't be the first time their fate hung in the balance. Colin had started out a legitimate businessman. Some days he still was, but he wasn't afraid to cash in on something reckless. None of them were. They all knew the risks. They'd all signed up for this life, in one way or another.

But not Capri. Capri hadn't asked for any of this, and now she was lying all bandaged up and woozy in the next room. His fault. Again. *His fucking fault.*

Brody slammed the glass bottle down on the counter with unintentional force, and it broke. All that remained in his hand was the neck of the bottle, and out of pure frustration he threw it. It hit a cabinet, leaving a long scratch in its wake.

Leroy eyed him warily, hand hovering over his gun—like the little prick had a chance in hell of killing him. Colin was on his feet, ready to grab him if it went any further. Brody breathed heavily, seeing red.

Every fucking thing he touched broke.

"Go and cool down, Shots," the captain ordered. His eyes were fierce, his hand on his holster.

Brody balled his hands into fists and realized his right palm was wet. It began to sting, and he looked down at the gash. The sight of it only added to his anger. He turned his glare on the captain, saying nothing, but staring him down, ready for a fight—*wanting* a fight.

"Don't think you're the only one upset about this," Colin told him. "But she knows as well as any of us what can happen in a gunfight."

"She doesn't know *anything*," Brody snapped. "What the hell happened to keeping her safe until we get her back to Ekon?"

"We needed her help."

"She ain't meant for this kinda shit."

"She handled herself just fine."

"She shouldn't have to handle herself at all!"

"Go, Brody," the captain told him again, voice icy, using his given name. It was enough of an indication that he was about to get himself booted.

Brody scowled. Leroy glanced between them, looking slightly panicked, like a child whose parents were fighting. But his hand remained on the revolver, and Brody knew if it came down to it the mechanic would at least *try* to shoot him.

And hadn't he promised to stay alive until Capri was back on Mars? He turned and stalked off.

CHAPTER 34

Capri woke feeling confused. She'd gotten used to waking up on the top bunk of Brody's bed. The security light from the corridor dimly illuminated the shapes of the lounge. They began to make sense in her fuzzy mind, and she remembered what had happened and why she was there.

She groaned and sat up, then repeated the sound as her aching head struggled to keep up. She pressed the heel of her hand to her temple. According to the clock on the wall, it was nearly midnight. She kept her throbbing arm close to her chest and stood, ignoring the wave of dizziness that crashed into her, warning her.

She needed water badly.

The chair Brody had knocked across the room still lay near the door. Capri stepped around it and made her way to the kitchen. She reached into the fridge for a bottle of water and turned to sit at the table. She almost dropped what she was holding.

Brody was sitting there, in the dark, watching her.

"What the hell are you doin'?" he growled.

His anger had faded to a simmer, but it was still there, still waiting. She sighed and sat down heavily in the chair across from him.

"I was thirsty."

"I left water in the room for you."

"Oh. I didn't see it."

Capri felt her cheeks flush with an innocent sort of pleasure. She'd never really felt cared for at the palace. She'd felt...*maintained*. His gesture was a simple one, but it made her feel very warm inside.

"Don't look at me like that," he said, sounding suddenly very tired.

"Like what?"

He didn't answer, just continued watching her. Capri took a long sip of water, careful to move her injured arm as little as possible.

"Have you slept?" she asked softly.

"You just got shot. You shouldn't be movin' around," he said, ignoring the question.

"You would be," she pointed out, finishing the bottle.

"Comes with the job," he said. "You don't belong out here."

There was no malice in his words. It felt like he was finally admitting a truth he'd known all along.

The amount of hurt she felt surprised even Capri. He'd put everything at risk to show her a different life, only to decide she couldn't handle it. That she was beginning to feel faint only served to illustrate his point.

"You took me away from Mars," she replied, tears pricking her eyes. "Now you want me to go back."

"I shouldn't have done it."

"I'm glad you did."

Brody shook his head and stood. "Come on."

She let him pull her to her feet and almost fell into him. He grasped her tightly around the waist, supporting her weight until she felt steady, but he didn't let her go. She couldn't see his face, but she could hear his breath, feel him nuzzle the tender spot beneath her ear, feel his lips brush her neck.

Capri relaxed against him, taking solace in his touch, his nearness, his comforting caresses. She was vaguely aware that he was lifting her, and she wrapped her legs instinctively around him, her injured arm tucked securely between their bodies and the other hooked around his neck. She was floating between consciousness and unconsciousness as he carried her down the corridor to his room, and she thought she'd like to be more aware of what was happening if he planned to bed her.

But he only laid her gently down in his bunk, and then the warmth of his solid body was gone. Her last conscious breath was of his scent; her last conscious thought that the pain in her arm was getting worse.

CHAPTER 35

Capri drifted into a nightmare. Blood, blank faces, and Sullivan. Brody was there, too, with his dark eyes and stubbled jaw. His expression was grim, as it often was, and he was trying to tell her something. He was close to her, gripping her arm and shouting, fighting to be heard above roaring wind. His hold on her arm kept getting tighter and tighter, but she couldn't hear him.

She tried to tell him he was hurting her, but the wind whipped her words away.

She'd read about tornadoes and hurricanes. This had to be something like that. What other force could wrench him away from her and carry his strong body into swirling debris? He was gone, and she was alone, but the pain remained.

In the same way she often came to realize she was dreaming, she realized the pain was genuine. She glanced down and found a bone sticking out of her arm, blood gushing from a torn artery.

She woke with a start.

Her fists were clenched in Brody's blanket. The man himself sat on a chair, watching her. His thick forearms rested on his knees, and he held a syringe between the first two fingers of his right hand. Maybe she was still dreaming.

"Arm hurting?" he asked.

Capri nodded.

"It's about time for another dose," he said.

She sat up obediently, and he stuck the needle in her arm. She lay back down, waiting for the pain to subside enough for her to sleep again. She was in and out after that. She remembered waking once, and the chair by the bed was empty. She came to again, and he was there. When the pain in her arm had receded to a steady, dull ache, and she finally felt like she could keep her eyes open for more than a few seconds, Capri tried sitting again. Her mouth was dry, her muscles stiff. Some of her hair had escaped its braid and formed a tangled mess around her head.

"How long was I out?" she asked as Brody handed her a bottle of water.

"A day and a half. We're headed back to Mars."

Capri froze mid-sip. It hit her quite suddenly that her feelings were no longer mixed. She didn't want to go back. But as Brody had said, what they wanted never seemed to matter. If she was returned, no harm would come to those aboard *Task Eternal*, and they'd be free to continue importing and exporting in the Kingdom. She'd never known Alexander to back out of a deal, and she wouldn't be the one to do it.

Besides, Brody had made it very clear she didn't have what it took to survive outside of the palace.

She finished drinking, swung her feet over the edge of the bed, and stood on legs that were steadier than she'd expected. He stood with her.

"I need to shower. I feel disgusting."

"You gotta wrap it."

She looked at him questioningly, and he gestured to the desk. She sat on the edge like it was an exam table while he rooted through the medical kit. He used scissors to cut the gauze around her arm, and she glanced down while he examined her repaired flesh. A row of neat, black stitches pulled her skin together. It was puckered, but it wasn't red, and the wound wasn't oozing. All good signs, she knew. He taped a fresh square of gauze over it and then pressed a clear plastic patch over that.

"Keeps it dry," he grunted.

She nodded and glanced up at him. He remained standing in front of her, blocking her. His eyes were on her lips again. She doubted he even realized it.

Her breath caught. She wanted nothing more than him, but she wouldn't take the blame. Not this time. He moved closer.

"I'm not asking for this," she breathed, forcing his eyes to meet hers.

His brow furrowed, and he started to pull away, but she caught his arm. "I'm not saying I don't want it."

He straightened then, regret flashing across his hard features. "I can't give you what you need."

"I know. I know…what happened. Since the last time we met."

His gaze narrowed, anger in his eyes. "Leroy," he muttered.

"It doesn't matter. Even if we can't have what we need, maybe, for once, we can have what we want."

"It won't last," he said.

"Nothing lasts," she agreed.

He studied her face, eyes still narrowed, before backing away like a distrustful animal, but Capri was through trying to convince him. She slid down from the desk and went to the bathroom, stripping off her clothes and letting the water run. She'd just stepped under the spray when the bathroom door opened and closed behind her.

The space was so small, she knew immediately that it was Brody. She'd probably sense his presence from a mile away. She felt his breath on her shoulder first, and then his fingers touched the crook of her elbow, gently pressing the arm she'd been trying to use to shampoo her hair down to her side. Her clumsy hand was replaced with both of his, and he scrubbed her scalp gently, lathering her hair from her temples to the nape of her neck.

She closed her eyes, relaxing under his caress. A moan escaped her, and she felt his teeth on her shoulder, a gentle nip—punishment, she imagined, for making him want her.

He tilted her head back so the spray could rinse the soap away, and then he began washing her body. She could feel the weight of his desire, thick and scorching against the small of her back. He attended to her front first, soapy palms skimming her breasts, kneading and tugging until her nipples formed tight peaks. Capri gasped for breath and squeezed her legs together, searching for relief. Brody washed the dirt and blood from her arms, her stomach, and then his hands found her thighs.

Instead of moving between them as she wanted, he slipped his hands behind her, teasing her, cupping her ass. He massaged the pliable flesh with his thumbs, running his slippery hands over and between the globes, scrubbing and enticing until Capri's whole body trembled.

Just when she was sure she'd burst with need, he spun her around and clutched her against him. She caught a glimpse of smoldering brown eyes before he kissed her, without hesitation or regret. He'd made his decision, at least for this moment, and Capri melted. He kissed her mouth with a desperation she'd never felt before. Her body quivered so that she was sure the only thing keeping her upright was his body against hers. His tongue swept over her lips, demanding entry to her mouth, before tracing her jawline and the sensitive flesh of her throat.

The noises he drew from her were animalistic, but she didn't care. She couldn't. She was too preoccupied by the heat between them. Once he'd thoroughly explored her skin with his mouth, he pulled back, adjusting her position slightly so that her left arm was pinned to her chest between them. Then, with a low growl, he lifted her, pressing her harder against the slippery wall and recapturing her mouth. It was cold against her back; Brody blazed against her front. The stark contrast made her shiver, honing her senses. The rest of the world was nonexistent. She lifted her hips, and he drove home.

Capri cried out. She'd never known it could feel like this, that she had so many nerve endings. She tried to keep their mouths connected, but she had to give up, throwing her head back, at the mercy of his strong and steady thrusts, of his lips on her neck, the grunts and groans escaping his own throat.

"Fuck," he breathed, and she knew he was close to the edge, to losing control, and that was enough to make her lose the fragment of control she'd been clinging to.

"No," she moaned. She didn't want it to end, she wanted this to last forever, but it felt too fucking good.

"Capri," he gasped, and his thrusts grew faster, harder.

At the sound of her name on his lips, Capri came apart. She bucked and shuddered and squirmed and screamed until Brody clamped his mouth over hers and shuddered his own release. They came down together, connected in every way they could manage.

Brody pulled away first, breath ragged, and he carefully lowered Capri's feet to the floor. Somehow, her shaking legs held her. He turned off the water and reached for a towel. He wrapped it around her and held her close for several minutes, until their hearts beat a steady rhythm once more, before pressing his lips against hers in what she knew would be their last kiss.

"Can you walk?" he asked.

For a moment, she considered lying, but she nodded.

"You should get some rest before we land," he said.

She nodded again and retreated to the bed, leaving him to take his own shower and refusing to let tears fall. He'd given her everything he could. Asking for more would be unfair—and life had been unfair enough to both of them already.

CHAPTER 36

"Capri."

Capri started awake. Had she heard that, or was she dreaming?

"Capri." Colin's voice sounded again, and this time she realized it was the intercom by Brody's bed. He, of course, was nowhere to be found. She pressed the button she thought would allow her to answer.

"Yes?"

"We're landing on Mars in a few hours. There's some things we need to discuss first. Get decent and meet me in the kitchen."

Capri's cheeks flushed. *Get decent?* Did the captain know what had happened between her and Brody? Or was he speaking generally? And why in the System did she care if anyone else on the ship had heard? She'd never cared before. But there was something about what they'd done that felt… sacred.

She got out of bed, favoring her arm, and dressed in a fresh change of clothes. She was glad Colin had called her to the kitchen. She was starving.

He was waiting for her, and when she sat down, he plucked a small bag from the table and tossed it to her. She caught it clumsily in one hand, and the objects inside clacked together. Ten small diamonds. She looked at Colin questioningly.

"You did a job. You get paid," he said simply.

Pride welled in Capri, so strong that tears pricked her eyes. For the first time in her life, she was holding her own money. He couldn't know how much it meant to her. Even she hadn't realized it would mean so much.

"Thank you," she said.

He nodded, the hint of a smile on his lips. Maybe he understood, after all.

"The other thing we need to talk about," he said, eyes so sharp on hers she had to fight the urge not to look away, "is Alexander. We haven't been able to make face-to-face contact since we got in range."

Capri felt a rush of uncertainty. "What does that mean?"

"We aren't sure he's still there."

The uncertainty morphed into panic. "But...either way, the agreement stands. Doesn't it?"

Colin's expression remained grim. "We can't be sure the last message we received was from Alexander."

"Well, it was from someone in the palace, and I don't believe Ekon would lie about this."

Colin raised an eyebrow. "Not even to get you back?"

Capri flushed, recognizing the naivete of her words. "I don't know. I don't know anything anymore. We should...go."

"Go?"

"We should run," she said urgently.

"We haven't been able to speak with Alexander, but Haddaway has made contact. He knows we're in range, and I have no doubt whatsoever that if we turn tail, he'll send cruisers after us."

Capri swallowed hard. Fear threatened to overwhelm her. "But... what's going to happen?"

"He'll take Shots, at the very least."

Capri was already shaking her head. "They can't—"

He leaned close and jabbed a finger into the tabletop to drive his point home. "They *will*."

"Does he know?" Capri whispered. "Isn't there a...a shuttle or something? Can't he get away?"

"You're panicking," he said, not unkindly. "What would happen then?"

She took a shaky breath. "They'd take you instead."

He nodded. "And for the record, no, we don't have a shuttle."

"So what do we do?" she asked, searching his brown eyes for some sign that he had a plan, that this would all turn out alright.

"We give them you. We give them Brody. Hopefully, that's the end of it."

"But—!"

He held up a hand to quiet her. "You'll be inside the palace. Play your part, and when the time is right you can help us get him out."

"I'll take a linker."

He was already shaking his head. "It's not that simple. They'll search you, and finding you've kept a way to keep in contact won't do you or him any favors. We need you to sit tight and wait for us to contact you."

Capri hesitated. Could she do that? Wait patiently for instructions when Brody's life hung in the balance?

"What if they kill him? What if they don't wait?"

"They'll wait. Shots has said Ekon uses…outside contractors for these sorts of things. It'll take a while to get someone in from the rebel planets."

Another thought, a worse thought, floated through Capri's mind. She looked down at the table, unsure if she wanted to voice it. "What if…he's lying to you."

Colin was quiet, and she lifted her gaze to his. There was an understanding in his brown depths, a pain she'd never seen. She remembered in that instant that Colin had lost a sister and a niece on the same night Brody had lost his family. He probably knew that his gunman had a death wish.

"It's a possibility. When Jill and Maxi died, he almost ended it. Then I guess he decided to let nature take its course. But I suspect in the last week or so he's found something else worth living for."

Capri wasn't sure she could hold back her tears. Colin seemed to understand. He stood, gave her shoulder a light squeeze, and left her alone at the table.

***

Capri shed her pants and boots, knowing the artificially controlled climate of Mars would be mild. She wore the dress she'd bought in Mexico Territory, brushed her curls until they shone, and tried to remember how to be a Lady of Mars. They'd gone from knowing what to expect to having no idea. Capri thought she'd had everything under control. She would go back, and they would go free. She had to remember how to be regal, powerful, how to take control.

She'd been able to do it often enough as the Prize. She should be able to do it now.

She joined Colin, Brody, and Leroy in the loading bay. Colin had opted to appear unarmed, but Capri knew there were weapons within reach no matter where they stood. Leroy bounced from one foot to the other as he checked the crates of goods bound for the palace. Colin hoped to use them as a reminder that their business relationship was worth something.

Brody was just a few feet away from her, grim-faced, fists clenched. He was likely itching to hold a gun, a knife, anything.

She knew how he felt—in limbo, eager to act. The silence was eerie.

The ship touched down, and Colin received word that the stabilizers were in place, but they waited to lower the ramp. He listened to Jax through his linker and relayed the information to the rest of the crew, his expression grim.

"Apparently there are a hell of a lot of guards out there. We've been ordered to remain unarmed."

"By who?" Capri and Brody asked in unison.

They glanced at each other, their gazes locking for the briefest moment.

"Haddaway," Colin responded. "Still no Alexander."

Capri moved forward to stand in front of the crew. Brody grabbed her arm to stop her, but she wrenched it from his grasp. "They won't shoot me," she told him.

His nostrils flared, and she softened her expression. "You're in my territory now. It's not about who's got the biggest guns. It's negotiation. It always is. And I'm the only advantage you have."

"Fine." It seemed to take every ounce of Brody's self-control to grind out the word.

She glanced at the captain, who nodded. Leroy's eyes flitted nervously between them.

"Lower the ramp," Colin ordered into his linker.

There were about twenty guards waiting for them at the bottom of the ramp, along with a medic and—Capri could have cried with relief—Briony. The guards all had guns, but they were pointed at the ground. Haddaway stepped forward.

"Lady Capri," he greeted.

"Haddaway," she replied coolly. "I want to make you aware that Alexander agreed to set these men free upon my return."

"Alexander didn't have the authority."

"He assured me that the King had agreed to the terms."

Haddaway's lips thinned. There was regret in his gaze. "The King has changed his mind. My orders are to question Captain Colin Wilkins and take Shots to a prison cell. Don't stand in the way, Capri. You won't win."

Capri hesitated, searching his face for sincerity. They weren't planning to take everyone. They weren't planning to kill Brody immediately. That was good. But it could still end so, *so* badly. She glanced behind her, into the loading bay. What if they just took off right now? Would Haddaway really be able to stop them?

"We've got cruisers standing by," he told her. "Anything other than full cooperation will make this ordeal much worse for everyone."

It wasn't a threat. Haddaway wasn't the type. He was just stating a fact. Capri met Colin's gaze, and he gave a short nod. Then, she looked at Brody. He stepped around her and held out his wrists for the handcuffs.

"I knew what I was doing," he told her under his breath. "I don't regret a goddamn thing."

Capri's heart twisted. If he died, she would regret so much.

Haddaway came forward to take Brody away, and Capri fought the urge to grab him, to hold him so they couldn't. Haddaway whispered something to Briony on his way past her, and the blond tucked her short hair behind her ears and began approaching the ramp, flanked by two guards. Capri's time on *Task Eternal* was nearly at an end.

"Capri," Briony said gently when she reached her, offering Colin and Leroy a nervous smile. "It's time to come home."

Capri swallowed her contempt. She'd missed her friend. She'd missed the fine food, plush pillows, and red wine. But it wasn't enough. It would never be enough again. But, somehow, she'd have to unbury the person she'd been just one week ago and pretend that this was everything she desired.

Briony wrapped Capri in a tight hug, and she forced herself to focus on the joy of seeing her again. She shot a final glance at Colin and Leroy and let Briony lead her down the ramp. She didn't look back again.

The medic gave her a quick once-over before they left the docks, speaking into a linker or recording device as he checked for injuries. He paused at the gunshot wound. Once he was satisfied she wasn't in any immediate danger, the young man allowed her to walk the short distance to a waiting car.

There were very few cars on Mars, and Capri knew the sleek, black sedan must belong to Ekon. Briony sat next to her on the bench seat, while a guard and the medic settled across from them. Briony held Capri's hand tightly, and Capri was surprised to find tears in the other woman's eyes.

"Capri, I'm so sorry." Her voice wobbled, and the tears fell from her lashes.

Capri didn't understand. "For what? What's wrong?"

"I *left* you. I'm surprised I'm still your Attending Lady. He should have banished me, too."

Capri pulled back to look at her. "You can't possibly think this was your fault. He can't blame you."

She shook her head. "I'm supposed to protect you. *You* are my priority, and if I'd done my job and stayed by your side, you wouldn't have been taken."

Capri couldn't believe that Briony had spent the last week in this sea of guilt.

"When I think about what you must have gone through, what they must have done to you..."

"They didn't do anything to me," she said. "And you couldn't have stopped him from taking me."

Briony's red-rimmed eyes flitted to the short sleeve of Capri's dress and the bandage peeking out from beneath the thin fabric. "What did they want with you, if not that?"

"It wasn't *they*. It was just one man. Acting alone."

"And what did he want?"

Capri looked out the window. "He thought he was helping me. Taking me somewhere safe."

Capri's voice caught as she spoke of Brody in the past tense, where he may very well remain. The thought of losing him in any sense was agony, and she had to be careful not to show it. She cleared her throat.

Briony remained skeptical. "You're defending them."

"I'm not. It was wrong. I'm just—" She was beginning to feel flustered, and she wasn't sure to how much the guards were paying attention. "I'm home, I'm in one piece, and let's just leave it at that."

Briony sat back in her seat, lips clamped shut, looking down at her clasped hands. Capri felt guilty. The blond had been her only friend and confidant for so long. But how could she tell her that she'd miss the man who had kidnapped her—and his crewmates?

"How are things here?" she asked, changing the subject. "Who else...besides Agatha...?"

Briony glanced at her again, then looked away. She'd been there in the aftermath of it all, and Capri hadn't. She was sure she was sifting through her own bloody memories.

"Faye. A few guards. Three citizens and two other Ladies you weren't close to."

"Did you know them?" Capri asked gently.

Briony nodded. "We were in the dorms together."

"I'm sorry."

"Faye's mother, it turned out, brought her here without her father's permission. She'd discovered that Faye was going to let that man who was pretending to be the guard—her boyfriend—have her."

"Have her?"

"*Have* her," Briony repeated, her tone leaving no room for misinterpretation.

"Oh. But she's so young."

Briony shrugged. "I don't know how it's done on rebel planets. But her father and that man came, I suppose, to rescue her. I think Ekon regrets taking on a Maiden at such an advanced age. I doubt he'll make the same mistake again."

"How did they get in in the first place?" Capri asked.

"No one knows. That's why King Ekon has been...worried lately."

Briony glanced at the guards across from them, and Capri could tell she was choosing her words carefully.

"Have I missed the funerals?" she asked.

"No. They were sent to Venus for cremation. When the ashes return, there will be a memorial service."

Capri nodded. She'd never attended a funeral before.

"Security has been tightened," Briony continued. "Alexander was released from his duties and banished."

Capri blinked in surprise. "Why?"

"He planted those guns for hire without Ekon's permission." Her dainty shrug seemed dismissive, but Capri couldn't tell for sure if she agreed with the King's decision.

"They kept him from being killed."

"Alexander undermined the King's authority."

"Who's the new advisor, then?"

Again, Briony paused while she determined the best way to answer the question in front of the guards. "There isn't one. Haddaway is taking on some of Alexander's duties in addition to his own. Our King feels he's able to see to the majority of his own affairs."

Capri didn't trust herself to respond with delicacy. Ekon was clearly shaken. Now was when he should be surrounding himself with more support, not less.

The car stopped, and a guard opened their door. Briony slid out behind Capri.

"I'll be glad to get back to the apartment," Capri said.

Briony hesitated.

"What is it?"

"You can't go back yet."

"Why not?"

"You have to go to the infirmary to be evaluated, and Haddaway will need to speak with you."

Capri struggled to keep her displeasure from showing.

The medic spoke. "It's standard procedure."

She glared at him. "How can it be standard procedure when this has never happened before? If Ekon wants me to be well-rested in time to receive the next Victor, I'll need time to recover."

The thought of going back to that, after all the freedom she'd had and all she'd shared with Brody, made her stomach turn. For one week, she'd been free to question everything, to make her own choices.

Now, she belonged to Ekon again.

"The bidding has been extended a week," Briony said.

"How kind." Capri was careful to sound only sarcastic enough that Briony would notice, and the corner of her Attending Lady's mouth lifted slightly.

"I'm afraid our entourage must be growing impatient. Better let our medic perform his duties." Briony smiled sweetly at the young man, who blushed and led Capri in the direction of an elevator that would take her to the infirmary. She felt a spike of fear and turned back to the blond.

"You're not coming?"

King Ekon ensured his Maidens and Ladies had regular health checks, but they were generally done in the comfort of their dorms or apartments. The last time she'd been admitted to the infirmary was after the rape, and suddenly the memory felt very fresh. Briony looked to the young medic, who shook his head slightly. She looked back at Capri with regret.

Capri set her shoulders and tamped down her fear. It would only be a cursory examination this time, she reminded herself. She wasn't a child. There had been no rape.

"I'll be close by," Briony promised.

Capri followed the medic, flanked by the guards. Her welcome hadn't exactly been warm.

In the infirmary, she was made to sit on the edge of a reclining bed. They checked her vitals, poked and prodded, saying nothing and asking nothing. Capri was an object for their perusal.

They told her to remove her clothing and examined Brody's handiwork on her arm with a critical gaze, muttering something about scarring. They put ointment on her abrasions and gave her a vaccine to fight whatever kinds of diseases she might have picked up while away. Capri kept her mouth closed, her back rigid, and waited for them to finish so she could speak with Haddaway.

She knew he'd have questions about the kidnapping and the time she'd spent on the ship, but she had her own reasons for wanting to talk to him. She'd remind him that Brody had been the one to save her from Sullivan, *twice*. He had been the one to save the King from that imposter, Tyler. He'd have to agree that his former subordinate should be released. He'd have to make Ekon understand.

"Remove your undergarments, please," the female medic requested.

Capri met the woman's gaze sharply. She was around Briony's age, but the thin, no-nonsense line of her lips made her look older. "Why?"

The medic who had met the ship—John, she thought his name was—blushed. He remained professional enough, but she doubted he got to see a Lady so intimately every day. Capri's skin crawled. The last person in the room was Dr. Churchill, the same man who had overseen her care after Sullivan. He watched her now, as if he resented her for wasting his time, and crossed his arms over his chest.

He explained the procedure to her with pained patience, as if she hadn't been through it once already. "We need to do an internal examination, to see what—if any—damage has been done since you were last within the palace walls. You'll put your feet up in the surgical stirrups, or if you prefer you may lie in the left lateral position. We'll simply check for evidence of…activity…and this will conclude the exam."

Capri's face flamed. "I wasn't raped," she said.

"We just need to be sure."

Capri was angry, so angry she was shaking. For once, the *activity* in which she'd participated had been entirely voluntary. She'd enjoyed intimacy with a man of her own choosing—and even that didn't belong to her. Ekon would take it, too.

"No," she said.

"Capri." Churchill's voice was sharp, and he took a step forward.

Would he force her legs apart? Who would stop him? She had to find some way to take control of the situation. *You are never powerless.*

"I want to see Briony," she demanded.

"After the examination."

"No. Now. Or I will scream. I will scream and fight, and I will tell Ekon that you—all of you—" Her glare landed on John, the weakest link. "—made inappropriate advances."

Churchill clenched his jaw. "John, please ask Lady Briony to sit in."

John, white-faced, scurried to find her. As promised, she'd been nearby and arrived within seconds.

"What is it? What's wrong?" she asked, ignoring the medical team.

"They want to perform an internal examination," Capri said.

"But you said…they didn't do anything to you."

"They didn't."

"Then what do you need to do an examination for?" Briony asked, rounding on Dr. Churchill.

"Because our King has ordered it," he said through gritted teeth.

Briony looked helplessly at Capri. Capri shook her head frantically, but what could Briony do? What could any of them do? Briony, especially, would never disobey a direct order from the King.

"Block the door, John," Churchill said casually, as he lifted a vial and a syringe.

"No!" Capri said sharply. "*Don't* block the door, John."

John hesitated. Churchill glared at him, and he stepped into place in front of the door.

"This is a sedative," Churchill said calmly. "I will chase you around the room and corner you if I have to, but I'd rather not."

They locked eyes for a long moment, and Capri finally lay back on the table. Briony grasped her hand. Capri squeezed back and looked at her. In that moment, she knew that Briony knew. Her friend wasn't stupid. Her protégé wouldn't be this upset if she hadn't slept with someone. But she said nothing in front of the medics, and they said nothing more to the Ladies.

They took their samples and recorded their findings.

And Capri began to hate. She hated the control Ekon had over her, over all of them. She hated him for monopolizing her youth, for demanding so much in exchange for so little. She hated the system and the man behind it.

By the time they'd finished, she knew she couldn't face another Victor. She couldn't stay here. She'd play her role for now, long enough to see Brody freed, and then, even if he wanted to wash his hands of her, she would leave Mars.

CHAPTER 37

There were few people Colin trusted, and he kept those people close. One of them, unfortunately, was Brody.

Colin had gotten away from the underprivileged planet of Ptolemy, received a good education, and made his own way in the world—all on the U.N.'s dime. In that first year of required service, he'd piloted their ships and moonlighted doing illegal runs with a friend whenever he could.

The jobs were a means to an end: *freedom*.

The U.N. had thought their offer of citizenship was too good to refuse. Make the rebel idiots feel indebted. Give them guaranteed employment, good pay, benefits, and comfortable living quarters.

Very few people in the scholarship program left after that first year, but Colin had. He had no love for the government that had abandoned Ptolemy after the Migration. His loyalties, if distant, lay with his home planet—but he was happiest aboard his ship, drifting in the in-between, away from the conflict and violence of Ptolemy and life on New Earth.

On his ship, he controlled his own destiny. He could aid the rebel planets by offering the basic necessities residents of New Earth took for granted, at a fair price.

Life so far had worked out in his favor, but Colin wasn't naïve. Most people from Ptolemy couldn't reject the darker side of life; they wouldn't have the same opportunities. So he hadn't thought twice about his sister and Brody making vows. The man was strong and capable. She hadn't found him in a drug house, he hadn't drunk overly much at the time, and he could provide for her.

Most importantly, Brody had loved Jillian—and Maxine, when she came along. It was maybe the only thing they had in common. It was why he'd helped with transport.

Then the gunman's moonlighting had caught up with him in the worst way, and now they were bonded by grief, as well. Brody was damaged, unpredictable, and a pain in the ass, but he was part of his crew. He was family. And as much as he'd brought this whole damn mess on himself, Colin wouldn't let him go without a fight.

The captain's greatest strength was strategy. It was why he allowed the guards to take his gunman now, choosing instead to keep the focus on trade relations. He wasn't sure what kind of punishment Brody would face, but he knew that staying on Ekon's good side was the only way they'd be allowed back on Mars—either to pick him up after he'd served his well-deserved time or, more likely, to bust him out if Ekon ordered execution.

Haddaway and two of his guards stayed behind while the others walked Brody to the palace. A gun was easily accessible on Haddaway's hip, but he didn't reach for it. The guards flanking him kept their rifles pointed at the ground. Good signs so far. No outright hostility.

"Haddaway," Colin greeted. "We'll offer the goods we promised to Alexander for twenty percent less than the agreed price. I know it won't make up for Shots' lack of judgment, but we'd like to keep Mars' business."

Haddaway's sharp eyes narrowed as he took the captain's measure. "Alexander is no longer under the King's employ. We'll accept the goods, if you consent to being questioned about your involvement in the matter."

Colin gave a short nod.

"You're not going alone, are you?" Jax's concerned voice sounded through the linker in his ear.

He didn't respond, but he knew why the younger man was worried. They had no insight into Ekon's state of mind, his level of outrage. He might not care so much that they had Capri with everything else that had happened. He might want all their heads on a platter.

The news of Alexander's dismissal didn't exactly bode well. Jax would just have to trust him.

"Why don't you come aboard and we can talk in the lounge?" he suggested, trying to stay on his turf.

Haddaway looked around the docks, and his eyes settled on a gray block of concrete, which housed the on-duty dock guards.

Haddaway would have similar concerns, and, for now, he also had the upper hand. If he wanted Colin to go off-ship, he would.

"How about over there? You can bring one of your men."

But Colin knew that if he brought Jax or Leroy, they'd still be outnumbered, and it would only prove to Haddaway that he felt the need for protection, that he might have something to hide. He shook his head.

The graying man smiled slightly, as if he'd passed some kind of test. Haddaway gestured to the guards and turned from Colin, trusting that he would follow. Colin glanced back at Leroy, who raised one sharp eyebrow but said nothing. He rarely questioned orders. Jax questioned them often enough but never twice. It was a necessary rule, if they were to maintain a relationship and Colin's authority in tandem.

He followed Haddaway to the small, dark building, used mainly for breaks and shelter—though the strange, still artificial air of Mars would never require shelter. There was the tinted globe of glass above them to remind him that the world was manmade.

Colin could never live in a place like this. It was, essentially, a stalled ship.

A guard entered in front of Colin to clear the room and ensure he couldn't trap Haddaway. He'd have done it the same way. There was a table against one wall, just big enough for two people. A mini-fridge and coffee maker sat on a counter, and on the opposite wall was a screen waiting for the pass code that would allow a guard to view the docks from inside.

Haddaway's guard stood by the door, alert and ready to spring into action if Colin stepped a toe out of line. Haddaway himself, however, seemed relaxed as he poured them each a cup of coffee from the carafe. All signs pointed to his precautions being just that: precautions. He sat down across from Colin. They might have been two friends catching up. Colin thought that was the mood he was trying to suggest, but the tension was there, around them, if not between them.

"The last time we spoke was to debrief about the shooting."

"I remember," Colin said.

"It was a bit underhanded, the role you and your men played."

Colin took a sip of coffee, unfazed. "We were hired by Alexander to do a job. It was his call whether or not to involve you."

"I suppose we were in the middle of debriefing when your crewman abducted the girl."

"I suppose we were."

"Were you trying to distract me?" he asked mildly.

Colin appreciated Haddaway's directness, and a smile touched his lips. He didn't like fucking around. "No."

"Did you know what he planned to do?"

Colin took a long sip from the steaming mug. "I don't think he had a plan."

"When did you find out about her?"

"Just after we left Mars. He'd stowed her away in his room. I told Alexander you and your men were more than welcome to come and get her."

"But you wouldn't bring her back."

"We had a schedule to keep."

"It wasn't strange that Brody left the party early, without a word to you?"

Colin held the handle of his mug thoughtfully, turning the ceramic object on the table, admiring the craftsmanship. He knew what Haddaway was implying: that his crew did as they liked, and, if they did, he must be an unfit captain.

Sometimes he wondered that himself. His ex-brother-in-law, his lover, and his lover's brother. Everyone had their role, and the ship functioned, but it was a complicated balance.

How much did Haddaway need to know about them? How much did he already know? The most important part of a good strategy was time; he couldn't answer with a knee-jerk reaction. He had to look at every possibility and choose the best one. It wasn't always possible in the heat of battle, but even when he had to make a quick decision, he did so calmly, thoughtfully, and with confidence.

This was not the heat of battle, and he took his time.

"Shots knows his job, and he got it done," he said finally. "I trust him. He doesn't have to tell me his every move."

"You trust him?" Haddaway seemed almost amused.

For a moment, Colin did feel angry—at Brody. His intelligence was being called into question because the man was a hothead, but he bit it back and answered patiently. "I trust him to fulfill his duties. He doesn't always make the best decisions on his own time."

"Do you think any of the rest of your crew knew what he was up to?"

Colin had to smirk at that. Brody and Jax worked well together, only because neither had any interest in further friendship. That left Leroy.

"No."

Haddaway sighed and sat back in his chair. "Okay," he allowed. "How was she treated in your care? We know she wasn't confined to the ship, despite the fact you were carrying the King's very precious cargo."

"She wasn't in my care. As I said, a representative of Mars was more than welcome to come and get her. She never left the ship against her will."

"Asked to do some exploring, did she?"

Haddaway's tone was dry, and Colin narrowed his gaze. Now they *were* beating around the bush, and he was irritated. "I have a crew to look out for and a business to run. I made it clear to Brody that I don't have time to babysit."

"Did you interact with Capri at all?"

"It's a small ship."

"So yes."

"Yes."

Haddaway paused. The conversation remained civil, but the air had changed. It could no longer be mistaken for a friendly chat.

"You entrusted her to the man who kidnapped her."

"Let's not pretend you two aren't familiar with each other," Colin said sharply. "He used to be your subordinate. Do you really think he would hurt the girl?"

Haddaway paused again, briefly, and Colin caught a glimpse of something like regret in the other man's eyes. "I don't. But Ekon will take more convincing."

"Will he kill him?" Colin asked.

Haddaway looked annoyed. He was supposed to be asking the questions.

"He might get out of it," he said. "If she's not too badly disfigured and if her story matches the one you both tell me."

Colin nodded. "What about the merchandise?"

Haddaway took a sip of coffee and then spoke again. "We can do business. For now."

CHAPTER 38

Brody sat in a windowless concrete cell beneath the palace. The person manning the front desk was the same grizzled veteran who had been working the night they'd hauled down Sullivan.

But this time, *he* was getting booked, *he* was getting pushed into the cell, and *he* heard the solid *thunk* of the steel door as it slid into place.

He sat on a cot that was too small for a man his size, breathing stale air and staring at the toilet.

He didn't care. He wouldn't sleep. His heart was pounding too hard in his chest. He could put a name to the feeling, but he wouldn't. It had been too long since he'd last felt afraid, and if he admitted the weakness, then all the time he'd spent training himself not to feel would be for nothing.

Death didn't scare him, if it came to it. It was the waiting that got to him—being left alone with his thoughts and no alcohol or action for distraction. The thoughts of his wife and daughter that he struggled to avoid, the familiar guilt, floating to the surface of his mind.

Old wounds. He'd expected that. But now there was a new wound.

Capri wasn't supposed to matter. It was bad enough being haunted by dead things, but she was still living, breathing, warm, and everything that made a person vulnerable. The surge of anger he felt, knowing she was right back where she'd started, back to being used by whomever Ekon deemed fit, was dangerous.

His anger was a selfish one, too. The idea that he might be erased completely, that others would know her as he had made him feel helpless, furious. She'd grown stronger, come into her own. One day, she might change her mind, escape this place, and run into the far reaches with someone. Someone else.

Anger, jealousy, *the urge to protect*, which had gotten him here in the first place…Each raw emotion drove home the message that he was still soft, still weak, still just as alive and vulnerable as she was.

He sat on the edge of the cot, booted feet flat on the floor, knuckles white where he gripped the metal frame. And he waited.

Hours later, the door slid open, and Haddaway appeared with a chair, his expression grim.

Brody remained impassive, glad to have a break from his own thoughts in whatever form it came. The older man just sat there, looking at him, as if he couldn't decide where to begin. Brody made the first move.

"Alexander's out?"

"Yeah."

"Who's the new advisor?"

"There isn't one. It's just me. Since you once worked for me, I'm sure this will be seen as some test of loyalty. He's been anxious to test people's loyalty since the shooting."

Brody raised his eyebrows briefly in feigned interest, but otherwise remained still as a statue, looking his former superior in the eye, waiting for him to speak. He did, finally, and he struggled to keep his voice calm.

"So, who fucked her?"

The gunman clenched his teeth and glared. He hadn't been expecting that, but of course Ekon would have her checked. He had to make sure his Prize hadn't been violated without his permission. Again, he found himself angry for her. Again, it made him angry at everything else. He remained silent.

"They found evidence of sexual activity," Haddaway continued. "Four men to one beautiful woman. Was it one of you? All of you? I hear she's not all that traumatized this time around. Maybe she's gotten used to having strange men inside her."

He watched Brody carefully as he said the last part. Brody knew the drill. Haddaway was hoping for a reaction, trying to gauge their relationship. His anger did flare, and he narrowed his eyes. He was sure it told Haddaway everything he needed to know.

"What did the girl tell you?" Brody asked.

"I haven't talked to her. Ekon's doing that himself."

Brody clenched his fists. He hated the idea of Ekon going anywhere near her, but what could he do about it from here?

"You already know it was me," he growled. "You have my DNA on file."

Haddaway sat as still as Brody for a moment, two animals, eyes locked.

"You probably could have gotten away with serving time. Maybe less if I vouched for you and reminded Ekon of the fact you saved his life not so long ago, of the fact you were a pretty valuable asset before you fell off the edge of the Kingdom. But you had to fuck her."

"Yeah," Brody agreed, lip twitching in a smirk as he remembered. "I did."

Haddaway stood abruptly. Brody stared at the wall behind him, sensing a lecture.

"You had potential, Shots. You could've had my job one day if you wanted it."

"What I wanted then ain't an option now."

"Well, I'm guessing this isn't exactly what you had in mind, either. You'd already won the girl for a night. Once wasn't enough?"

"Once was too damn much." Brody looked up at him then, angry, reckless, and struggling not to do anything stupid. Then again, if he did, maybe he could end all the bullshit sooner rather than later and have his old boss end him.

He held back. He still respected the man, for all it was worth. "You do what you gotta do, Haddaway."

The older man looked at him for a long moment. They both knew exactly what he'd have to do. He turned and left with a sound that made Brody think he probably felt like hitting something, too.

CHAPTER 39

They held Capri in the same room she'd been brought to after she was raped. She wondered if that had been on purpose, as punishment. It was meant to be a room for relaxation and recovery, but it felt like a prison. In the five hours she was made to wait, Briony was in and out to bring her a meal and change of clothes, but the door remained guarded. She wouldn't be allowed to leave the infirmary until Haddaway had taken her statement.

At least, she *hoped* she'd be allowed to leave then.

Briony had been gone for a while, to extract an update and demand that Capri be allowed to return to her apartment. She swept in now, carrying a dress over one arm. Capri had already changed into something comfortable and shapeless, though the craftsmanship was beautiful.

Now she was made to change hastily into a backless, chiffon dress. Briony spritzed her with scent and pulled her hair up into a loose bun in record time. Capri went along with it all, despite the trepidation she suddenly felt. She and Briony were a well-oiled machine. Plans had obviously changed, and she trusted her Attending Lady's judgment.

When the door opened again, it wasn't Haddaway who entered, but Ekon and his guards. Capri struggled to keep her expression neutral.

"He'll pay for what he did." The King promised vehemently.

Capri's heart stuttered. Of course they'd know it was Brody. His information was in the system from when he'd become a Victor. She struggled to remain calm, to fight back the desperation that would only anger Ekon.

She had thought she'd be having this conversation with Haddaway, and their transpiring would be conveyed impersonally to the King. He wouldn't be happy, but he wouldn't be here, looking at her with that same mixture of pity and disdain as he had when Sullivan ruined his plans four years ago.

She had to try and turn this around for Brody's sake.

"There's no need for that," she said, keeping her voice mild.

"No need?" Ekon looked appalled. "He kidnapped you, and he *raped* you."

Capri glanced at Briony, who was pale but quiet, refusing to demonstrate an opinion and risk betraying either of them. Capri's cheeks burned, but she looked at Ekon, using everything she had to try and convince him.

"He thought he was protecting me by taking me away from the shooting."

"And then he seduced you," Ekon finished.

"No. He won the auction."

"He had his night. No Victor is awarded the Prize twice."

"He didn't…we didn't…consummate that night."

The King stared at her in disbelief. "That's ridiculous."

"It's true!"

She snapped her mouth shut. That *had* sounded desperate, and Ekon's gaze turned suspicious. "You love him."

Capri felt Briony's eyes on her, too. It was too late to feign detachment, so she settled for something subtly scathing. "I wouldn't know."

"Once again, you've put me in a difficult position."

"I've never put you in a difficult position," Capri argued.

Ekon's gaze hardened, but he kept his control. She'd gotten too used to speaking her mind while away. "You've returned to me damaged beyond repair. You'll lose your status as the Prize. You'll be retired and serve another role."

It was supposed to be a demotion. Capri kept her gaze even. If he noticed her relief, he'd likely change his mind and come up with something far worse.

"And Brody?" she asked.

"Will die."

Capri's eyes dropped to the floor as she fought for composure. Ekon stepped forward, forcing her chin up so she had to look him in the eye. "You belong to *me*, Capri. Flaws and all."

Then he let her go, turned, and left with his guards. Capri stared at the closed door long after he'd gone. She couldn't react. The sensation was unfamiliar. Heartbreak. She didn't know whether to scream or cry.

Briony was there, just as she'd been when everything had fallen apart after Sullivan, and the smaller woman slipped her hand into Capri's.

"Let's go back to the apartment," she suggested gently. "We'll get you a glass of wine and a good night's sleep."

Capri turned and hugged her friend, holding her breath so she didn't burst into tears.

Briony patted her hair, arranged for someone to bring her things up to the apartment, and led the way out of the infirmary to a familiar set of elevator doors. Capri remained in a daze, still trying to process her grief, anger, and denial.

Everything seemed stuck on rewind. They were trying to send her back in time, back to her apartment, to when she had no real role in the palace...to when Brody didn't exist.

She wouldn't let them.

CHAPTER 40

Capri awoke with a start in the middle of the night, unable to remember the details of her dream. All she knew was there had been blood, a cage, endless space, and the feeling of falling. Her hand was tucked under her pillow, and she noticed for the first time that there was something unusual. Something rough and foreign touching her fingers. Paper.

She turned on a lamp and pulled the note from under her pillow, examining it. It had an unbroken wax seal—Alexander's—and her name had been scrawled hastily across the outside. She opened the letter and stared at the words that must have been jotted down and hidden before he'd left.

Sullivan = M's cousin.

Capri stared at the writing, trying to make sense of it. It took several moments to sink in. *M.* Marianne. Sullivan had been Marianne's cousin. Alexander must have kept it under wraps while he was loyal to Ekon—or while Ekon was loyal to him. Telling Capri was supposed to be some form of revenge, which could only mean one thing.

Ekon's own admission came back to her: *"Somehow she always manages to capture my queen."*

Marianne had set her up four years ago, all so she could remain the Favorite a little longer. That was what the note implied, and Capri didn't doubt it for a moment. Marianne was probably the reason Gina's dinner had become a bloodbath, as well, conveniently getting both the new Favorite and the Rising Favorite out of the way.

Capri shivered and pulled her knees to her chest, letting the note fall from her hand. How fucked up was this place? She'd never seen it so clearly until she'd left. She was angry and hurt, but the feelings weren't as intense as they should have been. Mostly, she felt hollow. Knowing Brody was just a few floors below her, waiting to die while she could do nothing, was killing her. Marianne was the past. Brody was the present.

There was no way she'd fall back asleep now. She needed to do *something*, something other than sit around and wait to hear from Colin. She stood and dressed in the dim light of her room. She'd lost her hold over Ekon. Who else could she turn to? Who else would listen?

As far as Capri knew, Haddaway was a good man, a fair man. If he wouldn't come to her, then she would go to him.

A guard stood outside her door.

"Where are you going?" he asked, but he didn't seem as if he planned to stop her.

"To the garden," she smiled wanly. "I can't sleep."

Typically, she would have Briony with her when she left the apartment, but he nodded and let her go. She walked away, expecting him to state her whereabouts through his linker, but she heard nothing. It struck her as odd. Why was he there, if not to keep tabs on her?

She counted herself lucky and headed down the stairs to the next floor. Another guard was stationed at the door.

"Welcome back, Lady Capri," the woman said kindly, hands loose around her rifle. "Where are you off to this time of night?"

"The garden," Capri answered again, and again the guard nodded and let her go.

The heightened security made her feel uneasy, but no one detained her. She forced herself to continue through the halls. Asking to see the head of security wasn't strictly forbidden, but it was an unspoken rule, and Ekon was already unhappy with her. She wasn't sure she wanted to take any chances with Brody's fate—or her own—by telling the guards the truth.

She reached the floor for the garden and hesitated. She'd intended to bypass it, but there was another guard, and he nodded to her. He was unsurprised by her appearance, even though Capri hadn't heard them alert one another.

If she'd known where to find Haddaway, she might have tried to bluff her way to him. He was either on duty, which meant he could be anywhere, or he'd be in his quarters, which she assumed were on the first floor. That was where Ekon housed the people he preferred to have close by. But she had no way of knowing for sure.

She quickly made the decision to stick to her story and enter the humid, botanical paradise. There was an exit on the other side. Maybe she could go that way and still achieve her goal.

She walked briskly along the winding path through the labeled trees and plants, but she found herself feeling uneasy again. She slowed her steps. The artificial atmosphere in the room was made so that the plants grew as naturally as possible, with night and day cycles. Right now, the gardens were dark and moonlit. Eerie.

She was not banned from walking in the garden at night. She and every other Lady had always been allowed to go wherever they liked—but now she knew that was only because Ekon had made their world so small. None of them would think of going anywhere other than the places he was comfortable with. They would explore the garden, library, or dining hall. They would call on each other. Always, the Maidens and unretired Ladies would have an escort, only because that was the way things were done.

The idea of venturing elsewhere was absurd.

At least, it had been.

She stopped, heart aching with the hopelessness that had to plague all caged creatures. She was being herded, forced to remain in the confines of the familiar. On the other side of the garden would be another guard. He or she would wish her a good night and offer to walk her back to her room.

Her mission had already failed.

Still, she didn't want to make it easy for them. She wasn't ready to admit defeat. So she wandered. There was a small waterfall, tall trees, and exotic plants. It was the only place on Mars besides the menagerie where living birds and bees could be found in something like a natural habitat. An owl hooted nearby. The garden was peaceful.

Capri reached out to brush the leaves with her fingertips as she passed, eyeing a tall, purple flower with mild curiosity. *Aconite*, the label read. After a while, she was aware of someone else. Her faith in the guards was weak. They'd proven themselves to be as useful as a security blanket—a brilliant defense against invisible monsters but useless against real ones. They were there to keep the girls in, not monsters out.

All of them except for Brody.

She shivered despite the warmth and pretended not to notice as the footsteps grew closer. Whoever it was matched her steps, trying to remain unnoticed, never coming closer than twenty paces. She had two options: try to reach an exit and ask a guard to escort her back or confront the person.

She came upon a long stretch of faux-cobblestone path and whirled around. Her stalker made no move to hide, and the fake moonlight was enough for her to make an identification.

"Haddaway," she greeted, keeping her voice even so he wouldn't realize how scared she'd been. "Just the man I was hoping to see."

His eyebrows lifted in surprise. "Is that so?"

"Yes."

"You were going the wrong way."

"I wasn't sure where to find you."

"I doubt they would have let you through the main entrance." His smile was terse. "I live off the main street, in an apartment with my wife and youngest son."

Capri's initial reaction was surprise, then embarrassment. She'd never given any thought to his home life. Why wouldn't he be married? Maybe she saw people as objects, too, at times. Haddaway had been there to serve the needs of the palace and nothing more, until this moment.

"I was home when I received a message that you were roaming the halls and acting strangely," Haddaway continued, not bothering to mask his exasperation.

Capri frowned. They were keeping close tabs on her after all.

"I won't keep you long," she said. "Can anyone hear us?"

"Not unless I want them to."

"Tell me what they'll do to Brody and how I can stop it."

Annoyance flickered across Haddaway's face. She doubted he appreciated being put on the spot when he should have been at home in a nice, warm bed next to his wife. But Capri's own bed was cold, her heart ached, and she couldn't muster the sympathy he probably deserved. She held her breath.

"There's nothing, Capri. He admitted it. His DNA was inside of you. Ekon wants him dead."

Pain lanced through her heart with surprising intensity, and she looked away to ensure she kept her composure. "How long does he have?" she asked.

"Maybe a few days. I won't do it. Ekon won't get his hands dirty. He'll have to call in some rebel gun-for-hire, since he's bent on killing the one he used before."

Silence stretched between them. She was stuck on one detail: *the one he used before.* Capri realized for the first time that Brody had been the one to kill Sullivan. It was one more link in the chain connecting them.

Haddaway watched her intently, as if trying to read her mind.

"There's no way to stop it?" she asked.

"Nothing short of breaking him out."

"Would you stop me?"

Haddaway shook his head, but it wasn't in response to her question. It was an admonishment. "Don't get in over your head, Capri. You're already on thin ice with the King. You'd never make it down there, and even if you did, you'd just be in trouble, too."

"What else could he do to me? Send me away like Alexander?"

Haddaway was silent, and Capri swallowed. She wondered suddenly if Alexander had been sent away at all. Haddaway spoke again, before her imagination could run away entirely.

"Is that what you want?"

Capri hesitated. Too much of his allegiance remained with Ekon. Total honesty wasn't an option. Once her business here was done, she had every intention of leaving. In the beginning, she'd thought she might be able to convince Ekon to let her go willingly, but he'd made it clear that he wouldn't. *"You belong to me, Capri. Flaws and all."* She'd never once thought, however, that he might kill her if she tried to run. There were so many Ladies. What did it matter if they stayed or went once he was done with them?

But it seemed to matter very much.

"I have ties here." Capri chose her words carefully. "I don't want to go anywhere." *Yet,* she omitted.

Haddaway shook his head, frustrated and tired. He massaged the bridge of his nose. "You mean Shots? You can't get involved with him. You think you love him? He loves you?"

Capri's face flamed. "It isn't just about him," she said sharply, cutting off his train of thought. He was asking questions she couldn't afford to consider.

"Who then?"

Capri hesitated. "Marianne," she said finally.

"Marianne," he repeated, incredulous. "You have ties to *Marianne?* You hate each other."

"I didn't say they were friendly." She took a deep, steadying breath, then thrust Alexander's note at him.

Haddaway was silent, but she could see that his brain was working as he read the words. He was checking facts, going over the years-old incident, trying to figure out if it could be true or if Capri had lost her mind during her short absence. Or did he think she was trying to distract him?

She could tell from the look on his face he had come to the same conclusion she had—that it was not only possible but probable.

"Don't get in over your head," he said again, voice softer now.

"I already am," she replied. "Do you think Ekon knows?"

"I don't know." He handed the note back to her. "But I do know that Ekon can do whatever he likes. He's the King. And he'll keep the peace with her before addressing the scandal with you."

It was similar to what Briony had said to her the night before Ekon bedded her, and she closed her eyes against the pain of the memory and the bitter taste of disappointment. She just wanted justice. For Brody, for herself.

"Then I'll go to the U.N.," Capri said. "He can only get away with so much."

Haddaway grabbed her by the arm and leaned in close, looking slightly panicked. Maybe he wasn't as confident in their privacy as he'd seemed.

"You have no idea how this place operates, Capri—not really. There is nothing to be done about Shots. There is nothing to be done about Marianne. Just stay put, play by the rules, and try to enjoy the gifts you've been given."

"Is that what you do?" she asked. "You play by the rules and just hope he doesn't decide to make you the next scapegoat?"

He shook his head and stepped back. "I've got my family to think about. I'm not a hero."

"I can see that."

He ignored the jibe. "I'll take you back to your room."

Capri let him lead her away from the gardens, fighting a despair that threatened to drown her. Haddaway wouldn't help. Ekon wouldn't help. She would have to help herself. When they got to her room, Haddaway made eye contact with the guard on duty and nodded, as much a warning to keep an eye on her as a greeting. She ignored them both and entered the apartment.

Her head was buzzing with lack of sleep and swirling emotion. She needed time to think and to plan. She needed more sleep. Instead, she found Briony sitting on the edge of the mattress in her dressing gown, back straight and legs crossed, mouth pinched with worry. She didn't stand, but she looked at her Lady.

"Where have you been?"

Capri glanced at the clock by her bed. She'd been gone for two hours. At the U.N., the sun would just be rising.

"I went for a walk," she answered, sitting carefully next to her friend.

A knock sounded on the door, and Briony stood to answer it. She returned with a tray of tea, fruit, and soft-boiled eggs. Capri had gone to the alcove to pour a glass of wine. She sat with her friend, who eyed her drink of choice dubiously.

"I'm going back to sleep," Capri explained. "I'm very tired."

Briony took a sip of steaming liquid from one delicate cup. After spending time on an industrial ship with only the bare essentials, even that tiny china cup seemed absurd.

She watched her friend for a moment and considered opening up to her, but she was worried her frustration, anger, and sadness would make her say something hurtful. She felt too much like she had after Sullivan, when she was angry at the world and Briony had taken the brunt of it. And why shouldn't she be angry? The betrayal ran deeper than Capri had ever imagined.

But Briony deserved more than that side of her, so Capri held her tongue.

"What happened on that ship?" Briony asked after a moment. "You had sex with someone? Willingly?"

Capri swirled the dark red liquid around in her glass and watched the ripples. "Yes."

Briony paused. She seemed to sense they were on tenuous ground.

"Was it the man that took you? The big one?"

"Yes."

"You have...feelings for him?"

"Yes."

"Are you sure?"

The question was gentle, but Capri bristled. The blond suspected she'd been brainwashed.

She drained her glass. "Yes."

"Capri." Briony reached out to cover Capri's hand with her own.

She pulled away. She'd scream or cry and she didn't want to do either. She tried to ignore the hurt look on her friend's face.

"I'm just trying to understand," Briony said. "I'm your friend. Help me understand."

Capri stared at her empty glass, too tired or tipsy to defend against her friend's gentle assault.

"He used to be a guard for the palace," she said finally. "The one who caught Sullivan. He won the last auction."

"The one who rejected you?" Briony was trying to keep up with the bombardment of information.

"Yes. He didn't know it would be me, and he couldn't go through with it. He wanted to save me—to save *someone*—and that's why he took me. We had sex before we came back to Mars. He's the first man I've ever wanted, and now he might die for it."

Her voice was bitter but not bitter enough to hide the waver at the end of her words.

"Oh, Capri," Briony breathed. "I am so sorry."

She wrapped her in a hug, and Capri bit her lip, struggling to keep her emotions in check.

"I'm tired," she said.

"I'll let you sleep."

CHAPTER 41

Over the next two days, Capri made every attempt to fit back into palace society. She attended a luncheon with Ladies who wanted to hear about her experience with the monsters who had kidnapped her. She walked in the gardens, visited the masseuse and manicurist. She accepted condolences for the loss of her position.

Briony was the only one who knew she spent her time behind closed doors ruining that manicure while she wondered what would become of Brody. Did Colin know he'd been sentenced? Should she try to tell him? Sitting, waiting, and hoping were torture, but risking a message could mean putting her ability to help them in jeopardy.

Ekon couldn't know just how fully her allegiance had shifted.

She had to pretend she didn't care. If she could convince everyone she'd followed Haddaway's advice and learned to be grateful for the life Ekon bestowed upon her, then she would be in a better position to help Colin infiltrate the palace.

She'd promised to help Colin, to trust him. She'd relinquished control over Brody's fate, and it was agonizing. But the truth about Marianne belonged to her, and the less she was able to do about Brody, the more she contemplated the part Marianne had played, the ripple—no, the fallout—of her actions. The auction would never have come to pass. No innocent bystanders would have died on the night of Gina's birthday. Ekon would not be so afraid and unpredictable now.

Brody would not be in a cell, waiting to die.

It all came down to Marianne, and there was no telling how much more damage she could cause. She had to be stopped.

When mingling with Ladies, gossip was currency, and in exchange for vague details about her time away from Mars, she learned that

Marianne was in need of a new Attending Lady. A plan formed in Capri's mind, but its execution required a meeting with the King.

The opportunity came in the form of a sealed message, so like the invitations she'd received to the upper dining hall when she was held in higher esteem. Only this time, when she held her breath, waiting for Briony to open it, it wasn't excitement and anticipation she felt—it was hope and fear. Somewhere the gavel had dropped, and he was inviting her to receive judgment. They were both to see him that afternoon to discover their new roles.

Briony didn't ask Capri's opinion on her wardrobe as she usually did; instead, she stood in her Lady's closet, biting her lip as if struggling to reach a decision. Then, she held up a familiar, royal blue dress.

Capri looked from Briony to the dress and back again. It was the one she'd worn the night of her seventeenth birthday, the night Ekon had appointed himself the first Victor.

"I'm not sure this will work the way you want it to," she told Briony.

"I know he's changed, but he still knows a beautiful woman when he sees one. Perhaps the reminder of your night together will... appease him." Capri frowned at the memory, and Briony shook her head. "You have to work on that."

"What?"

"You've changed, too, Capri. You have to hide your thoughts."

Capri only grew more sullen. She'd never had to hide her feelings from Brody. She felt the loss of that freedom more keenly now.

"I'm more honest," she argued.

"Ekon doesn't want honesty. You know that."

Capri relaxed her face and smiled. Briony raised an eyebrow, looking amused and annoyed, and Capri knew that her expression was convincing.

"Better," Briony conceded. Then she turned serious, clasping Capri's hand in her own to be sure she had her full attention. "I know there is tension between the two of you. He's a jealous man, a possessive man, and your relationship will never be the same. But this is your home. You *must* do what you can to make it easy on yourself."

Capri's once-future loomed before her. She'd live a long, empty life in the palace of Mars and then die in her sleep, a shell of the beauty she'd been, with no other accomplishment than having once been a Lady.

Once upon a time, she'd have chosen that fate gladly. Now it felt like a disturbing dream. After being with Brody, she knew what home felt like, and it wasn't this. But she couldn't tell that to Briony.

"If you think wearing the dress is for the best, I'll do it."

"I do," she said firmly.

Briony helped Capri slip into it. The garment still fit as well as it had two years before, though the bandage on her arm was in stark contrast to the rest of her fair skin. Briony found an arm cuff in silver that covered the imperfection well enough, though the friction was far from comfortable.

Capri sat down at the familiar vanity and Briony braided her hair, weaving the beads made of precious metal into her brown curls. Her Attending Lady's fingers lingered for a moment in the soft strands, and when she glanced in the mirror, there were tears in her friend's eyes.

She reached back and covered her hand, putting all of her gratitude into a gentle squeeze. It was the last night they'd be in the roles they'd sustained for four years. If Capri let herself feel too much, this new loss might devastate her. She had to stay focused.

Briony spritzed her with scent, something floral that Ekon liked, and checked her own reflection in the mirror. Capri took a turn and straightened her shoulders. She was radiant and more than deserving of Ekon's attention, but she just couldn't muster the demure, worshipful look that had once come so naturally. She felt confident and powerful in her own right, and no matter what kind of pretty things Briony adorned her with, he wouldn't like that.

"Are you ready?" Briony asked, and Capri realized the blond had been waiting for her.

She smiled, and they linked arms. "Ready."

A guard escorted them to Ekon's chambers and let them into the parlor. Capri spotted a decanter of whiskey on a shelf behind Ekon's large wooden desk, and it was enough to make her lose focus, to think of Brody. Pain lanced through her. What was he doing now? When would Colin act?

She looked away, forcing herself back to the present. This meeting wasn't about him.

One of the King's valets offered chairs and tea. Two guards stood at each of the three doors in the spacious room. There was furniture made of real wood, the smell of leather—luxury that few people in the Kingdom had the opportunity to experience.

Briony accepted the tea but remained standing. Capri followed suit. She knew that they would make the most impact that way, their beauty on full display like exquisite mannequins.

Ekon came through one of the doors a short time later, escorted by Haddaway, who nodded to the Ladies. His eyes lingered on Capri's briefly, a warning, before he stood at a respectful distance.

The King was dressed in trousers, a collared shirt, and a long blue jacket. He offered the pair a small smile. For a moment, he looked like the old Ekon, the one who hadn't realized his dynasty could come crashing down around him at any moment. But his grin was wry, and though appreciation gleamed in his eye, caution was stronger.

"You both look lovely this evening."

He let his eyes stay on Capri, and she knew that he was remembering their night together, just as Briony had planned. She hid her revulsion.

"Please sit," he said smoothly. His words weren't a request, and they obeyed their King.

Capri sipped her tea and watched him carefully. Ekon had been angry with her at their last meeting. He'd recovered his composure, but she knew his feelings weren't changed. He demanded the attention of nearly fifty women and girls, she'd slept with as many men and women *at his request*, and he would treat her as if she alone were impure.

"I trust you're getting used to being back?" Ekon asked Capri.

Capri could see right through the polite words to the question he was really asking: *I trust you've been behaving.*

"Yes, thank you," she responded.

"Good."

"This tea is delicious," Briony said, and Ekon rewarded the blond with a genuine smile. He had a soft spot for her. He'd looked at Capri that way before she'd slept with a man from whom he was unable to profit.

"It's a special blend, imported from China Territory. I'll have some sent to your room."

"That's very kind, King. Thank you."

"Of course."

He cleared his throat and turned his attention back to the both of them. "I'm afraid other obligations won't allow me to linger long, so I'll make this quick."

"We understand." Briony spoke softly and inclined her head gently. Once more, Capri forced herself to follow suit, appearing pleasant and curious, nothing more.

"Marianne is in need of a new Attending Lady, and you are both in need of a new position."

Briony opened her mouth to speak, but Capri interrupted with a derisive snort. She knew Briony would volunteer for the position, to save her the misery of being stuck serving the wretched cow, but she couldn't let that happen.

Ekon's attention snapped back to Capri, and his eyes narrowed. Still, he remained in control, his tone patient and pleasant. She was afraid of inciting his anger, but this was why she'd come. If there was ever a time to act confident, it was now.

"What do you find so funny, Capri?" he asked.

"Nothing, King. I'm just not surprised." She kept her tone flippant and glanced at her manicured nails.

Briony caught her eye and gave her a look that said very clearly: *Shut up!* Capri kept her attention on Ekon, who seemed to be choosing his words carefully.

"You never liked her," he said.

"There's not much to like."

Briony splashed tea on her dress, trying desperately to end the conversation. "Oh, dear!" she exclaimed.

But neither Ekon nor Capri acknowledged her, letting a valet help her clean the skirt.

"What is it about her you find so threatening?" he asked.

His tone was curious, but the smirk on his lips told her he was looking for a reaction, and much to her chagrin, he got it. Capri's pride flared, and her nostrils with it. That was all, but it was enough.

His expression changed to one of satisfaction and he sat back in his chair, taking a long sip of tea.

"You'll be Marianne's new Attending Lady, Capri, and move into the adjoining room tomorrow. She's been ill as of late, and it's made her…disagreeable. However, I expect her to be ready when I call and to make an appearance at the memorial. You'll make sure of that. I don't want unfounded rumors concerning her condition and whereabouts."

"Of course, King," Capri agreed, allowing her bright façade to falter slightly. It worked in her favor now for Ekon to think she was unhappy.

Briony had given up and merely sat there, watching the exchange, the spiced tea growing cold in her hands. Ekon rose, and he held out a hand as if he wished to help Capri rise. She set down her tea, smiled demurely, and took his hand. He helped her to her feet—then pulled her hard to him, pressing her against his body to whisper in her ear. She was caught off guard and gasped at the sudden closeness, recoiling slightly before she could stop herself.

She glanced at Haddaway, who looked displeased by his King's behavior but didn't make a move to stop him.

"You don't want me in that way," he murmured in her ear.

She didn't answer. She didn't need to. She only held her breath and waited for him to release her, but he wasn't done yet. He slid a hand down her arm, squeezing the cuff slightly and making her wince. He breathed in the scent of her hair and then looked into her eyes once more.

"Marianne's illness can get in the way of our amorous activities."

Capri swallowed but held his gaze. "It's a good thing there are so many available young Ladies. I am well aware that I am too sullied for you."

He released her, and she stepped back. She was ready to flee, but she had to wait to be dismissed.

"I am still entitled to you if I want you," he reminded her in such a gentle tone that she almost didn't register the threat it encompassed. "Don't forget that. You may go. I'll speak with Briony alone."

Capri glanced at her friend, who looked so scared and hurt on her behalf, and tried to offer a reassuring smile. Then she turned and left the room while she was still able to walk straight-backed, head held high.

As soon as the elevator door closed behind her, she stopped fighting and let herself slide to the floor, feeling all the fear and loathing she'd forced back when Ekon had pressed their bodies together.

When the door opened again, she was standing, and no one could tell that she had broken down.

CHAPTER 42

Capri's new apartment was smaller, the furnishings simpler. The bed was meant for just one person, but it was plush and comfortable. She'd fallen in status, but a Lady could only fall so far. She still garnered some luxury.

Briony's last act as her Attending Lady had been to weed out the majority of her more daring outfits and have the remaining garments sent to her new room. It wouldn't do for Capri to upstage Marianne.

She sat on the edge of the bed and tried to make peace with her new role. The idea of waiting on the conniving woman was unappealing, but it had to be done. She'd known Ekon would assign her to Marianne. He'd been looking for a way to punish her, and she needed an excuse to be close to her.

A soft knock sounded on the door to the hallway, and Briony slipped into the room. Her tenure was over, but she'd offered to come as a friend, to help her get settled. They hadn't talked much since their meeting with Ekon, but Briony swept into the room and barely looked at her before picking up a long dress and hanging it in the closet. Capri took hold of a few garments and stood with her friend to hang them.

"What happened after I left?" she asked, breaking the silence.

"I'll be attending another young Lady."

"Will you let me know where?"

"It's the same apartment." Her tone was clipped; she still wouldn't look at Capri.

Capri hung two more dresses and pretended not to notice when Briony rearranged them. Another woman would be in the room that held so many mixed memories for her. She wasn't sure how she felt about that.

"Well, someone will be very comfortable."

Briony made a noise of polite acknowledgement. Capri had had enough. She took her friend's arm and turned her so they were facing one another. She couldn't divulge her reasons for doing what she did. She wouldn't let Briony get involved. The only way a secret worked was if there was one keeper, but she couldn't stand the tension between them.

"I'm sorry," she said. "I didn't want you to get stuck with her."

"I'd have handled it better than you."

"You're probably right."

Briony threw a dress on the bed in frustration. She lost her cool so rarely that the movement startled Capri.

"I know you better than anyone, Capri. Anyone *here*, at least," she allowed with a trace of bitterness.

Capri stared at the dress on the bed for a moment, gathering her thoughts. It was the dress she'd been wearing when she was transferred from the ship back to Mars, and she was filled with sudden longing.

"What are you doing?" Briony asked softly, green eyes searching her hazel ones. "You did this on purpose, and it wasn't just for me. How will this help him?"

She meant Brody, and Capri's heart contracted painfully. It wouldn't. Again, the idea of making a break for it, rushing the prison, and getting him out on her own flashed through her mind. But it was a fantasy, nothing more. It was agony to do nothing, but if she trusted Colin—and she did—she had to wait.

"You just have to trust me," she told Briony. "I'll be okay."

Briony glanced at the door that would adjoin her room and Marianne's. She would report for duty the following morning. Briony's gaze slid back to hers. She still looked hurt, but Capri could sense she was relenting.

"Fine," Briony conceded. "Are you ready for tomorrow?"

Capri attempted a smile. "Of course not. I've been too busy being pampered by you these last four years; I never bothered to learn your secrets."

To Capri's relief, an amused smile touched Briony's lips. "I'll give you some pointers."

CHAPTER 43

Capri did her own hair the next morning, braiding her curls at the temples and pulling the plaits back in a practical style. She chose a long, gray dress paired with comfortable flats. No jewelry, no scents, no frills. She was striking despite the lack of adornment.

Marianne would hate that.

The corner of her mouth lifted slightly. She approached the door to her Lady's room, took a deep breath, and knocked.

Her first day's instructions came directly from Ekon. She was to go in at 8:00 sharp, whether Marianne was awake or not. Her Lady was to bathe, eat, and drink ginger and peppermint tea. If the nausea persisted, Capri was to go to the infirmary for something stronger. She must be discreet.

Marianne had to be ready for a visit from the King in the evening. Capri knew well enough what that meant.

There was no answer on the other side of the door. Capri knocked again, louder this time. The door was made of heavy wood rather than steel, and it dampened the sound of her fist. It was just the beginning of the luxury in Marianne's apartment.

"Come in," called a groggy voice.

Capri walked through. Marianne sat in a four-poster bed amidst a sea of rich cream-and-emerald bedding. It could have fit four people comfortably, but she was alone, so pale Capri almost mistook her for an uncovered pillow. Ekon hadn't exaggerated her illness.

Marianne's expression was one of accusation. She hadn't been expecting Capri.

"You," she snarled, but her voice was so weak it sounded more like a squeak.

Capri almost felt sympathy, pity, things the other woman did not deserve. She didn't respond immediately, instead taking a moment to survey the room and collect her thoughts.

There were rich oak details and even a few live plants she'd likely be responsible for keeping alive. Marianne did not have an alcove in the back as Capri had had, but there was a separate room with a table for two and a small kitchen—for the servants' use, Capri was sure. Marianne would never lift a finger.

A crystal chess set sat on top of a wardrobe, reminding Capri of the unsettling conversation she'd had with Ekon two years before. It was safe to assume Marianne's closet and bathroom were up to the same over-the-top standards. These were the chambers of a queen, meant to be an escape for Ekon as much as a home for Marianne. Quite suddenly, Marianne bent over a porcelain container by the bed and dry heaved. When she'd finished, she spit into it and wiped her mouth with the back of her hand. Her voice was hoarse and bitter.

"This is a punishment for both of us."

"Why would he punish you?" Capri asked.

"For this. This *illness.*"

Capri didn't reply. For all she knew about Ekon these days, Marianne could be right. She felt conflicted. How could she kill a woman who seemed half-dead already? And if she couldn't, what the hell was she doing here? She'd never intended to stay Marianne's Attending Lady for long.

"Come on. Let's get you cleaned up." Capri helped the shaking woman out of bed without bothering to hide her impatience. She was angry that her resolve was wavering, that she'd found her once-regal archrival in such a pathetic state.

"Bring my receptacle," Marianne managed.

"I'm not cleaning that up."

"It's your job."

"No."

"I'll tell Ekon."

"You can tell him when you see him tonight, but I doubt he'll be able to come up with a worse punishment than you."

Marianne's pale face turned a shade whiter. "Tonight? But...he knows I'm ill."

Capri remained unsympathetic. "You wanted to be the Favorite, Marianne."

She took her Lady's thin arm and helped her to the bathroom. Marianne went in to dump the contents of the pot and relieve herself, and then Capri ran a bath for her. The blond raised her arms to wash her hair, but she shook so hard that Capri had to take over.

Once she was clean and robed, Capri moved to the call box. "I'll have tea and crackers sent up."

"If you must," Marianne muttered, sitting down heavily in a chair and sipping a glass of water.

Capri made the order, stripped the bed, and found fresh linens. She threw the soiled sheets and blankets, along with Marianne's sweat-soaked nightgown, into a basket to be taken to the laundry chute.

"We'll go for a walk after you've eaten."

"No," Marianne protested sharply. "No one can see me like this."

"You won't get better by staying in bed," Capri said. She paused, trying to sound nonchalant when she asked her question. "What's wrong with you, anyway?"

Marianne averted her gaze. "No one knows."

Capri didn't believe her. Mysterious illnesses didn't exist. The doctors on Mars came straight from the medical schools on Venus, which meant they were some of the best. But she didn't contradict her.

"There might be something in the infirmary to help," she suggested.

"I'll be fine."

"We'll walk up and down the hall," Capri said. "At least I'll be able to say I did my part."

"Fine."

"Ekon won't be happy with either of us if you don't make an appearance at the memorial."

"He's made that very clear already. But you're likely to get it worse than I do if I'm not there."

"Maybe," Capri agreed. "Or maybe he'll give up on you and find a new Favorite. I can't fall much farther, Marianne, but you've got a long way to go."

The blond gave her a scathing look. A knock sounded on the door, and Capri gave her a polite smile. "That will be the tea."

***

That night, Capri brushed and combed Marianne's long blond hair until it shone. She placed rubies around her slender neck and put more makeup on her skin than she might have before the illness, to mask the dark circles and sunken cheeks. She helped her slip into a red dress.

Normally, black would suit her better, but in her current state it would only make her look witchlike.

Marianne studied her reflection with a critical eye and pursed lips. Even she had to admit she looked spectacular, considering she'd thrown up again just an hour before. Capri had called for more ginger tea and crackers, but she suspected her Lady was still fighting nausea.

"It'll do," Marianne said at last.

Capri inclined her head slightly. "Champagne and glasses are on the side table. Should I look in on you after he leaves?"

"No. I'll see you in the morning." Marianne glanced at her for the first time since she'd begun dressing, and her gaze was sharp. "This time, if I'm sleeping, don't wake me."

Capri raised her eyebrows briefly in response and went to her own room. Marianne was disobeying Ekon with the command and asking Capri to do the same.

Maybe this was her quiet way of retaliating. Maybe, under different circumstances, Capri would experience a feeling of camaraderie. They would put aside their differences and fight the good fight together.

But this was the woman responsible for the single worst moment of Capri's life. She was the reason for every lost hope, every unkind Victor, and every nightmare.

Marianne could rest in the morning—but she couldn't be allowed to live.

CHAPTER 44

The meeting between Marianne and Ekon began with talking, laughing, and some convincingly playful murmurs from Marianne. But when they got down to business, it was clear Ekon was the only one enjoying himself. Although the heavy wooden door between their rooms dampened the noise, it couldn't mask it all.

Empathy cut Capri deep. *She doesn't deserve it,* she reminded herself. Still, tears pricked her eyes, memories of her own unwanted Victors in her mind. A whirlpool of emotions formed in her chest, threatening to suck down her resolve.

Brody wouldn't think twice about it. Marianne would already be dead. Hadn't she learned anything from her short time with him? If no one would serve justice on her behalf, she'd have to do it herself. Marianne's current state was no excuse for past crimes.

A muffled cry sounded from the next room, and Capri stood. She had to get out. She glanced briefly in the mirror and slipped out of the room, nodding to the guards in the hallway. There were more than usual, due to the King's visit.

She walked slowly, running her fingers along a gilded railing, heading nowhere in particular. But she soon found herself wandering toward the end of the hall, down the stairs, intent on searching through the kitchen store cupboard for something she could use against Marianne.

Capri silently recited her reasoning. Marianne was responsible for Capri's downfall, Faye's murder, and Gina's injury. She wouldn't stop. Brody would have already done the deed, but Capri had to be careful; she had to be subtle. If she got caught, she'd end up in a prison cell right next to him, unable to help the crew of *Task Eternal* free him. Saving him—and, hopefully, herself—had to remain the priority.

She stopped on the landing where Sullivan had begun to seduce her, where Brody had rescued her for the first time, though she hadn't known it then. With renewed purpose, she continued to descend, acknowledging a guard as she passed through the kitchen door. The guard didn't seem surprised to see her. It struck her as strange.

It wasn't unheard of for Ladies to fetch something from the kitchen, but it was unusual. They could call for whatever they needed to be brought to them. It made her think of the night she'd met with Haddaway in the garden, how no one had seemed surprised by her presence then, either.

Had cameras been included in Ekon's security upgrades? If Briony knew about them, she'd have mentioned them. Before the massacre, the Ladies had been afforded some privacy and trust, but these were different times. There would always be before the shooting and after.

She glanced at the ceiling for the telltale glare of a lens but found nothing.

"Can I help you?" a round-faced cook asked cheerfully, hands folded in front of her flour-dusted apron.

Capri lapsed easily into a relaxed demeanor, meant to put people—*Victors*—at ease and convince them of her acquiescence. "I'm looking for ginger tea," she said. "My Lady isn't feeling well."

The cook gestured to a closet. "It's just in there. Do you mind having a look yourself? Everything is labeled. I just have to get these cakes out of the oven."

"Of course. Thank you." Capri nodded and stepped through the open doorway.

She felt uneasy in the dim room. Gaining access alone was what she'd hoped for, but it had been too easy. She began examining the shelves.

One held spare uniforms and extra pots and pans. The selection of herbs, spices, and teas was expansive, and she wracked her brain, trying to think of something useful. She reached for the ginger tea and paused as a draft moved her skirt. She followed the shelves around a corner and found a door that led to the warehouse. At the far end was another open door, and beyond that lay the docks.

She glanced behind her. She was the only one in the storeroom, and there were no guards. She could leave right now and send word of Brody's impending fate to *Task Eternal*. She could make sure they knew. And then, after getting him out, she could use the same route to escape.

She pulled back suddenly, as if she'd been burned. *This* was why she'd been let into the storeroom. It was a test. That was the only explanation. Even if she couldn't see them, there *must* be cameras. It also meant she couldn't pilfer anything dangerous, even if she found something stronger than nutmeg.

She left quickly, holding the tea she'd come for in one hand, in plain view, so no one could suspect she'd been there for other reasons. She left the kitchens and considered going to Briony. Although she couldn't reveal everything to her former Lady, her steady presence helped her feel centered.

But it was late, and her friend would be adjusting to life with a new Lady. Capri tamped down a wave of jealousy.

She wandered again, until she found herself in the garden. This time, there were others milling about. A group of girls from the Maiden Dorm had been taken to see the moon flowers. Some Ladies acknowledged her and offered friendly smiles, while others whispered to their companions.

Capri's demotion was common knowledge, as was her appointment to attend the most disliked Lady in the palace. For all she knew, her tryst with Brody was common knowledge, too.

None of it would have happened if it wasn't for Marianne's interference. Brody would never have walked into the stairwell or into the closet. He wouldn't have been her Victor that night because there would have been no Prize. He wouldn't have taken her from the palace because she'd never have been anything other than one of Ekon's Ladies to him.

If it weren't for Marianne, her heart wouldn't be broken.

Tears pricked her eyes, and she found herself alone on a familiar path. She stared at the purple flowers again. *Monkshood. Wolfsbane.* Aconite had been mentioned in some of the books and poems that had made up Capri's required reading, as well as books she'd chosen herself. She reached out and picked a handful of the soft, purple hoods and tucked them into the same, small box that held the ginger tea.

Marianne was already sick. She'd already decided poison would rouse the least suspicion.

Capri took the winding paths back to the entrance of the garden. A wave of dizziness washed over her, and she stumbled slightly. A guard watched her with concern but not suspicion. Ekon's surveillance didn't reach that far, then—if it existed at all. She pushed through the feeling and wondered if it was her conscience making her feel off or if the plant was just that powerful. It seemed to come with its own warning that killing someone else meant killing a bit of oneself, as well.

Is it worth it? the plant was asking.

Capri shivered and held the box more tightly as she approached her room. There was only one guard now, which meant Ekon had finished with Marianne and left. In the safety and solace of her room, Capri shoved the box underneath her bed, stripped, donned her robe, and lay down to sleep.

She released a long breath into the darkness. She had time to answer the question the plant posed. And if she answered yes, now she had the means to go through with it.

CHAPTER 45

Brody could tell the days were passing only by the guards' shift changes. He'd been there for three days with nothing to occupy him but his thoughts. He was given just enough food and water to keep him alive, just so they could kill him.

He thought maybe they wanted to drive him insane before sending him to be executed. His thick beard, the scent of unwashed man, and his natural tendency to snarl when his life was threatened would be enough to convince any jury that he was unstable, a threat to society.

But this was Mars. There was no jury. Ekon's was the only word that mattered, and he wanted him dead. Once, Brody had been the man the King turned to when he needed someone put down, so he knew exactly how it would happen.

He would be led to an old closet lined with plastic sheets. A guard would cuff him to a chair, facing the door, and some gun-for-hire would walk through that door and shoot him between the eyes. Cleanup would be a breeze. It would be like he never existed.

That was fine.

This was the agony. Ekon had to know what he was doing, leaving him like this, with nothing to do but think about his future, his past, his mistakes. Capri. Losing her. Losing her to *him.*

He had to stay active, keep his mind busy, or regret would overwhelm him.

He did push-ups and pull-ups. He propped his thin mattress against a wall and used it as a punching bag until his knuckles were bruised. It was something, at least, to keep his thoughts at bay, to tire him out so he could sleep at night.

But he still had his breaking point, moments when his shaking body, fueled by too few calories and on the brink of dehydration, just couldn't take any more, and he had to stop. He had to sit down. He did feel vaguely drunk in those moments, but not drunk enough, and it was in those moments that he considered giving the King one last middle finger and finding a way to off himself.

But he couldn't do it. He told himself it was because he couldn't cheat Jill and Maxine out of their revenge. That day on Ptolemy, after he'd killed Sledge with his wife's gun, he'd put the barrel in his mouth, then removed it again. It wasn't enough. He deserved to suffer through life a little longer. He'd begun to believe that his fate was in their hands, and they'd decide when he got to die.

He'd always known it would be early and violent; since their deaths, he'd been ready for it, maybe even waiting for it. But now, he had to admit he no longer felt the same way, and it was all Capri's fucking fault.

He cared. He'd cared from the moment he realized she was the Prize and had seen the single, unfair path ahead of her. He'd just wanted to show her another, give the girl a choice, drop her somewhere and never see her again.

But his reckless decision had backfired in the worst way. Her touch, her scent, those eyes—everything about her was ingrained in him. He knew his death would hurt her, and he didn't *want* to hurt her. Maybe this had been Jill and Maxine's plan all along, to make him feel again, to twist the knife, before letting him die. He wished they'd just get it over with.

It was during one of these dark moments on the third day that the door to the prison cell opened and Haddaway appeared. The gunman didn't betray his surprise and continued glaring at the wall, but he knew the other man wasn't supposed to be there.

"Shots," Haddaway greeted.

Brody only grunted, exhaustion and suspicion preventing him from making more of an effort.

"Thought you might appreciate an update. Maybe a meal."

Brody glanced at him and noticed the two bowls he carried. Haddaway dragged a chair into the room and sat across from him, just as he had that first night. Brody reached for the steaming bowl of chicken and broccoli, and he couldn't hide the fact that he was famished. He shoveled the food into his mouth and then accepted the bottle of whiskey Haddaway offered him with a gesture of thanks. He took a few swallows and handed it back, feeling more like himself.

Haddaway still didn't speak. Brody leaned back against the wall, his long, broad legs stretched out in front of him, arms crossed over his chest.

"This some kinda last meal?" he asked.

Haddaway took a sip from the bottle and met Brody's gaze. "Not yet. You've got five days."

Brody nodded slowly, considering the other man's words. "Any way to speed that up?"

The other man snorted and shook his head. "Leave it to you."

Brody shrugged. "Sittin' here in my own stink ain't my idea of fun. There's no sense puttin' it off."

"Ekon has it planned during the memorial service. Some kind of poetic justice, I'm sure."

Brody grunted, and the two sat in silence. "Thanks for lettin' me know," Brody said finally.

Haddaway nodded, but he made no move to leave. Brody waited. If there was anything he had right now, it was time.

"Capri's gotten more ambitious since you took her away," the older man said.

Brody's eyes shot up. "You talked to her?"

"She came looking for me. Seems to have some ideas about getting you out."

The gunman smirked. "I'm touched."

"Seems to have some ideas about Marianne, too."

"Marianne? What about her?"

"Capri thinks she was responsible for her attack."

Brody narrowed his eyes, trying to make sense of the girl's accusation. "Why?"

"It turns out Sullivan was Marianne's cousin. Explains how he got the job and landed in the palace so fast. I'm sure Marianne asked Ekon for a favor."

Quite suddenly, Brody remembered the floral scent that had always seemed to linger on Sullivan, and it made sense. It all made sense. He'd been meeting with Marianne, planning Capri's downfall. He leaned forward, fists clenched.

"Aren't you the fucking head of security? Shouldn't you have maybe picked up on that?"

"So you think it's true?" Haddaway asked, unperturbed by Brody's anger.

Brody had never harbored such bloody thoughts toward a woman. "Yeah, I do."

Haddaway took another long sip of whiskey. It wasn't like him to drink more than a glass on the job. Something else was eating at him. Something more than past crimes, something more than seeing an old friend in a concrete box.

"What are you gonna do about it?" Brody asked.

Haddaway swirled the brown liquid around in the bottle. "Nothing."

"Coward."

"I know." He raised his eyes to Brody's. "She has a new position."

"New position?"

"And she's been restless, dissatisfied. Any idiot can see it. You might have ruined her for this place, Shots." Haddaway raised the bottle briefly in salute. "Thanks to your little affair, Ekon's declared her damaged goods. Now she's an Attending Lady."

"Good," Brody grunted, and he meant it.

No one would touch her again—unless *she* wanted them to. He could go in a little more peace now, knowing that. He downed the rest of the bottle, welcoming the hazy feeling he'd spent the last days searching for.

"To Marianne."

Brody went cold and stared at the man across from him. He realized exactly why Haddaway was there and why he was acting so out of character. "Did she ask for it?"

"I'd say she manipulated her way into it pretty damn effortlessly."

Brody licked his lips and leaned forward. His heart pounded. Haddaway couldn't touch Marianne. Ekon wouldn't. Capri would be pissed. If she was in this position by any means other than pure coincidence she could only have one plan in mind.

"Are you gonna stop her?" he asked.

Haddaway looked at Brody as if he was searching for something. "She means something to you, doesn't she?"

"That ain't an answer."

"I don't know. I joined the palace guards fifteen years ago for two reasons: to serve my King and deliver justice. Lately I'm only doing one of them."

Brody was tense, waiting. Finally, Haddaway met his gaze. "If she's discreet, I don't think I will."

The gunman relaxed. Haddaway stood and gathered the dishes.

"I'll see you in five days, Shots," he said.

Brody grunted, and then he was left alone with his thoughts again. This time, instead of the haunting images that usually seeped into his brain, he saw Capri and tried to imagine her plan. Just a few weeks ago, he could never have believed she had it in her to kill someone.

But now, since he'd taken her from Mars and watched her learn that she was made of more than Ekon had led her to believe…maybe she could.

Marianne deserved to die, but Capri didn't deserve to have blood on her hands. He clenched and unclenched his fists, wishing he could do the deed for her. Kill Sullivan again. Kill Ekon.

He wished he could do anything other than stay in one place, waiting to die, thinking of her.

He stood, propped the mattress against the wall, and slammed a fist into the thin padding.

CHAPTER 46

Leroy was shoulder deep in *Task Eternal*'s elevator gears. The metal cage was stuck halfway down to the docks on New Earth, where they'd stopped to refuel before going to Mercury. Having to jump the rest of the way down to the ground was undignified to say the least, and the captain hadn't been happy about it. Leroy bit his lip as he reached farther, feeling where the bits and pieces were misaligned.

To their surprise, the crew had been given a job by King Ekon: pick up building supplies from Mercury. The kingdom, conveniently, was the farthest place from Mars, except for the prison planet of Alcatraz, and it didn't take them long to reach the conclusion that Ekon wanted them out of the way.

Because he intended to kill Shots.

No great loss, if you asked Leroy.

He pulled his arm out of the open panel and touched the linker in his ear. "Did you turn off the power to the loading bay?"

"For the third time, yes," Jax replied.

"I'm just asking. Do you want me to lose a limb?"

There was a silence, just long enough to be offensive. Jax had always been good at getting the desired effect without speaking much. Leroy, on the other hand, used too many words. He knew that. He'd been called annoying plenty as a kid, and he lived in constant fear that now, even as an adult, he hadn't kicked the label.

Maybe that was why he hated Shots so much. He didn't sugar-coat anything. He just told Leroy he was everything he feared, like it didn't matter, like they were all as dead inside as he was. He still couldn't understand what Capri saw in him. But if Jax had taught him anything it was that people couldn't help who they fell for.

He and the captain didn't talk about it much. They weren't showy. It kept things professional, and it kept Leroy from feeling like a third wheel. But he knew Colin was the last person his brother would have chosen to be with. Jax was all lists, rules, and order. Falling for a superior was messy. Jax was supposed to be under the captain—*figuratively.*

Leroy smirked at his own joke and fitted the wrench to the gear. He pulled hard, muscles straining, and felt the gear shift, tighten, and fall back into place. He smiled with satisfaction and touched his linker again.

"You can restore power."

"I already did."

"What?"

"Kidding."

Leroy glared at nothing and jammed his finger into the button on the control panel. The elevator clanked down to the ground. He called it back, then released it once more. Satisfied with the results, he put everything back together before calling it back to the loading bay. His back was to the metal cage, and the captain's voice made him jump.

"Leroy."

"Shit," he muttered, spinning around. "Captain."

"Anyone could have climbed on."

Leroy's cheeks flushed. "Sorry."

"I need to talk to you," Colin continued, plugging a few notes into a reader before slipping the thin sheet into his back pocket. "The contractors on Venus can supply everything we need for Mars."

"That's lucky, but won't that be more expensive?"

"We won't see a profit."

Leroy burned with irritation. "What's the point?"

The captain narrowed his gaze. "The point is this is the only chance we have at saving Shots from execution. Is everything on the ship in working order?"

"As far as I know."

"Good. Then you'll go back to Mars. Use a fake name. Land at the far docks. You're the only one who might be able to get the information we need to get him out."

Leroy was frozen. He felt so many things: proud that he was being entrusted with something so important; afraid of traveling through space alone for the first time; angry that he was expected to do something so risky for a man he doubted very much would lift a finger to help him.

The captain was waiting for a response. Leroy wondered briefly if he should voice his thoughts, but he'd never been one to keep from saying things he shouldn't. "Wouldn't it be easier just to…hire someone else?"

Anger flickered across Colin's face, but Leroy could see the question didn't come as a surprise. He wondered what that said about him and felt slightly ashamed.

"If you're ever in the same situation, should we just hire someone else?"

"All due respect, Captain, I don't think you'd ever find me in a similar situation. He got himself there."

"You might not like him, but he's a member of this crew." Colin was always careful not to let the fact they were also family by marriage play into it. "Do I need to make this an order?"

Leroy knew he wouldn't win this one. He hadn't expected to, but it was a way to air his grievance.

"No, Captain," he muttered.

"Look through the work rosters from a few years back and see who he worked with at the palace, who he might have been friendly with. There could be someone willing to take a message to Capri."

Leroy perked up. He might see her again. He was suddenly very glad the captain hadn't listened to his complaints.

"We'll talk more over dinner. Pack so you're ready to leave after. I've booked you passage for tonight."

CHAPTER 47

By "booking passage" the captain meant he'd rented a camper ship for Leroy to use. These were tiny ships mainly used by middle-class families to see some of the sights outside of New Earth. They held enough fuel to travel twenty-four hours without stopping.

Leroy had ridden in one once when he and Jax were small. They'd gone to Venus to see some famous fountain because their parents had thought they should go off-planet at least once in their lives; they'd never imagined their sons would travel the System for a living.

There was a dock on the far side of Mars for those on unofficial business, who were there just to visit family and friends or see the shops, restaurants, menagerie, and the less lived-in parts of the palace. There was enough space for about twenty ships and a guard booth.

Leroy held his breath during check-in, but his false documents passed inspection. They took his picture, which was standard practice, but he clearly wasn't on any kind of watch list. He tended to fade into the background compared to Colin and Brody. Even Jax, sometimes. People took his twin more seriously. In this case, it was a good thing.

There was no time to waste.

His original plan had been to join a tour group at the palace. He could sneak off and hack into the mainframe easy enough. But thanks to the shooting and tightened security, the tours had been put on hold and that was no longer an option. However, he'd done his research, and he knew that most of the readers at the Mars bars and restaurants were connected in some way to the palace in case they needed to send out official announcements.

If someone was highly skilled—and he was—they could hack into the network and get the information they needed that way.

He tossed a backpack over his shoulder. The guard at the booth would only find a few essentials—and one door latch from *Task Eternal.* He studied the object for a moment, then shrugged and put it back in the bag, waving Leroy through.

The mechanic breathed a sigh of relief and walked into the first bar he came to. His plan worked beautifully, and he had a belly full of beer and the information he needed in no time.

Tamara Ellis frequented the bar nearest the palace docks after her shift, and one month ago she'd shared a drink there with Broderick Davis.

Leroy walked until he was able to catch a tram, watching the people of Mars while he moved closer to his destination. Everyone had their place in the perfect, manmade hive. No one was idle. Everyone was happy, confident. They dressed in similar clothes to one another and looked perfectly content as they went for an evening stroll or watched children play on swings.

It gave Leroy the creeps. Even in U.S. Territory on New Earth, it hadn't been that perfect, that efficient. He'd had to read a book called *The Stepford Wives* at school once, and he thought everyone around him now could be robots.

The palace must be different. He couldn't imagine Shots—or Capri—fitting in out here.

He reached the bar and pushed the door. He admired the wood accents and other luxuries that were plentiful enough on New Earth but didn't often extend to places like this. He'd had it pretty good on New Earth. Traveling on *Task Eternal* had shown him the other side of things—how those on the rebel planets lived—but the Kingdoms were always a step above everyone else. They resembled gated communities, some part of the U.N. so detached they barely had to follow the same rules.

It was never more obvious than here, where the King was allowed to have a harem—and now a prostitute—with no repercussions.

Even now, as he took a seat at the bar and glanced down at the reader the barman provided, there was an advertisement for the King's Auction.

"Lager, thanks," he said when the bartender came to take his order.

He offered the automatic smile that came from years of practice. He'd been the class clown, of course, always ready with a smartass remark and shenanigans. Somebody had to counteract Jax's enduring solemnity. He never knew anything other than being the yang to his brother's yin—even when his brother wasn't there.

The bartender brought the beer, and he promptly downed it.

"Another?" the bartender asked, hand on the empty glass.

Leroy nodded, face brightening as his target appeared at the entrance. "And your fifth-best whiskey on the rocks."

He waved to Tamara and smiled as if he'd known her all his life. The woman, still in uniform, looked behind her to see if the greeting could have been meant for someone else. Her gaze narrowed, turning suspicious, and she approached the mechanic with caution.

"Do I know you?"

"No, but you know Shots."

Tamara backed up a pace. "Are you a newsman? Have you come to shit on his name, too?"

Leroy wasn't sure what to say. He'd been prepared to spend a fair amount of time and drinking money to discover the woman's allegiance. That was another thing to be said for rebels. They were direct.

"No," he said, recomposing himself and getting into the forlorn character he'd expected to have a few hours to ease into. He looked sorrowfully down at his drink. "He is—was?—a crewmate of mine."

Tamara hesitated. Then she seemed to come to a decision and sat down on the stool next to him. She remained tense, on guard, but Leroy didn't think it would take long to convince her that he was a friend.

"Is," she said gruffly, eyeing the untouched whiskey in front of him. He slid it over. She took a sip and continued. "I don't know exactly when he's set to die, but I know he ain't dead yet."

Leroy nodded and took a sip from his own glass, looking down at it once more. Then he glanced at her, as if determining whether or not she could be trusted. "Do you know a Lady named Capri?"

Tamara snorted and took a long sip of her drink. Her nails were well manicured. The whole of her was somehow a meeting of masculine and feminine that he found appealing.

"Everyone knows Lady Capri. Shots is dying for her, ain't he? I'd be surprised if he's the first." Her brown eyes shot up. "Were you on the ship with them, then?"

Leroy couldn't keep the flush from his cheeks, but he nodded calmly. Tamara went back to the drink. "Then you might know what I mean," she said.

The mechanic didn't want to divulge too much, but the observation hit home. He nodded again and took a long sip of beer. It was a struggle for him, it went against his nature, but he had to keep his answers short and sweet.

He also had to be as honest as possible, if he was to be believed. "I do."

Tamara raised her eyebrows in a casual, commiserative salute, and Leroy saw his opening to expose his ulterior motive. "They were in love."

For all he knew, the words were true. The guard's eyes shot up from her glass at that, and suspicion settled itself in her hard features once more.

"I doubt that."

"It's true. I have something of his I think she'd like to have. It might bring her some comfort."

Tamara swirled her drink around in its glass, considering his unspoken request. "I ought to report you, you know," she said.

Leroy was shit when it came to masking his feelings, and he was sure he looked scared. A smile twitched the corner of her mouth. "I won't. If you tell me how it is you knew about me."

As close to the truth as possible, he reminded himself. "I'm good with computers. Shots mentioned you a time or two when he was still at the palace. Seemed like the two of you were at least on good terms."

Tamara glanced at his bag and finished the drink. "What is it you want me to give her?"

He pulled the latch from the front pocket and displayed it on his palm. Tamara took it gingerly between her thumb and forefinger, as if she thought it might explode. "What is it?" she asked again.

"Trust me. It'll mean something to her." He hoped his words were true.

The woman looked hard at him, still trying to make up her mind, but she closed her fingers around the object and slipped it into her pocket. Leroy nodded his gratitude and ordered another round.

Tamara lifted her glass. "To Shots," she said.

"To Shots," Leroy agreed.

***

Leroy returned to the little camper vessel two hours later, legs wobbly and vision blurred. He probably shouldn't have ordered that last beer, but his mission had been accomplished. The next step was in Tamara's hands. He could afford to celebrate.

He only hoped Capri would recognize the latch from the first time they'd met. She was observant, skilled at what made people—men, lovers—tick. She'd understand he was sending her a message and look deeper. She had to. Otherwise, Brody was dead and he'd failed.

He climbed the short, folding stairs that led into the small craft—and stopped dead. Haddaway was seated casually on one of the bottom bunks. Leroy felt a wave of dizziness, and it had nothing to do with the drinking.

Haddaway would know exactly who he was and could guess why he was there. Had Tamara ratted him out after all? Leroy cleared his throat, but his voice cracked slightly.

"I didn't give you permission to board."

A humorless smile touched Haddaway's lips. It didn't make the mechanic feel any better. The other man stood, and Leroy held his breath.

"Leroy," he greeted. "I was glancing through our list of guests on this side of the Kingdom, and your photo caught my attention."

Leroy said nothing, afraid he'd give something away.

"What brings you all the way out here?" Haddaway's gaze was hard, unblinking. He reminded Leroy of a school principal.

"Just had some vacation to burn," he said with as much confidence as he could muster. "Thought I'd come and see the sights."

Haddaway nodded, eyes holding a glint of disappointment. He'd expected a better lie. Leroy felt the blood drain from his face. One word burned in his mind, and the pain was searing—*failure.* This was the end of his solo missions, and it was only his first one.

But Haddaway turned away, hands clasped behind his back, posture impeccable. A military man. Leroy recognized the signs. The older man gazed through the side window at the rest of the dimly lit dock.

"You know Shots will be executed."

Leroy swallowed, forcing his mind back to the present, away from his fears. "I wasn't sure," he lied.

Haddaway nodded, almost approving, but probably just deep in thought. "I expect you aren't here to try and sabotage that."

Leroy snorted, easily digging up his disdain for the gunman to convince the senior officer. "Of course not."

"Good. Because Ekon insists on having tightened security at the memorial, which means I don't have as many guards as I'd like to transfer Shots that night." He turned to Leroy. "If anyone knew that, something could easily go awry."

Leroy stared at the man. Haddaway wasn't an idiot. Why was he telling him this? He forced himself to nod. "He made his choices. He deserves what he gets," Leroy said automatically, not entirely disbelieving the words.

"Good." Haddaway nodded again, turned, and exited the camper.

Leroy stood where he was for a moment, stunned. There was only one explanation for Haddaway's visit and strange behavior: he was on their side.

CHAPTER 48

Capri waited until 9:00 the next morning to enter Marianne's room, knocking out of courtesy before letting herself in. The protégé-to-friends dynamic had worked for her and Briony, but that would never be her and Marianne. Marianne required a firmer hand, and she was happy to give it.

The sound of retching greeted her, and, again, she struggled to ward off sympathy. She had to remember the woman was a monster. Capri held her nose and approached the bed. Marianne looked worse than the previous day. The blond groaned, barely able to keep her eyes open. Her lips were dry. Capri pinched the skin on the back of her hand, and it took a while for it to sink down into the rest of her pale flesh.

She needed care beyond what Capri could provide. She turned to use the phone.

"Infirmary," came a clipped female voice.

"This is Lady Capri. Lady Marianne is very dehydrated and needs to be taken down. She can't walk on her own."

"We'll send a team."

"Thank you."

Capri hung up and turned to find Marianne's narrowed gaze on her, but it was hard to find the other woman threatening with her head lolling against the side of a floral basin.

"I won't go," she croaked.

Capri ignored her and put a cup of water to her lips. She sipped, but it came back up almost immediately. Again, she had to remind herself that Marianne was not to be pitied, even as tears streamed down the other woman's gaunt cheeks, further depleting her resources.

"You have to go," Capri said firmly.

"I do not. People will see. People will know."

"There are already rumors. Some people think you're dead. I don't know why you're so scared. If you don't accept some kind of help, you really will be, and you can attend the memorial service as a corpse."

The woman's nostrils flared slightly, but it was the only sign of annoyance she could muster. Capri touched Marianne's damp forehead as her eyes fluttered shut. She wasn't feverish. Capri wasn't an expert, but she was well-read, and she just couldn't imagine what the condition could be.

A possibility came to her suddenly, and she frowned—maybe she hadn't been the first to consider poisoning Marianne.

The door opened then, breaking into her thoughts, and two medics entered. Capri recognized one as John, the young man who had been assigned to her when she'd returned to Mars. He avoided her gaze, his cheeks pink.

They did a cursory exam, which prompted Marianne to wake up and vomit.

"I won't go," she protested again.

The medics glanced at one another and tried to coax her, but she wouldn't budge. Neither of them seemed keen on taking the King's Favorite by force. A weak woman of her status, thrashing and vomiting her way to the infirmary, was a scene neither wanted to be a part of.

The female medic suddenly rounded on Capri. "Can't you do something?"

Capri shrugged. "Do you really think I hold any sway?"

They finally left an exhausted but triumphant Marianne and went to the sitting area to confer. In the end, they called down to the infirmary and brought the equipment to her.

Once she was hooked to I.V. fluids and an anti-nausea drip, Marianne fell asleep. Capri turned to the female medic, who was packing her bag.

"Hasn't anyone figured out what's wrong with her yet?" she asked.

The medic paused, looking from John back to Capri. "She's pregnant, Lady Capri. It's not widely known, but I thought you would have been informed."

Capri swallowed hard. That was impossible. Precautions were taken. "What do you mean, pregnant? Does Ekon…the King…does he know?"

"Of course he knows."

Capri shook her head, still disbelieving. "But he's not yet forty-five."

The medic shrugged. "I was surprised, as well, but for some reason he's decided to keep this one. Now, as I've said, it's not widely known."

Capri nodded numbly and turned back to her Lady while the medics made their exit. Pregnant. She should have realized. But the King had strict rules. He would choose a Lady—or Ladies—with which to produce an heir next year. Now, she had to consider the fact that she wouldn't only be killing Marianne but also her baby.

She felt the fragile purpose she'd found slipping away. She couldn't do it. She knew she couldn't do it. It meant that, once again, Capri had nothing to distract her from Brody's impending death. She was here, caring for a woman she despised, for no reason whatsoever.

Marianne would get away with everything.

Capri was in a daze, trapped, panicked. She had to get out of there. Tears swam in her eyes as she stumbled from the room. Ekon had to realize that Marianne was manipulating him, that she was quite effectively picking off any Lady who challenged her. Why did he let her do it?

She wasn't sure where she was going, but she needed to move; she needed to do *something.* She found herself at the staircase, and she stumbled down to the next floor, not even glancing at the guard stationed there.

She couldn't think about the cameras, couldn't think about Ekon's increased paranoia. Capri came to a stop in front of her old apartment. She'd never had a guard outside unless she was entertaining a Victor. Marianne had the best apartment in the palace, save for the King's penthouse suite, and required—or at least *believed* she required—additional security.

But there was a guard outside of her old room now. Who exactly was the new occupant?

Capri gave the guard a sideways look, but he didn't stop her from knocking on Briony's door. It took a few moments for the blond to respond. Capri thought she must be attending her new Lady.

At last, her friend's head popped through the door, and Capri tried to smile, tried to act normal. If Briony would only let her in, she'd reveal everything. She needed a friend now more than ever. "Hello," she said.

"Capri!" she said. "It's good to see you. What do you need?"

Her speech was too quick, too impersonal. Something was wrong. Capri's smile wavered. "I was hoping we could talk," she said uncertainly. "I could use a friend."

"I'm sorry, Capri, but my Lady needs me today. Where is yours?"

It was her turn to glance around Capri, as if expecting Marianne to suddenly appear. Maybe that was why she was acting so strange. Maybe she just didn't want to be near Marianne.

"She's sleeping." She imagined the two of them talking over tea. By the end of their chat, Capri would somehow feel okay again, just like she always did. But Briony's expression remained polite, and she kept the door partially closed.

"Who is your new Lady?" Capri asked.

"Oh. Gina."

Capri brightened. "Really? We should have lunch together. I can come back later. We'll go down to the dining hall."

Gina's voice sounded from inside the room. "Briony? Who is that?"

"No one!" Briony called hastily over her shoulder.

When she turned back, Capri was already stepping away.

"Sorry to bother you," she said, hoping her former friend heard the hard edge and not the tremble.

She turned on her heel and walked away before Briony could see the tears in her eyes. She thought she heard a regretful "Capri..." behind her, but she didn't stop.

What had happened? Hadn't they sorted out their differences over the meeting with Ekon? Had Briony simply decided Gina deserved her full dedication? That the friendship they'd shared for four years wasn't worth keeping?

Instead of feeling calmer, more centered, Capri felt more lost than ever. Again, the urge to go down to the prison, to see Brody, to do something, *anything* overtook her. She ducked into the stairwell and made it down one flight before coming to her senses. *No.* She had to wait. She planted her back against the cool wall in the shadows beneath the stairs and finally let her tears fall.

Her self-assurance was all she had left, and she was dangerously close to losing it. After indulging in self-pity for a few moments, she took a deep, gasping breath and wiped at the tears with a long sleeve of her dress. Losing friends would only make it easier to leave, and that was her goal. She should be grateful.

She had to stay focused. She had to trust herself.

She moved to leave her hiding place just as the door on the landing opened. A strong hand shot out, grabbed her arm, and pulled her back into the shadows. In the dim lighting, all she could see was a guard's uniform and blond hair. Fresh terror assaulted her, and she struggled.

"Lady Capri!" The gruff, urgent—but distinctly female—voice reminded her that Sullivan was dead. The guard's eyes were almond-shaped and long-lashed, but the skin was sun-roughened, hair cropped short, lips thin.

Capri recognized her as the guard who had replaced Sullivan, and she waited, one foot pointed toward the door but curiosity holding her fast. Tamara relaxed her hold once she felt confident that Capri wouldn't take off running.

"I have something for you. From Shots."

Capri's heartbeat quickened. "What is it?"

"Some piece of junk, if you ask me. A friend of his said it would mean something to you. I worked with him for a while, and...I liked him. Least I could do for the poor bastard."

She slipped something solid and metal into Capri's hand, and she closed her slender fingers around it. She didn't look at it immediately and grasped Tamara's arm to keep her from leaving, fear and panic rising. It was a last token. Did that mean...?

"Is he dead?" she asked breathlessly.

Tamara shook her head, glancing over her shoulder. "Not yet."

Then she was gone. Capri forced herself to take a deep breath and opened her hand. But instead of finding something to remind her of Brody, she found the latch to the cockpit door of *Task Eternal.* She furrowed her brow. It could only be from Leroy.

Her confusion gave way to excitement. They were here. They had a plan. She held the rectangular object tightly in her hand, anxious to take it back to her room and examine it for clues.

She hesitated on the first stair and glanced around, paranoia creeping in again. She hadn't passed Tamara on her way to Briony's room. How had she known where to find her? If there were cameras, someone should have seen the exchange between them and come to investigate.

The small hairs on the back of her neck stood up, and she shivered. She *wasn't* paranoid. Something strange was going on in the palace. Something new. All she had was instinct, and all her instinct could tell her—for now—was that she needed to be careful.

CHAPTER 49

Once she was safely back in her room, Capri sat on her bed and stared at the metal object in her palm. Her hands shook as she separated the pieces with minimal force.

There were tiny etchings between two rivets. If she hadn't known to look for them, she would have missed them. She dug out a reader that had been shoved in the drawer of her vanity and held it over the deconstructed latch. Using her thumb and forefinger, she enlarged the image until she could read the words: *Doc's. Tues. 23:00.*

They'd come. She'd see them again. The joy and relief she felt was so overwhelming she thought her heart might burst. Her emotions were fried, and tears fell again easily. She tried to stay quiet. If anyone here discovered she'd found a shred of hope, they'd find some way to snatch it away.

A bell rang nearby, signaling that Marianne was awake and required her presence. Capri tucked the reader back into the drawer and hid the latch in the box with the aconite. She took a moment to look in the bathroom mirror, to wipe her face with a cool cloth and compose herself. Her hazel eyes were red from crying, her face drawn and tired from the emotional toll of the day.

She doubted Marianne would notice. She was too deep in her own misery. Capri took a steadying breath. She had a new challenge now: meet Leroy without getting caught. Considering she couldn't take ten steps without someone knowing exactly where she was, it wouldn't be an easy task. But at least she was finally able to act.

***

Capri had decided to leave the palace through the warehouse, the way she had with Brody on the night of the shooting. Her other choices were the bustling front doors of the palace, and she was not confident in her ability to hide in plain sight, or the private entrance she'd used after returning to Mars, which was perhaps more heavily guarded than the main doors.

In the warehouse, there was enough activity to provide some cover but not enough to require fooling many people, and she could choose from two points of entry: through the storeroom, which she'd already decided was an obvious trap, or the side hall, where Brody had taken her. It also helped that she'd experienced escaping this way once before.

A lot of things had to go right, and that meant she needed a plan—and a disguise.

She walked with purpose down to the kitchens wearing a shift dress, the plainest garment she owned. Her hair was in a messy bun with strands hanging strategically in front of her eyes to mask the fact that she was anything other than a servant. The kitchen workers would know her, but she didn't need to fool them. She only needed to fool the cameras.

A girl, maybe fifteen years old, greeted her at the door this time. She was new and flushed with the excitement of being so close to one of the King's Ladies.

"Can I help you?"

"I need ginger snaps for my Lady."

The girl turned toward the storeroom, eager to assist, but Capri stopped her.

"I don't want to interrupt you," she said quickly, trying to exude an air of authority. "I know where they are."

The girl hesitated and then stepped aside with a timid smile.

"Thank you," Capri said, and then, to cinch the girl's loyalty: "You're very pretty, you know."

The girl's round face turned bright red, and she laughed in surprise. Then the head of the kitchen called sharply to her, and she scurried away to stir something. Capri released the breath she'd been holding and slipped into the storeroom. She took a spare hat and apron and hid them beneath her dress. She grabbed the ginger snaps, so as not to raise suspicion, and left the way she'd come.

There was a second door in the stairwell, and it led to the hallway she planned to use, the one reserved for busy chefs, bakers, runners, and servers. She pressed her ear against the door and waited for the sounds of movement to subside. When she was sure no one was watching, she donned the hat and apron and pushed it open.

If no one looked too closely she could pass for the girl from the kitchen.

Capri walked confidently along the shelves of dry goods and grabbed a bag of sugar, keeping an eye out for something that would help her get to the warehouse exit the next evening. If her outfit fooled the cameras now, the same method should work again.

She found what she was looking for on one of the forklifts: a hat that was part of the official uniform of the palace warehouse workers. She tucked it into the apron and hurried back, keeping her head down and nodding as someone else came through the door. She didn't look at them, afraid they'd realize she was an imposter.

Capri took a deep breath, held on to the bag of sugar for dear life, and made it through. The person didn't pause. Then she hurried to the door that led to the stairs, glanced behind her to make sure no one else was in the passageway, and removed the hat and apron. She left the bag of sugar in a corner.

She tucked the disguises neatly beneath her dress, and no one tried to stop her as she returned to her room. With each step she took, relief and triumph replaced apprehension.

The first part of her plan had been a success—or so she thought.

Haddaway was leaning against the wall beside her door, waiting for her. Capri swallowed a wave of despair. Maybe he was there for another reason. The look in his eyes, however, told her he'd recognized her in the warehouse. She wouldn't meet Leroy, after all. Brody would die. She might be headed for a concrete cell herself.

She forced her feet forward and made her face an emotionless mask. She wouldn't crack, wouldn't make it easy for him. He'd have to admit he was monitoring the Ladies.

"Haddaway," she greeted coolly. "What can I do for you?"

"Why don't we talk inside?" he suggested.

Capri hesitated. Her eyes slid to the door of her room and then back to him. She knew by now what happened when she was alone with a man. Haddaway seemed to know where her mind was, and his expression softened. Capri wasn't sure which was worse, the fact that deep down she was still a scared little Maiden or that he pitied her for it. She nodded quickly, attempting to disguise her emotions with impatience, and ushered him in.

One corner of the small room was designated as a sitting area with two chairs and a small table, and she gestured for him to sit. Then she turned her back, poured one glass of wine and one of water, slipped her burdens discreetly into the drawer beside the corkscrew, and regained her composure.

Haddaway accepted the water with a nod of thanks. His gray eyes never left her; they were watching, searching, dissecting. She remained on guard, sitting still and silent in the opposite chair, waiting for him to speak.

"What were you doing in the warehouse today?"

Anger flared. It was the confirmation she'd been searching for.

"Helping the kitchen staff," she said, daring him with her eyes to press her.

Haddaway raised an eyebrow, like a parent waiting for a child to confess the truth. Maybe it was the same look he used on his own children. Maybe it was effective in his house. But they weren't in his house, she was no ordinary young woman, and his look only incited her.

"Where are they, Haddaway?" she asked, gripping her glass until her knuckles were white. There *had* to be cameras. He couldn't deny it anymore. Still, for a moment, he only watched her.

"You two are more alike than I realized," he said at last in a quiet voice. "You're both just looking for a hold, aren't you?"

Capri's fire went out. Of course he was talking about Brody, and his words only drove home that fact that she would never see the gunman again. It had been his plan all along, to take her somewhere and leave her, for her to be without him. Despite herself, despite *him*, he'd managed to steal a piece of her heart.

Haddaway would extinguish the last of her hope.

"Where are they?" she asked again, pleading.

"I don't know what you're talking about." Haddaway looked her in the eye, confused, convincing, but he *had* to be lying. "I'm just here to remind you that for your safety, you must stay in the confines of the palace."

Capri snorted and downed half the glass of wine in one gulp. "Bullshit."

Haddaway stood, but he didn't leave. "What is it you think you know, Capri?"

"I'm being watched."

"There are no cameras, Capri."

She glanced up at him, unimpressed with the lie. Again, his face betrayed nothing, and she narrowed her eyes. "I'm not an idiot. I'm not paranoid."

"No, you're not," Haddaway agreed. Maybe he was only trying to appease her. "How have you been feeling, by the way?"

Capri looked up from her wine, the sudden change in topic making her suspicious. "Fine."

"Good. The vaccine is doing its job."

"Is there some health crisis I should know about?"

"No." Haddaway shook his head, a cryptic smile touching his lips. "Enjoy the rest of your day, Lady Capri. And stay put."

He left. Capri remained where she was, sipping the rest of her wine, trying to make sense of the strange conversation. He hadn't searched her or the room. He hadn't mentioned the things she'd stolen from the kitchen and the warehouse. She sat up suddenly, an icy chill creeping up her spine.

He didn't know about the hats and the apron. He didn't know about the aconite or the message from Leroy.

They couldn't *see* her. They just knew where she was. At all times.

The vaccine. All the ladies had received one, just after Capri was taken. A precaution, they'd said, against any viruses she might bring back with her.

She pulled her dress off quickly and stood in front of the full-length mirror, examining the tender flesh of her upper right arm where she'd received the injection. She pressed down on the skin with her fingertips, searching for...she wasn't sure what, exactly, but she found it. A small, hard bump beneath her skin.

She had to get it out—Capri knew that much—and she'd have to do it herself, in secret. She forced air into her lungs, breathing deeply until the shock subsided enough for her to form a plan.

She dressed again and opened the door to Marianne's room. Her lady was still sleeping soundly. Capri moved silently to the prep kitchen behind the table where Marianne ate with Ekon. The small space had everything a chef might need—including a set of very sharp knives.

Capri examined the steel blade of a paring knife, and her stomach turned. It would be a small price to pay for freedom. With luck, it could mean Brody's freedom, too.

She wrapped the object in a clean napkin and slipped back to her room, making sure the hall door was locked. Then she stripped down to her underwear and marked the bump with a calligraphy pen. She inspected the knife for cleanliness and could put it off no longer.

Everything felt hazy. Adrenaline pumped through her, making her heart beat at an alarming rate. Her hands trembled. It felt as if her reflection belonged to someone else. All she could think of was the bullet when it had been cut out of her, the sounds of her own screaming. But this object was small, skin-deep, more akin to a splinter.

Another memory surfaced. Her father, taking a needle to her finger, the point black where he'd burned it to sterilize it. She didn't remember her father well, but she remembered she'd trusted him. She'd trusted him enough to hold still and let him pluck a sliver of wood from her small finger.

She should trust herself as much.

She closed her eyes, took a steadying breath, and then looked at her arm. *Now or never.* She placed the tip of the knife against her skin and pressed down. The sharp blade went deeper than she'd intended, and she winced—but the worst was over. She laid the knife on the napkin and pressed firmly on the injured flesh until a trickle of blood ran down her arm.

A tiny glass capsule emerged through the incision. She held the tracking device in her palm. It was the size of a grain of rice, so unassuming, yet so very sinister.

Capri remained transfixed for a moment on the translucent shell, the copper wiring. The betrayal. Then she wiped the knife clean, placed it in her vanity drawer, and used the napkin to stop the bleeding. She tightened a ribbon around her arm using her teeth, and then she chose a new dress, one with long sleeves. No one would notice the wound—at least not yet.

She placed the napkin in the garbage chute and turned to the last piece of evidence that needed dealing with: the tracker.

There was a locket that Ekon had given her the day she'd moved up to the Maiden Dormitory. It was tradition—everyone received the same silver locket with the King's portrait inside. She hadn't liked the weight of it, the chain around her neck, so she hadn't worn it often. Some kept it under their pillow for luck or tucked it safely in a drawer. Some wore it regularly, hoping the King would notice their devotion.

She found hers in a box in the back of the closet, and she placed the tracker inside, behind the portrait of the man who had placed the foreign object in her arm to control her. She clasped the chain around her neck, slipped the heart into the front of her dress, and let down her hair. She looked at herself in the mirror. She was pale and shaky, but otherwise no one would know the small but heavy weight she carried.

Regret squeezed Capri's heart. She knew that every other Lady— maybe even the children and Maidens—had had their privacy invaded in the same way. But she couldn't tell them. She could say nothing, at least not yet, or she would compromise her own mission.

She needed to meet with Leroy and free Brody. Maybe she'd even manage to free herself.

What would she do when she left Mars? She'd asked Brody that question, and he hadn't been able to give her an answer. He'd made it clear he thought she couldn't survive the life he led. But the answer came to her now, as if it had always been there. She would do exactly what she'd suggested to Haddaway in the garden. Go to the U.N. Expose Ekon. They couldn't know about the trackers. If they did, they wouldn't stand for it.

If Capri made it out, she'd tell them everything.

CHAPTER 50

Leroy chose a table in the corner of the bar to wait for Capri. He wore cargo pants and the cleanest shirt he owned. His leg bounced, and his eyes moved from his beer glass to the door, over and over, until he was sure he had to look unhinged. His chest felt tight. He kept forgetting to breathe.

Capri had made her choice clear. She'd even thanked him for not having expectations. But he couldn't help the feeling of anticipation, like he wasn't waiting for help with an important mission but for a date to arrive.

The door opened, and his breath caught. Capri's dress was simple, A-line. She wore a hood and the boots she'd acquired on her voyage with the crew. She was trying to look ordinary, but her curse—the curse of all Ladies—was that they never really could. One look at those silky brown curls and stunning eyes, and she would attract attention.

She saw him, and relief flooded her face. She walked so fast she was nearly running, and Leroy barely managed to stand up in time to catch her. He closed his eyes for a moment and held her tightly. He let himself pretend, just for a moment, that she belonged to him.

When she pulled away, there were tears in her eyes. Her voice trembled. "I wasn't sure I'd see you again."

He bit his lip to keep his soaring heart in place. She was speaking only as a friend. He smiled and glanced around, but no one had taken notice of them. She seemed to remember then that they were on a covert mission and sat down across from him.

"Is everything okay?" he asked.

"No," she replied. "Ekon's lost his mind. He implanted trackers in us."

"What? Were you followed?" Leroy glanced around, looking for uniformed guards.

"No. I was tipped off before I left."

Leroy released his breath. He'd never felt this much responsibility before, and he wasn't sure he wanted to again. There was so much at stake—and more variables than he'd realized. "That's lucky."

"It is."

Leroy realized the implication very suddenly. "Wait, *in* you?"

Capri swallowed and looked down at the reader in front of her. It would remain blank until she touched it. "Yes. I got it out."

"Shit." He looked around the table, searching for something encouraging and sympathetic to say instead of his usual bullshit. He could think of nothing. He slid his beer her way. "You need this more than I do."

Capri laughed before raising the glass to her lips, and Leroy felt relieved. Maybe his bullshit was exactly what she needed.

"So what's the plan?" Capri asked.

Leroy fought a grimace. "You know he's supposed to…"

"…die," Capri finished, and her expression turned eerily blank to keep her pain from showing. She chugged the rest of the beer and set the glass down on the table.

"Yeah. That. Haddaway came to me, and he told me security will be light during the memorial. He'll be transferred from his cell at 7:00pm."

Capri nodded, thinking she understood what he needed. "I'll find a way to get you guys in."

Leroy gave her a lopsided grin, almost apologetic. She had no idea what he was about to ask. "It's just me. Jax and the captain will come later with *Task Eternal* to act as decoys. We need *you* to get him out."

"Oh." Leroy watched as surprise, fear, doubt, and finally determination flashed in her eyes. When she spoke again, her voice was steady. "Okay."

"I made you a stun gun," Leroy continued, producing a small, rectangular box from his pocket. "Just press this button and shove it somewhere soft. Whoever gets the shock will drop."

She reached out, hand hovering over the object for a moment before she took it and slipped it into her pocket. She looked at him again, awaiting further instructions.

"It's not enough to knock them out," he said. "How do you feel about inflicting head wounds?"

Capri swallowed and looked mildly queasy at the suggestion. "Not good."

"Then it'll have to be a drug. Propofol. Ketamine. Midazolam."

"I'll get my hands on something from the infirmary."

"Great. Once you get to him, he'll know the best way out."

She nodded. "I'll do my best."

Leroy smiled wanly. "I know you will."

The words came out sadder than he'd intended, and she noticed. Her cheeks turned pink, but she reached across the table and squeezed his hand. As she pulled back, she brushed against the reader, and it turned on. An advertisement appeared for the King's Auction. Her face turned white, and she wobbled dangerously in her chair. Leroy shot forward to grab her arm, but she waved him away.

"I'm okay," she said, but her voice was a gasp.

"What is it?" he asked, glancing down at the ad with her. "You don't need to be embarrassed. We knew you'd be...back to that again."

He shrugged to show her it didn't make a difference to him.

"I'm not," she whispered.

Leroy hadn't been expecting that. "Oh."

She stood suddenly. "I have to go."

He wanted to stop her, but they'd discussed all they needed to. He couldn't hold her. She checked that her hood was in place and then turned back to him.

"I'll get him out," she said, with more confidence than she'd shown before. She attempted a smile. "Maybe one day I'll make it out, too."

Then she was gone, before Leroy could tell her he'd take her wherever she wanted to go.

CHAPTER 51

Capri hurried back to the palace in a daze. She'd found a tram heading in the right direction and hopped on the back, keeping her head down and alighting a few blocks from her destination.

She had to take every precaution until she was safe within the palace walls again. She had to stay focused, even as shock, hurt, and anger coursed through her.

It had been naïve to think the auction would end with her. She'd been a valuable source of income. She knew now why Briony had avoided her, why she'd kept Gina away from her. She was trying to keep it a secret, to save Capri the anguish of knowing that her own role hadn't changed in the slightest. Briony would teach Gina to entertain rich men and women, all of whom would have different tastes and expectations, in the name of the King.

Briony would teach her, and the next Prize, and the one after that.

Gina didn't deserve that future. None of them did. But now it was crystal clear that there would always be a sacrificial lamb in Ekon's flock—because they were disposable, and he was greedy.

Capri forced her mind to quiet as the docks came into view. Getting out had been easy enough. Getting in would depend on confidence and luck, like much of her life so far. She took a deep breath, relaxed the muscles in her face and shoulders, and pulled back her hood. She tilted her chin up and adopted an air of regal authority as she approached the guard at the footpath entrance.

There were two ways into the palace: the front gate and the docks. She was counting on the likelihood that the guards stationed at the docks hadn't been briefed on the tracking devices. The fewer people who knew about the devices, the less chance there would be of a leak, she reasoned. The guard looked bored until he caught sight of her.

He shifted a bit so he was more upright. His cheeks turned pink.

"I'd like to come in," she said.

The young man's brow furrowed. "I can't do that without seeing proper identification."

"You know me," Capri said, and he glanced around, as if hoping someone else would come along to share the responsibility. Then he squinted.

"Lady Capri," he said finally. "The one who was taken."

She nodded.

"You aren't supposed to leave the palace."

"Well, I did," she said briskly. "And now you need to let me back in."

"I'll need to run this by—"

He reached up to touch his linker, and Capri cut him off. "If you tell anyone about this, I will tell them you let me out."

He looked stunned. "They won't believe you."

"Are you willing to take that chance?"

He paused, considering, and Capri took a gentler tone to smooth the feathers she'd ruffled. "I'm only trying to get back to where I belong. No one will be the wiser, and you'll get home on time instead of sitting in an interview room—or worse."

"Go," he grunted.

"Thank you."

She replaced her hood and walked through the docks until she found a truck heading for the warehouse. She hopped on the back of it, concealing her body behind boxes, and placed the stolen hat on her head for good measure. Once inside, she employed her trick of passing for a kitchen worker, grabbed another bag of sugar, and entered the walkway.

Capri took off the hat and apron and made to go through the door to the stairs. She was almost safe, if she could retrieve the necklace before any guards saw her and realized she wasn't where the tracker indicated.

But the door opened, and the large, round figure of the night cook blocked her way. He eyed the burdens in her arms, a clear sign she'd been up to something. "What are you doing here?"

Capri's mind was racing. She could go through the kitchen rather than the stairwell, but it was almost guaranteed someone would see her and call the guards. She wouldn't risk the plan failing and Brody dying. The cook knew who she was, knew her former role, and was pathetically easy to read. She knew what he'd ask for in return for his silence. She dragged her eyes back to his beady blue ones, waiting for him to say it.

"Decided to take a little tour of the warehouse, huh?" he asked, sneering. Again, she didn't speak, and his eyes narrowed to slits. "The guards don't have to find out."

He looked pointedly at her chest. She slipped her hand into her pocket and felt the comforting weight of the stun gun.

"Let's go, then."

He moved forward, and she took a step back, trying to hide her sudden burst of fear. She shook her head, relying on his eagerness to control him.

"I'll take you to my room. You'll want the full experience of bedding a Lady."

He paused, and she could see his tiny mind working. He'd have an even better story to tell his friends if he did as she suggested. He nodded, and she led him to the stairs. She paused at the second-floor landing, and he looked at her with suspicion.

"We'll take the far elevator," she said. "But I need you to distract the guard."

He nodded and went through the door ahead of her. She couldn't hear what he said to the guard, but when he beckoned her through, he was gone. One obstacle down.

On their left was the entrance to the botanical gardens, and another guard stood outside of the doors. She walked a few paces and then ducked suddenly behind a pillar, feigning a sudden change of heart.

"I'm sorry," she whispered. "I can't."

"Oh, you're gonna," he growled, and he leaned forward, threatening with all his body language to take her then and there.

She jammed the stun gun into his groin and let him drop into the hallway. The guard's hurried footsteps approached, and she snuck around the pillar, hurried down the hall, and entered the gardens. He might tell the guards she'd been the source of his injury, but she doubted he'd be stupid enough to let Ekon know his dick had been so close to a Lady—even a ruined one.

Besides, her tracking device would show she'd been in the garden the whole time.

The locket was buried in a hidden grove that was popular for meditation and yoga. She dug it up quickly and slipped it around her neck. Relief made her knees weak, but she stayed standing. To anyone who was tracking her, it would look as if she'd had an extended stay in the gardens.

Now that she was safely back in the palace with the locket around her neck, she let her focus shift to the information she'd discovered at the bar. She balled her hands into fists and went to the elevators, ignoring the medical team crouching over the fallen cook. She got off on the fourth floor and headed straight for Briony's door.

She knocked sharply. There was no answer. Her former Attending Lady was probably sleeping, but Capri knocked on the door again, demanding her attention. After a few moments, it slid open, just a little. Briony's expression changed from one of annoyance to one of surprise—and guilt. Capri recognized it now. But even as her cheeks turned pink, her mouth formed a thin line of resolve.

"It's not a good time, Capri. The memorial is in just two days, and we—"

"I know what you've been hiding from me."

Briony's eyes widened, and she opened her mouth as if to protest.

"Don't," Capri said. She couldn't stand being lied to again.

Briony's shoulders slumped, and she opened the door fully. Capri entered and dropped into the familiar sofa near Briony's digital window. It was raining against the pretend pane; the sound of it floated from speakers nearby, the air smelled of it.

She found herself wondering what real rain was like. She wasn't sure she remembered. Snow, wind, sleet—she wanted to know it all now. The desire for freedom was a hunger pain, gnawing and insistent.

"How did you find out?" Briony asked, sitting down on the other end of the sofa.

"Does it matter? You knew I would."

"I knew it would upset you."

"I was more upset when I believed my only two friends wanted nothing to do with me."

"Oh, Capri." Briony moved closer and reached out to squeeze her hand. "I'm sorry."

"Ekon has gone too far," Capri said, looking down at their still-joined hands.

The blond's brow furrowed, and she lifted Capri's fingers to examine them more closely. There was dirt from the garden beneath her nails, and she pulled away before Briony could begin asking questions.

"What does Gina think of all this?" she asked. "Is she alright?"

Briony shrugged. "She's only had one Victor so far, and she wasn't...traumatized beforehand, as you were. She's doing the King a service, and he's rewarding her well."

"Was it the scarring?" Capri asked bitterly. "Ladies can no longer have a single imperfection?"

Briony's smile was half-hearted. "We never could. You know that."

Capri pursed her lips, tamping down her anger.

"He did have her first, shortly after I was appointed her Lady," Briony continued. "It's part of what's kept her so agreeable, I think."

"He can't keep doing this," Capri said fiercely. "Having his 'collection' is bad enough, but this...The U.N. can't possibly support turning the palace into a brothel."

"I doubt they know anything about it. The Prize's identity is anonymous to outsiders, so even if they caught wind of the auction, they wouldn't know it was someone different, and they won't make a fuss over one girl. Anyone who knows the truth won't report it. They'd risk the same fate as Alexander or your Brody."

Pain lanced through Capri, but she forced it back with a grimace. "He's not 'my' Brody."

"You know what I mean." Briony's voice softened. "I can't say I thought I was doing the right thing by not telling you. I was waiting for the right moment, for a sign, for *something*. It never came. I should have been braver. I'm sorry."

A knock sounded on the door, and the two women glanced at each other. Most people were in bed at this hour. Capri was reminded of her recent, unauthorized outing. What if Haddaway had been lying? What if there were cameras after all? A second tracking device? What if the cook had opened his mouth, or the guard from the docks?

If Briony noticed her anxiety, she said nothing. She opened the door to find a guard standing on the other side. Capri held her breath, and then he held out a folded note with a familiar seal. It was for her. She squeezed her hands into fists a couple of times to stop them from trembling, and she took the note with a nod of thanks.

She read through it and breathed a sigh of relief. It had nothing to do with her.

"I have to go," she told Briony. "We'll talk later?"

Her friend nodded. "Of course."

Capri nodded in return and left to go back to her own small apartment. She was still hurt, but at least they were on their way to mending.

CHAPTER 52

Capri waited until the next morning to reveal the note's contents to Marianne. Thanks to the medication, she had been sleeping soundly when Capri returned to her room. Once she felt confident she hadn't been missed, she fell into her own bed.

Too soon, she woke to the sound of a bell ringing, did a quick check of her hair, and put on a robe. Capri was still exhausted from her adventure outside of the palace and the confrontation with Briony; all she wanted was to go back to sleep. But Marianne—and the note—wouldn't wait.

The blond was sitting at her vanity with the lights on. For the first time, she'd pulled back the curtains on her digital window, which stretched from floor to ceiling on the wall beside her bed. The scene was of a bright sunrise over a lush, green jungle. It might have been a wild planet like Alcatraz, or it might have been a scene from Old Earth. The Amazon, she thought it had been called.

A lot of Ladies liked the windows. Even though they were on a giant, floating spaceship, they could fool themselves into thinking they were anywhere. It was no longer enough for Capri.

Marianne was also dressed in a robe, applying some kind of face cream. She was still pale, and her hand shook, but she was able to function. The PICC line remained in her arm. If she couldn't hold down food and drink today, she would be hooked up again.

"There you are," she said with a brief glance in Capri's direction. "I need a bath, and send for more ginger tea and snaps."

"You must be feeling better."

Marianne laughed, but the sound ended in a grimace. "I have to try, or the medical team will never leave me alone."

"You're attending the memorial, then?" Capri asked as she threw some discarded clothing and bedding into a basket.

Marianne glared at her in the mirror. "I've already spoken with Ekon. He knows I'm in no condition to go."

"My instructions haven't changed."

The blond snorted. "I don't care about that. You might be reprimanded, but he won't touch me."

Capri pursed her lips. It would be easier to slip out the following evening with Marianne out of the way. She felt a brief pang of disappointment. She had wanted to attend the memorial, too, to give Lady Agatha and the others a proper sendoff—but when made to choose between the dead and the living, the living had to win out. For now, Brody still fell into the latter category.

"Ekon will touch you, either way," Capri informed Marianne, leaning casually against a sturdy bedpost.

Marianne turned in her chair, suspicion in her brown gaze. "What is that supposed to mean?"

She held up the note and raised an eyebrow, leaving no room for her to doubt the note's contents. Marianne stood to grab it and read the schooled handwriting. Her eyes widened in disbelief. "He can't. I can't. It will kill me."

"Then tell him no," Capri suggested lightly.

"And risk losing everything?" Marianne retorted. "I don't expect *you* to understand. You haven't had him the way the rest of us have. You've never had the pleasure of his company. Of his *favor.*"

Capri nearly revealed everything she knew. Her exhaustion made her volatile. It was Marianne's fault she'd never been a proper Lady, and now she had the gall to stand there and degrade her for it.

"I *have* had him."

Her comment had the desired effect. Marianne froze. "Liar."

"It's true," Capri said. "And as the only other Lady who has ever bedded other men, I can tell you with absolute certainty that *the pleasure of his company* is mediocre at best."

Marianne slapped her. If the blond had been at full strength, she might have tasted blood. Capri was too pleased to have gotten under Marianne's skin to feel offended.

She gave her Lady a terse smile. "I'll run your bath."

***

They didn't speak of the incident again, and the following morning Marianne wasn't able to speak much at all. Capri found her throwing up again. She called the medical staff to give her fluids, but she declined the anti-nausea drip on her Lady's behalf.

"It makes her feel worse," Capri insisted.

The medics protested, but she held her ground. She needed the excuse to visit the infirmary.

The fluids provided enough relief that Marianne slept, leaving Capri to her own devices again. Tonight was the night, and despite outward appearances, her stomach was in knots.

Capri stood in her room, toying with the locket around her neck. There were three parts of the plan to save Brody. They all needed to go smoothly, and they all relied on her. She had no one to talk to. Though Briony, unknowingly, had a part to play, she couldn't speak to her about it. Their friendship was still strained. The timeline was too tight.

She forced herself to push back the feeling of loneliness, to stop worrying and start acting before Marianne woke up. She went down to the infirmary and approached the medic at the front desk.

"My Lady Marianne needs some anti-nausea medication."

The woman smiled politely and nodded. "Of course. Let me just check her records and find something suitable."

She disappeared through a sliding door, and Capri caught a glimpse of what lay beyond: storage closets, mostly, and no other people that she could see. She was the only one in the waiting room, which she'd been counting on. Illness was rare in the palace. She had a rare insight into the workings of the infirmary and knew there were no guards within, only medics.

Why waste resources protecting the medicine on the inside when it was so carefully guarded on the outside? By the time Ekon discovered a reason to increase security, it would be her doing, and the task would be complete.

Capri hid her locket beneath a cushion and stepped boldly through the same door as the medic. She'd just found the closet of sedatives when she heard footsteps. She hid inside the door, fingers on the vials of propofol, trying not to breathe. The waiting room door opened. The woman stepped out, paused, and then came back, passing by the closet again.

Once the footsteps retreated, Capri hurried out to the small waiting area, grabbed the locket, and hid in the bathroom until the medic returned to her post.

The vials and a syringe were tucked safely in a hidden pocket of her dress, and she could only hope their absence wouldn't be noticed until Brody was free. She straightened her hair and clothes and stepped out.

"I was wondering where you went," the woman said pleasantly enough.

Capri smiled apologetically. "Sorry. Bad timing."

She took the medicine with a quick thanks and went straight back to her room. All that remained now was to execute Brody's rescue.

CHAPTER 53

Capri had never been to a memorial service before. She looked in her closet for something suitable, something bold and beautiful. It had to appear as if she had every intention of attending this celebration of life, down to the last detail. She chose her own ensemble and went to Marianne's room to choose hers.

This time, she had no qualms about waking the sleeping beauty. The mark on her cheek was still visible. Their mutual animosity lay out in the open.

"Rise and shine, Marianne," she said, turning on the lights.

Marianne hissed and hid under her pillow, like a vampire trying to block out the sun.

"Go away," she commanded.

"No. I have medicine for you."

Marianne grudgingly accepted the pills and a glass of water. Capri went to her Lady's closet to sort through options for her meeting with Ekon. She turned to get the blond's opinion, but she'd fallen asleep again.

Capri sighed and decided to let her rest a while longer.

She had known this would be the worst part of the day. She had nothing to do for hours and so much riding on her actions later. Capri ate a small lunch in her room, went for a walk in the garden, and tried not to think too much. She couldn't concentrate long enough to read.

The other Ladies and courtiers were busy with last-minute details and gossip. Capri had the halls and gardens mostly to herself. Finally, she'd wasted enough time that it was late afternoon, and she could once again attempt to wake Marianne and dress her.

"I don't like any of these," she said, waving a hand at the three choices laid out on the bed before her. She hadn't even looked at them. Capri had chosen a red ball gown, a slinky black dress, and a dark blue number layered in embroidered tulle. The last choice would have been especially flattering.

Capri gathered her patience and hung the last dress back in the closet. She pulled it out again, and this time Marianne curtly nodded her approval. Capri bit her tongue and helped her Lady dress. Her color was better since she'd rested and rehydrated, but she was still too skinny. Her knees trembled as she stood to allow Capri to shimmy the fabric up her long legs, slip the sheer fabric over her arms, and close a hidden zipper.

Capri wasn't sure how she'd make it through Ekon's visit.

She immersed herself in her work at Marianne's vanity, applying the woman's makeup, pinning her thick hair into a low bun at the nape of her neck, and choosing a pair of teardrop earrings and sandals to complete the look. For that hour, she was Capri's canvas and nothing more. She put all the effort into her that she would have into any masterpiece.

Marianne looked herself over, searching for something to criticize, but she could only nod again—acceptance and dismissal. Capri was nearly through the adjoining door, mind already on getting herself dressed and completing her mission, when Marianne's voice stopped her.

"Capri." The tone was cool and familiar, a sure sign that Marianne believed she was about to deliver a scathing blow to an opponent. Capri bristled, ready to defend, but she waited obediently to hear what her Lady had to say. "What would you do in my position?"

The question was unexpected, and she proceeded with caution. "What do you mean?"

"Would you really have the King bed another woman? Risk falling out of his favor after you'd worked so hard to gain it?"

Capri paused. The energy between them warned that this was some kind of trap. She tried to keep her response vague and neutral. "He always seems to come back to you, doesn't he?"

Marianne nodded. The blow never came, but there was something strong and sinister about her. She looked very regal indeed, thanks to Capri's hard work. "You may be right. Thank you."

A shiver ran down Capri's spine. She turned to go again, but again Marianne's voice stopped her. "I'll ask him to dismiss you after tonight."

"Good," Capri replied, her mind already back on the task at hand.

She closed the door and focused on making herself look presentable—no, *stunning*. Stunning distracted. Stunning was rarely questioned. She donned a striking empire gown with a black corset top and green satin skirt. There was a high slit in the thick, cool fabric, but the floor-length style and wide bow in the back kept it just in the category of eveningwear rather than lingerie.

She left her hair loose but made sure each curl was perfect. She fought the part of her that knew stilettos would look best and settled on a pair of black, low-heel ankle boots. The rest of her ensemble would make up for the necessary faux pas.

She was just putting the finishing touches on her makeup when she heard Ekon in the next room. She paused. They'd be eating now—or, at least, *he* would. Marianne would settle for a sip or two of soda water. The voices were quiet at first, murmurous, seductive. Then they grew louder.

Maybe Marianne was putting her foot down, after all.

Capri ignored them, rubbing oil on her arms and chest in a thin layer, making her skin scented and supple. In just a few minutes, she could leave the room and go upstairs to Briony without drawing suspicion. Most attendees would arrive early. Even if Marianne came looking for her, her absence from the adjacent room wouldn't be suspicious.

She placed a silver armband over each wound and was still clasping the eye hooks on her bodice when the door to Marianne's room burst open. Ekon stood there, looking wild, shirt pulled apart and pants undone. Capri's surprise was replaced with a familiar fear.

She stared at him, wide-eyed, waiting for him to speak. She kept her hands over her top, shielding her breasts from view.

"Don't act so shy," Ekon said, voice disturbingly controlled despite his appearance.

Capri glanced over his shoulder. Marianne stood there, smiling triumphantly.

"You've let our secret slip."

She didn't answer him. There was nothing to say. Capri remembered their conversation from when he'd appointed her to this position with disturbing clarity. She waited like prey in the face of a predator, itching to run but unsure of which direction to take. So, like prey, she would waste too much time in indecision and die in the end.

"No matter," he murmured. He removed his shirt and took a step forward. Capri held her ground, but inside she was screaming. *Not again, not again.* "Marianne tells me you've volunteered to take her place tonight."

The other woman still watched them, arms folded, a smirk on those thin, dry lips that appeared so full and lush thanks to Capri's handiwork. She felt the betrayal like a knife—quick and painful. She'd never trusted Marianne, but she'd stupidly believed she was no longer a threat. Once again, she'd underestimated her. Once again, Marianne would be the cause of her pain and humiliation.

Anger and hatred filled the wound. Baby or no, Marianne didn't deserve to live.

Capri's eyes slid back to Ekon's, even as she knew it was hopeless, even as she knew she no longer had any hold over him. "There's been a misunderstanding."

"How unfortunate," he replied. "However, I require a bedmate, and I'm eager to prove my capabilities to you. I believe I've learned some new tricks that might satisfy you."

His eyes locked on hers, and any sliver of hope she'd had of escaping the situation vanished. He'd been rejected by Marianne and made to feel inferior by Capri's own stupid words—likely thrown in his face by the blond during their argument.

He was out of control and angry on many levels, and he would win this battle of wills. Their eyes remained locked as he pulled his erection through the flap of his pants and stroked it once, twice.

"On your knees," he commanded.

Capri clenched and unclenched her fists. Her first instinct was no longer to succumb. She wanted to fight. She wanted to claw Ekon's eyes out with her freshly manicured nails and then go for the other woman's throat. Marianne seemed determined to watch, to witness her rival's humiliation for herself this time.

Maybe Capri could do it. Maybe she could win. But she didn't have the time.

This could be done in a matter of minutes, and then she'd still be able to catch Briony before she and Gina left for the memorial.

She could still free Brody. She'd come this far—too far—to let her pride stand in the way now. She forced herself to remember the bigger picture.

She obeyed her King.

She knelt down and opened her mouth. He was rough, unforgiving, punishing. He grabbed her freshly styled hair and pulled. Tears welled in Capri's eyes. Her heartbeat was fast and erratic, like the organ was trying to jump out of her chest to save itself.

She felt dizzy and ashamed—and angry. A vision of Brody flashed in her mind, and with it came a flood of emotion. He was always angry. If he ever found out about this, he would be angrier still. If he found out the reasons, he'd feel guilty.

She could save them both the trouble if she would just *act.*

She came to life—the prey in the predator's claws—and she bit down. Ekon screamed, a strangled sound, and he jerked back, removing himself from her mouth. She only had a moment of sweet relief before he raised his hand above his shoulder and brought the back of it down against her cheek.

This time, Capri did taste blood. His palm hit her other cheek with a hard slap, and he didn't seem ready to stop the assault. His eyes were filled with fury; he was too far gone to care about the fact that he was damaging part of his precious collection.

She scrambled away from him, back against the vanity. She shoved the chair at him, and it stopped him long enough for her to reach in the drawer and grasp the knife. The sharp tip glinted in the dim light of her room. He stopped, and she saw Marianne in her peripheral, hands over her open mouth. She was stunned. Scared. *Good.*

Capri stood and backed away from Ekon, who held up his hands. His expression was one of anger, indignation, skepticism—but he held perfectly still, unwilling to risk her wrath if he was wrong.

"You would kill your King?" he asked quietly, calm and controlled once more. He didn't look at all remorseful for what he'd just done. The two of them deserved one another, Capri decided.

"That depends on my King's next move," Capri said. Her voice shook, but the hand holding the knife was steady.

Ekon put his wounded, flaccid penis back in his pants, buttoned his shirt, and glanced behind Capri, using her mirror to fix his dark hair.

Every movement was precise, never betraying fear, but he wouldn't move closer. When he was satisfied with his appearance, his eyes slid up the length of her body, pausing at her exposed cleavage before finally meeting her gaze.

"I'll deal with you after the memorial," he said. He turned slightly to glance at Marianne. "And I won't be bothering you again."

Then he was gone. Pride, she imagined, had kept him from calling out to the guards during the altercation. She turned her furious gaze on the blond, who shrieked and closed the door. Capri wanted to rip it open and cut the other woman's throat. She could do it. Right now, with all the pain, anger, and adrenaline pumping through her, she could *do* it.

But if she was going to help Brody, she had to go. Now.

She set the knife down and looked in the mirror again. There was nothing to be done about the red marks on her face. They would bruise, and they would be ugly. She dabbed her bleeding nose and lip, fixed her hair, and finished clasping her bodice. She retrieved the supplies she'd need for the night's events from the box under her bed. Then she placed the locket around her neck and opened the sliding door to the corridor.

A guard was there, waiting for her. Capri's heart beat hard in her chest. He would keep her in the room. But his expression was mild, and he held out his hand.

"I need to confiscate a knife from you."

Capri released her breath and gave him the blade. He let her pass, assuming, she hoped, that she would be going to the memorial before accepting whatever fate Ekon decided to hand out this time around. They knew—or *thought* they knew—exactly where she was at all times. As far as they were concerned, the whole palace was her prison.

Anger flared in Capri again, but she kept it sealed within herself, saving it for later. She walked quickly to the elevator and prayed Briony would still be in her room. She was, and she exited Gina's room to talk to Capri in the hallway. Her brow furrowed as she managed to tear her eyes away from her former protégé's dress and focus on her face.

"My God, Capri, what happened? Was it Marianne?"

"In a way." Capri's voice was bitter. She was already reaching behind her neck to unclasp the locket. "I'll explain later. I need you to do something for me."

"Anything," Briony agreed without question.

"Wear this."

Briony held out her hand, and the locket and chain pooled in the center of her palm. She looked bewildered. "I don't understand."

"I know. I'm sorry. Just promise me you'll wear it. Don't take it off for any reason. I'll come back for it."

"Capri—"

"I have to go. I'm sorry."

She turned and ran for the stairs, glancing at a clock in the hall. She had ten minutes to make it to Brody while avoiding the guards and anyone else who might let slip that she wasn't attending the memorial with her best friend at all. That's how it had to look.

She felt for the full, capped syringes taped to her thigh. Their cylindrical shapes were reassuring. She removed the stun gun from her other thigh, biting her lip as the tape ripped soft, unseen hairs from her skin. She had to be ready.

It would all be over in just a few minutes—one way or another.

CHAPTER 54

In the end, there was no last meal. A guard brought Brody bland soup and bread for breakfast and then nothing for the rest of the day. Even if Haddaway hadn't tipped him off, he'd have been able to figure out tonight was the night he'd die. The steel door wouldn't open again until it was time to take him to the little room with the chair.

There was a knot deep in his stomach—anger, guilt, regret—and he worked it out the only way he knew how. He beat the mattress to death for the last time. His bruised knuckles protested, but he carried on. Soon, he'd no longer feel them. With each *smack* of his fist against the padding came an image: Jillian. Maxine. Capri. Jillian. Maxine. Capri. Capri. Capri.

Sweat dripped down the back of his filthy t-shirt. His beard itched. He was an animal, wild and ready to burst from his cage, even if it meant running toward his own death.

The door opened behind him, and he stopped mid-punch. The air was still except for his labored breathing. He was shaking, the last of his energy spent fighting nothing and everything.

He squared his shoulders, set his jaw, and turned.

At least Haddaway had the balls to transfer him to the death closet himself. He held out a pair of restraints. Brody glared at them, then at Haddaway. It wasn't in his nature to make things easy for a person who was trying to kill him, but he placed his wrists together. There were two armed officers behind the head of security.

Again, he considered jumping them, making them kill him, making their job messy.

But the older man was already cuffing him. He motioned for Brody to follow with a jerk of his head. The gunman growled low in his throat, but he obeyed. Once, he'd begged for this, but now something held him here. He hated that. The images flashed through his mind again, this time to the rhythm of his own heavy footfalls. Jillian. Maxine. *Capri.*

The group passed the booking desk, and the officers paused. Brody glanced over, only mildly interested in whatever was causing the delay, but his head jerked up at the sight of Capri. The sudden onslaught of emotion was more than he'd felt in the last week, more than he'd felt in years.

It was more than he'd ever wanted to feel again.

The intake guard was slumped over his desk. Capri stood beside him, straight-backed and beautiful in some fancy green dress. Her eyes were wide and terrified, her cheeks freshly bruised.

"Lady Capri," Haddaway said. "Are you alright? What happened here?"

"It was horrible," she gasped.

But she didn't move. Something was off, something in her posture, in the breathy tone of her voice. She was putting on a show. *Why?*

Haddaway had been the one to say it, five days before. *Seems to have some ideas about trying to get you out.* Suspicion triggered an adrenaline rush, and Brody felt strong again. He flexed his muscles, testing the strength of the handcuffs in case he needed to protect himself, to protect *her.*

But she didn't need him.

Haddaway approached with caution, and she threw herself into his arms. He dropped to the floor in some kind of spasm. The guard to Brody's left lunged forward to restrain her, but Capri plunged a syringe into her neck, and the guard was on the floor and woozy in a matter of seconds. She injected the same into Haddaway's arm before he could fully recover.

The last guard opted to hang back but had his finger on his linker. Brody elbowed him hard in the ribs and looped his cuffed hands around his neck. Capri rushed over and found a vein with shaking fingers, injecting the last of whatever had been in the syringe. He slumped against Brody, and he let him go without killing him. This was her show, and she seemed intent on letting them live.

Capri whirled around, making sure there were no other guards coming, and then her hazel eyes finally settled on his. He hadn't thought he'd be this close to her again, the bare skin of her arms and chest so near to him he could feel the heat radiating from her. Her face was close enough for him to see that the split lip and bruised cheeks weren't fake.

Anger clouded his vision, and he brushed a thumb over the marred flesh. She closed her eyes and shuddered in response to his touch. He had questions, but she spoke first, unfastening his wrists as she filled him in.

"*Task Eternal* is acting as a decoy. Leroy has another ship at the far docks. He'll be waiting for you."

"Let's go," he said, voice rough with disuse but still commanding.

Something like regret flickered briefly in her gaze. She shook her head, and the handcuffs clattered to the floor. "I have something I need to take care of."

Brody held her gaze, recognizing the anguish like he was looking in a mirror. He took her by the arm, making her hear him.

"You go down this path, and there's no goin' back."

Capri's lower lip twitched, like she was remembering the abuse that split it. She was looking at him, but she was lost in whatever had happened. His hand tightened around her arm, as if he could make her listen by forcing his will into her skin.

"Go, Brody," she whispered.

"Not without you."

"Don't let this be for nothing." Her tone was sharp. There was no reasoning with her.

He wanted to knock Capri over the head, inject her with whatever she'd used on the guards, *make* her go. But he couldn't. It was her decision. He wouldn't take that away from her—not again. He'd thought he'd never see her again, smell her again, feel her again. He hadn't wanted to. Every time they connected it was harder for him to let go. He growled low in his throat and forced his fingers to unclench. She stepped back before he could change his mind, eyes lingering on his just a moment longer.

Then, she turned and ran.

He watched her retreating form, the way the ludicrous skirt billowed behind her, before grabbing the nearest rifle and making his own escape.

CHAPTER 55

Capri retraced her steps, using the stairs, counting on most of the palace being distracted by the memorial on the sixth floor. The guard stationed outside of Marianne's door was unavoidable, but Capri had the element of surprise. He was shocked to see her; her tracking device showed that she was by Briony's side in the upper dining hall.

She used the last dose of propofol to subdue him. Her vision was blurred, her nerves electric. Her breath came in short, enraged pants. She took the guard's gun and went through her own room to access Marianne's apartment. She turned the doorknob. It couldn't lock, since an Attending Lady's presence might be required at a moment's notice, but something on the other side was blocking her entry. She stood back and kicked. The force knocked a chair from its place beneath the doorknob.

The blond shrieked and threw herself on the bed, as if she were a child playing hide-and-seek, thinking no one could see the yellow hair poking out above the pillows. It was pathetic, and it made Capri hate her even more.

Capri took aim and rested her finger on the trigger. She breathed in, just as Brody had taught her.

"Wait!" Marianne begged, holding her hands up in front of her. "I'm pregnant. You'll kill him. You'll kill him, too."

She moaned—fear, nausea, or both—and hugged her stomach in a way that tugged at Capri's heartstrings. She took aim again, determined to ignore the woman's protests. Then, to her dismay, she hesitated.

It should have been a quick, practical decision. The woman before her was evil, and she needed to die. The baby inside her would be raised by evil parents in this evil place. She was doing it a favor.

"I know you're pregnant," Capri said, but her voice shook.

The blond whimpered and turned away, protecting her stomach as best she could. Was it maternal instinct? Or was she simply protecting what Ekon found most valuable? Capri tried to squeeze the trigger, but she couldn't. Her resolve melted away. Brody had been right, after all. She was too soft. Drained and defeated, she let the gun fall to her side.

"You know it's a boy?" she asked dully.

"I do," Marianne said, breath and voice coming fast. "It *has* to be."

Capri nodded, tears slipping down her cheeks and stinging the places where Ekon's blows had cut her skin. "I hope that's true. You know as well as I do Ekon only has one use for girls."

"That's sick," Marianne whispered. "He would never. She would be a princess."

"She would be a *commodity*," Capri corrected.

Marianne didn't dare argue when the other woman had a gun in her hand.

"Your time is limited," Capri continued. "Think about what the pregnancy will do to your body. The birth. You aren't even a good breeder. He'll never touch you again. You're the cocoon for his butterfly, and that's it."

Tears tracked down Marianne's cheeks. She shook her head. "That's not true."

"You know it is. You, of all people, know how cutthroat this place is. You, of all people, know why you should take your baby and run. If you care about him or *her* at all, Marianne, you'll find a way out."

The blond swallowed, her dainty Adam's apple prominent against the thin, pale flesh of her neck. "I'll live?"

"The *baby* will live. You've made sure everyone standing in your way has fallen, one way or another. But someday, you're going to stand in *his* way—and you'll fall the hardest."

She turned and went back to her room, shutting the door behind her. She felt dizzy. Marianne was supposed to die, but the baby had thrown a wrench in her plans. Maybe it *would* be a boy and grow up to be like his father. Maybe it would be a girl and grow up to be like her mother. Or maybe the baby would bring change with it.

There was no way of knowing, so she couldn't do it.

She imagined Marianne would be calling the guards now. Capri would take Brody's place on death row. Ekon already had the hired gun waiting; death would come quickly for her.

She dropped the gun suddenly and doubled over. She couldn't breathe. In her mind, she sifted through the whirlwind of variables to find one, just *one*, that ended in her survival—but there were none. What a waste. What a fucking waste she turned out to be.

Suddenly, someone pounded on the door, and she jumped. The guards. Then a familiar voice said, "Capri! Capri, open the door! It's important!"

Briony. The fog disappeared, and Capri opened the door. She threw herself into the other woman's arms.

"Oh, thank God!" Briony said, holding her tightly. "I overheard Ekon telling one of the guards to arrest you as soon as he could spare the manpower. You don't have much time."

Capri pulled away, wiping at her eyes, fighting the chattering of her teeth as the adrenaline left and hopelessness seeped in. "I'm already out of time."

"Why? What's going on?" Her friend was in earnest.

"I tried to kill Marianne."

Briony's eyes widened. "*Kill* her?"

Capri swallowed hard. "She had Sullivan rape me, and she tried to have Ekon do the same tonight. She killed Faye. She tried to kill Gina. She's a fucking monster, Briony."

"She *what?*" Briony's eyes filled with furious tears. "Oh, Capri…"

"I couldn't do it." Capri swallowed again, trying desperately to maintain her composure and failing. "I'm sorry. I couldn't do it. I'm sure by now…the guards—"

"You have to go," Briony said quickly, desperately. "Now."

"There's no point. I'll just be going to them instead of making them come to me. It's better this way."

They held tightly to each other's arms, tears streaming down both their faces. This would be the last time they saw each other. The door opened, and Briony shrieked. Capri shut her eyes, unable to face her fate as bravely as she'd hoped. Then her friend shook her, and she opened her eyes to find Brody, gun in hand, looking as wild and dangerous and unmoving as ever.

Relief crashed into her—and anger. "I told you to go!"

"Come on," he said.

Capri turned to Briony, and she caught sight of the locket. "The necklace," she said quickly, holding out her hand.

Brody was already pulling her in the other direction. She spoke as quickly as she could while Briony hastily unclasped the chain. "The vaccines you received. Ekon's put trackers in us. Don't tell them anything!"

They clasped hands one last time, and then she was out the door, stepping over the body of the guard she had incapacitated and two more whom Brody had killed.

She tossed the locket down a garbage chute as they ran for the stairs.

CHAPTER 56

Brody and Capri moved through the halls together, armed with the rifles he'd taken from his incapacitated escorts. His chest felt tight. He knew he would fail her—because he *always* failed. The only person he could keep alive was himself, even when he didn't want to. But he had to at least try. He kept thinking if he could just get her somewhere safe, he could let her go.

But nowhere was safe.

The kitchen was a madhouse. Cooks and kitchen workers rushed to finish the feast that would follow the memorial. He and Capri slipped through the side hall to the warehouse. By now, someone would have discovered the guards' bodies. They had to get as far as they could as fast as they could.

This time, they were playing by his rules. He shot a guard in the warehouse and felt Capri flinch beside him. It was confirmation enough that she hadn't been able to kill Marianne, and a part of him was relieved. She deserved better than a life that was tainted with blood, like his. The guard at the gates received a quieter death, out of necessity. He left the rifles with the body and exchanged them for a pistol.

A thick crowd of people had gathered outside the palace. Residents of Mars and others, from more distant places, wanted to show their respect for those who were killed. They wouldn't be allowed into the main event, so the crowd would remain. It might provide them with cover, or they might draw too much attention by moving in the opposite direction of its flow.

They stayed on the edge and kept their heads down. It was a strange sort of ambience—quiet, despite the number of people. There were murmurs and singing, feet shuffling. The mourners were waiting for the service inside the palace to end. Ekon had agreed to give a speech.

Suddenly, there was a commotion at the front doors. Brody's head snapped up, eyes sharp as he assessed the threat. Someone was trying to get past the guards, maybe a distraught family member who wasn't satisfied with saying goodbye through the palace walls. He breathed a sigh of relief. It had nothing to do with them.

Capri kept a vise grip on his hand as they made their way to the shadows of the main strip. The area was nearly deserted. The guards would search *Task Eternal* first, which was docked by the palace. They wouldn't be combing the streets—not yet.

But Capri didn't seem able to relax. She stopped suddenly, releasing his hand, and doubled over. She was shaking, arms wrapped tightly around her heaving ribs. Now that they'd found a fragment of safety, the panic she must have been holding back crashed into her full force.

He clenched and unclenched his fists, fingers itching to comfort her the way they usually did to pull a trigger.

"We can't do this now," he said. "We gotta keep movin'."

She nodded and forced her body upright, fighting for control. She tried and failed to hold back tears, but she still didn't break completely. She couldn't stop shaking—shock or something. He wasn't sure she could walk. He just had to stop the shaking. That's all it was.

He wrapped one arm around her waist and slipped the other into the slit of her skirt. He held her tight against him, hand on her thigh, skin on skin, grounding them both. Without hesitation, she buried her face in his chest and held on to his shirt. The only sounds were her soft gasps and his own ragged breathing.

Her erratic heartbeat slowed to match his. It felt too good, holding her like this. No one had fit into his arms this way since Jill. The flash of memory, of the last time he'd held his wife close, was enough to make him break the hold. He let go as if he'd been burned. Anger, guilt, wanting—and stronger feelings he couldn't bring himself to think about swirled within Brody, and he struggled to shut them down.

"Let's go," he said, turning on his heel and leading on through the shadows.

They'd gone about a block when a tram stopped beside them. Brody put a hand on his gun. Capri stayed behind him, but she didn't seem to have the capacity left for fear. She stood slightly out of the way, eyeing the vehicle warily.

It was empty except for the driver, whose face was shielded by a hat. He lifted his head, and Brody relaxed.

"Shots," Leroy greeted. "You look like shit."

"Fuck off," he replied.

Capri and Brody slid into the seats behind the mechanic, and he drove them back to the tiny ship. Brody drew his gun as they approached the guard booth, but there was no one inside.

"It'll look like the tram driver did it," Leroy said, voice disturbingly chipper for someone who had just killed one man and framed another.

Brody glanced at Capri, but she was looking the other way, shoulders slumped, still shivering although she couldn't be cold on the climate-controlled satellite. He reached out to take her small hand in his calloused one, and her fingers closed around his automatically. But she still didn't face him.

The tram stopped, and Leroy jumped out, holding out a hand to help Capri step down. She released Brody and stood for a moment with the mechanic. Brody walked ahead, pausing at the fold-down stairs to look back. Leroy was whispering something in her ear, and she gave the twin a weak smile.

Brody clenched his jaw, anger and jealousy flaring as he watched them, even though he had no right to her. He didn't *want* a right to her. Leroy jumped on the tram again to take it back to wherever it had come from.

As Capri turned toward the camper, Brody turned away and went inside.

CHAPTER 57

"I'm here for you." That's all Leroy had said, but it meant the world.

To know she had someone outside of Mars she could count on made the prospect of striking out on her own a little less terrifying. She knew she didn't mean nothing to Brody, but he was fighting his own battles, and she wouldn't put the pressure of expectation on him.

If she was leaving, she'd have to be able to make her own way.

Once inside the small ship, she sat down on a bottom bunk. Brody had settled into the cockpit to view their surroundings, check for coordinates—to look for any information, she imagined, that would give him some sense of control. He must be as exhausted as she was, but he was still moving, still searching, still avoiding her.

She watched him dig around in a small fridge and come up with a ready-made protein pack. He shoved hard-boiled eggs, cheese, and cold bacon into his mouth like a starving man. He probably *was* starving.

Leroy returned, pulling up the folding stairs as he went. "*Task Eternal* is gone," he said, voice rich with his usual infectious excitement. "We've gotta go before the U.N. catches up to them and finds out you're not onboard."

He went to the pilot's chair to plug in coordinates, ignoring Brody's presence in the co-pilot's seat. "We'll stop at New Earth to refuel, then rendezvous on Venus. He turned briefly to shoot Capri a grin. "Once we're back onboard the ship we'll figure out what to do with you."

Capri gave the mechanic a sad smile and shook her head. "I'm not going with you."

Brody spun around to stare at her, but she kept her eyes on Leroy.

"What do you mean?" Leroy asked.

"I'll stay on New Earth. Ekon's out of control. Someone needs to go to the U.N."

"They've never cared about the shit he's done," Brody growled.

"It's worse now," she said, finally meeting his gaze.

His brown eyes flitted to her cheek.

"More than that," she said softly.

The ship was taking off. Leroy turned in his seat to concentrate, but she knew he was listening.

"There's another girl acting as the Prize now. As long as he can make money from the auction, he'll keep going. He also injected us with tracking devices." Brody's gaze dropped to her right arm. He was realizing that both pieces of jewelry were being used to cover wounds. "And Marianne is pregnant. He'll have an heir—or a girl."

As always, Brody's face revealed little, but his jaw was tight as he absorbed the information.

"Haddaway thinks it's a bad idea," she admitted. "But I have to try."

The ship was sailing on its own now, but still Leroy said nothing, facing the screens instead of her.

"Did Haddaway say it was a bad idea or a pointless idea?" Brody asked finally. "Bad means there might be trouble."

Capri's cheeks grew hot as she lied. "I'm not sure."

He held her gaze. Brody knew her too well. He always would. He'd seen her at her worst often enough, and he'd brought out her best. They'd always share a bond, but their lives were traveling in opposite directions.

She couldn't think about the fact she'd never see him again, or she'd cry. Leroy turned then, and she turned her gaze to him. He gave her a weak smile. "I'll miss you, Capri."

"I'll miss you, too."

***

Capri had only meant to close her eyes for a moment, but exhaustion took her, and she slept for hours on the small bunk. By the time she woke, the interior lights were off, and Leroy was snoring in the bunk opposite.

She spotted the back of Brody's head above the pilot's chair. It was his turn to make sure the small ship stayed on course. Through the video screens, she could see stars, an occasional meteorite or piece of space trash, and another ship in the distance.

She joined him, sitting in the seat beside him. It was a simple vessel, meant to be flown by families with a temporary license. She was surprised to find she knew what the gauges meant, what some of the levers did. She'd learned more than she'd realized during her short time away from Mars.

Brody glanced at her. Capri thought it might be his only acknowledgement until he handed her a snack bar and a bottle of water. After that, he kept his eyes on the screens, and she ate slowly, staring at the screens with him in silence. He broke it.

"What happened?" he asked in a low voice, so as not to wake Leroy.

His voice was deep, and she felt it more than heard it. He was looking at her right cheek, which stung more than the left. It must have looked worse, too.

"He tried to use me."

"Tried?"

"Tried."

He grunted, and she caught the dark look in his eyes before he turned back to the screen. His thoughts were on murder, but they both knew killing a King was a great deal more involved than killing some thug in an alley or a greedy rebel.

That was why she had to take him down another way.

"You're set on it?" he asked, and she nodded.

He nodded, too. Then he turned back to her, and she saw something else there, something she felt, too. Her heart fluttered. This was no time to play coy, no time to play games. This was a last chance.

She stood, lifted her voluminous green skirt, and slid her leg slowly, tantalizingly over his lap until she straddled him. He responded by moving the seat back, giving them more room to maneuver.

Leroy had had the foresight to bring some of Brody's belongings with him, fresh clothes and a tote of guns, but no one had known Capri would be leaving with them. She'd be stuck in the same grimy dress for the foreseeable future.

She didn't mind. She needed that dress. The small diamonds she'd earned during her stay on *Task Eternal* were sewn carefully into the seams. Brody was toying with the satin fabric now, deep brown eyes boring into hers. She was relieved that he seemed to be done with talking, too, done with denying. She just wanted to kiss him forever, imprint the memory of him on every cell of her body.

She closed her eyes and leaned forward to run her tongue along the seam of his lips. He groaned and opened his mouth, his own tongue darting out to taste her while his hands wandered higher, stroking her waist, then continuing their journey to undo the eye hooks at the top of her bodice.

Capri moaned into his mouth as he freed her breasts and explored them, running his hands over and between the soft mounds. He tugged her loose curls, pulling her head back and breaking the kiss so he was free to tease her nipples with his tongue and teeth.

She whimpered softly, moving her lower half against him. He grunted and moved his hand so it was cupping her cheek, his thumb landing on her lips, a gentle reminder that they weren't alone, that they needed to stay quiet. Capri nipped the pad of his thumb lightly and he pressed it into her mouth as he continued raking his teeth over the sensitive flesh of her nipples.

She licked and sucked his finger, and his erection strained beneath her. He pulled back, releasing her, and looked her in the eye while he licked her saliva from his thumb. Their ragged breathing was the only sound save for Leroy's reassuring snores.

Capri had never wanted a man more in her life. She was sure she'd never want another man as much again. Before she could dwell on the thought, on the impending heartbreak, Brody slipped a hand beneath her skirt and slid it up her inner thigh. She gasped when he reached her center, stroking her through her thin underwear before nudging it aside to dip a thick finger between her folds.

She rose up slightly, allowing him better access, and he slipped a second finger inside of her. She bit her lip hard to keep from crying out as he hooked them, finding her pleasure point with ease. She writhed against him, suddenly very frustrated that she was topless and at his mercy when he still had so many clothes on.

Capri grasped the bottom of his t-shirt and tugged it up just enough to slip her hands underneath, to feel the rough hair of his chest and abdomen scrape tantalizingly against her palms. He growled low in his throat and removed his fingers, sucking off her juices before leaning forward to kiss her neck. While his lips teased the sensitive flesh beneath her ear, his hands continued to work, moving under her dress, toying with the seams of her underwear, until she felt a tug and heard a rip.

She brought her hands up to touch his face, to run her fingertips through his short beard and hair, before letting them slide down the front of his shirt. She pushed him away, just far enough to reach the fly of his pants. He pulled his erection through, and Capri poised herself over him.

They looked into each other's eyes. Desperation flickered in his brown depths, and a muscle twitched in his jaw. For a fleeting moment, it all seemed so simple. He could come with her; they could be together. The words were on the tip of her tongue, but she recognized the haunted, pained look in his gaze. She cared far too much to ask too much of him.

They couldn't have everything, but they could have this.

Capri lowered herself onto him, hands sliding to his shoulders to grip them tightly, throwing her head back as he came to rest fully inside of her. Her body trembled, and she stopped for a moment, basking in the simple ecstasy of being so close to him, of her body pulsing around him. She lifted herself and came down again, and again, she paused. Brody made a noise of frustration and slipped his hands beneath her skirt once more, grabbing her ass and taking over.

She gasped softly in time to his tantalizing rhythm, trying to stay quiet while Leroy's snores continued a few feet away. Brody's breath was heavy, his muscles tense as he guided her movements. She kept her hands clasped around his neck, gazing into his dark brown eyes as he stroked the deepest parts of her, things said and unsaid hanging between them.

His dark eyes moved to her swollen lip. He leaned forward slightly to brush a kiss against the wound, then took her mouth hard, sweeping his tongue inside, cleansing and possessive. Capri brought a hand to his beard, stroking his cheek, memorizing the way he felt.

She wanted it to last forever, but the momentum was already building between them, desperate and electric. She dug her nails into his back, and he groaned, bucking against her, losing control. There was no stopping the wave now, and they crashed together, shaking and panting and swallowing each other's noises of pleasure until it ebbed.

For a long moment, they held each other, foreheads touching. Then, Brody released his hold, and she removed herself from his lap to stand on shaky legs. She bent down to retrieve her torn underwear, trying to convince herself she didn't feel the loss so keenly, while he stood and zipped his pants. Then, he pulled her to him by the waist, grasped her hair gently, and tugged so she was looking up at him.

"You take the next shift at the helm," he said, letting her know in the simplest way that he believed in her.

Pride and sorrow swelled in Capri's chest. Then, he landed a kiss on her forehead and left her alone.

CHAPTER 58

The ship touched down on New Earth in one of the rural docks of U.S. Territory. They were hours away from the U.N. District. Capri only had her fake papers from Mexico Territory, courtesy of the data ring Leroy had kept on him since her departure, and Brody was a wanted man. They couldn't afford to draw attention to themselves by landing in one of the better-guarded docks.

She was ready to go. Brody sat in his bunk, cleaning his guns maybe a little more aggressively than usual. He wouldn't stop her. Maybe a part of him wanted to, but this was the choice she'd made.

Giving in to tender feelings would kill him—and her, in the end. He couldn't be the one to save her. Not again. He had to say good-bye, let her try to make it on her own. It was what he'd planned from the start of this goddamn mess, anyway, and now it was what she wanted, too.

Leroy hugged her tightly, freely, and she kissed his cheek. Brody looked away, picking up a familiar snub-nosed revolver and handling it with more care than the other weapons.

"Take this," the mechanic said, and he looked back in time to watch him hand Capri a linker. "It only works in atmo, but you know we'll be around eventually."

Annoyance and a familiar jealousy surged through Brody. He rubbed the barrel of the gun hard, as if the cold steel beneath his fingers could somehow seep into his heart and reinforce it. The force of whatever the hell it was that drew them together time and again was intense. But no more.

Capri lingered at the top of the steps and looked back at him. Her hazel eyes were clear, determined, but in the thin line of her mouth there was regret. She didn't speak. He had nothing to say. He stood, stone-faced but far from unfeeling, and approached her. Just like that, her eyelids lowered and her lips parted slightly, unconsciously. He watched her mouth and considered tasting it one last time, but he stayed strong.

He held out his parting gift, and she accepted the revolver with a nod of gratitude.

Then she was gone.

Brody went back to his guns while Leroy refueled the ship. He had to focus on the relief and not the loss. He had to forget the girl.

This had to be the end.

ACKNOWLEDGEMENTS

Eric, this wouldn't have happened without you. Thank you for "letting" me write, investing in me in every way, and having confidence in me when I had none. I love you, and I love that, together, we get to show **A** and **S** what it looks like to set goals and reach them.

Mom, for teaching me to love reading and being the first to believe in me.

Dad, for understanding the struggles of a frustrated artist (and the margaritas).

Sean, for convincing me at a young age that nerd stuff is cool.

Becs, for always keeping my books on your shelf.

Kacie, for spending many a weekend writing fanfiction with me, which contributed heavily to my inability to stop writing, ever.

JP, for being my writing buddy and keeping it real.

Amy, for reminding me that reading is supposed to be fun.

Jan, for providing me with a home away from home so I can, occasionally, escape the daily demands of marriage and motherhood.

Lynsey, who motivated me to make this manuscript better without making me feel discouraged. If there are still parts of this book that are imperfect, it's probably because I ignored one of your suggestions.

COMING SOON

Instead of helping Capri take down the King of Mars, the U.N. wants to sweep his transgressions under the rug—and his former Prize along with them. With killers on her heels, Capri calls on Brody and the crew of *Task Eternal* for help.

Their meeting should have been brief, just long enough to find Capri a safehouse, but the U.N. has other ideas. They catch up to her and haul Brody, Capri, and Leroy to the wild, inescapable prison planet of Alcatraz.

Leroy struggles to communicate with Jax and Colin, their only hope of rescue, while Capri is separated and forced to confront a past she'd nearly managed to forget. Brody is frantic, finally accepting that the only way to keep Capri safe is to keep her close—if only they can reach her in time.

To top it off, the trio discovers that criminals aren't the only thing the U.N. is hiding on Alcatraz.

Subscribe to my Substack for sneak peeks and release dates!